Survival Rout

⁓ ❦ ⁓

EARTHSIDE

ANA MARDOLL

SURVIVAL ROUT by Ana Mardoll

Copyright © 2016

All rights reserved.

ISBN: 978-1-5446094-5-4

Published by Acacia Moon Publishing, LLC

Cover illustration by James, GoOnWrite.com

Books by Ana Mardoll

THE EARTHSIDE SERIES

Poison Kiss (#1)
Survival Rout (#2)

REWOVEN TALES

Pulchritude

To Mom and Dad,
my fiercest advocates and the
first to see beauty in my scars.

CONTENTS

CHAPTER 1 1

CHAPTER 2 12

CHAPTER 3 22

CHAPTER 4 32

CHAPTER 5 42

CHAPTER 6 54

CHAPTER 7 66

CHAPTER 8 76

CHAPTER 9 86

CHAPTER 10 97

CHAPTER 11 108

CHAPTER 12 119

CHAPTER 13 129

CHAPTER 14 139

CHAPTER 15 149

CHAPTER 16 160

CHAPTER 17 171

CHAPTER 18 180

CHAPTER 19 189

CHAPTER 20 200

CHAPTER 21 211

CHAPTER 22 222

CHAPTER 23 232

CHAPTER 24 242

CHAPTER 25 251

CHAPTER 26 262

CHAPTER 27 272

CHAPTER 28 282

CHAPTER 29 292

CHAPTER 30 301

CHAPTER 31 314

CHAPTER 32 323

CHAPTER 33 334

CHAPTER 34 344

CHAPTER 35 354

CHARACTERS 373

CONTENT NOTES 374

CHAPTER 1

Aniyah

"Aniyah, can I borrow Timmy for Labor Day weekend?"

I've only just hung my purse on the back of the bar stool when Miyuki pops the question; she hasn't even waited until we've sat down. I tear my eyes away from Timothy—who nods at us in warm welcome but is too busy filling drink orders at the other end of the bar to rush over—and stare at her.

"Miyuki, that's not until September! Anyway, what do you want him *for?*" I ask, not bothering to disguise my mystified tone. I'm grateful he's too far out of earshot to hear us over the noise of the band, because I can't imagine what he'd think of her question.

She sniffs in a pretense of haughtiness and perches on the edge of her stool, pulling at the hem of her sweater where it rides up over the curve of her stomach. Miyuki is taller than me when we're on our feet, but on the barstools we're almost eye-to-eye. She aims an arch gaze at me over the top of her rectangular-framed glasses. "Well, you're not going to be using him, are you?" she points out in her most reasonable tone of voice, leaning closer so I can hear her. "Unless you asked him to fly out to Atlanta with you?"

"I don't think dating over the summer justifies the price of a plane

1

ticket, especially when we'd just end up spending the weekend at the public pool with my folks." I settle into my own hard vinyl chair, wishing for the umpteenth time that the stools here were more comfortable. Timothy sometimes brings me a little travel pillow that he keeps under the bar to brace my back, but it doesn't do much good.

"Besides, you know we're not serious, right?" I add the qualifier quickly, anxious to downplay the importance of Timothy. "We're not at any sort of meet-the-parents stage yet."

I can't quite meet her gaze, opting instead to pick at a stain on the bar, my fingernails flicking crusty sugar from the varnished wood. We haven't spoken, she and I, about the night she spent in my bed last week, nor have we repeated the experience. But she must have noticed that I haven't gone out with Timothy since it happened, opting instead to stay home so I can study for summer finals—a 'studying' that mostly involves lying on my stomach in bed and staring at theorems I can no longer concentrate on.

She flashes a triumphant grin at me. "Well, yeah, that's why I feel pretty comfortable asking to borrow him, Ani," she teases, leaning over to nudge me with her shoulder. My hands instinctively grip the edge of the bar for balance, but she moves slowly to telegraph the gesture and her touch is as light as a feather. "If you two were engaged or something, it would be so very awkward."

My lips part in an answering smile to her own wide grin, unable to remain serious in the face of her teasing. "Okay, okay, you can borrow him," I relent, laughing in surrender. "But why do you want him? You don't even like him!"

Her hazel eyes dance as she feigns a scandalized expression. One hand reaches to flip her hair over her shoulder in that dismissive way of hers, but she's still getting used to her new pixie undercut that left the top shaggy but shaved everything up the back; her fingers meet only soft baby fuzz. "Aniyah! For shame. You know I adore Timmy." Her wry grin is unrepentant. "He pays for our drinks."

I roll my eyes in acknowledgment of her damning faint praise, and she laughs with me; yet I can hear the strain in her laughter, a tiny forced note just audible under the raucous music flooding the mostly empty bar. "Miyuki, you know I can't say no to you," I point out, my tone gentler than before. "But won't you tell me why?"

She doesn't answer right away. Leaning her elbows on the counter, she rests her chin on her hands and stares at the brightly-lit liquor bottles lining the back wall of the bar. "Truth is," she admits in a low voice, "I've been informed I have to put in an appearance at John's house for the holiday weekend. Since he hasn't yet written a check for the fall semester, the usual threat looms."

My breath catches in instant sympathy. I've met Miyuki's father on the rare occasions when he's come out to our apartment rather than summoning her to his palatial lake house. In none of these visits has John endeared himself to me, and my antipathy appears to be mutual. Withholding financial support is a favorite tactic of his, and I know Miyuki's driving goal is to finish her degree in physical therapy as quickly as possible so she can shed the last of her dependency on him.

"Oh, Miyuki, I'm so sorry. That sounds miserable." I reach out to touch her arm, wishing I had more to offer than commiseration. "But... you want *Timothy* to come with you?" I'm still confused on this point; although she gets along with Timothy, they don't interact much apart from me. He's my summer boyfriend and she's been my roommate since freshman year. Their relationship, such as it is, seems defined by that loose connection alone.

She shrugs but her shoulders are stiff with tension. "Well, you know how John is," she says, waving her hand in airy dismissal. "He'll love Timmy; he's white and male and gainfully employed while working on his master's degree. They can talk about what a darling housewife or adorable secretary I'll grow up to be, while I catch up with Okaasan in peace. She'll be visiting too, for my sake, so it won't be total hell."

I remember the meaning of that one: *Mother*. Over the past three years, Miyuki has been picking up the language her mother, Yumiko, was forbidden to teach her as a baby. John hadn't wanted his child speaking words he didn't know and, according to Miyuki, John always got his way. Yumiko had stayed for the sake of their daughter but filed for divorce the same week Miyuki moved out to start college. Miyuki had been ecstatic, breezing through freshman year with a wide smile that never left her face.

She visits Yumiko at her studio apartment once every couple of weeks now, and devours vocabulary books in her spare time. I help make flash cards and compliment her attempts to incorporate kanji into journaling. Sometimes she brings me along for her visits, but I try not to get in their way. I'm glad she has this chance to connect with her mother but remain privately astonished by John's actions. My own parents didn't always agree on how to raise me, yet I can't imagine one of them denying me my heritage.

"So you want Timothy to play your decoy boyfriend for the weekend?" I ask, the familial scene she describes slowly solidifying in my head. "The plan is to throw him at John so that John will be in a good mood and the weekend won't be miserable for everyone else?"

Miyuki shrugs, her shoulders set in a defensive hunch. "It's just for a couple of days and it wouldn't be hard. Timmy knows me well enough to play the part and he's ridiculously good with people. Anyway, he's watched movies at our apartment with us at least half a dozen times! He can just imagine he was there for me instead of you." She takes a deep breath, not meeting my eyes. "Besides, I don't know any other boys who'd do it without wanting something in return."

"Oh." My cheeks heat as her meaning sinks in. "No, he wouldn't." I reach out to touch her again, wishing we were home so I could wrap her in a proper hug. "Of course you can borrow Timothy. I mean, you're going to have to ask him if he *wants* to spend Labor Day with you," I amend, glancing down the length of the bar at the smiling man working his way steadily down to us, "but I'll let him know it's important to me. I can't imagine he'll refuse. Free food, right?"

4

She grins, relief palpable on her face underneath the playful scorn she quickly affects. "Aniyah! Food is the least of the treasures on offer! You haven't even seen the remodeling that's been done on the lake house; I guarantee he'll come out for that alone. John just bought the most ludicrously expensive boat and he'll want to show it off. What could be more fun than barreling at breakneck speed all over the lake, polluting the environment like proper manly men?"

"Maybe you'd better let *me* sell this to Timothy," I observe in my driest tone. "You're not helping your case one bit."

"Sell me what?" He reaches the end of the bar where we perch, having finished with his paying customers. Flashing me a warm smile, he adds, "Hey, babe, I've missed you! What are you girls up to tonight? Any chance I can convince you to come back to my place for a movie after I close up?"

"Well, in answer to your first question," I tell him, "it just so happens I have an exciting limited-time offer: Emma here wants to take you boating for Labor Day." Miyuki bestows a wry grimace, but doesn't interrupt my sales pitch. "And, uh, a movie sounds tempting, but I've got work tomorrow," I add, grimacing in apology.

It's not a lie; I do have work tomorrow. But even if I didn't, I think I'd still want to go to my home instead of his. I feel off-balance from the noise, the band, and the presence of the other patrons. I'd rather snuggle Miyuki on our couch, chasing away her family woes with a liberal application of ice cream and shitty movies. I don't want to be here at this bar, struggling to remember to switch over to her first name for Timothy's sake. It isn't his fault, of course—the use of her middle name is reserved entirely to her mother and, after I asked about it last year, to me—but lately I find it increasingly difficult to switch.

"Oh, that sounds fun," Timothy agrees in his easy way, leaning against his side of the bar. "What's the catch? And what do my two best girls want to drink tonight? We've got a new sour green apple Cosmopolitan I'm supposed to be pushing."

Miyuki has gone quiet, taking off her glasses and wiping them with her shirt to avoid eye contact. "That sounds great, thanks," I tell him, flashing a grateful smile for the both of us. If he notices Miyuki's awkward silence, it doesn't show on his face as he strides off to prepare our drinks.

Once he's out of hearing, I slump in my seat and sigh. "You know, if you take him out to the lake as your fake boyfriend, you're going to have to be nice to him," I point out, giving Miyuki a stern look.

She twists her lips as though she's tasted something bitter. "I'm nice!" she protests, shoving her glasses back up her nose. Her hands fuss with the composition notebook she carries—one of her many journals—playing with the ballpoint pen she leaves clipped in the binding coil. "It's just: does he always have to call us 'little women' or his 'best girls'?" Her voice is so low I can barely hear her over the noise of the band; as near as it is to closing time, I hope this is their last song. "John does that to me and Okaasan, and I hate it."

I bite my lip, glancing up to reassure myself that Timothy isn't close enough to hear. "I don't think he means to be condescending; he's just trying to be friendly. Do you want me to talk to him about it?" I can hear the reluctance in my tone; we're racking up a lot of favors from Timothy today.

"No." She sighs and doesn't meet my gaze. "The problem isn't Timothy, not exactly. Aniyah, do you ever think about whether you might not be a woman at all?" Her low tone has turned strangely urgent. "No one ever really asked our opinion on the subject; people just assume."

"What, like, do I think I'm a man?" I'm thrown by the direction this conversation has taken and I smile at her, expecting a joke. Yet if there's a punchline here, I don't get it. I frown at her, a sudden thought striking. "Miyuki, are you saying *you're* a man?"

There's a transgender man in my math department, so I know gender isn't always what you're labeled at birth. He was nice and gave me less shit than the other boys in the department did, but never did I think I might be like him. I was a girl, and all this time I'd assumed Miyuki was too. Sure, she kept her hair cropped short and hung around the apartment in baggy sweaters and boxer shorts, but she always wore makeup when we went out together and she owned at least a dozen skirts.

She shakes her head at my question, shoving her bangs back from her eyes as she stares down at the counter. "No! Do you ever think you might not be a man *or* a woman? You might be neither, or a little of both, or something else entirely." She drags her gaze up to me, watching my face for a reaction.

"How would that work?" I'm trying to keep my voice neutral but I'm flailing. I can't tell where she's going with this or if it's purely hypothetical. "What would you call yourself, if you weren't a man or a woman?"

"Well, there are other words," Miyuki insists, defensive now. "There are nonbinary genders for people who don't fit neatly into one or the other. Lots of cultures have them! There's genderqueer and genderfluid, and then you have demigirls like me who are part-girl but also something else that isn't girl at all, and look here!"

Yanking her pen free, she clicks the point and begins to draw on her wrist, her usual method for note-taking when she's working on an idea that isn't fully formed and ready to commit to her journal yet. She picked up the habit as a child, washing words away from John's prying eyes.

"You've got these pronouns that everybody knows, right?" she says. She's hunched over her arm and talking quickly, almost to herself. "*She, her, hers, herself.*" She prints the words in neat tiny letters on her arm. "Well, there are other pronouns, new ones people have made up. Neopronouns like *xie, xer, xers, xerself.*" These go on her arm under the first words, the ink dark against her fair skin.

"Zee?" I repeat, straining in my seat to see the tiny letters. She pauses her hurried writing to look up at me, her face unusually vulnerable. "Miyuki," I say, hesitating as I search for the right thing to say, "is this a new piss-off-John thing? Like the purple dye you put in your hair sophomore year?"

Hurt flashes in her eyes as soon as the words leave my mouth. "No," she mutters in a dejected tone, looking away from me. "I'm not going to tell him. You know how he is; he'd just mock me for it."

I could kick myself for being such a heel. "Hey. Sorry! If it's a secret, it can be just between us," I promise, reaching out to touch her wrist. She looks up at me and I give her my warmest smile. I still don't understand a word of this, but if it's important to her I'll damned sure learn. "Like your middle name, right? 'Miyuki' and 'xie' with me, 'Emma' and 'she' around everyone else. That's easy enough, yeah?"

Her hazel eyes shine at me from behind her glasses in the low bar light. "Aniyah, I fucking love you," she says, a slow grin spreading over her face. The words don't mean anything; I know that. Miyuki has been saying she loves me for years. It's just a thing she says to me, her roommate and best friend, and a sentiment I'm used to echoing back without thinking. It's not meant to be taken seriously.

So why does my heart leap now when she says it, her joyful eyes holding my gaze such that I can't look away? And why do I feel so guilty when I hear Timothy's voice at my elbow cheerfully announcing, "Here you go!", as he plunks down our free drinks? I jump in my seat, as startled as a cat, hoping none of my thoughts show on my face when I smile at him.

I like Timothy, even if this thing with him wasn't meant to be serious. He's older than us, working on his master's degree while we're still undergrads. It was supposed to be a simple summer fling, easy and sexy and fun, but then everything got tangled up with emotions. He's sweet and understanding and easy-going, willing to accommodate me when my back pain flares up and kind to Miyuki even on her snarky days. I haven't stopped liking him just because I like someone else. I don't think my brain works that way.

My fantasy would be for the three of us to agree I could be with both Timothy and Miyuki without giving either of them up. But I'd need to sit down and talk to them individually, and I don't know how to ask permission for something like that. I'm not ready to lose Timothy, but when I sit here with my fingers lingering on Miyuki's wrist and feeling the warmth of her skin under my own, I *know* I can't let my chance with her pass me by. I want to be able to take her home and kiss her and share a bed together without worrying that I'm cheating on someone else. And it's not right to keep racking up favors from Timothy if he's expecting exclusivity from me. Better to be honest with him now than to hurt his feelings later.

"Well, what do you think?" he asks, breaking through the turmoil of my thoughts with a cheery grin. He nods at the drink in front of me. "Go on, drink up. I didn't make it too cold and your brain is too big to freeze anyway, babe."

"Says you." I snort and take a long swig of the sour apple cocktail. Miyuki is already sipping at her own drink while she doodles a flower on her inner arm, an activity that keeps her attention away from Timothy while he leans on the bar. "It's good, yeah."

My praise is automatic and instant; I don't want to hurt his feelings, after all. Yet I find myself frowning at my glass when the first quick gulp slams hard into my stomach. The drink isn't terrible, but the alcohol burns my throat and there's a bitter aftertaste under the sour flavor. Free is free, and I don't want to be ungrateful, but something feels wrong even as I take another careful sip.

"It's a little strong, isn't it?" I observe, looking at Timothy with confusion. It's not like him to double the liquor in our drinks. We visit for a light buzz before bedtime rather than wanting to get smashed. If he's trying to treat us to something stronger, he ought to have asked first; he knows we have to drive home.

He grins at my question, unconcerned. "Is it? I made it the same as usual. The juice is pretty sour, I know. I keep telling management we need to rim the glasses with sugar. Take another sip. I think you'll like it once you adjust to the taste."

I don't want any more, but neither do I want to be rude. I gulp down another mouthful as quickly as I can, hoping the bitter aftertaste won't hit so hard if I don't let the drink linger on my tongue. Already I'm starting to feel light-headed; the room seems too hot and too close, and stirrings of nausea rise in my stomach.

"Sorry, maybe it's me. I don't feel well." I push the half-finished drink away and try to offer him an apologetic smile but I can't seem to turn my head; my neck feels weak and my chin heavy. "I think I'm going to be sick," I add, hearing confused panic rising in a voice that sounds too distant to be mine.

"Ani?" Miyuki's voice is hazy under the noise of the bar; a wavering sound that comes from far away. "Aniyah, are you okay?"

I sway in my seat, my mouth opening to answer only to find I can't form the words. Timothy's voice comes from my left, moving around behind me as he leaves his post at the bar. "She's having a bad reaction to the alcohol," he says, his voice low and urgent. "Was her back hurting more than usual today? She probably took two hydrocodone pills instead of just one. We need to get her to the hospital, quickly."

I'm trembling, the soft shaking of my limbs the only movement I can manage; I can't even frown at his words. He's wrong: I've taken only one painkiller today and that was this morning. I've been on opioids for years and I know when I can have a single glass of liquor. What's more, I've experienced complication side-effects before, and this hazy paralysis seizing my limbs and muddying my brain isn't right. If I'd taken alcohol too soon after my medication I'd feel drowsy and slow, but not frozen in place.

"Aniyah, hang on; we'll get you to a doctor," Miyuki reassures me, placing her hand on my arm. There's something wrong with her grip and it takes me a minute to register she's shaking almost as hard as I am. She tries to stand and nearly falls, catching herself by sweeping her arm out and clinging to the bar for support. Her flailing knocks her notebook and pen to the floor, their clatter ringing in my ears.

"Craig, help Emma, won't you?" Timothy says. His voice is too calm, a surreal contrast to my pounding heart. His hands are on me, yanking me to my feet. Out of the corner of my eye, I watch a burly man in his mid-thirties hop down from his nearby seat. I hadn't noticed him before—just another patron at the bar—but he seems perfectly at ease wrapping his meaty hands around Miyuki's arms in a tight grip. I expect her to protest and push him away, but her eyes are half-closed and she looks almost asleep.

"Just a little tipsy," Timothy pronounces, shuffling me to the door. My legs are wooden, but somehow I manage to place one foot in front of the other.

What's happening? My thoughts are thick and muddy, but I know something is very wrong. Timothy shouldn't be like this, all cool collectedness and calm orders, as though he'd expected us to become sick like this. And *why* are we sick? Was there something wrong with the drink, some ingredient gone bad or rotten? Why just us, when surely other patrons must have had the same cocktail before we arrived?

The realization hits me along with the warm night air: Timothy *put* something in our drinks. I hear Craig behind me, pulling Miyuki along. Her feet drag loudly against the asphalt in her drugged stupor. The parking lot is empty of people—or, at least, I think it is; my vision blurs at the edges and I can't lift my head. Timothy guides us towards a black van with dark windows that I've never seen before.

We're being kidnapped, is my last thought before the drugs steal my vision and I black out.

CHAPTER 2

Keoki

I'm nursing my second beer and trying to decide whether to visit the men's room before or after I order another basket of cheese fries when she walks in. She's gorgeous; perfect brown satin skin and dark flashing eyes that deserve their own dedicated love song. Her hair is shorter than mine but otherwise identical: kinky curls flying in every direction. Maybe it's narcissistic to love what you see in the mirror, but I always say there's no arguing with good taste. She climbs her bar stool like she's scaling a mountain and in doing so claims my rapt attention. I love interesting people, and this girl moves like she has a story.

Strange for her to come in so near to closing time. Is she someone's ride? I glance at the clock on my phone. It's getting late, but I don't want to leave without talking to the band. Until they finish for the night, I've got time on my hands and nothing to keep myself awake except people-watching. I could order coffee, but I'm trying not to turn nocturnal. I've gotten away with laxity over the summer holiday—hauling boxes and taking inventory down at the warehouse isn't so taxing that I have to be vigilant about keeping regular hours—but when fall classes start I'll need to go back to a normal sleep schedule. Still, I'm off work tomorrow and can sleep in to make up for tonight; Dad won't bug me before noon.

I settle back with my beer and shoot off a quick text to let Dad know I'm still alive but I'll be home late. He's been cool about not hassling me, and I give him props for respecting my personal space. Really, getting to hang out with him again has been the best thing about moving down here to attend school in Texas. He was super enthusiastic about the suggestion that I live with him, and I know he's missed Makuahine and me, never once skipping a phone date and sending regular checks back home. I can't be angry at him anymore for leaving us; now that I'm older, I get that he had to travel where the work went.

We could have gone with him when he retired from the Air Force to become a defense contractor, but Makuahine didn't have it in her to leave O'ahu. The younger, long-ago versions of Dad and Makuahine—just plain George and Kailani before they had the best son in the world—swore to stay together for better or worse, but Texas wasn't included in the deal. Now that I've lived here a couple of years, I can't say I blame her. I miss the beach, the weather, the people, the look and feel of home. The food is different, too, and as much as I like all the Tex-Mex, there are days when I would kill to taste a proper Spam musubi again. *Maybe I can fly out over Christmas break for a few weeks.*

I take another swig of my beer and pray this song is the last of the night. I came out here to watch the band, specifically the bassist; he's a cute local boy, and a friend in the music department swore he was worth checking out. His technique is great—fast and artistic without being flashy—but there's only so much he can do to make up for the lead's flat vocals. I've been gritting my teeth, determined to hang on till closing time, because I want to talk to him about his playing style. I'm converting over to bass after several years on guitar, but still struggling with the switch from playing with a pick to just my fingers. Fingers give you a beefier tone and more control over the sound, but a pick is faster and I'm still attached to mine.

My fingers stray to the worn leather cuff on my wrist, the soft material so close in color to my skin that the bracelet almost fades into me. On the inside of the cuff, nestled against my arm, is a tiny pouch that carries the brass pick Makuahine had engraved for me before I left Hawai'i, bearing my name and a proverb she'd found. *Damn, I miss her.* I definitely have to fly out there this year. Maybe I can surprise her with a visit. It'd be awesome to pitch up on our porch and lift her up in a swinging hug when she answers the door. Hell, maybe I could persuade Dad to come out with me; for all that they've been separated for years, they love each other too much to divorce. I think she'd like to see him. I know I'd like to see them together.

A loud thumping noise on the stage grabs my attention. The band has finished and they're starting to break down their gear. The scrawny-looking drummer sorts out his kit from the shabby house equipment, and I wonder if it would be cool to offer my help. I'm strong enough to play roadie, but I might come off a little creepy; not everyone wants to be cornered by amateurs and groupies after a gig. Maybe I can just slip the bassist my number before he leaves and offer to buy him a beer sometime. I think that approach might be less pushy than *"Hi, let me carry that amp for you"* and snatching equipment out of their hands.

Satisfied with this plan, I slide my gaze back to the cutie at the bar. She's got a friend with her, a girl with a freckled nose and short black bangs spilling over sexy librarian glasses. Something the girlfriend said has made her smile, alighting her face with sunshine. I wonder if she's the type to enjoy adventurous holiday escapes and romantic walks on the beach. That'd be a good pick-up line, right? *"Hey, I'm flying out to Hawai'i for Christmas and need a girl to take home to momma; do you know anyone who'd be interested?"* I think I could probably pull it off with a proper application of confidence and a goofy grin to cushion the delivery.

She'd laugh, I decide, watching the tiny smile that never leaves the edges of her lips. When her girlfriend looks down at her hands, her face troubled, my cutie reacts with a touch that is one hundred percent sweet sympathy. The belated thought hits me that they might be together, like, actual girlfriends and not just girls-who-are-friends. Not that it's any of my business, but it's a solid reason not to saunter over and throw down a pick-up line unless I get an indication it would be welcome. There's a fine boundary between confident and creepy, and I don't want to be a jerk.

Tragically, no such invitation seems likely to be issued; all the while I've been enjoying the view from my table, neither of them has even looked my way. I blame the bartender for monopolizing their attention. He's had his eye on them since they walked in, working his way down to their end of the bar and then parking himself while trying to make a play for my crush. The girl with the librarian glasses studiously ignores him by doodling on her arm while he talks, and my crush hunches over her drink and glues her gaze to the counter to avoid making eye contact, hoping he'll take the hint and leave them alone.

It's not until she pushes her drink away and balls her fist into her stomach that I realize she's actually sick, her pained body language more than just a manifestation of her desire to be rid of the bartender. My hands pat uselessly at my pockets but I don't have any antacids on me. I could offer to run down to the nearest gas station, but she might not want to take pills from a total stranger. She stares hard at the counter and I think she's about to hurl, but then the bartender helps her out of her chair. I figure he's going to guide her to the toilets while her girlfriend pays their tab so she can take her home.

Then I see the girlfriend sway in her own seat, and I realize *she's* sick, too. She lurches woozily forward, knocking her notebook to the floor as her hand sweeps out to catch herself. Before I can hop up to help, a big burly dude is already out of his chair and steadying her. Which is nice of him—very Good Samaritan and exactly what I'd be doing myself if I were a little quicker on the draw—except the way he holds her bothers me. I stare at them and realize his hands don't hesitate like they should. He grips her as if he handles sick girls all day, instead of like a random dude helping out a stranger. Before I can process that thought, he and the bartender lockstep the girls out the door as fast as they can move.

Where's the fire? I wonder, frowning at the door as it closes behind them. None of this makes any sense. Two girls become violently ill as soon as they get their drinks, and instead of helping them to the bathroom the bartender ejects them with the help of what seems to be an off-duty bouncer. Why? Were the girls underage? I could have sworn they were over twenty-one, but girls can do amazing things with makeup. I got pretty sick the first time I drank liquor, and if the bartender had been too busy flirting to check licenses, he'd want them off the premises as soon as he realized his mistake. Safer to bounce them than risk someone reporting him for serving minors and losing his license.

Yet walking them outside just moves the problem to a new location. Neither of those girls looked anywhere near fit to drive. Maybe the bartender will call them a taxi, but he hasn't exactly struck me as the responsible type. I sigh and glance back at the band. They're almost finished loading up, carrying their gear out to the back parking lot rather than through the front. If I go chasing after those girls, I won't be able to catch the bassist and this whole night will have been a waste. But I don't want a drunk driver on my conscience. I toss a couple bills on the table and head out, swinging by the bar to scoop up the fallen notebook.

The front lot is deserted this time of night, with not a soul to be seen and only a handful of parked cars. I'm confused when the heavy night air first hits me; I'd expected to hear retching and vomiting, or the high rapid babble of drunk conversation, yet the lot is silent. For a moment I think I'm too late, that they must have driven off; but if they've already gone, where are the bartender and bouncer? Then I hear faint sounds under the hum of the air conditioner units: soft scuffling noises and low voices trailing out from the side alley between the bar and the next building over.

Is someone fucking? It's a stupid thought, but the first thing that pops into my mind at the furtive noises; there's a muffled quality to the voices that doesn't sound at all like someone asking a sick girl if she's okay. I hesitate, running through a short list of scenarios, none of which are good.

16

I'm the last person to ruin someone's fun but those girls are underage, drunk, sick, or some combination of the three, and that's *not* okay.

I hug the building, stepping silently around to the side alley. I figure I'll duck my head around the corner and assess the situation before I make any noise; I don't want to startle anyone into a panic if the girls are in danger. When I reach the edge I peek around the side, my eyes straining to see in the dark. The alley is wider than I'd realized and tall buildings on either side cast the entire area into deep shadow. I can only just discern movement at the far end of the alley: two tall shapes huddled around a dark van.

"—objections are noted, Craig. Just finish tying those knots."

"I'm just saying I don't like surprises. Thought you called me out here for a beer, not for a public snatch from your own bar. You want me to tell them you're *trying* to get caught?"

"You do and I'll break your fucking teeth. Do you know how long it took me to find her? I didn't pick this one for her looks. I spend a couple goddamn months being sure she's the right one, only for her to ghost on me. My options were to do it tonight or lose her forever, so less talk and more rope."

Holy shit. I jerk my head back and flatten myself against the brick wall. I thought I'd been prepared for anything I might see, but my heart is pounding against my ribcage like it wants to get out. *What's the plan here, genius?* I'd been figuring some loud yelling would scare off the kind of guys who like to manhandle drunk girls. Worst case, I could throw a punch; it's been a few years since I hit anyone, but it's like riding a wave: it comes back when you need it. But I don't know what to do about ropes and vans.

You hear stories on campus about kidnappers who prey on college girls. You never know if the stories are urban legends, but they tell girls to walk in pairs and carry pepper-spray. No one tells you what to do if you actually witness a kidnapping taking place. Should I go back inside and get help? I don't know if anyone will believe me, and I don't want to risk these guys driving off while I try to rouse the bar. I can't even see their license number from here, so I'd have nothing for the police to track if they got away.

But I have my phone, I realize, hand flying to my pocket as I pray the battery isn't dead. It lights at my touch and I press it close to my ear, angled away from the alley so they won't see the glow. I've never dialed emergency services before, but of course I know the number and I punch it in as quickly as my fingers can move.

"911, what is your emergency?"

The woman's voice on the other end of the line is weirdly comforting in its normalcy, but my blood still pounds a staccato rhythm in my ears. My voice is so soft I can barely hear myself, and even then I fear I'm too loud. "Ma'am, there are girls being kidnapped."

"What is your location?"

It's such an obvious question, crisply asked with expectation of an immediate answer, but I'm thrown by it. *Where the fuck am I?* I don't remember the name of the bar. I'm not a regular, I only came for the band tonight, and my brain blanks in panic. "I-I don't know, it's a bar, I'm outside a bar—"

"Can you see a street sign? An officer has been dispatched to the vicinity of your mobile."

I can't think, I can't seem to breathe. I twist my head to view the nearest intersection, its forlorn lights blinking at the empty street, but I can't find a single sign. Half of the small streets around the campus edges are missing their signs; they get stolen to decorate dorm rooms and the city is slow to replace them. I feel fresh panic rising, but if there's a car coming maybe I can give them directions and have them retrace the route I took to get here. "It's not on the main road; I had to turn right off of—"

My world explodes into pain and a throbbing red cloud obscures my vision. There are no conscious thoughts in my mind, no words or images, but other senses dutifully report in: I hear the clatter of my phone hitting the ground and the hard crunch of a shoe coming down on glass. The crunch is too close to my ears, the sound ought to come from lower down, but then my nerves relay the rough grit of the parking lot under my fingers and I slowly register that I'm kneeling on my hands. *What the fuck was that?* I've taken a punch before and recognize the pounding throb in my temples, but this was like being blindsided by a hammer.

"Goddammit. We've got ten minutes, maybe less. Pull him back into the alley, Craig."

I'm hoisted up by hands that feel like stone mitts. I'm too woozy from the blow to struggle effectively and let myself go limp, figuring he'll drop me and have to drag me into the shadows—anything to slow them down—but my dead weight doesn't even faze him; the bouncer hurls me over his shoulder like I'm a sack of flour.

"Don't like the look of this one," the low voice rumbles underneath me. "You want me to kill him and throw him in the back?"

He shrugs his massive shoulders and I'm tossed hard on the ground, my vision spinning again. We're beside the van, the tires so close I could reach out to touch the mud in the treads. The side door of the vehicle is wide open and I can see the girls sprawled on the matted carpet. Their eyes are closed and they've been tied up with that brightly-colored rope people use on boat docks. The bartender stands nearby, glaring at me with cold anger.

"No, we're going to have to port over from here," he says, shaking his head in annoyance. "Might as well bring him with us."

"But the usual place—"

"Craig, I don't need you driving around with three bodies in the van if cops pull you over," the bartender snaps. "I don't *want* to pull a portal here, but it's better than the alternatives. You'll have to take them in by yourself. I'll port back, close the bar, and answer any questions if police show up."

My head is still pounding. I press my hand to the side of my face, registering dully that the slick wetness under my fingers is blood. "Dude, I told them everything," I slur, dragging my swimming vision up to meet the bartender's gaze. "What you look like, the name of the bar, your friend here. They're gonna catch you. Let us go and you'll just be facing an assault rap instead of murder. You can be smart about this."

The beefy bouncer cuts me off, though I'm not sure he's even heard me; his slow rumbling voice seems to respond about two minutes late to everything. "You want me to take all three of them in by myself? You don't even know if he's changeable, Tim. What if he's one of the ones who can't handle it over there?"

The bartender snorts, but his cold eyes don't leave mine and I know he heard me loud and clear. "Then you'll only have to carry in two bodies and not three," he says. He clasps his hands together in front of his chest, and for a moment I think he's praying. "But after all the trouble he's put us through, I fucking hope he survives," he adds in a low tone.

There's something wrong with the periphery of my vision. I shake my head, trying to clear my eyes. *Probably a concussion,* I think with a wince, but I've never experienced one like this: white mist is filling my vision, swirling in the air around us. It can't be real; aside from the fact that it must be eighty degrees out here, mist wouldn't be bright white in the middle of night in a dark alley. Yet the mist grows until it forms a thick wall that encloses us in a glowing bubble.

The manifestation of white mist is enough to make me worry about the state of my bruised brain, so what I very much do *not* need right now is for these two dudes to begin shifting and changing around the edges. The bouncer, already two heads taller than me and as broad-shouldered as an ox, begins to grow. A sandy-brown texture ripples over his skin as everything about him widens and his edges sharpen to angular points, until I could swear he's a giant made of rough-quarried stone slabs. *No wonder that punch took me down,* I think, staring at the strange apparition.

The bartender, too, grows a little taller, but he doesn't harden out into a half-man, half-rock monster; instead, his facial features shift and his hair grows brighter until each blond strand is shimmering like real gold. I've seen the stuff in candlelight, the way the metal glows, and there's nothing quite like the real thing. Before, he seemed impossibly bland and boring with nothing interesting or noteworthy about him, yet now his face clarifies into one of the most beautiful I've ever seen. He's still not my type, but for those cheekbones I'd make an exception on principle.

"What the—?" Words are inadequate to encompass the mist, the strange blond beauty, and the beastly rock-creature.

"Lights out, kiddo," the man with golden hair declares, grinning at my confusion. "Craig, put him under for the trip."

"Right," responds the beast, his voice like the slow grind of gravel. His impossibly huge fist swings towards me; I can feel the momentum behind it and have just enough time to know that this will hurt in the morning. Then the impact hits home and I'm out like a light.

CHAPTER 3

Aniyah

"Hey. Wake up!" A demanding hand pats my cheek as bright sunlight casts red spots on the back of my closed eyelids. I groan, trying to work out why I feel so groggy. It's rare for me to sleep late into the morning. *Why didn't my alarm go off?*

"She's coming round. Slap her again."

Another pat against my cheek, the hand cool and strong. "Wake up, do you hear me? We haven't got a lot of time. Imani, how's the other one?"

"Stirring slowly, but we'll get her awake. C'mon, sweetie, there's a good girl."

Girls' voices, unfamiliar and too many. *The other one? Other than me? Do they mean Miyuki? Is she here? Where are we? Oh god, Miyuki!* Memories flood back, jagged and broken at the edges, a flash of disarrayed images: Timothy, golden hair and bright smile, leaning against the side of the bar. Green liquor hiding bitter poison in my glass. Heavy, unfamiliar hands restraining me before hurling me into darkness.

My eyes fly open in panic. I twist my limbs wildly to no effect: I'm tied from chest to foot, rope biting the skin of my arms and ankles when I struggle. "Miyuki!" Her name is a hoarse cry on my lips, my tongue too dry to shout properly. I turn my head to look for her but the world spins around me. Cool hands reach to hold me down; I try to yank away but searing pain shoots through my spine at the motion.

"Hey! Hold still, you're going to hurt yourself. I know you're scared but I need you to listen to me."

I freeze, less from her words and more from old familiar instinct; if I keep twisting like this, I'll pull a muscle in my back and be bedridden for a week. But holding still while restrained is harder than I'd ever have imagined. Animal panic rises in my blood, uselessly urging me to struggle against the ropes even as my mind knows better. *I must calm down, or I'll never get free.* Blinking against bright sunlight and the lingering dizziness, I turn my head slowly to look around me and my jaw drops open in surprise.

I'm in some kind of cave. Sun spills from a wide shaft set high in the ceiling, bathing the curving reddish-brown sandstone walls in warm light. In the very center of the cavern, a long table has been cut from the rock and its mineral deposits sparkle in the glow of the sunny spotlight. The table has been set with bowls of fruit I don't recognize and spiced meats which cause my stomach to clench greedily. The wall on the far side of the cavern glistens with moving water, the silent stream feeding a natural pool below. The water looks clean and inviting, and my dry tongue aches with need at the sight.

I've been laid out on a stone platform roughly the length and width of my full-sized bed back home, leveled off about three feet from the ground. The slab is set back from the light so that I am sheltered in cool shade. Red nylon ropes hold me bound, but I'm relieved to see I'm still dressed; whatever Timothy did to me while I was unconscious, it didn't involve the removal of my clothes. When I turn my head to the right, I see Miyuki similarly trussed and lying nearby on an identical rocky altar and beginning to stir awake.

Around us are the girls I heard before: four young women who can't be much older than I am. *No, five,* I amend when my eyes sweep the back of the cavern. The fifth girl is slender and tall, with olive skin and light brown hair swept up into a ponytail. Her ear is pressed against a set of enormous ornately-gilded doors dominating the far cave wall. She looks frightened and alert at her post, like a rabbit poised to run. Her body is liberally covered in an impressive array of tattoos that will be easy to pick out of a police line-up, and my inspired plan to make a collected witness grounds me against the steady panicked roar in my ears.

Yet there's something *wrong* about her. Aside from the fact that she's standing in a warm sunny cave that ought to be in Arizona or on a movie set, she's dressed in what looks like white gauze. The other girls are dressed in the same filmy cloth, as though they'd collectively decided that clothes were too much of a hassle and just wrapped themselves in translucent bath towels instead. The diaphanous fabric does little to hide the outline of their bodies, and embarrassed heat rises to my cheeks. *Why would Timothy kidnap us only to drop us off at a day spa? What is this, some kind of cult?*

I yank my gaze to their faces, which I resolve to memorize as fast as I can; if I'm going to be kidnapped, I'll make damn sure everyone involved goes to jail for a long time. Yet my determination almost immediately falters when I study the girls nearest Miyuki. A pretty black girl with a compassionate face and short ringlet curls bends over her, gently touching her face as she stirs. Another girl hovers nearby looking impatient to help; with long auburn-red hair and thick curves all over, she looks like a model for one of those specialty plus-size stores at the mall where Miyuki buys her in-betweenie jeans. The girl pinches Miyuki's glasses between her fingers as though she's holding them for her. Nothing about either of the girls seems hostile.

Who are these people? Nearer to me, a petite blond white girl sits on the cavern floor by the glittering table, her chin resting on her fist. She returns my stare with zero interest in her dull green eyes, and a belated realization strikes me: she doesn't seem to mind I've seen her face. None of them have, which can't be a good sign. My eyes flit back to the nearest girl, the last of the five: a short Asian girl with wavy brown armpit-length hair. Her eyes probe me like flint knives running over my skin, and her hand is poised to pat my cheek again—yet, as with the others, I don't get a sense that she wants to harm me.

"Hey," she says, her voice firm. "I know you're scared, and I'm sorry, but we don't have much time before he comes. I need you to tell me everything about yourself, about where you're from."

"Who are you?" My voice rasps against my dry throat. "Where are we? Look, if you let us go, we don't need to tell anyone."

There's sympathy in her determined eyes, but not nearly enough to distract from her purpose. "I'll answer all your questions and protect you the best I can, but we don't have much time. I need to know your name and where you're from. Are you from the University?"

"The university? Yes, I— We both are." I peer at her in renewed confusion, my temples throbbing with the residual effects of whatever drug Timothy gave us. The way she says it, *'the University'*, sounds wrong to my ears. She says it as if there's only one, like it's more important than a mere school.

She nods in a manner probably meant to reassure me, but I'm too freaked out to appreciate it properly. "And your name?" she presses. "What's your name? What's hers? You said 'Miyuki'. Is that her name?" To my right, Miyuki groans softly and stirs at the sound of her name. I twist my head to look, but my interrogator grasps my chin with cool hands and forces my gaze back to her. "Please, I *need* to know."

I can't work out her angle with these questions. If we've been kidnapped, wouldn't we have been taken for a reason? The only one I can think of is ransom; my parents don't have that kind of money, but Miyuki's father is loaded. If they kidnapped us with specific intent to shake down John, they'd need to be sure they have the right girl—and of course Timothy would have called her Emma, not Miyuki. *No wonder they're confused.*

"My name is Aniyah," I tell her, trying to keep my voice steady. If all they want is ransom, we can survive this. I don't give her my last name; I don't want them to get greedy and hound my parents for money they don't have. "My friend over there: yes, I call her Miyuki but her first name is Emma. *Emma Miyuki*, you understand? Her dad is going to want both of us alive, not just her; I'm a close friend of the family. He's rich enough to pay anything you ask, so let's just stay calm. What should I call you?" I don't want their real names, but maybe if I can forge a bond with this girl they won't hurt us.

"I can't tell you that yet," she says, shaking her head. Her voice is low, almost furtive. "I *will* tell you, but later. Right now, I need to know everything you can tell me about yourself and about her. Is there anything you don't want forgotten?"

Forgotten? None of this makes any sense: this cave, her clothes, the urgency behind her questions. A suspicion I've been trying to keep at bay now worms forward: are these girls captives, like us? Maybe someone is coming to kill us, Miyuki and me, and the girls want to be able to tell our story later if they survive. I shiver against the ropes that bind me, blinking back unhelpful tears.

"I don't understand. Please let me go. Take off these ropes. Tell me who you are and where I am."

The blond girl scoffs, the sound dull and flat. "She's not going to tell you anything, you know," she says to the girl who questions me. Her voice lacks any interest or inflection. "Look at her; she's too scared. Can you blame her?" I hear the sounds of the other girls whispering to Miyuki, trying to coax her to lucidity.

My interrogator ignores her. Leaning forward, she takes my face in both her hands. I try to move away, but I'm tied too tightly to escape. "Listen to me, Aniyah," she says, her voice solemn. "I will not lie to you, not ever. I need you to trust me right now. Tell me about yourself. Is there anyone you love? Do you have family, any parents or siblings? What's your favorite color? Your favorite food? If you could be anywhere else right now,

26

where would you be?" Her tone speeds up, becoming more urgent at the litany of questions.

What is this, freshman orientation? I try again to turn towards Miyuki—I need to know she's okay, I need to see what they're doing to her—but this girl holds me in an iron grip. "You're not making any sense!" I protest, blinking away the hot tears that spring up to blur my vision. "Am I in *love*?"

"Aniyah, I need you to answer me," she persists, holding me in place.

"Yes, I have family! I'm an only child and my parents don't live in the area; they're not rich, you won't get any money from them! My favorite colors are yellow and black. I like pizza with pineapple. Where would I rather be right now? What do you expect me to say: 'There's no place like home'? Please take me back to the university campus! Or *anywhere* but here! Now let me see Miyuki!"

I throw answers out quickly, desperate to satisfy her so she'll let me go. Out of the corner of my eye, I see the blond one straighten where she sits, the bored flatness of her expression showing the tiniest spark of interest. "That's a new one," she murmurs, watching me with narrow eyes. "Ask her about pineapple."

The dark-haired girl doesn't look away from my face. "Good! That's good. What can you tell me about your friend? Does she like the pizza with pineapple? Where is her home? You said she has a father; does she live with him? Do you all live together at the University Campus?"

My answers tumble from her lips in a stilted jumble, repeated by rote as though the words don't carry the same meaning for her as they do for me. *Forget Oz, this is Wonderland,* I think, my breath coming in hard gasps now. Whatever is wrong with this girl, she's not in any position to help us.

"Listen to me," I say slowly, enunciating each word as I hold steady eye contact with her. "I need you to untie these ropes. Can you do that?"

A flash of frustration crosses the girl's face at my tone, and I hear the blond one sigh. "She's checked out," she says, her tone returning to the flat boredom of before. "Maybe the other one—"

"He's coming!" A fearful yelp comes from across the room. The dark-haired girl releases my face and I twist to see the tattooed girl running over from her place by the doors. "He's coming, I heard him," she hisses, her voice high and anxious.

"Balls," the blond girl observes in a dark tone.

"We only just got the other one to come round." I hear a low protest near Miyuki and twist my head in time to see the big red-headed girl drop Miyuki's glasses down her cleavage.

"We're gonna be okay. Take your places! Now!"

The order from my interrogator is no less authoritative for her low volume. The tattooed girl scurries to the table in the center of the room, plunking down to sit cross-legged on the floor. She then pretends to pick lazily through a bowl of fruit for the ripest offering. The blond girl crosses the room at a fast clip, dropping her gauzy dress to the floor and sliding silently into the far pool; once in the water, she makes a show of washing her hair. Over by Miyuki, the other two girls scurry to different corners of the room.

I have only a handful of seconds to register the panic rising in the room. Their leader whirls back to me, grasping my chin in her hand again. "Let go of me!" I hiss, my voice low to match theirs.

"Aniyah!" The fear in her wide eyes scares me more than anything else thus far. "I need you to close your eyes and pretend to be asleep. Please. Please trust me. He'll kill me if he knows we spoke."

I can't breathe, the ropes too tight against my chest. I shake my head, trying to escape. I don't know how to accept her frightening words, but I can't look away from her direct gaze. Two heartbeats later, I nod my assent, squeezing my eyes shut to block her out. *Let this be a nightmare, please. Let me wake up now.*

I can't pretend to be asleep when I'm nearly hyperventilating, but her hand moves away from my chin and something warm touches my forehead—a damp cloth, soft and soothing. The warmth seeps into me, the muscles in my face relaxing in response. My breathing evens out to a soft cadence that might be mistaken for sleep as long as my eyes stay closed.

There's a scraping sound, metal against stone, and the temperature of the room sharply dips. I still hear Miyuki stirring behind me, but otherwise the room is deathly silent; I realize with a shiver that the girls are holding their breaths. A sibilant voice issues from the direction of the doors. "You girls didn't call for me. Should I be angry." It's not a question; there's no uptick in the silken voice.

"That one has only just begun to stir, Master. This one is still asleep. We did not wish to bother you." The voice is the girl who questioned me, but her tone is softer now, deferential with a touch of simper.

I hear the whisper of heavy cloth on stone, and an encroaching chill raises bumps on my arms. There is a long pause, the silence heavy in my ears. I have to force myself to breathe normally and not hold my breath. "This one is awake," the strange voice murmurs, the tone still utterly without inflection.

"No, Master," the girl contradicts, almost chirruping in her denial. "Her eyes are closed, see?"

"Her eyes are closed because she is pretending," the voice says. "Diamond, this is why you would be useless in the Arena; you are a fool. All girls are. Now let me work."

She's already saying "yes, Master" in that high little-girl voice of hers, shot through now with contrition, when a hand grasps my throat. I cough violently for air at the sudden assault, uselessly jerking against the ropes that bind me. My eyes fly open and I find myself staring into the face of a horror I have no name for.

The creature she called 'Master' stands eight feet tall. His hand encircles my neck and lifts me high into the air. He's shaped like a human—two arms, two legs, a torso—but there the similarities end. He's paler than white, the color of nocturnal grubs who have never seen the light of day. He holds me level with what I would call his head, except it looks nothing like a head should. Bald and hairless, with a wide slit cut in parody of a mouth, and two tiny red-rimmed holes set in a flat expanse where a nose ought to be. There are no eyes, not even the shape or suggestion of eye-holes, yet I know the creature is staring at me even as I stare wide-eyed back at him. Around the edges of his head jagged hooks of ugly metal protrude from his skin, as if a canvas was meant to be stretched over his face for painting.

I would scream but there is no air. I can't kick or fight against the ropes; I can barely breathe because of the pressure around my throat. *I'm going to die. I've been kidnapped by aliens and I'm going to die. I don't want to die here!* I suck a thin thread of air through my nose, struggling not to pass out.

The creature tilts his head as though studying me, but there's nothing kind about his curiosity. "Yes," he murmurs, his lips barely parting to allow the whispering hiss to escape. "She was worth the wait. Powerful spotters are so hard to acquire. This one will see to the edge of my arena once she is awakened. Diamond, you will take good care of this one."

"Yes, Master," she agrees, her eyes obediently downcast. "And the other one? May we keep her? I know the boys will like her; did you see her pretty freckles?"

He spares the tiniest of glances for Miyuki. "Common stock. No rare talent to develop. Hardly worth the expense to keep. Easier just to eat her." He pauses. I have to fight for every breath I take while he remains frozen with me still dangling in his iron grip. "If you think the boys will like her, I will allow it."

Eat her? Keep her? My eyes fly to Miyuki, taking in how wan she appears on her slab, trussed up in red rope that looks so much like blood in my swimming vision. *Miyuki, are we going to die here?*

Memories swirl through my mind, fast and frightened, the last flash before I die. I drove us to the bar. I'd wanted to see Timothy in a neutral place where we wouldn't be able to talk about anything heavy, where there'd be no chance of going to bed with him again until I'd sorted out my feelings for Miyuki. I'd trusted him, cared for him, and he turned around and kidnapped me and my best friend. No, not just my best friend. She's the girl I care most for in the world, the person I live with and love and made love to.

I should have told her, I realize. *When she said she loved me at the bar, I should have said it back to her. I should have told her I meant it.* I'll watch her until death comes, I decide, even as my vision swims sickeningly again.

Yet death doesn't come. There's a pulling sensation in the back of my mind, a strange draining like the swirl of water in an emptying tub. It's a sleepy feeling, reminding me of lazy sunny days when I would spend the summer with—

With?

There were summers, I remember those. Mama would drive me out to the country to spend two weeks with—

I can't recall. I feel a quick spike of fear, but it fumbles and slips away into the drain, there and gone again in a flash. The hazy nothingness spreading through my mind brings a numbing calm that deadens where it touches. Why should I be afraid of a silly little thing like a memory not existing? Certainly there's nothing fearful about the gentle soporific whirl in my mind, lulling me down into a warm darkness.

My vision clears for just a moment and I see a pretty girl with short dark hair and a splash of freckles on her fair face, lying bound in red rope on a slab of sandstone. She's staring blearily up at me with soft hazel eyes, though I'm not sure if she sees me. I smile at her, wishing to be polite, and think we might get along if we came to know each other. Then the inviting darkness drags me down and takes my vision with it.

CHAPTER 4

Keoki

I groan, the sound a dry scratch in my throat, and clench my eyes tighter shut against the intense sunlight beating down on me. *It's the middle of the day. Did I fall asleep?* I have a fleeting feeling that this is bad, but I'm not sure why. My head pounds with a dull thudding pain, and all my thoughts seem fragmented and incomplete, as if I've been smashed into a million pieces and put back together poorly.

My hands move at my sides and I feel the familiar brush of sand beneath my fingers, but the sand is wrong. It isn't soft and rounded like sand should be but rather rough and crumbly, the grains too large and strangely fragile. When I pry my eyes open to look—squinting against the sun and ignoring a low roar rumbling in my ears—the grains clinging to my skin aren't the soft pale buttermilk color sand should be. Instead, my hands are dusted in a dark burnt ocher flecked with tiny crystals that catch the light. I stare at my hands and the strange sand coating them, and try to work out how I know these things.

I know what hands are and that these are mine, and I know what sand is and that this sand is wrong. The knowledge came when I felt the coarse texture under my fingers and opened my eyes to see the tiny particles on my skin. Information flowed to me freely as though it were always inside me, just waiting to pour out. But what I don't know is *how* I know these things, or where the information came from in the first place. I don't remember being taught any of this, and I can't imagine where you would go to learn that sand should be soft and yellowish-brown rather than rough and burnt-golden.

In point of fact, I don't remember *anything* before waking just now. There's a darkness in my mind where the jagged thoughts come from, but poking at that mental spot sets off a throbbing ache behind my temples. I wish I knew if that were normal, and if everyone else feels this way. I assume there's an *everyone else*. I don't remember ever meeting another person, but I can't be the only one in existence, can I? *But where are they? And where am I?* I pull myself up to a sitting position in the rough sand, squinting against the blinding brightness that fills the sky and glints off the crystalline ground.

I'm in some kind of valley. Sheer mountainous walls enclose the area on all sides, framing the land in a vast oval of towering stone. The ground beneath me is unwaveringly level, smooth sand stretching in every direction without the slightest hint of a slope. All around me, giant spires stab up through the sand at random intervals, jagged fingers of sandstone reaching five times my height. Sloped wooden platforms wrap around the spires like ramps, leading up to the top and supported by thin sun-bleached poles.

A loud clatter sounds in the distance behind me, the screech of something solid scraping stone. I whirl to face the noise, but the sound is drowned out by a deafening spike in the rumbling roar which has been filling my ears since I awoke. Like the sand, the low rumble had felt vaguely familiar while still being entirely wrong, and I had set aside the wrongness of it until I could get my footing under me. Now the roar rises to an unnatural crashing pitch that builds on itself without dying, and I realize that the cacophony is coming from the cliffs that ring the valley.

I bring a hand up to shade my eyes, peering at the dark walls surrounding me. I hadn't bothered to study them before, dazzled by the sun and more interested in the strange spires. Now that I take a moment to let my eyes adjust, I'm surprised to see movement blanketing the walls: colorful shapes throbbing with living vibrancy in time with the frenzied roar. *People*, I realize, my breath catching at the sheer number of them, exploding the population of my world from one to thousands. *It's everyone else.*

I turn in a circle to see them, so close to me and yet too high to reach. The cliff walls are set with tiered ridges for sitting and standing, each row placed further back and higher up so everyone has an unobstructed view of the valley where I stand. The people clustered on the ridges look more comfortable than I feel down here, and I wonder if I could get up there. Only then do I notice they're all turned towards me, clapping and cheering. This feels oddly right, as though I've seen a crowd arranged in rows on rising seats like this before, yet I don't understand why they're all so pleased. *Have I done something good?*

The lowest row of the nearest wall is close enough for me to see the expressions of the people there. One of them, a girl with hair so vibrantly orange I think she might actually be aflame, leaps to her feet and excitedly waves a scrap of red cloth—some kind of pennant, I realize, the word entering my mind without any context. I study her eyes for some kind of clue, only to realize she's not actually looking at me. It's hard to tell from this distance, but I think she's looking at something behind me.

Turning to follow her gaze, I get the briefest glimpse of the thing before it bowls me over: golden-brown shale coats its legs and arms like armor while stone shards form the jagged shape of what might be a head, if you were flexible on the whole needs-to-be-round concept. Then its massive weight slams into me like an oversized fist and I'm sent flying. I hurtle through the air and everything is a blur of dark cliffs and bright sky until gravity reasserts itself and I skid through the rough sand, raking deep scrapes into every bit of exposed skin and ripping my clothes.

My vision swims while I crouch on my hands and knees in the sand, sputtering for breath. *What was that?* I drag my gaze up from the ground, shaking my head until the world stops spinning, but when I get a good look at the thing I don't know what to call it. No identifying words come flooding forward, though I can name the individual pieces: stone, rocks, jagged, brown, *wrong*. It's a creature, a monster, roughly human-shaped and yet thoroughly inhuman. Yet I can tell those words aren't unique to this thing; it's a monster because I don't have any better words for it.

And it's running towards me, I realize, fresh panic spiking through my blood. The creature rushes me in a heavy lumbering gait, its long arms swinging with each thudding step. One impossibly huge fist pulls back to strike again, and my hands scramble uselessly against the sand, trying and failing to push myself up.

I need to run, dodge, roll, *anything* to get away, but time slows in preparation for the blow and I know it's too late. The monster is too near and too fast, and my mind is still sluggish, not yet recovered from that first heavy hit. If the incoming punch is anything like the last one, I'm pretty sure it'll put me down and out. *Am I gonna wake up in a different valley and do this all over again?*

"Hey!" There's a shout over the roar of the crowd, the sound coming from my right side; out of the corner of my eye I see a blur of fast movement in the direction of the call.

I blink and almost miss it: a guy with shaggy black hair, decked out in some kind of leather armor, speeds between me and the creature. He crouches low to grab a handful of sharp sand which he hurls directly into its face. The crowd roars in approval and the monster stumbles back, shaking its head and clawing at rough clumps of sand streaming down the jagged rocks comprising its face.

My unexpected savior skids to a halt next to me, pulling me to my feet with a quick jerk on my arm. "Wake up, newbie, before you get yourself killed; nobody's gonna save you out here!" he yells. He barely glances at me, his gaze firmly fixed on the creature. His words aren't technically a true statement, given that he's just done exactly that, but the gist is received loud and clear.

"Uh, thanks," I manage, my own attention pretty equally occupied by the angrily roaring monster. It still claws at its face, but I have a feeling this reprieve won't last forever. "Do you have any pointers on the whole staying-alive thing?"

I spare a glance at him, searching his face for answers or at least some spark of recognition. He's paler than me, his skin fair with warm undertones. Straight black hair spills over into dark eyes so unreadable they seem almost sorrowful in their emptiness. Bits and pieces of him seem familiar to my rattled memory, but the overall whole is a blank to me; if I knew this guy before, I don't know him now.

He snorts at my question, as if it were the stupidest thing I could ask. "Get a weapon," he advises, then turns on his heel and kicks off at a sudden run.

I stare after him, wasting a few precious seconds to gawk. He's *fast*, the shifting sand under his feet doing little to slow him down. He makes a beeline for the nearest of the huge stone fingers that stab up through the sand, his feet pounding on the twisting wooden ramp in a hard staccato rhythm as he dashes up the spiral walkway. *What in the world is he doing?*

Movement nearby reminds me that I don't have time to watch him. I wrench my gaze back to the stony creature, studying it warily. Loose sand streams off its strange body and rough hands continue to claw at its rocky face, but the flailing has slowed and become more controlled. The monster straightens from a crouch and sets its legs in a determined stance, its rocky head turning slowly around as if seeking the source of the most recent attack.

Oh, this probably isn't good. My heart is beating wildly with the need to put as much distance as possible between myself and the monster, but I don't want to draw attention with any sudden movements. I peer at it, wondering how it senses its prey. There are no visible eyes or ears on

36

the creature, nothing but rocks clumped together in a messy heap that shouldn't hold together the way it does. *Can it see me, or hear me, or smell me? Does it feel vibrations in the sand, or sense moisture in the air?*

I take several careful steps backwards, moving tentatively farther away a few inches at a time. The crumbly ground shifts under me with each step, making it difficult to walk, yet my legs know this feeling. *I can do this,* I realize. *I could run, even.* Then its blank face swivels my way and I freeze in place, hardly daring to breathe. I hold perfectly still for a dozen heartbeats while an eyeless face seems to stare at me, then it resumes its slow scan of the valley. *Okay, it can't see me. Small comfort.*

The crowd is cheering and catcalling so loudly I can barely hear myself think. If I can't creep away, I have a dilemma: run or stand my ground and hide. Running appeals to the fear singing in my blood, but I remember how fast the creature moved when it hurtled into me with a body-blow that sent me flying. As comforting as it is to know I can run on this sand, that ability won't do me any good if I can't outrun this monster.

But if I don't like my chances of running away, what else can I do? There's enough distance between myself and the creature such that it can't simply reach out to grab me, but I won't be able to stay motionless forever. Eventually it will sense me and close the small gap separating us. Maybe I could distract it in some way, like throwing sand in its face again. *What did that guy say? 'Get a weapon'?*

I look around, but there's nothing here that fits that word, only sand and rocks and sun. I twist my head to find the guy, picking out the nearby wooden platform he'd been running up. He's reached the top and his hands are patting all over the enormous spire as if looking for something. Suddenly his hand snakes into a hole near the very top, and I see the bright flash of metal as he draws out what my mind instantly identifies as a sword: sharp, long, pointy, and meant to be stuck in things.

Before I can wonder what he plans to do with that, he takes off running back down the platform. At the second loop from the top around the stone spire, he leaps into empty space like he thinks he's going to fly, tucks his knees up into his chest, and turns an honest-to-god flip in the air while the crowd roars in sudden approval.

The shale creature whips around at the hard *whump* in the sand where the guy lands, but as fast as a lick the sword flashes out, reflecting light as it swings. Metal connects with stone in a resounding crash and the creature's head is swept clean off in a burst of tiny rocks and rubble. Underneath the explosive clamor is the ugly sound of metal breaking and the top half of his sword tears off, flying wildly through the air to embed itself in the sand nearby.

I'm pretty sure my eyes are wide enough to pop as I stare at the guy who has now saved me twice. "Hey, thanks, man," I tell him. I'm holding back a grin, feeling light-headed with relief. It's all I can do not to tease him for saying nobody would have my back out here when he seems to be doing just fine on that score. I still don't know where we are or what's going on, but at least I've made a friend.

He doesn't return my smile, though. Doesn't even look at me. His dark eyes watch the headless stone monster while his hands grip the broken sword, panting for breath where he stands. It hits me in a slow way, the thoughts sluggish in my throbbing head, that the monster hasn't fallen down the way you might expect something missing a head to do.

In fact, I realize with a dawning horror as the words *oh shit* flit across my mind, it's still moving. A fist the size of my own head and covered in rough bulky stone swipes out and catches the other guy right in the stomach, sending him reeling back in pain.

"Hey!" I move before I have time to think whether this is a good idea, launching myself hard into the back of the thing in an attempt to throw it off balance. It stumbles under my weight and twists to try to face me—determined to meet this new threat head-on, I guess, but minus an actual head.

I move with it, wanting to stay behind and out of reach of those heavy hands, but my feet stumble in the sand churned by its flailing footwork. I slam into the monster but this time I grab on; my skin scrapes against stone as I frantically search for handholds, footholds, any kind of purchase. The creature writhes, reaching around behind to grab at me while its body shakes under me in an attempt to knock me off. I hold on for dear life, pretty sure this was a stupid move but fully committed to it now.

Scaling my way up its back while trying to avoid the clumsily groping hands, my fingers sink under one of the wide shale plates that armor its body. I curl my hand around the lip of the rock in an attempt to keep my hold as the creature rears in another attempt to buck me. But instead of anchoring me in place, the thick slab tears away and I feel a rush of vertigo as we lunge back. The heavy slice of stone goes flying behind us to land with a loud thump in the sand as I scramble to stay on.

What the—? My scrabbling hands find exposed skin where the shale plate had been, smooth and brown and slimy under my fingers. The texture is spongy and I poke at it—only to feel the creature writhe under me in instant response as though I'd touched a nerve. *No wonder the sand in its face bothered it so much, if the entire body is soft under these plates.*

Grimacing in concentration, I lean in closer to avoid the fumbling hands still seeking me. The kernel of an idea is forming in my mind, a plan more proactive than just hanging here. I shift position until I can hang on with one arm, using my free hand to tear away more slabs. I grab and pull and toss them in a furious frenzy of strength I didn't know I had, gritting my teeth so hard my head hurts from the pressure.

The monster bucks harder under my assault, desperate now to throw me off. My handhold and toeholds tremble and the shale slabs become precariously loose under my weight. "Shit!" The word rips out of me in a panic, my body twisting wildly as another slice comes away in my hand and I nearly fall backwards.

"Hold on, newbie!"

I can see him just over the shoulder where I cling: he has one fist balled into his stomach where the creature hit him, but damned if he isn't still holding that broken sword. The creature is too occupied with me to notice his approach as he races forward and drops to his knees, his momentum sending him sliding between the monster's thrashing legs. I hear the sword connect down low, the shattering crash sweet music to my ears.

The creature pitches forward and lands kneeling on all fours in the sand, or rather, on all *threes*; two giant hands and one remaining leg hold it up, the other leg ripped away in the attack. I ride out the crash like a wave, elated to realize that I don't have to worry anymore about those clawing paws. My hands scramble over its exposed back with fresh purpose, ripping out more of the huge stone slabs as my arms bulge visibly with thick cords of muscle.

"Here!" I yell to the other guy, pointing to exposed skin. "Can you do anything with that?"

He's watching me with wide eyes, ducking to dodge the heavy stones I'm haphazardly chucking behind me. "Yeah," he pants, his voice barely audible over the screaming crowd. "Watch out!"

He darts forward, leaps over the creature's remaining leg, and runs on a light step over its back. His jagged sword, badly abused, dips low and drags a deep cut in the area I've opened. Dark ichor spurts from the monster where the blade tears open spongy brown skin, and viscous fluid coats my hands and his weapon. The creature thrashes once more and then stills beneath us, steaming softly in the hot sun.

Ecstasy at finding myself alive and mostly unharmed sends a shot of pure pleasure to my throbbing brain. I leap off the corpse and whirl to face the other guy, pumping my hands in the air as the crowd screams with delight. "Did you see that?" I yell. "Did you see what we did? You're amazing, you know that? Fast as fuck!"

He seems momentarily surprised by my joy, blinking once before sucking in a deep breath and dropping his ruined sword in the sand. A wry grin breaks over his serious face, a lopsided smile which curves over the right side of his mouth and makes him look arrogant and handsome all at once. "You ain't seen nothing yet, newbie," he brags, his gaze sweeping me from head to toe. "You're one of the strong ones, I see. The crowd likes those. Keep grinning just like that; no one likes a sore winner. They love you right now."

"Is that a good thing?" I lift my head to look at the cheering crowd surrounding us on all sides. I'd been smiling already, of course, but before his words I'd been happy *with* them, not *for* them. I pump my fists into the air once more and am rewarded with a renewed chorus of frenzied cheers.

"Keeps us alive," he says with a shrug. "C'mon, I'll introduce you to the other boys."

He turns to walk towards the far end of the valley and I trail in his footsteps, happy to follow. As we round one of the thicker stone spires, I'm granted an unobstructed view of an elaborately wrought metal portcullis set into the stone wall and find myself shivering in spite of the heat. There is something menacing about the giant gate; as dangerous as this place has been, I have a foreboding that the exit might take me somewhere worse.

"The other boys?" I echo, anxious to keep my guide talking.

"Yeah, there's a bunch of us," he says with a shrug. He glances back at me and blows a puff of air through his lips, his long bangs stirring momentarily away from his dark eyes. "Nice to meet you, newbie. Don't worry if you don't remember your name; we'll get you a new one. Mine's Tony. Welcome to Arena."

CHAPTER 5

Aniyah

"Mmmm, thirsty."

My tongue is swollen in my mouth, the back of my throat dry. My hand reaches out seeking water but brushes soft silk instead. I keep searching, my fingers stubbornly feeling for something I can't quite visualize in my mind, but only rough rock meets my touch where the expanse of silk ends. I jerk my hand back with a gasp and open bleary eyes to find myself sucking on wounded fingers, two of them scraped enough to draw tiny beads of blood to the surface.

"Steady," says a calm voice to my left. I turn to see a girl with fair skin and wavy brown hair standing beside me, holding a bowl in one hand. She pulls from the bowl a white cloth soaked in water and leans over to drape the material across my neck. Coolness soothes my skin while a deeper warmth spreads through my throat, easing the painful scratching sensation.

"You're going to be okay." Her dark eyes study me with dizzying intensity. "Do you remember anything?"

I stare up at her, blinking as my vision clears. I'm in a cave, all brown sandstone and cool shade, save for where brilliant sunlight spills from a large shaft rising up through the high ceiling. The slab I'm lying on is hard

42

and flat, covered with a silken pad that does nothing to lessen the dull ache in my lower back. Where the silk ends there is only bare sandstone. And while I have words for all these things—stone, silk, pain—I have no memory of ever seeing or feeling them before.

"No. Where am I? Where is this?" I struggle to sit up, but bending at the waist is hard for me and I have to roll to one side.

"I've got you," she says, moving to help me. "Sit steady. We're trying to wake the other one too, and it'll be easier to explain to you both at the same time. Chloe, how's she doing?"

"She's coming round," answers a voice to my right. I hear a low moan, but if there are words in the sound they are too soft to distinguish. "What's that? Imani, did you catch what she said?"

Another voice answers, warm and kind. "She said she's thirsty. Hana, they need water."

"Heather, bring us some water?" The girl who steadies me makes the request, her voice as firm as her grip on my arms.

"I'm comfortable. Get it yourself." Indolent words drift from a blond girl lounging on the floor in the center of the cavern, her back set against a slab hewn from the same stone as the walls and beds. Sun pours from the ceiling, setting the table behind her alight with tiny sparkling minerals and embedded crystals, while the sun-drenched girl glimmers a delicate yellow under the spotlight.

The dark-haired girl beside me sighs. Her face is in shadow here in the shade, but I hear the annoyance in her voice and can just discern her delicate arched eyebrow. "Sappho, can *you* get us some water?"

"Sure thing, Hana." A chirrupy voice answers, high and soft all at the same time. A girl with cool olive skin and thick brown hair caught up in a messy ponytail runs fleet-footed to the far end of the cavern, snatching up two slender gourds sitting on the lip of a pool fed by a quiet waterfall.

I press a hand to my throbbing temple, wishing the pain in my head would subside. *Hana, Chloe, Imani, Heather, Sappho?* I repeat the words in a soft litany, wishing they sounded familiar. The thought strikes me that if they all have names surely I must have one of my own. *Why can't I remember it?* The emptiness in my mind confuses me, making me feel dizzy even when the room is perfectly still.

The girl with the water hurries back to us, the white gauze draped around her body doing little to hide the tattoos that cover her from neck to ankle; I find myself staring at a naked mermaid inked with bold red fish scales on her left shoulder. "Hi," she says shyly when she reaches me, handing me one of the water-filled gourds. "I'm Sappho." Bright blue eyes watch me with curious interest from beneath thick lashes.

"Uh, hi," I answer, sipping carefully at the liquid. The water soothes my swollen tongue, the throb in my throat subsiding almost immediately. "Oh! *Thank you*, I needed this," I tell her with a grateful sigh.

"Go tend to the other one," Hana prompts, and Sappho offers me one last shy smile before darting away.

I turn my head to follow her and see another bed with another girl, who is likewise struggling to sit up. Two more girls wrapped in the same flimsy gauze are helping her: one with richly dark skin and teeny-tiny black curls covering her head, the other an immensely curvy girl with a riot of red hair that tumbles to the small of her back. Yet it is the girl on the bed who grabs my attention, the one they called 'the other one'.

Who is she? I don't know the reclining girl, as I'm quite certain I've never seen her before. Yet she seems out of place here, different from all the others. She's not wearing the white gauze the others are draped with, instead dressed in a skirt patterned with soft pink flowers and a thin gray sweater that would be uncomfortably warm if the knit on the sleeves weren't wide enough to leave her skin open to the air. Unlike the other girls, she wears shoes on her feet: blocky sandals that raise the heel and lace up her calves.

I frown, confused by the way my mind supplies all these words without a single memory to support the knowledge. I just *know*, without understanding how I know. This puzzle deepens when I look down and

44

register that I am just as wrongly dressed as she. I'm wearing a bright orange shirt, black jeans, and black closed-toe flats; articles of clothing I don't recognize and can't remember donning.

"Why am I dressed in these things? What is going on?"

"Can you stand?" Hana asks, her voice gentler than before. "C'mon. We'll get you two caught up. Chloe, Imani, can you bring her over to the table?"

Hana helps me off the bed-slab, her arms wrapping around me when I wobble. She's smaller than me but undeniably strong; together we walk to the table, my muscles remembering what my mind does not. Yet the effort is tiring and I collapse onto a thick cushion once we reach our destination, grateful to be allowed to stop. The other girl, the one in the skirt, is guided next to me. She sits down tentatively, watching me with wary eyes from under a mop of short dark bangs.

The others arrange themselves around the table, each claiming a cushion. Hana sits cross-legged across from us, her expression grave. Sappho leans forward with her elbows on the table, watching with bright eyes. The two who helped my counterpart to the table, Chloe and Imani, sit on either side of us, the slender one smiling kindly as though to soften some imminent blow. The blond girl, Heather, doesn't move from where she's been lounging against the table, still detached from the rest of us.

"Okay, introductions first." Hana speaks in a steady voice, with an air of having done this before. "Hello. My name is Hana. You've already met Sappho." She gestures to the blue-eyed girl with olive skin and colorful tattoos. "She brought you water just now. This is Imani." The girl with the warm brown skin and kind smile nods at us from my right, her dark curls bobbing slightly with the motion of her head.

"Nice to meet you again," she says. Her voice is gentle but I blink at her words. *Again?*

Hana pauses only long enough for Imani to speak. "Over there is Chloe." The big girl with glorious red hair nods at us, her dark brown eyes steady and arresting. "And this one here is Heather." The blond girl allows her bored gaze to drift over to us, but doesn't nod or smile.

I realize that no name has been forthcoming for myself or the girl beside me. The question sounds foolish to me even as it reaches my lips, but I have to ask anyway. "Do *we* have names?"

Hana looks me straight in the eye and doesn't laugh. "You do. Your name is Aniyah. And your names are Emma Miyuki," she adds, turning to the girl who sits beside me.

"Emma... Miyuki?" She repeats the words, looking a little thrown by this revelation.

I sympathize, turning my own name over in my head. It doesn't sound *wrong*, but shouldn't it sound familiar? No illumination sparks to confirm this knowledge; she might as well have told me my name was 'Orange Shirt' for all the recognition I feel.

"Why do I have two names? Everyone else only has one." The girl beside me looks faintly skeptical, her head tilted to one side as she looks in Hana's direction.

Hana nods, acknowledging the point. "Well, we're not sure. When you were brought in together, she—", to my surprise, she nods at me, "—told us your name was Emma Miyuki. She said Emma was your first name, but that she calls you Miyuki. Your father is rich, she told us, so we talked about it while you were asleep and we think maybe you were able to buy a second name."

The other girls nod at this, looking varying degrees of convinced. *Is that how second names work?* I'm not sure; everything seems muddled up in my brain.

The hazel-eyed girl looks at me then, frowning in confusion. "You... call me Miyuki?"

I shrug, feeling helpless. "I-I don't know! I don't remember you. I don't remember saying what she says I said. I don't even remember *my* name is Aniyah!" My voice rises, scratching my sore throat.

"That's normal," Imani breaks in, stroking my arm soothingly. "We know you don't remember anything. We were the same way, just as confused as you are now. Each of us has been right where you're sitting, asking the same questions. We'll tell you everything we know and you can take it in as slow as you need."

"It's okay to be a little scared," adds Sappho, her blue eyes sympathetic. "I mean, if you feel that way. No one will think any less of you. We understand."

"But you don't *need* to be." Chloe's rich voice is as solid as the ground beneath me, supportive and firm. "We're going to take care of you. You're one of us now."

I look around the table at each of them, trying to organize the chaos in my mind. "One of you? You've *all* lost your memories?"

"We've all had our memories *taken*," Hana corrects, the hint of a growl in her voice. "We were stolen away by the Master of Masques. He brings girls here and strips their memories away. You don't remember, but we met when he hauled you in; we woke you up and asked you questions. Tried to save whatever memories we could. That's how we got your names."

"We're not supposed to do that," Chloe adds, looking grimly triumphant.

"If he knew, he'd probably kill us," Heather observes, breaking her silence. Her voice is cool, despite the threat implied by her words. "So try not to mention it."

Hana gives her a thin-lipped look and turns back to us. "Don't tell *anyone* your real names. You can use them only in this room and then only with us. Do you understand?"

None of this makes any sense, and I don't know where to start. The girl with hazel eyes—*Miyuki?*—speaks before I can. "If we were stolen away, where did we come from?"

"We're not sure," Hana admits, her brow creasing with frustration. "He drugs the girls before they're brought in. Everyone we've questioned has been too afraid or too incoherent to give clear answers. But we know it's somewhere else."

"It's called the University," Imani adds, her warm voice turning firm. "People study there and learn things."

Sappho nods eagerly. "And you live at the Campus. That's where you eat and sleep with your family."

I turn this over in my head, nodding slowly; that sounds vaguely right, but it's as if there's a haze around the words in my mind, an outline without details. "What kinds of things do you learn at the University?" I ask, trying to fill in the edges of the word, to sharpen the mental picture. Yet when I look around at them, none of the girls meets my eyes. "You don't know," I realize, my heart sinking a little.

Heather turns flashing green eyes on me, roused from her torpor. "More than what you can learn here, which is nothing at all," she says sourly.

"Heather!" Sappho takes a deep breath, poised to argue, but Chloe breaks in before anything more can be said and leans closer to Miyuki.

"Hey, Emma?" she says, her rich voice carrying over the table, shutting down the brewing disagreement. "Or do you prefer Miyuki? Either way, there's time to decide. You were wearing these when you came in. We kept them safe for you while he changed you; they look fragile."

From the gauzy material wrapped around her chest Chloe pulls a thin, glinting metal frame with two opaque rounded rectangles: 'glasses', my mind helpfully pops up to name. Miyuki stares at the offering while hardly seeming to breathe, then she delicately opens the hinges and guides the glasses to her face as though she'd performed the action a thousand times before.

"Oh!" she breathes, her voice suffused with relief. "I can see you all so much better now, *thank you*."

I blink, transfixed by the way her hazel eyes look the tiniest bit larger behind the frames. "You couldn't see me before?"

She reaches up to brush hair away from her eyes. Her expression is softer now, less wary. "You were all fuzzy around the edges; everything is so much sharper now."

48

"If you want to keep those, you'll have to hide them from Handler when he comes in," Heather says, her bored voice turning stern.

Miyuki jerks around to look at her, confused by the sudden order. "Why?" One hand reaches up to touch her glasses.

"Who's Handler?" I add, mildly surprised by the demand in my tone. I feel very protective towards this girl, which is odd considering she's a stranger to me. But if we were brought in together and I knew her names, we must have known each other before all this. *Were we friends?*

Hana frowns and leans forward on the table. "There's no easy way to explain this," she says, picking her words carefully. "You are now the property of the Master of Masques. He owns this place," she waves her hands to encompass the large cavern, "and a lot more that you haven't seen yet. Outside, there's a place where boys fight and people bet on them: that's the arena."

Miyuki blinks at her. "We have to fight?"

"No." Hana's flinty eyes flash with irritation, though it doesn't seem aimed at us. "The *boys* fight. We girls are kept as prizes. When the boys do well, we're sent to them as a reward."

"We don't get to say 'no'," Sappho adds quietly, running her hand over one of her tattooed arms.

"Handler *says* we're not allowed to refuse," Hana corrects firmly. "Handler doesn't come into the rooms to watch." She turns back to us. "Handler is our keeper. The Master put him in charge of us. He comes to collect us when one of the boys is awarded a prize, and he brings food and clothes and things we need."

"He'll be here soon," Imani murmurs, tracing slow circles over the rim of an empty bowl.

Hana nods, looking solemn. "He comes to process the new girls, to chain them and collect their old clothes. We're not allowed to keep things from before. Heather's right about your glasses; we'll have to hide them when he comes."

Miyuki's fingers cling protectively to the hinge of her glasses, and I'm gripped by fears of my own. "They're going to take our clothes?" My palms are sweaty on the rough rock lip of the table. "But they're the only things we have, the only connection to our memories!"

"Aniyah—"

Imani reaches out with her hand to squeeze mine, but a sound behind us makes her freeze. The noise is heavy and loud, a scrape of stone that sets my teeth on edge. Beside me, Miyuki starts upright and fumbles her glasses into her sweater sleeve before whirling around to look. I turn with her, ignoring a sudden painful stab in my spine at the movement.

Along the far wall sit two giant double doors, ornately gilded in strange tracing patterns that jar not even an echo of recollection in my mind. These metal doors scrape open to allow a man to stalk through. Tall and somber, he's cloaked in a hooded robe that covers every part of him except his hands and face. His skin is ashen gray and lined with dark veins, until he steps into the light and I realize they aren't veins at all, but carved lines forming deep furrows in his skin. I realize with inexplicable horror that the furrows in his hands and face match the alien patterns decorating the eerie golden doors.

He approaches us in a slow, stately walk. His eyes are closed, their lids bearing the same ridges as the rest of his face, yet he seems to see without difficulty. "Diamond, why are the new acquisitions still dressed?" His voice is low with disapproval. An overwhelming fear stabs my heart as he draws closer.

Hana jumps to her feet. "Well, they were very thirsty, Handler," she says, her voice high and breathy. "And then they were hungry. We were thinking about having a bath, but we just washed—"

"Enough." His voice cuts over hers and she falls silent. "They are to be chained and named, by order of the Master." Without warning, he turns his head to me and I take an involuntary step back, his unseeing gaze setting my nerves on edge. "Wrists out, girl," he orders, stepping towards me.

I don't think I could do it—I hardly understand the demand—but Imani is there to steady me with her warm touch. "Like this, hon," she says, her hands guiding my elbows forward until my wrists jut out awkwardly in front of me.

The man towers over me as his gray hands reach out to seize mine. He draws a glittering chain from his robes and wraps it around both my wrists, tightening the metal until I cry out in pain. He does something I can't quite see, his hands blocking my sight as he works over my wrists. The tightness lessens to mere irritation, and a hard *snap* cuts through the air. Then he releases me, dropping my arms without warning.

I drag my wrists up to my face and see two slender chains embedded with strange gems I cannot name. They turn a deep green in the light, almost as green as Heather's eyes, but melt into a thick inky purple when I shade the chain with my hand. The chains could be taken for pretty bracelets were it not for the fear and pain I feel.

"Alexandrite," the man declares, his voice hard and cold. "Rare, of course. Only quartz for the other," he adds, moving without preamble to Miyuki. His hands draw out another set of chains as Chloe steadies her. "Your chains are set with smoky quartz, as that was all we had on hand at short notice. Too good for you, but the boys won't know the difference. Quit whimpering, girl." Another hard crack breaks through the air. Miyuki sags against Chloe when he moves away, staring bleakly at the chains on her wrists.

"Diamond, I will return shortly with the third meal. Have their clothes ready for disposal. I must attend an arena fight, a minor one for which your presence is not required. However, there is a new fighter in the ring. If he survives, the Master will wish to reward him. I leave it to you whether to send one of the new girls to be broken in; I know how competitive you are over fresh blood." His last words are cut off by the screeching doors, the scrape of metal against stone sending shivers up my spine.

I hold perfectly still, my lungs struggling to breathe again in the wake of the tangible fear trailing our terrifying keeper. Miyuki pulls out her glasses to study her chains more closely, frowning at the murky white-gray gems adorning her wrists. "What do they mean?" she asks, looking up at Hana with a frown. "Quartz, Alexandrite, Diamond? They're stones, aren't they?"

"Precious stones," Hana answers, thinning her lips. "That's what they call us. We have to learn the words, have to use them around the Master and Handler and the boys, but they're *not* our names. We don't ever use those words here when we're alone."

I swallow at her words, my throat dry again. *And if the Master overhears us using our names, we die,* I think, Heather's warning ringing in my ears. Yet at the same time, I'm glad. I'm grateful that these girls risked their lives to save my name, that I haven't been reduced to nothing more than a gemstone I don't recognize, this strange purple-green alexandrite.

No, I think, closing my eyes in a silent vow, *that will never be my name.*

"So that's it?" Miyuki asks, her voice smaller than before. "There's no choice? I have to answer to Quartz?"

"Outside, yes. But not in here. Not with us." Hana extends her arms, palms facing up, and pulls away the scraps of gauze that cover her wrists. Flashing brightly against her skin are matching cuffs of silver chain embedded with clear stones that wink with a thousand inner facets. "The Master calls me Diamond," she says, studying the cuffs with a cold expression. She flips her hair over her shoulder, defiance hidden in the flow of those soft rippling waves. "But my *name* is Hana."

"Amethyst," Imani whispers next to me, pulling off her own gauze and raising her hands as fists to show dark purple gems. When she meets my gaze, I see an answering flicker of rebellion deep in her sorrowful eyes, even as the delicate features of her face maintain a sympathetic smile. "But my name is Imani."

"Sapphire," Sappho chimes in, snorting as she rolls her eyes. Sparkling blue circles her wrists when she raises them for us to see. "But my name is

Sappho," she says triumphantly. "It's written on my skin. No one can ever take it away."

Chloe tosses her own red tresses, anger flashing in her deep brown eyes. "Ruby," she all but spits, lifting her hands to display flashing fire. "But my name is Chloe."

The last one, Heather, is silent for a long moment. Eventually she drags her wrists to the table, metal striking stone with a dull *thunk*. Her eyes are as brilliant green as the gemstones embedded in her chains, yet her gaze is dull as it slides over her cuffs. "Emerald," she says in a flat voice. "You can call me Heather. And we really ought to get your clothes off, unless you want to be punished on your first cycle."

"But why rush the fun? There are always plenty of chances here in our vault," she adds, her dry sarcasm edged with despair.

CHAPTER 6

Keoki

The iron gate set into the wall enclosing the valley is twice my height and as wide as I am tall. Metal grinds against stone as the gate rises into the wall, and I recognize the strange sound I heard earlier before it was drowned out by the roar of the crowd. *This must be how Tony entered the arena,* I realize, staring up at the huge gash carved into the side of the mountain.

Behind the gate waits an inky darkness I'm hesitant to enter, but Tony strides in without apprehension. Not wanting to seem afraid, I follow him at a matching pace and hope I look appropriately confident. I'm momentarily blinded by the plunge from dazzling sun-flooded arena to cool shadowy cave, but I hear Tony's steps on the stone just ahead of me and manage to follow without banging into any inconvenient walls.

After a few strides, my eyes adjust and I see the flicker of flame coming from torches set into the walls at regular intervals. Nor is that our only source of light; the walls and ceiling are coated with a phosphorescent substance that glows a cool greenish-blue around the welcoming yellow fire. The combined light doesn't compare to the glaring sun and glittering sand at our backs, but I can see well enough to avoid rough spots in the floor and pick out the shape of Tony ahead, his walk confident and easy.

He seems to know exactly where we're going, which is comforting when shapes rise up from the shadows: strangers approaching us, their features vague in the flickering firelight. I have a moment of wariness, unsure how to respond to this fresh influx of people into my world. Then I catch laughter, welcoming and teasing, and my muscles relax at the familiarity of the sound even before my mind catches up. *More boys. The ones Tony said he'd introduce me to.*

A laughing voice, thick and rich, calls out as they approach. "Hey, Tony, you picked up a new addition? You hear that, Justin? You don't have to be the newbie no more."

I squint to pick out the owner of the voice from the approaching shapes: a guy about my height but with a slighter build, his arm draped teasingly over the shoulder of another boy our age. The owner of the voice is dark, his skin a richer brown than my own, and his hair is styled in tiny cornrows beaded at the ends. Scruff covers the top of his lip and traces the bottom of his jaw, framing a wry mouth complimented by dancing eyes.

"'Bout time, Christian," comes the glum answer from his companion, low and almost defensively surly. He's taller than his laughing friend, his shoulders hunched in irritation at the friendly arm draped over him. Black kinky curls fall to his shoulders and into narrowed eyes that watch me with suspicion.

"Aww, Justin, don't pout," returns Christian, amused and teasing. "You'll always be a newbie to us."

"Tony, seriously? You were saved by a newbie?" A new voice rings out; teasing, but with a competitive edge. From the shapes around us I pick out a boy with white skin verging on the edge of a tan, and light sandy hair cropped short against his skull. He grins in the firelight, bright teeth flashing in a taunting smile.

"Go fuck your hands, Lucas," Tony snaps. "I wasn't *saved* by anyone. He lined me up for a kill, that's all."

"It was a good kill," observes another voice, friendly and warm, with the air of someone trying to smooth over an argument before it can start. "Good assist, too. Jumping on its back like that, tearing off the armor with your bare hands? Gutsy. The crowd loved it, you could tell." A strong hand claps around my shoulders and I jump in surprise at the unexpected side-hug.

"Uh, hey, thanks," I offer in response to his praise. I turn my head to pick out my new friend, trying to be cool about the whole hugging thing. His face is white against the flickering firelight, much paler than Tony's fair coloring, and he's taller than us both. His brown hair is straight instead of curly but otherwise as long as mine, brushing his broad shoulders whenever he turns his head. Unlike the other boys he wears cloth wrapped over his chest and stomach, but even multiple layers can't hide his sharply-defined muscles.

He'd look intimidating, I decide, were it not for the wide smile spread across his face, his teeth perfectly white and straight save for one crooked outlier on the upper right side, twisted in such a way as to make his smile faintly goofy and wholly approachable. "Name's Reese," he says, giving me another friendly squeeze as we walk. "Don't guess you remember yours, huh?" he asks, glancing sideways at me.

I shake my head. "No, I just woke up and here I was."

"Yeah, that's how it goes," he says easily, as though this were no big deal, and maybe it isn't. "C'mon, we'll get you patched up and dressed. Warm meal coming soon, I'm betting, and you can have Alpha's room to sleep in."

"Who's Alpha?" I ask, not sure I like the idea of sharing rooms with a stranger.

"He died, about three matches back." Tony's cool voice drifts back to me, not bothering to turn his head.

"You'll last longer than he did," Reese predicts. "Alpha was always kinda full of himself. Not a team player. Welcome home, newbie."

The tunnel we've been walking through suddenly widens out around us, and Reese's welcome echoes through the expanse of a huge cavern. I stumble to a halt, causing Reese to pull up short as well, and blink with surprise at the disorienting play of light against darkness. Above our heads is a vast blanket of black, the sound of our footsteps echoing up to a ceiling too far away to see. The phosphorescent moss coating the walls climbs into the inky void and disappears in the distance, the faint glow not strong enough to reach us.

Although the ceiling is lost to my eyes, I can see perfectly well around me. Thin pillars of stone shoot up at regular intervals throughout the cavern. Their tops disappear into the darkness but their middles are ringed with torches. The flames dance and flicker, their light spreading through the enormous cavern to bathe the area in a welcome glow. Around the sides of the room, heavy wooden doors have been cut into the stone walls, their iron hinges glinting dull black in the torchlight. To the left, not far from where we spill out from the tunnel into the cavern, a smaller passage leads off into darkness.

In the center of the cave, the stone floor has been dug out and a large rectangular pit has been filled with sand—*real* sand, soft and pale in the torchlight. A man with warmly tanned skin and a sparse beard spread thinly over his chin waits in the center of the pit. Relief flickers in his eyes when he sees Tony stride into the cavern at the head of our group, and the man walks toward us. His gait is hindered by a limp in his right leg, for which he uses a thick cane made from dark glossy wood.

He smiles when he sees me, but the warmth he projects doesn't reach his tired eyes. He approaches me and Reese, leaving Tony to stalk over to a series of hooks set in one of the stone pillars where he begins shucking off his leather armor and hanging it on the hooks. "Welcome home," says the man, echoing Reese's words from earlier. "My name is Matías. I'm the teacher here. You're newly awakened?"

He's older than us, though not so much that my brain wants to call him 'old'. I recognize him as a man, while the others possess a wider variety of words: *boy, guy, dude, bro*. Matías extends his hand and I reach out to clasp it with my own, the gesture familiar to my muscles if not to my brain.

"Uh, I guess so," I tell him, feeling a little off-balance. "I was just saying, I woke up in the arena out there. I don't remember anything before that."

Matías nods, leaning on his cane for support. "That's normal," he says, his tone gentle. "Happened to all of us. You're one of us now, an arena fighter. You'll be introduced to everyone, though it looks like you have a head-start there," he adds, his smile turning wry, "and we'll get you re-dressed. You can't keep your old clothes, but sometimes there are clues in them. Strip down?"

I blink at the request, not sure how I feel about this. He's said it like this is perfectly ordinary, and maybe it is; out of the corner of my eye, I see Tony still undressing out in the open as though the rest of us weren't even here. He pulls away the last of his armor and then tears off the cloth that lay underneath, dropping the sweaty material carelessly on the ground and grabbing up fresh clothes to wind around his waist. Distracted, my eyes linger to count the scars on his back with a worried frown. He's strong and lithe, and I saw how fast he moved out there. What could have cut him badly enough to leave those marks?

"C'mon, you can lean on me," Reese says, offering me his muscular arm as support. "Christian, come help the newbie? Justin, you check his—"

"His shoes, yeah. I know," interrupts the kid with the luxurious dark curls, his voice sour.

"Oh, hey, uh," I start to object, but Christian is already squatting on the floor, pulling the shoe off my left foot and handing it up to the dour-looking Justin. I wobble and lean against Reese, deciding it wiser not to topple over. "*Why* can't I keep my clothes?"

"They just get ripped up during practice," replies Christian, chuckling as he tugs at my other foot.

Matías nods at this. "The buckles and loops are a hazard. Too easy for something to grab you and pull you in."

The guy with the light sandy-brown hair, the one who had taunted Tony, watches me undress with a dry expression. "Not that there aren't plenty of ways to kill you at a distance," he adds helpfully.

"Lucas, let the newbie get a name first before you start in on him," Reese suggests, his hands moving to help me. "Pull this over your head." Between the two of us, we get my shirt off and Reese checks it carefully as though searching for something. "Nothing special here," he mutters to himself. "Christian, have you and Justin got anything?"

Christian looks up from where he squats on the floor, his hands moving quickly over one of my abandoned shoes while Justin stands nearby doing the same with the other. "We've got options, but nothing promising," Christian says, not looking up from his meticulous examination.

"Well, unlike Alpha, he hasn't got any tattoos." I look up to see Tony strolling over, watching me with his unreadable dark eyes. I'd already been mildly uncomfortable with the guys stripping me down, but now I'm suddenly very aware of how naked I am. I'm taking on faith that I'm easy on the eyes—at least as handsome as any of the other guys here—but standing here stripped bare in the torchlight would be easier if he'd smile or joke or *something*. Anything other than that cool steady gaze I can't get a solid read on.

"He hasn't," Reese agrees, appearing not to notice my discomfort. "And there's nothing in his hair, at least not that I can find." He pats over my head trying to be gentle, but his rough fingers catch in the tiny corkscrews that spill over my shoulders. I wince at the sudden tug and wish I hadn't when I see Lucas smirk.

I don't want to look weak, so I focus on Tony and the white cloth he's tied about his waist and which drops to just above his knee. I wonder if they'll let me dress soon, and if I'll have the same wrapped cloth as the others. I play with words in my mind, wishing I could determine where they came from. *Shoes, pants, shirt, briefs*; these are the things being taken from me. The words for what the other boys wear are different: *skirt, wrap, cloth, towel, sarong, lavalava.*

This last word rolls around my mind like a sweet special treat, something just for me and not for the others. *How do I know these things? If I could just figure out the source—*

"Oh, now here's something!" Reese's voice breaks through my thoughts, his hands patting at a leather cuff on my wrist. I hadn't noticed it before, but when he fumbles with the snap and takes it off, I *feel* the absence of it.

"No, I-I need to keep that," I tell him, reaching out for the thing I didn't even know I had until I'd lost it.

He doesn't hand it back, but his eyes soften. "Hey. We just need to look at it, okay? Only for a bit." I don't like being separated from it, but I can't think of a good reason to tell him no. I ball my fists into the sides of my legs and try to act cool as he hands it over for Matías to examine.

The cuff is soft brown leather, almost the exact color of my skin. The leather is smooth, and the tiny stitches along the side are so small I can barely see them under Matías' gently probing fingers. The brass snaps that held the cuff closed glitter warmly in the firelight, and I notice another snap along the center length of the cuff. This central snap holds in place a tiny rectangular flap of material which folds over the front of the cuff, forming a small pouch.

"Something inside?" Christian guesses, even as Matías carefully thumbs open the flap. He taps the cuff and a thin piece of metal slides out, the warm glimmering brass falling into his hand.

"Look!" Tony orders, but we're already staring at the tiny engraved words.

"What does it say?" Justin asks, craning his neck to see.

Matías takes it gingerly between his fingers, holding it up to catch the light. "'Life is a song; love is the lyrics,'" he reads. "And on the other side, one word: 'Keoki'."

"It's a pick," I breathe, almost trembling with the effort not to snatch it out of his hand. "You make music with it." I'm sure of this, though I can't quite work out *how*. Something to do with strings and fingers, with practice and skill and magic.

"Is that your name?" Reese asks, his voice hopeful. "Keoki?"

I blink at him; I'd been focusing on the pick, not the words. *Is that my name? Keoki?* I'm not sure. It's *a* name, but it doesn't instantly sound like *my* name. Surely a name should feel more certain than this, something you know in your heart. *But what other options do I have?*

"Uh. Yes," I agree, feeling a surge of relief when Matías hands back the cuff and pick. I nestle the pick back into the cuff and fasten it around my wrist, breathing easy again when it's secure.

"Well, better that than shoes," Christian says with a grin, nudging Justin with his elbow before stretching in a bored way. "Christian," he adds by way of introduction, fingering a little rectangle of white bone that hangs on a silver thread around his neck. I peer closer and see his name in letters going down the pendant, ending in an engraved cross that tugs vaguely at my blank memory.

"Reese," Reese repeats, handing over a thick cloth square and helping to wrap it around me. He lifts his wrist and I see he has a bracelet, too: shiny silver beads on a leather string, the letters of his name spelled out one bead at a time.

"Lucas, and you'd better remember, newbie," Lucas tosses off, holding up thin stamped steel tags that dangle from a dull metal chain around his neck.

"Justin," the younger kid mumbles without enthusiasm, his hands fumbling with a bit of torn cloth that I can't see well in the light; I catch a big red "J" alongside black and white lettering that seems strangely familiar to my eyes. The cloth is ragged at the edges, like a tag torn from a shirt. *Or a shoe,* I realize.

I look up at Tony, expecting him to join in the litany of names. "Tony to you," he says, his voice tinged with defiant pride. He reaches into the knot at his waist and pulls out a tiny rectangle of cloth, printed with fine letters.

I peer at it in the firelight, my lips moving with the words. *Property of,* written in a soft curving scroll and ending in a tiny colon; on the next line, in bold straight letters: *Anthony Suen*. Soft threads fray at the edges of the rectangle, as if it had been pulled away from a larger piece of cloth.

"Where did you—"

My question is cut away by the screech of grinding metal on stone, a sound that sets my teeth on edge and causes the boys to jump. Christian hastily kicks my clothes into a small pile, while Matías moves to stand between me and the sound. The group of us turns to face the far wall where a pair of doors—taller and wider than the little single doors dotted around the cavern, and so tightly wrapped in scrolling black iron that I can barely see the wood underneath—opens with a ponderous lack of rapidity.

"Good match. That was a good show for the crowd. Very well done." The voice is low and dull, and I hate him even before I see him. His manner is different from the way the other boys praised me, as if I weren't a person at all but just a piece of entertainment. Then he walks through the opened door and into the firelight and it's all I can do not to recoil. It's not his gray skin or even the cuts in his face and hands; scars don't bother me. It's the pattern of the strange swirls, the sickly fear emanating from him and the way he looks directly at us even though his eyes are tightly shut.

"We've collected his clothes for you, Handler," Matías says in a deferential tone.

"That's good," the intruder says, pushing forward a wheeled cart. He towers over it, taller than all of us by more than a head. On the cart are bowls filled with bread and spiced meat, tantalizing steam rising from the offerings. "That's very good, Teacher. That's why we keep you alive. Clothes on the cart."

Reese and Christian jump forward to pull bowls off the cart and hand them around while Matías picks up my clothes from the ground and deposits them as ordered. His knee doesn't allow him to bend, but Justin squats on the floor and hands up the articles to him, flinching whenever the gray man turns his way.

"The new one did well," Handler observes, swiveling his face to me.

"The Master has decided to keep him; the crowd enjoyed his creativity. He needs a name for the betting cards, and we haven't used Granite in a while." He chuckles, a soft dry cough of a noise as emotionless as his empty voice. "Not that you boys care, but we have to call you something, don't we?"

Matías nods at him, his stiff outline scrupulously polite. "Thank you, Handler. Granite is pleased to have performed well. We are grateful for the warm meal."

"Good," the towering creature says flatly, not looking in his direction. "We like obedient boys. The hot food is reward for his performance, and a Prize will be sent to his room. Eat quickly; rooms by fourth bell and sleep at fifth bell." With that, he turns and pushes the cart out of the cavern, the giant doors scraping closed behind him.

I shiver once he's gone, despite the warmth of the torches. The other guys ignore me, scarfing down food as quickly as they can. Reese eventually looks up, nodding at the bowl he'd placed in my hands earlier. "Hey, you need to eat. Won't be any more food until first bell, and it won't be hot then."

None of this stuff about bells makes any sense to me, but I tear off a piece of bread and try to choke it down. It's good, hot and fluffy, but my stomach is still clenched from the fight earlier and from the invasive presence of that man just now. I chew the bread without any enthusiasm and chase it with a bite of meat.

"What do you look so glum for?" Lucas snaps at me, tearing into his own food with decidedly more verve. "You get a Prize. Some of us have to wait until Auction, you know."

I'm not sure how to respond; I don't know what kind of prize they're talking about, but it must be something good to make him so jealous. "Well, of course I get a prize," I tell him, taking a large bite of bread just to spite him. "I was awesome out there. I'm good enough to be rolling in prizes."

Christian chuckles. "Now there's an ambition," he says, nodding with solemn approval as his eyes dance.

I think of Tony then, how he helped me in the arena and how Lucas had taunted him, acting as if the kill hadn't been his. I remember how fiercely he'd asserted his usefulness. *Why isn't he a getting a prize?* I wonder. But I can fix that. I jerk my thumb at him, the gesture including us both. "And I'm gonna share my prizes with Tony," I tell Lucas, taking another bite of meat and looking him right in the eye.

Reese chokes at my declaration, coughing hard and needing to be pounded on his broad back by Matías. *Shit,* I think, realizing I've misspoke but with no idea how. Christian smirks and Lucas glowers at me, but Tony just watches with those dark eyes. Once again, I have absolutely no idea what he's thinking.

"Are we, uh, not allowed to share prizes?" I ask Reese, trying to sound nonchalant.

Matías opens his mouth, looking grave, but before he can speak the sound of a bell rings out through the cavern. The noise is deafeningly loud and I drop my bowl so I can clap both hands to my ears. The bell clangs four times in total before fading into blessed silence. None of the other boys seem surprised; they set down their food and drift off towards the smaller wooden doors set in the walls. Each of them moves towards a separate door and they all seem to know where they're going.

"Wait, what are we doing?" I ask, panic rising at the thought of being left alone.

Reese pulls me up by the elbow, his coughing fit having subsided. "Shit, we forgot the tour. Real quick, 'k? Big tunnel leads to the arena; that's the gate where you came in. Smaller tunnel there slopes up to a little cave over the gate; they put a slit in the rock so we could watch the fights. Doors are private rooms. You're here," he adds, directing me to a nearby door. "This was Alpha's old room, and yours now. That was fourth bell, so we gotta clear out of the cavern so Handler can clean it. Fifth bell will ring in a bit and you have to sleep then. We'll see you afterward, at first bell. Got all that?"

I nod, feeling a little frightened by all this but trying to be cool. "Uh, sure. Bells. But what about this prize thing?" I don't really care—there's nothing I want right now except to stay with these guys—but it had seemed important.

He shakes his head as he strides to a door just down the wall from mine. "You'll be fine, kid," Reese calls back over his shoulder. "Just, uh. Be nice to her?" Then he slips into his room, closing the heavy wooden door behind him, and I'm left alone.

CHAPTER 7

Aniyah

"Heather's right; we have to hurry." Hana brushes her hands on her gauze skirt as she stands. "Handler said he'd be back soon with third meal; that doesn't give us much time. Chloe, Imani, help me undress them. Sappho, Heather, you go through their clothes looking for words. Check the necks and sides—"

"We know the drill," Heather snaps. Despite her earlier indolence, she unfolds herself quickly from the ground. Hana thins her lips but hurries to our side of the table, her hands flying over my body in a complicated dance with Imani's own gentle movements as they begin to strip me. On my other side, I see Chloe helping a frozen Miyuki out of her shoes and skirt.

I ought to protest, fighting to keep my clothes as long as possible, yet I don't want to alienate the only friends I have. They'd spoken so casually about punishments, about the Master being willing to kill us for any infraction. *Is that really a thing that happens?* If so, how many other girls have stood here before me, stripped by these expert hands such that there's an established drill they follow? I don't know what to believe, except to hope these girls really do have my best interests at heart.

Our clothes are pulled away: shirts, shoes, and panties all stripped off and handed to Sappho and Heather. When we're stripped to the skin, Hana flashes an apologetic smile. "Stay here. We'll get you fresh clothes in a while, but we don't have much time to look through your old ones." With that, she hurries to the splash of sunlight where the others are sorting through the pile of our belongings.

"There's nothing new here," Sappho complains, peering at the inside collar of my shirt. "The same words as usual, but they still don't make sense; I'm sure navy is a blue color, not orange, and none of these are old or faded!" The other girls ignore her, digging deeper into the pile, but their expressions are grim.

A soft touch on my arm causes me to jump; I spin on my heel to find myself face-to-face with Miyuki, her hand outstretched toward me.

"Sorry," she says, "I didn't mean to startle you. But you have— Does it hurt?"

I stare at her, frowning in confusion. "Does what hurt?"

Miyuki hesitates, biting her lip. "You have a scar. Here, let me?"

She reaches out and takes me by the shoulders, turning me around until I'm facing away from her. "Here," she says, and I feel her finger touch my back, just below my right shoulder blade. There's a small rut there; I can *feel* it, the way her finger dips into a tiny valley of skin. Then she traces down and around my side, her finger traveling over uneven bumps as she follows the track of the scar. She ends facing me again as the cut stops at my hip, just under the curve of my belly.

"There are words here," she says suddenly, bending to study my hip.

I lift my arm out of the way, craning my neck to look with her. "There are? What do they say?"

It's a vulnerable feeling, having my own body described to me by a stranger. Yet with the others occupied as they are, we're wrapped in a sort of privacy. Again I wonder who this girl was to me before our minds were blanked. Has she done this before, seen me up close like this? Or is this the first time she's read the words inked into my skin?

"'Bent not broken'," she reads aloud. "Written in cursive, all lowercase." Her finger lightly touches my skin, following the trail of tiny letters underlined by the last few inches of the long scar. She looks up at me, brushing the hair from her eyes. "What do you think that means?" she asks. "A scar like this had to be something serious, right?"

I close my eyes, wishing I could disappear inside myself to emerge with the answers. My body feels like my body: there's a heaviness in my lower back; a tightness in my neck and shoulders; a dullness along my side where the scar tissue cuts a path from front to back. There was pain before, when I twisted to see Handler as he entered, and I had struggled to sit up straight when Hana woke me. But I have no frame of reference for whether any of that is normal or not, no reason to believe I'm bent *or* broken in any way.

"Aniyah?" she whispers, reaching her hand out to touch my arm.

I open my eyes, offering a smile in place of the words I can't find. With her arm outstretched, I see her chains glint dully in the shadows and I notice something else: writing on her skin, though not the deep ink of a tattoo. The words are smudged, as if water and a determined finger could swipe them away. "What's that?" I ask, craning my neck to see.

She looks with me, her gaze dropping to her arm, her fingers reaching tentatively to hover over the words. Four little columns of two rows, grouped together: *she, xie; her, xer; hers, xers; herself, xerself.* Next to them is a tiny flower in black ink. Something about the words tugs at the vacuum where my memory should be; I can't place them, but have the feeling that they're important.

"What do you think they mean?" I ask, but before she can answer me, voices are raised behind us.

Heather stands next to the pile of our clothes, her bare feet set in a stubborn stance as she and Hana angrily stare each other down. Imani and Sappho kneel on the ground, folding our clothes and wearing expressions of quiet disappointment. Chloe is missing, and it takes me a moment to find her in the shadows near the waterfall where she gathers up stacks of flimsy cloth in her arms from a wall niche. New clothes, I realize, my heart sinking at the reminder that our old ones are soon to be taken.

"I said, *I'm going*," Heather states loudly, with the air of someone repeating herself.

Hana's dark eyes flash with determination. "You are *not*. Handler said the fighter is new, and you know I have dibs on the new ones."

"You had the last one," the blond girl counters hotly. "We agreed to take turns. Now it's my turn."

"*You* said we would take turns," Hana corrects her. "I didn't agree then and I'm not agreeing now. I get all the new ones, and that's just how it is."

Imani stands, wiping her hands on her skirt. "Handler will be back soon," she says quietly. "If he hears you two arguing, he may take the choice away entirely. No one wants that."

"Then I guess Hana needs to see reason," Heather snaps, her eyes narrowing.

Hana steps closer to her, staring up at the taller girl without fear. "Heather. I am not going to argue about this with you," she says, her voice low and firm. "If you want to do it the hard way, I will choke you unconscious and tell Handler you're taking a nap. Is that what you want?" Stillness ripples through the cavern in the wake of her threat and Sappho tucks her knees under her chin, looking away from the fight.

Chloe ignores them, crossing the cave with stacks of cloth piled across her arms. Imani joins us in the awkward silence, helping Chloe unload her burden onto the nearby stone beds before turning back with a long cut of cloth in her hands. Gently the two girls wind the soft material around our waists, breasts, and arms. Multiple pieces form layers over each other to cover us, and Miyuki and I spin obediently in place, watching and memorizing the folds and knots that keep our clothes from falling away. While we dress, Heather stares balefully at Hana, frustration trembling through her shoulders.

The silence is broken by the screech of metal on stone and every spine in the room stiffens. The golden doors grind open and Handler shuffles in, pushing a silver cart along the rough ground. Bowls adorn the top of the cart, each holding warm fruits and scented meats that make my stomach growl at the smell. He wheels the cart to the table, silver glinting in the sunlight that bathes the center of the room.

"Clothes," he orders without preamble, his voice as flat and emotionless as before. Sappho gathers up the tidy stacks of our former life, while Imani and Chloe leap forward to unload the bowls of food. Our clothes and shoes are piled on while the gray man waits with closed eyes. His head turns, his sightless gaze picking out Hana without difficulty. "The Prize?"

"Me," she says, stepping forward. Beside her, Heather grits her teeth so hard I can almost hear the enamel grinding, but she doesn't argue.

Handler chuckles, but there is nothing pleasant in the sound. "Greedy Diamond, always so eager. Come on, then." He leads her out, the silver cart scraping against the floor as they go. The doors shut behind them with a finality that makes my heart clench, and a strange bell clangs out with deafening loudness: four heavy tolls, like a memorial marking this moment.

I whirl on my heel, my hands clapped to my ears. "What is that? What's happening?" I shout over the sound reverberating through the cavern, my arms shaking. Nearby I see Miyuki, eyes wide as she jams her glasses back on and stares helplessly at the doors that separate us from Hana.

Imani takes me by the shoulders, lowering my hands gently from my ears as the ringing fades. Reaching out to touch Miyuki's elbow with her other hand, she guides us to the table and helps us sink onto the cushions lining the floor. Sappho pushes two bowls of steaming meat in our direction, her blue eyes avoiding mine.

"You need to eat," Chloe says, taking a seat opposite. "Third meal is the last until first bell. That won't be for a long time." She reaches without enthusiasm for a bowl of plump fruits.

"But where is he taking her?" Ignoring Sappho and Chloe, I reach out to grab Imani's hands. "Imani, where has Hana gone?"

70

She squeezes my hands in an attempt at reassurance that isn't reflected in her eyes. Sitting this close to her, I can see a kaleidoscope in those depths; countless beautiful shards in a dozen hues of brown, tiny flecks catching the light whenever she moves her head.

"She's been sent to a fighter as a reward," she says, faltering a little. "They brought in a new boy at the same time they brought in you two. He didn't die in the arena, so he gets a prize; something to entice him to fight well next time."

"The fighters are supposed to please the crowd," Chloe adds, her voice low. "Make a good show. Earn lots of betting money for the Master. But boys need incentives: hot food, softer blankets for their beds, Prize girls."

Imani reaches out to brush a curl away from my eyes. "That's us, Aniyah. We're Prizes. Hana volunteered to be the Prize for the new victor. We'll see her again at first bell."

Beside me, Miyuki's breathing is audibly uneven. "Wait, but," she protests, shaking her head. "Food and blankets make sense, but what does it mean that she's the Prize? We're people, not food!" Miyuki looks around the table, her eyes wide. "What do boys *do* with Prizes?"

"Whatever they want," Heather says darkly, throwing herself onto her cushions by the table. "That's the whole point. Handler takes you to a room, pushes you inside, and shuts the door behind you. Your job is to stay alive until first bell, which is particularly tricky with the newbies."

Chloe sighs and begins to comb out her luxurious hair with her fingers. "Hana is just trying to protect us, you know," she observes in a weary tone. "Be angry with her all you want, Heather, but you know she's the logical choice: they can't hurt her."

"They can't *harm* her," Sappho corrects quietly, her fingers playing anxiously over a waxy blue fruit plucked from her bowl. "It still hurts. It always hurts."

"Everyone but me," Heather adds in apparent agreement, picking up one of the servings of spiced meat. "Which is *why* I should go first."

I stare at them, trying to make sense of all this. "What does that mean?" I look at Imani, the one I trust to make some sort of sense. "They can't harm Hana, but they can hurt her? They can't hurt Heather at all? Are these rules they have to follow?"

Imani hesitates, choosing her words carefully. "No, this is not about rules. Do you remember how Handler spoke of rare gems and common ones when he chained you?"

I nod, frowning at the change in topic, and she continues. "He was referring to your talent. Aniyah, you have a rare talent; something that took the Master a long time to find and which he's trying to awaken in you. Because of that, he ordered us to take good care of you. We all have talents, though not as rare as yours. Sappho, do you mind?" There's a request in her words, as though asking for a demonstration.

The blue-eyed girl sighs and extends her arm over the table, her gaze fixed upon a bowl of fruit on the far side. Instead of stopping at the end of her reach, her hand *keeps going*, stretching impossibly long. As it passes in front of us her arm narrows but continues unchecked on its way. When she reaches the far end, Sappho grasps the lip of the bowl and drags it back to her as if this were nothing unusual.

"Sappho is stretchy," Imani says, her voice soft at my elbow. "The Master says it makes her more pliable for the boys, and a better dancer when we entertain."

"But how—" I turn to her, the question dying on my lips when I see her face.

A stranger sits at my elbow where Imani had been before: her lips fuller, her skin glossier, her soft black curls each now as long as my hand and sticking out in every direction on her lovely head. Her ears, her eyebrows, her forehead, her nose: every feature of her face except those perfect arresting eyes is subtly altered; she is no longer herself.

"Imani?" Miyuki breathes her name, and I'm pathetically grateful to hear my own astonishment in her voice.

The stranger smiles. "It's me," she murmurs before letting her face shift back to what it was before, her features rearranging themselves like soft clay. "I can... well." She shrugs, her smile turning rueful. "Easier to show than to tell. It's supposed to keep me fresh for the boys; always a new face, if they want one. Comes in handy for telling stories, too."

"Can you all...?" I turn my head to Chloe, studying the bigger girl intently. Adrenaline pounds in my ears as I wait for her to grow bigger, or stretch to the ceiling, or send her long hair tumbling down to her ankles.

Chloe snorts, not bothering to look up. She picks up one of the wooden bowls, and dumps the fruit out onto the table before a loud *crack* rips through the room. Her hand clenches hard against the bowl and the thick wood crumbles into splintered chunks.

"Whoops," she says dryly, opening her fist to let the broken pieces clatter into a heap on the table.

Miyuki's eyes widen behind her glasses. "Amazing," she breathes, reaching out to poke at one of the chunks. "Can you do that any time you want?"

"Wait," I put in, blinking in confusion. "What does that do for the boys?"

Chloe chuckles, the sound deep and rich in her throat. "Any time I want, Emma," she affirms. "Aniyah, you'd be surprised how useful a pair of strong arms and legs can be."

Heather reaches out to toy with one of the sharp pieces. "And I," the blond girl murmurs in a flat voice, "Can't. Be. Hurt." Her gaze holds steady as each word is punctuated by a sharp downward stab of the wooden shard into her outstretched arm. The first two stabs whiten her already pale skin, and the third cuts into her arm with a vengeance, red blood welling up from the gash.

"Heather!" Sappho springs from her seat, running to fill another gourd with water from the pool before darting back to kneel beside the girl. "You could have just told them, you didn't have to show. Even with the water, it'll take at least a cycle to heal!" She fusses over the other girl as she washes the wound, but Heather's face has resumed her bored expression; she hadn't even flinched when the shard pierced her.

Miyuki swallows hard; when she speaks, her voice is unsteady. "And Hana has that? She can't be hurt by the boys?"

Imani sighs, turning back to us. "She can't be *harmed*. If she'd done to herself what Heather did just now, Hana would heal up in a heartbeat, right as you watched. But it would hurt her, as much as it would hurt you or me."

"The problem with new fighters," Chloe cuts in, chewing grimly on a pink fruit, "is whether to send Hana, knowing they can't damage her permanently, or to send Heather since she can't feel pain. We can't guess in advance if a newbie is going to be decent-but-clumsy or actively sadistic after an arena kill. Ideally, we'd send Heather to the clumsy guys since they can't hurt her by accident, and we'd send Hana to the kill-happy fighters since they'd have their work cut out for them trying to injure her. But we can't tell in advance."

My hands grip the silk cushion under me and stuffing slides beneath the surface under my fingers. *If I gripped the material any tighter, would I tear it? If I were as strong as Chloe, I could.* "We have to worry," I sound the words aloud slowly, my voice hoarse in my dry throat, "whether the boys are going to deliberately wound us or just accidentally hurt us very badly?"

Imani touches my arm again, calming me. "Only the new ones. Once they've been here awhile, they get to know us. We work out a system to keep everyone safe, like Hana going first. And you'll be taken good care of," she adds.

"We'll be taken—"

I start to echo her only to stop when my brain catches up with my tongue. She doesn't mean *we'll* be taken care of, Miyuki and I; she means *I'll* be taken care of, because of some rare talent, something only I can do. I close my eyes, swallowing my words as I try to wrap my mind around this fact.

Whatever rare talent I have, I don't care; I don't want it. I know I *ought* to care. If I were smart, I would nurture it and do whatever I could to help awaken it so I'll remain unharmed. But it seems profoundly unfair that I should be protected more than the others. Can my talent help Hana if she's being hurt right now? Can it do anything to stop Heather's bleeding as Sappho wraps gauze over the wound? Is it only a stroke of luck that I am safe here while Miyuki is in danger?

Handler had called Miyuki 'common'. Will the fighters look on her with similar contempt? How much danger will she face when she's chosen to go? Heather had said the boys could do whatever they wanted, but what *do* they want? Vague sensations flash through the darkness of my mind, an idea of what I might do with a boy whom I liked, or liked to look at. But a violent stranger, angry after a kill, is a different matter. A shiver traces down my spine, the sensation trailing pain. *Is this my life now? Our lives, together?*

Miyuki's soft voice cuts into my thoughts, quiet and determined. She's scooted her cushion closer to the table, her fingers tracing over the rough surface. "What are we to do until she returns?" she asks, carefully avoiding any suggestion that the calm, steadying girl who woke us might not return at all.

"We wait," Chloe says simply, lying back on the floor and gazing up unblinkingly at the bright sun that bathes her in light. "That's all we can do."

CHAPTER 8

Keoki

The room on the other side of my door is a cave: a tiny enclosed space of low lighting and cool air, as well as the first moment of privacy I've had since I woke. Though I'd wanted to stay with Tony and the others, I have to admit it's nice to have a moment alone to breathe without being watched. I haven't forgotten this room belonged to another boy before me and I'm not sure how I feel about the death of a total stranger, but I'm too tired to feel anything more than gratitude for what I've been given.

There are no torches, but I can see my way around. The walls and ceiling are covered in the glowing blue-green moss that seems to grow everywhere in these caverns. The room is no wider than ten strides from the heavy wooden door to a cloth curtain that hangs on the opposite side. Pushing the sheet aside, I find an alcove carved into the far wall; this is set above a wide stone bench that I would assume is for sitting except that the curtain baffles me. Then I see the large hole cut in the center of the bench and a neat stack of cloth strips sitting beside it. *Bathroom,* my mind suggests, but the label is tentative; after all, the curtained alcove is hardly a room and there's nothing here I could call a *bath.*

Water *is* here, for which I'm grateful. To the left of the door, equidistant from the entrance and the alcove, a brass bowl has been set into the wall. A stream of water trickles from the ceiling to collect in the wide basin. The overflow disappears into a damp patch of sandy earth below. The quiet burble of water is calming music to my ears, and I drink deeply from the bowl before dipping my hands into the water and splashing some on my face. The little stream continues uninterrupted, slowly replenishing what I take away.

A flat slab of silvered metal has been set in the wall above the bowl. As my eyes adjust to the darkness I catch my reflection in the mirror, blurred by the constant trickle of water. My fingers reach out to touch the strange face and brush only cool wetness; not a single memory accompanies the sight. *Well, at least I know I'm handsome.* Set in a niche below the reflective metal is a soft, sudsy stone and an odd little blade set on the end of a flimsy stick. These do bring back flecks of memories, but when I rub at my chin there isn't enough fluff there to necessitate a shave. *Maybe later?*

On the right side of the room and directly across from my water bowl, a large niche has been cut into the cave wall, wider across than I am tall. Stone rises from the floor to about knee-height and the wall curves down from the ceiling to stop a head above my own, but the space between my knees and my head has been completely carved away. The cut is clean, and extends so deeply into the wall that I can't see where it ends; the light from the ceiling is too dim to reach all the way to the back.

It's a bed, I realize. The stone has been lined with a thin pad big enough for two or even three people to lie next to each other in the darkness. A blanket, thick and fuzzy, lies folded at the end of the pad along with a bolster pillow that extends from the lip of the opening to the back wall. As with everything else here, there is a lingering sense of mismatch between the word and the reality. I'm not sure what's wrong, just that 'bed' doesn't quite describe a hole in a cave wall lined with a flat pallet and a single solitary blanket.

I'm touching the blanket experimentally, feeling the soft fur and wondering if I can place the animal it must have come from, when I hear a noise behind me. I whirl to see a slender girl slip through the door. At the sight of her, my breath is stolen away.

She's smaller than me—shorter than all the guys, if I had to guess—with smooth skin and soft curves outlined in the faint light. Brown hair spills down her back in gentle waves, and dark eyes glint up at me. She's wrapped in some kind of see-through cloth that just barely covers anything important. Then she shrugs her shoulders and even that falls away, and she's standing there in naked glorious beauty.

"Wow." It's a stupid thing to say, but my tongue is tied just looking at her. Lower down, beneath my sarong, I feel an instant stirring reaction, and I hope the thicker material of my own clothes won't give anything away. *Or should it? Should I even be dressed right now?* She's naked, after all; perhaps I'm supposed to be as well.

"I am called Diamond," she murmurs, crossing the distance between us and sliding her hands up my arms with easy intimacy. Chains glint on her wrists, the tiny white gemstones catching the dim light as she moves; the word 'diamond' drifts through my mind as a word separate from her name. "I am yours until first bell."

I swallow hard at her words, trying to clear my head and finding it difficult to do so. "Mine to do, uh, what with?" I ask. I force out a little laugh, hoping to turn my ignorance into a joke.

She smiles up at me, her hands caressing my shoulders and causing a fluttery knot to gather at my stomach. "Why, anything you want," she answers, her voice low and easy. "Is there anything you would *like* to do with me?"

I don't have words for it, nor an image in my mind, but the tug at my groin makes me think I could figure something out. I clear my throat, wishing she weren't standing so close to me, that she didn't smell so sweet. "So you're a... prize for doing well out there?" I can't help myself; I reach out to touch her shoulder, feeling silken skin under my fingers. More than anything else since I awoke, this feels perfectly right.

"I am," she says warmly, her dark eyes flashing. "There are many Prizes and I am the Diamond Prize. Do I have the honor of being your first?"

The way she asks makes my cheeks burn, making it sound as though I'm more amazing than I am. "Yeah," I manage, hoping she can't feel the heat from my face, "but that makes *me* the lucky one, right?"

Her answering smile makes my stomach flip over. "Let me?" she asks, reaching around behind me. Her fingers deftly pull apart my cloth wrap, dropping it to the floor. Before I can react her hands are on my stomach, pushing me with surprising strength for her size. My legs meet stone and I fall backwards onto the bed in a sitting position, where roughly all of my mind is immediately taken up with the question of whether I need to protect the exposed part of my body that feels very vulnerable in the open air.

"I know what to do with that," she murmurs in a coy voice before dropping to her knees onto my discarded skirt and taking me deeply into her mouth.

A wordless sound rips out of me that had started life as a "what?" but comes out as a helpless "wuuuh" noise. My hands bury themselves into the bed-pad, because the alternative would be to grip her hair for support and I'm not sure if that would hurt her. She bobs her head slowly, her tongue swirling around the length of it, and the pleasure that tears through me is like hot steel piercing my mind. This is familiar; I've experienced it before and I can't imagine how I ever could have forgotten.

"That feels *so* good." I manage to rasp out the words in a hoarse voice. "T-Thank you." It seems a strange thing to say, but for all that the lashing of her tongue feels beautifully right I have no memory of the etiquette in this situation. *Can* I tangle my hands in her hair? A part of me very much wants to, but I have no way of knowing whether she would like that.

Her mouth pulls off, the sudden absence of her warmth ripping an involuntary groan of disappointment from me. Yet she doesn't move away. She remains kneeling there, looking up at me. "I am so glad I please you," she murmurs, her smile warm and easy. "At first bell, when I must leave you, Handler will ask how you enjoyed your Prize. It would mean so much to me if you tell him I made you happy."

"Oh." I blink down at her, as images I didn't want in my mind at this particular moment flood in anyway: that creepy guy with the strange face and the way he spoke to us like we were meat. "Yeah, I'll tell him that," I promise, wincing with pleasure when her tongue darts out to caress me. "Diamond, as far as I remember, you're the best thing that's ever happened to me." She giggles and I'm rewarded with another plunge into her warm mouth, gasping under the welcome assault of her tongue.

I'm just about to reach out and try some hair-touching when she pulls off me again. This time I manage not to groan, but the effort is immense. I'm achingly grateful for everything she's doing with her mouth and hands, but her sudden stops are going to be the death of me. *Maybe she doesn't realize. Should I be telling her what I want?* She'd made it pretty clear that she wanted to make me happy, after all.

She aims a sly smile up at me, her fingers moving over my stomach. "I won't be the best thing that's ever happened to you for very long," she teases. "An amazing fighter like you will have so many Prizes."

"Do you think so? Well, I *am* pretty strong." I'm not sure how I should respond to her praise, but I'll agree with anything she wants if it means more of that tongue. I receive another lick and a smile, the combination sending shivers up my arms.

"There are other Prize girls here," she murmurs, still gazing up at me. "They're good girls, all of them, but some of them are frightened or confused. New here, just like you." Another long lick then, from the very base to the tip then circling around the top until I'm ready to tear the bed-pad apart in the intensity of my grip. "Will you do me a favor?" she whispers. Her eyes hold mine like shining pools in the darkness.

I can barely focus on her words for the blood pounding in my ears. "Uh. Yes? I mean, of course I will. What would you like?"

She gives me the sweetest smile I could imagine, her pink tongue darting out once more. "If you ever have a Prize who doesn't want to play, will you treat them gently for my sake? Tell Handler they were good, even if they were not. I know it may seem a tiny bit unfair, but I *promise* I'll make it up to you the next time we're together, you and I."

A pause hangs in the air between us, the cave silent save for the constant trickle of water. I feel a heightened awareness, almost like I did in the arena when time had seemed to slow. I'm conscious of the throb of my heart thrumming through the lower parts of my body and the gentle rise and fall of her breasts as she breathes. Her earlier words echo in my ears: *Handler will ask how you enjoyed your Prize.*

What would he do her in the morning if I told him she'd been bad? What would happen if I said I hadn't liked her or that she'd been rude to me? I remember the way Matías had moved to stand between me and Handler when he arrived with our food. I recall how quickly the boys leaped to obey his commands, flinching away from the fear gathered around him whenever they stepped too close. I'd felt threatened by his presence, by the power he seemed to hold over us—a threat that loomed especially large after the fight in the arena and the news of my predecessor's death. *Is this girl under similar threats?*

"Oh. Hey." My voice is hoarse and I have to clear my throat to speak. "Hey, I ain't gonna tell stories on any girls, okay? If someone is, you know, scared or whatever? I won't tell on her. I get it." I give her a smile I hope is reassuring. "We're all friends here, right? We have to stick together."

Her smile is brighter than the arena sunlight, and she nods vigorously before dropping her head to engulf me with fresh enthusiasm. I hold my breath, thinking she might stop again to speak, but this time she keeps going. A wave of relief rushes over me and I half-close my eyes, leaning back on the bed against my elbows. I can't imagine being more relaxed than I am right now as she works.

Works?

Why did that word pop into my head? She's not working; she said herself that this was play. She's been all smiles the whole time, clearly having as much fun with this as I am. I open my eyes, looking down at the soft curtain of wavy brown hair bobbing enthusiastically between my legs. Well, maybe not as much fun as *I* am, I admit as another wave of pleasure ripples through me, but she's enjoying herself. She's happy to have come here.

Except she didn't come here, did she? She was *brought* here. Handler announced a Prize would be sent to my room. This girl, Diamond, is that Prize. She'd said I could do anything to her. I'd thought she was exaggerating, but now I'm not so sure. I'd wanted to tangle my hands in her hair and wondered whether it would hurt her; I'd thought about asking if she'd like that. Would she have told me the truth? Or would she have allowed something that hurt her rather than risk a bad report to Handler?

She's smiled at me all this time and even initiated this: stripping her clothes off, pushing me down onto the bed, dropping to her knees. But how much of a choice did she have about any of it? How much of what she's doing right now is to protect herself? Is she making me happy because it makes *her* happy, or is she doing it so she won't be hurt? The answer is clear if I'm honest with myself: she *is* working, and I let her do so without asking if she was happy about the situation.

"Hey, listen." I take her by the shoulders, pulling her away from me as gently as I can. Trying not to curse myself for calling a halt to the most pleasurable moments of my new life so far, I study her face in the dim light. She looks up at me with a quizzical smile and the gentle curiosity of her expression hardens my resolve. I don't know what I want to see in her eyes, just that her polite sweetness isn't passion.

I clear my throat again, fumbling for words. "You, uh. You don't want to be here. Doing this. Do you?" I give her an apologetic smile, trying not to scare her.

She lowers her eyes, her gaze dropping to the floor. "I am very honored to be your Prize," she murmurs, her voice still warm and flirtatious. But she doesn't dive forward, or lock her lips onto me again. She doesn't say *'yes, I need you and I need this, please don't make me stop'*. I don't know if that's what she would say, but it's what I need to hear; from her or anyone else who'd do this with me.

"It's okay," I whisper, giving her another smile. "Can we start over? I never introduced myself. My name is Keoki. Well, we think it is." I tap the leather bracelet on my wrist and give her a goofy shrug. "You're called Diamond?" She nods silently at the question.

She looks so beautiful kneeling on the floor, but now that I study her closely I can see tiny goosebumps on her shoulders and arms from the chilly cavern air. My hand moves in a casual way to cover myself, knowing I'll feel better with my sarong wrapped around me. "Why don't we put our clothes on again and we can lie down and share this blanket? There's only one, but I think it's big enough for both of us."

Diamond watches me, her expression giving away none of her thoughts. "Okay," she says, her voice lower than before, and more serious. She pads over to pick up her clothes and drape them around herself. My own movements are faster and without grace: wrap, tuck, and dive under the cover. She slips under the blanket with me then, taking half of the long pillow without hesitation.

I notice she doesn't offer to take the inside wall where I lie and she doesn't touch me under the cover. She lies on her side and watches me, her face in shadow now that the cave lighting is at her back. "Handler says you fought well out there," she tells me, her voice soft. "You survived."

I laugh without amusement. "That's what they tell me. I gather that's how you get ahead around here? Fight good; get food and... stuff." I fumble awkwardly at the end, remembering she was part of those promised rewards.

She's cool about the gaffe, not acknowledging it. "Eat, but don't stuff yourself," she advises. "Train, but don't wear yourself out. Sleep as much as they let you. Don't *just* fight; put on a good show for the audience. That's how you stay alive."

The lump in my stomach sours until I wonder if I'm going to vomit. Tony, Reese, Diamond; they all talk about my death as something I can avoid as long as I do everything right. *What happens when I don't?* But I smile in the dark and try to sound cheerful. "Is that how everyone else manages? The other boys, I mean."

"Some of them. They stay alive because they're good fighters, or good entertainers—which is not always the same thing. Or else they're useful; that's how your teacher stayed alive, even when he was too injured to appear in the arena anymore."

"There's seven of us, right?" I ask, biting my lip as I count heads and names from earlier. "Does that change a lot? They said there was a guy before me who died; am I his replacement? But there were more than seven doors out in the main cavern."

She shakes her head against the pillow. "They bring in new fighters now and again. There's been up to twelve at once, at least as long as I've been here. The Master has to balance the profitability of the bouts against the cost of keeping you fed well enough to fight." She tilts her head, and I can feel her studying me. "Do you know your talent yet? Sometimes they take time to surface."

"My talent?" I blink at her shadowed face. "Oh! Uh, Tony said I was strong? I pulled the armor off a rock monster so he could stab it."

I think I've impressed her; there's fresh interest in her voice when she speaks. "Crowds love strong fighters. Especially if you were paired with Tony. He's nimble, with finesse to supplement a partner's raw strength."

I feel my shoulders relax a little. It's easy talking to her about Tony and the others; much easier than dwelling on my impending death and her task here with me. "Have you seen him fight, then?"

"We watch most of the matches. The Master keeps us on display near his throne. We see you well enough, but given the sun and the distance and how busy you are down there, you might not see us. We weren't out there this cycle, but I imagine we'll watch your next fight."

Next fight. I hadn't really thought ahead to that, though I suppose I should have. Fighting is what fighters do, right? The brooding mood that has been threatening to pounce now settles around my temples, reigniting the headache I woke with earlier. I wonder how long it's been since I opened my eyes in the arena; it feels like an eternity ago.

The girl in my bed seems to sense my mood, or perhaps it's written on my face more clearly than I'd like. "Keoki?" she whispers, my name soft on her tongue. "You should sleep now. You're safe in here until first bell, I promise."

"I'll try," I tell her, unsure how well I can deliver. My groin is still throbbing from where we stopped earlier—though after all this talk of death and fighting, I'm not sure I'd want to continue even if she did. *And she doesn't. And that's that.* So I close my eyes and let all the fatigue I've been pushing away since the fight wash over me, dragging me into dreamless sleep.

CHAPTER 9

Aniyah

Hana was gone and would not return until first bell. I sit on my cushion by the stone table, numbness fogging my mind. *What if she doesn't come back?* I barely know her, but she saved my name at great risk to her own life. I don't want to imagine she might die out there on the other side of the golden doors.

Across the table, Sappho fusses over Heather's bleeding arm. The blond girl holds perfectly still throughout her ministrations, looking bored. When the wound is wrapped and the end of the gauze tucked into place, Sappho douses the area one last time in water from the pool. She frets over the gash, her hands fluttering around the wrapping several times to reassure herself the bandage has not come loose.

"Eat up, Heather," Chloe orders, her voice flat in the wake of Heather's dramatic demonstration. She pushes bowls of fruit and warm meat in our direction also, her nod encompassing myself and Miyuki. "You two as well," she says firmly. "I know you don't feel like eating, but you'll be hungry later if you don't."

Miyuki reaches for a bowl of spiced meat, picking out plump bites with her fingers and eating without relish. For my part, I tuck away a bowl's worth of tiny bright orange fruits I don't have a name for. They're tasty—

sharp on my tongue, but with a sweet aftertaste—yet I can't really enjoy them. The danger hanging over us robs me of any comfort from the food, and I feel physical pain from sitting on the floor. I find myself squirming between bites, trying and failing to ease a persistent ache in my lower back.

Imani misinterprets my squirming and touches my elbow with a kind smile. "Let me show you two the restroom," she offers. As we've both eaten all we want, Miyuki and I follow her to the far side of the cave.

A flat stone wall stretches between the heavy golden doors and the waterfall, and for a moment I'm confused as to where she's leading us. Then she reaches out to touch the rock and it *ripples* in her hands. I jump, and my startled eyes adjust to recognize brown canvas. A huge curtain hangs from the ceiling, the shade on this side of the cavern just dark enough for the material to create the illusion of a wall.

"There's just one toilet for all of us," she says, holding the canvas back. The cave curves sharply behind the curtain, carving out a private area about six paces deep. A long stone bench juts out of the wall, with a hole carved in the center and strips of cloth stacked nearby. "Everything goes down the hole. We pour water in after. Don't worry about the cloths; Handler brings more at first bell. Go ahead. We'll have a bath when you're finished, and then we'll all go to bed. We put the curtains up before fifth bell."

I blink at her. "We'll have a bath *together?*" This doesn't seem to fit my idea of the word.

Imani smiles at my question. "It's more like swimming. Or wading, if you can't swim. It'll be okay," she assures me.

I don't consciously remember swimming but I must have done it before, as my body knows exactly what to do from the moment I dip my feet in the water. I feel vulnerable being naked in front of the other girls, knowing they can see the scar on my back. So I let my body take over, sinking low into the water and swimming quickly out to the deeper end of the small pool, keeping my back pointed towards the privacy of the far wall where the waterfall trickles down.

"Aniyah! Aniyah, wait for me!"

Sappho splashes out to join me, waving in her enthusiasm. I'd expected Miyuki to come out, but she squats on the shallow shelf near the lip of the pool, scrubbing silently at her arms and ignoring the rest of us. Imani sits near her, knees pulled up to her chin and the water reaching almost to her chest. Chloe drifts on her back in the deep water near the center, her long hair spreading in all directions around her.

"I'm not going anywhere," I point out to Sappho, spreading my arms and treading water. Despite my earlier funk, I have to laugh at her infectious exuberance to reach me. "Unless there's an underwater tunnel or some such thing."

She giggles, catching up to me with quick strokes. "Nope!" she says, shaking her head. "We've looked. There is a bottom, it's just pretty deep."

"That's too bad," I tell her, but I hadn't really expected anything else. Wherever we were brought from, wherever the University is, I wouldn't think we could just swim there. Still, a thought nags at me. "Where does the water go?" I ask, turning my head to look at the waterfall behind me. "Why doesn't the pool overflow?"

"We wondered about that, too," she says, undoing her ponytail and leaning back to dip her hair in the water. "One of the other girls—we called her 'Lane'—said the rock is porous. Water goes through, even though we can't."

I bite my lip, unsure how to phrase the obvious question. "What happened to her?"

Sappho stares up at the ceiling as she floats, avoiding my eyes. "The fighter she was sent to had a bad dream. Strangled her before he realized he wasn't in the arena. He couldn't live with the guilt, so he threw his next match. We saw him die, but only learned what had happened to Lane afterwards."

I cover my mouth as I listen in horror. Sappho sighs, a world of sadness in the sound. "We never knew her real name, just a tag on her clothes. Same as with Heather; they were both brought in before Hana was. Hana came up with the idea to wake newbies before their memories could be taken. She even woke herself up! Too strong for the drugs. It was amazing—and a little scary, knowing we could be killed."

There's pride in her voice as she talks about Hana, admiring her bravery. "You were there for that?" I'd assumed Hana was the oldest from the way they all deferred to her.

She smiles, sorrowful reminiscence playing over her soft features. "Oh, yes. I was here for Hana, and Chloe and Imani after her. Heather was here already when I was brought in, which makes her the oldest now. And I've been here for others. They're gone now, though."

How many? I think, and immediately push the thought aside. *No, I don't want to know.* I'm sad enough already about a girl I'll never meet and whose name I'll never learn. "If Hana arrived after you, how did you know your name?" I ask, casting about for another topic.

Sappho grins at my question and bobs in the water until she's vertical again, inches away from me. I'm very aware of how naked we both are, but the close proximity doesn't seem to bother her. "I had my name tattooed on me," she brags with a giggle, "along with everything else."

She's not lying about that. Her entire body is a canvas of shy maidens, beautiful mermaids, horned succubi, and twisting dragons. Tiny black birds fly across her collarbone and rise over her shoulder while colorful little butterflies climb the back of her neck into her hairline. She extends her left arm to me, twisting so I can see the soft inner flesh of her upper arm. Words are there, a scrolling script written in letters so small I have to squint to read them in the shade.

I alone of all things
fret with unsluiced fire
and there is no quenching
in the night for Sappho

"It's a poem," I realize, looking up at her. "But it doesn't rhyme."

"It's *my* poem," she replies with a laugh. "It doesn't need to."

"Sappho, are you ready to help with the curtains?" Chloe's voice drifts over the water. I glance up to see her already out of the pool and toweling her hair dry.

"Yeah!" Sappho chirrups, twisting back to face the shore. Grabbing my arm on an impulse, she yanks me forward. "C'mon, Aniyah, you can help too."

I wince when she pulls me, sharp pain shooting up my spine. Drawing back, I try not to yelp as I disengage from her grip. "Coming," I manage to choke out, biting my lip against the throbbing ache that settles in after the sharp pain recedes. She gives me a funny look, concern mingling with confusion, but splashes forward, trusting me to follow.

The curtains are made from the same heavy brown canvas used to cordon off the toilet. Chloe climbs onto one of the stone beds clustered on the side of the cavern furthest from the golden doors. Heather stands nearby, listlessly handing up armfuls of rough cloth to her. I'm impressed that the pain in her wounded arm doesn't bother her, only to remember she can't feel it. I can't decide whether I'm unsettled or envious.

Sappho chooses a bed nearer the center of the room, where the slope of the ceiling is higher. She climbs up and raises her hands above her head, her arms stretching to become almost as long as I am tall. As Imani hands up the cloth, Sappho affixes the material to hooks set in the ceiling, creating a shelter around the stone platform. "We'll need to do two extra for the newcomers," Imani reminds her. "I think we have enough cloth, but we should ask Handler for more when he comes at first bell, just in case."

"What are the curtains for?" I ask, toweling off by the pool. I'm last out of the water but Miyuki lingers by the edge, fiddling with her clothing. "Are you okay?" I add in a softer voice, anxious not to disturb the others.

"I'm fine." Her smile is kind, yet hesitant. "Actually, I was going to ask you: do you want help dressing?"

90

I hesitate at the unexpected offer. "You're sure you don't mind?" I don't want to be a bother, but I'm grateful for her assistance; my back still throbs painfully and the twists and turns needed to wrap our clothes around us are more difficult than the other girls made it look.

Heather doesn't turn around, handing up more cloth to Chloe. "To block out the sun while we sleep," she says in answer to my earlier question. "It's easier and more comfortable to sleep in the dark."

I hadn't thought of this. I tilt my head to peer up at the hole in the ceiling where sunlight floods in. Only the table in the center of the cavern lies directly in the light; the beds have been cut farther back into the shade. Still, I imagine it would be difficult to relax with all that glittering brightness nearby.

"Doesn't the sun ever go away?" Miyuki asks from behind me, tucking the last of my wrap into place. The uncertainty in her voice mirrors my own; I'm not sure why, but the idea of a sun that always shines seems somehow odd.

"Nope." With Heather's help, Chloe hops down from the bed she's standing on and mounts the next bed down the line to start anew. "What you see here is what you get."

"It's darker in the boys' rooms," Imani cuts in, handing another armful of cloth to Sappho. "There's glowing moss on the ceilings, but the beds are cut into the walls and it doesn't grow there. Some of the girls noticed a long time ago that they slept better in the dark. Handler eventually brought curtains."

"He gives us things if we ask for them?" This is a new idea, one full of possibilities.

Heather snorts at my question. "If we ask hard enough," she spits, her voice sour. "We stopped eating. After the first two girls were punished and we still wouldn't eat, we got our curtains."

I stare at her, my thoughts in turmoil. I can't imagine what punishments would make the listless girl turn so thoroughly acrimonious, and I don't think

I want to. Yet even more difficult to imagine is anything being so important to me that I would take such a risk. *Could I willingly suffer for curtains?*

"Was it worth it?" Miyuki asks. She sounds as curious as I feel, but her voice is steadier than mine would be.

Heather shrugs. "We're all going to die anyway," she says, reverting to her hollow tone. "Better to be well-rested when it happens."

"That's enough of that," Chloe says, brushing her hands on her skirt. "No one is dying this cycle, Heather. Sappho, help me with the two empty beds by the wall; those'll be for Emma and Aniyah. We'll get you two all set up and then you need to sleep. Fifth bell will ring soon."

I don't feel tired but I nod anyway. I look at Miyuki, and the hazel eyes behind her glasses are as dull as I feel. She offers me a sad little smile, and I return it; they're trying to make us comfortable, I know, and it's not their fault they don't have much comfort to offer.

When the curtains are up, Imani helps me onto the thinly-padded stone slab that is my bed, giving me a little rectangle of cloth for a blanket. "It doesn't get cold in here, but sometimes we get chilly during sleep. Try to rest. We'll get up together at first bell to eat. It'll be okay." She squeezes my hand in a reassuring way before ducking out through the hanging canvas that darkens the tiny world around me.

I can't imagine how I'll be able to sleep. The curtains help to create a closed space; light is blocked out, and I hear only slight shuffling noises as the other girls settle in. But I'm still overwhelmed by all this. I've been kidnapped and brought here against my will. My memories were taken from me, leaving me unsure of even my own name. Now I'm a piece of property, to be used by boys I don't know until I die.

I might have been able to push that aspect away to dwell on later were it not for the tangible absence of Hana. I met her only long enough to know she saved my name, and then she was taken away. I don't know if she'll be back, and that frightening possibility makes the danger I'm in feel far more immediate. *If this place can kill a girl who seemed so strong, what chance do I have to survive?*

The curtains around my bed rustle. A small ray of light squeezes in before the darkness falls back into place with the addition of an intruder's barely-visible outline. "Aniyah?" I hear Miyuki's soft voice. "Can I sleep with you? I don't want to be alone right now."

She can't see the rueful smile on my face, but perhaps she can hear it in my voice. "You too, huh? Yes, I think there's room." I manage to work myself onto my side and scoot over to make space for her. I don't know how I can ever sleep with hard stone pressing painfully into my spine through the thin pad, but at least I'll have company.

"Thanks," she whispers. She slips in beside me with movements more graceful than any I've been able to make. Up close, I can see her despite the darkness; her freckled face is drawn into a nervous frown. "This is all pretty scary, isn't it?" She tries for a smile but doesn't succeed.

"I'm terrified," I agree, a chuckle escaping my throat. There's a weird relief in admitting it, not having to pretend for the other girls that everything is normal and I'm fine. "Where are your glasses?" I ask, belatedly noticing her face is naked.

"I can't sleep in them," she says, her voice fretful. "If I roll over, they might break. So I wrapped them up in gauze and left them on my bed." She bites her lip. "Do you think that's a safe place to leave them? If I put them on the floor, I'm afraid someone will step on them."

"I think the bed is safe," I say slowly, considering the limited options available. "They said that was *your* bed, right? I don't believe anyone else will go near it before we wake up again."

She nods, cushioning her head with her arm. "I'm so afraid of losing them," she admits in a low whisper. "I'm more afraid of not being able to see than I am of anything else. What if they fall down the toilet? What if that man, Handler, takes them away?"

On impulse, I reach out to touch her shoulder. "Hey. He won't. Okay? I won't let him."

Her eyes widen at me, studying my face in the dark. "Why would he listen to us? You heard what Heather said, didn't you? They had to starve themselves just to get curtains!"

I flash a broad smile, attempting to look reassuring and determined all at once. "They said I was special, didn't they? I have some rare talent, so he wants to keep me healthy and happy? Well, he can keep me happy by taking good care of you." I find her hand and give her the same gentle squeeze Imani offered me earlier. "I'll make sure you're safe, I promise."

She holds on to me, her hand cool after the bath. "Thank you," she whispers, summoning a brave smile. "Aniyah."

My name rolls over her tongue like a sweet fruit she's savoring, lending the word warm familiarity in her mouth. "Do you remember me at all, even a little?" I ask, watching her face for some spark of recognition.

Her smile softens, becoming almost bashful. "No," she admits, shaking her head. "But we must have been something to each other, right? We were kidnapped together and we knew one another. We weren't strangers when we were taken."

"Friends, maybe?" I hazard. "Not sisters; we know that much."

Miyuki chuckles but then sobers, her eyes watching me intently. "Aniyah, I'm wondering if we were very close. I think we might have been." Her thumb strokes the soft underside of my wrist, carefully avoiding my chains. "You used my second name, the special one that goes with the words on my arm."

She looks so earnest that I want to understand, but I don't quite follow what she means. "I saw you washing them away while we were in the pool. Did you figure out what they meant?"

Her eyes are wide in the dark, solemn and eager all at once. "I think so. I think those words are a part of me, a part of *Emma Miyuki*. I think the top row was for Emma and the bottom row was for Miyuki. Two names, two pronouns."

I turn this over in my head, nodding slowly. "You think your father bought them when you got your second name?"

94

"Maybe," she agrees, though she seems less sure on this point. "But I'm certain about the division. I think *Emma* and *her* and *she* were given to me first for everyone to use. Then I added *Miyuki* and *xie* and *xer* later as something special to share with people I care about. Aniyah, I think you were one of those people."

I squeeze her hand again, in no hurry to let go. "Well, you *do* seem pretty special," I tease, hoping she can hear my smile even if she can't see it.

She returns my grin, but her eyes retain a kernel of worry. "I must have known we were being kidnapped and tried to save everything by writing on my arms. But I must not have had time to finish. If Hana hadn't woken you, I'd have lost both my names."

The anxiety in her voice is more than I can bear. I let go of her hand to wrap her in an awkward hug. It's tricky to pull off while lying on my side and my spine twinges with fresh pain, but the cost is worth it. "Hey." I touch my forehead to hers so she can see my eyes without her glasses. "You didn't lose them, though. We did good. We saved the important stuff. We know I'm Aniyah, and we know you're Emma Miyuki."

"We saved the important stuff," she agrees in a soft whisper, tears welling up in her smiling eyes. She's quiet for a while but then her gaze slides away, reluctant to meet my own. "Aniyah? The other girls are already calling me 'Emma'. But can I still be 'Miyuki' with you? I know we don't remember each other, but I'd like to save that part as well."

I stare at her, our breathing the only sound in the dark bubble we've made for ourselves. Despite the fact that I've been calling her 'Miyuki' in my mind, her name isn't familiar to me; it's simply a word I used because I was told I'd used it before. With my memories gone, I don't know this girl or her names or the words she uses to describe the different parts of herself. Any relationship we might have had is lost now, leaving us no better than strangers.

Yet she's soft and cool in my arms. Her face is so close, I can see the little specks of freckles splayed across her cheeks, their color so much like the warm hazel of her eyes. When she smiles my heart beats faster, and when she looks sad I want to hold her and chase the sorrow away. I can't take away the danger surrounding us, and I can't make our memories return. But I *can* do my absolute best to protect her and make us both as happy as possible in this grim place.

"You can still be Miyuki to me," I promise, my voice low. "I'm happy you want to share yourself with me."

She looks up at me—no, *xie* looks up at me—xer eyes shining with unshed tears. "I'm glad you're here with me, Aniyah," xie whispers. A trembling smile spreads over xer face, wry and laughing all at once. "I know it's just the worst thing to say, to be glad you're caught in this mess with me, but it's true."

I laugh with xer, exhaustion and fear making my limbs rubbery. "I can't think of anyone else I'd rather be here with, Miyuki." It's a joke, of course, since I can't remember anyone else, but it's also perfectly true. Xie grins at me and snuggles closer into our hug, closing xer eyes.

We're quiet after that. Xer breathing slows and deepens, eventually turning into a gentle snore against my neck. I close my eyes and smell the soft scent of xer hair, letting myself be lulled by the rhythm of xer breathing. I'm unsure if I'll be able to sleep through the pain which has grown into a constant and unwelcome companion, but I hold Miyuki close and cling to the hope that we might wake to a better world than the one we've seen so far.

CHAPTER 10

Keoki

A single bell, loud and clear, jars me out of my sleep. I sit bolt upright in bed, breathing hard as a blur of memories assault me: the arena, Tony, Diamond. Panic grips me, but I try to steady my breathing and let the wave of feelings and sensations wash over me. I don't want to push the memories away; I'm anxious to ensure nothing has been lost and that whatever wiped my mind before hasn't struck again.

I'd fallen asleep after going to bed with Diamond, too exhausted after the fight to keep my eyes open. The tolling of fifth bell had jostled me awake, but she'd made gentle shushing noises and I'd slipped back under almost immediately. I vaguely remember her getting out of bed at some point and moving quietly about the room, but the recollection is hazy and indistinct. This lack of clarity worries me, but perhaps sleep-memories just aren't as vivid as waking ones. Anyway, there's no way to know and nothing I could do about it if I did, so the only course of action I can see is not to fret over it.

I slide out of bed and stretch my legs, rubbing grit out of my eyes. Diamond is nowhere to be seen and isn't behind the bathroom curtain, so I have to assume she left while I was asleep and probably won't be back. This gives me a moment of disappointment; I'd have liked to tell her goodbye. Yet she'd said we would see each other again. *If I win another match and she's my prize.*

I don't want to think about fighting or prizes, so I direct my attention to the nearby bathroom where I'm pleased to find I remember what to do with the hole in the stone bench. A little more trial and error is required to discover that my water bowl detaches from its niche in the wall, but once the metal basin pops out into my hands I'm able to lug it over the hole and flush away any lingering mess. Afterwards, I shave while the basin refills and manage not to nick myself more than twice.

I'm pretty proud of myself, all things considered: even without memories, I'm keeping myself and my room clean like a real winner. I'm just looking around the room and wondering what else I might do to tidy up—*Rinse my clothes? Fold the blanket on the bed?*—when I'm startled by a loud rap on the door and I jump to open it.

Reese's wide smile greets me from the other side. "Hey, kid, food's here. Get it while it's cold! Your girl make out okay?" He cranes his head, trying to look into the room behind me while not wishing to seem obvious.

"She's not here," I tell him, though the room is small enough that he's probably come to that conclusion already. "I think she left a little before the bell rang."

He nods. "Yeah, they do that," he says, shrugging. "They gotta squeeze in a nap before the bouts. Assuming there is a bout. Not like we usually get any warning. Who, uh... who'd you have?"

I wonder why he cares, but there's no reason not to tell him. "She said her name was Diamond."

Reese visibly relaxes at my answer, his broad shoulders loosening. "You got Diamond? She's great," he enthuses, his grin widening. "Ought to be a fighter herself. If you get her again, you should ask her to train you; she knows stuff even Matías doesn't know. Now, c'mon! Gotta eat before practice starts."

98

I wonder if we mean the same person. I can't imagine asking the short girl who knelt between my legs to train me in any kind of fighting, but I follow him out into the cavern without argument. "What kind of food do we get? Is it different from what Handler brought before?" This seems by far the most important topic, my stomach gurgling in greedy expectation.

His voice takes on a wistful tone. "We only get the good stuff after someone wins a match. Otherwise, it's cold cuts and stale leftovers; not very tasty, but it'll still fill you up. Newbie alert, everyone be nice!"

This last is said as we round one of the columns that stab up through the cavern floor. On the other side, the guys sit on the ground or lean against columns of their own, each of them eating out of wooden bowls the size of my hand. Reese scoops up two free bowls from the ground, handing me one and nudging Justin with his foot to make a place for us to sit.

"Look at him! He didn't sleep at all, you can tell," Lucas announces, shaking his head at me with a knowing grin. "You'll be hopeless during practice, newbie. Was she at least worth it?"

"Who'd blame him?" Justin complains sourly, moving grudgingly in response to Reese's nudging. "At least you've all had one; I still haven't gotten a Prize."

Christian laughs. "That's why you need more practice, kid," he teases Justin, picking a long sliver of cold meat out of a bowl with his fingers. "If you actually *won* a fight, rather than boring the challenge to death, you'd probably get one. Who'd you get, anyway?" he asks, looking at me with a grin.

"He got Diamond," Reese answers for me, tipping his own bowl directly to his mouth.

"Diamond!" Christian laughs again, puckering his lips in a mock kiss. "Come back when you've had Ruby. Round and soft and perfect, with thighs that could break you in two."

"Don't listen to him," Lucas butts in, shaking his head at me. "Emerald is the best, and only a fool would think she wasn't. She's the prettiest of them all, and she does anything you want without a peep."

"Lucas, just because *you* like them quiet—"

"Save it for practice."

Tony cuts in, his voice low and curt. He leans against one of the columns, picking at his food without any enthusiasm. He hasn't once looked at me since I walked in—a fact I know with perfect certainty because I've been watching him. I'd give just about anything to know what he's thinking; he'd been almost friendly in the arena, but his demeanor has been distant and cold since then. *Did I do something wrong?*

I clear my throat, swallowing the last of a particularly chewy chunk of gristly meat. "When is that, actually? Practice, I mean."

He turns his eyes on me at last, dark and unreadable. "In a hurry? C'mon, then," he orders, stalking off before I have a chance to reply. I throw a glance at Reese, who just shrugs and continues eating. My own bowl is only half-finished, but despite my previous hunger my stomach wants no more of this bland food. I scramble to my feet after Tony, ignoring the chuckles and groans that follow in my wake. *I'd rather practice than talk about girls, anyway.*

I catch up with him at the big rectangle cut into the center of the cavern, the one filled with sand that is everything sand should be: soft and tiny-grained and yellow. Matías is here as well, slowly pacing the perimeter of the pit and occasionally stopping to draw lines in the sand with the tip of his cane. "Hey!" I call to Tony's back, walking faster in order to gain ground on his more casual stride. "What do we do in pract— *whoa!*"

I'd thought Tony had moved fast in the arena, his every action so skillfully precise that not a single movement was wasted. But that was nothing compared to what Matías does now as he suddenly speeds across the sand. My eyes can't follow him properly, the rapidity of his approach causing his body to blur at the edges. He crosses the pit in the span of a few heartbeats, darting up the stone steps that lead down into the sand. My hands come up in a defensive posture, but far too slowly; I'm pushed hard up against the nearest column, the length of his cane pressed across my throat as I struggle to catch my stolen breath.

"We practice staying alive," Matías says, his voice low as he stares down at me with solemn eyes. He studies my face, and I wonder if I've failed some test by losing to his unexpected assault.

"Okay, yeah, that makes sense," I agree, trying to sound unfazed; not an easy task, given the fact that I still can't breathe freely and I'm pretty sure everything he just did was impossible. Still, I manage to pull off a casual tone. "I didn't know we'd started yet. Obviously." *Not that it would have made a bit of difference if I had.*

A warm chuckle floats back to us, and over Matías' shoulder I see Tony watching me with a smile on his face. "You've gotta admit he doesn't fluster easily," he says, approval creeping into his voice. "Teacher, your knee is shaking. You shouldn't show off like that, not for practice."

Matías snorts and backs a step away, lowering his cane from my throat in order to lean heavily on it. Now that there's space between us, I see Tony is right: Matías' knee is trembling violently. "Oh, hey, do you need help?" I stammer, my hands coming up in preparation to steady him.

He turns away from me, picking each step with care as he walks slowly back to the sand-pit. "No," he answers, his voice firm. "If I need help, I will ask for it. We'll pair the two of you up to practice for now. I assume everyone else is still eating?"

"And fighting over girls," Tony says, rolling his eyes. "You know, important stuff."

He strides over to the column where Matías pushed me. I'm not injured or even really winded, yet he extends his hand in an offer to pull me up. I grasp his arm, my muscles remembering the movements, and he rocks me forward off my heels until I'm standing almost nose-to-nose with him.

He's the tiniest bit taller than me, unless you take my curls into account—in which case I win. His eyes are almost black in the torchlight, but there's warmth in them now that he's smiling. *What changed?* I can't predict his moods or understand them. He'd been friendly in the arena, only to turn cold when we entered the cavern; then he'd acted sullen when

I came out of my room, only to be my best mate now. *Does he just like seeing me get beaten up? Because if that's the case, maybe we could work out some kind of schedule.*

"Well, there are worse things to fight over," Matías observes, breaking into my thoughts. "Left side for you two?" He's still picking his way over the sand, his back to us as he speaks in the mildest of tones, yet Tony's spine stiffens and he backs a step away from me as though he'd been stung.

I blink at him, thoroughly confused. *What did I do now? Or was it something Matías said?* All these mood-swings are killing me, because either I'm doing something wrong around Tony or all the other guys are. Then my breath catches as a new thought slams into place: *The other guys.* The cause of Tony's discomfort isn't what anyone is saying, it's just that they're there at all.

Every time he clammed up and turned cold was when others were around, or when he was reminded they were present, as with Matías speaking to us both just now while we were standing toe-to-toe. *He doesn't feel comfortable in large groups,* I realize, fighting an almost irresistible urge to break into a broad grin. *He's shy.* Not a jerk, not an aloof untouchable fighting god, just perfectly and adorably shy.

"Well?" Tony prompts, frowning at me. "Left side good for you? With you here, there's six of us, so we can have three pair-matches. Christian likes to take the center to do his thing, so that leaves left and right sides."

"Left is great," I agree, my voice cheerful to my ears now that I've solved the mystery of the handsome moody boy. I follow him out into the pit, sighing with contentment at the sensation of real sand sliding between my toes—it's gritty and scratchy and I'll need to wash later, but I feel as though I've come home.

"Wouldn't want Christian unable to do his thing," I add as we come to a stop where Matías is drawing starting marks in the sand. "But, uh, how does this work? Do I get to see *your* thing?" I flash a grin at Tony, wondering if the question will ruffle him.

102

He rolls his eyes. "You've already seen my thing," he says dryly. He strides to the nearest side of the pit, bending to grab up a handful of little bundled cloths. There are maybe a dozen in total, all of them rolled and knotted until they look like thick little fingers. "Raise your arms." I tilt my head at him, but when no further explanation seems forthcoming I shrug and do as I've been ordered.

Once my arms are out of his way, Tony unrolls the little cloths and wraps them around me. One goes around my waist while another is wound like a sash over my shoulder, crossing my chest once before loosely tying at my hip. He wraps two more around my wrists and steps in closer to bind the last one around my neck. I give him a wide grin, my face a finger-width from his, but he ignores me.

"I feel so pretty," I tease when he steps back to survey his work. "Do I get to tie *you* up now?"

I'm rewarded with another eyeroll. "No. Teacher does."

He hands the remainder of the cloth to Matías, who gives Tony his cane to hold. Our teacher moves slowly around him, tying the cloth in identical configurations to my own: waist, chest, wrists, neck. I watch Tony turn to facilitate the binding, my eyes lingering on the deep scars carved into his back. When the final sash is in place Matías tugs on the knot, collects his cane, and heads to the side of the pit. He climbs the stone steps out of the sand and leans against a nearby column, his sharp gaze settling on us.

"So, what are we supposed to do now?" I look at Tony for guidance and my eyes nearly pop out of my head.

Tony is sitting in the sand performing what looks like the most painful stretches imaginable. His legs extend directly out and he's bent over double, so that his hands grasp his feet and his forehead touches his legs. As I watch, he move his legs until they're stretched out on either side of him, pointing in opposite directions as he leans forward to hover his nose directly over the sand.

"Please tell me I don't have to do that," I beg, my inner thighs aching just from watching him.

He snorts, sand swirling away from his breath. "No. This is my warm-up."

I watch him with open curiosity. "So what *are* we doing? And where'd you learn that?"

"Came in knowing some of it," he says with a shrug. He pulls himself up to a standing position, brushes off, and begins a pattern of lunging forward on one foot only to step back and repeat the movement with his other leg. "One of the girls, Sapphire, helped me get better. As for what you and I are doing, we don't use blades on newbies. Too easy to hurt someone. So we're gonna play grabbers instead."

"Grabbers?" I touch the cloth bow he's tied across my chest.

"Grabbers," he repeats. "Wrists are a disarm, because you can't hold your weapon if your hands aren't attached. Stomach is a gut-cut. Chest is the same, but across your chest. Neck is a throat-cut or heads-off entirely, so watch your neck. Oh, and we start *now*."

He throws himself at me so suddenly I don't have time to think. My hands come up in the same defensive posture as when Matías attacked, and just as before I'm too sluggish. Tony doesn't move with the teacher's impossible blurry speed but he's still *fast*, with not a single movement wasted. His hands shoot out and grab me by the wrist, then his fingers wrap around the cloth like claws and *yank*. He dances away from me in the space of a breath, waving the torn cloth like a triumphant flag.

I stumble back, putting distance between us. I can't believe how calm he is; he's not even breathing hard. "How do you *do* that?" I ought to be pissed at the unfair sudden start of the game, but getting to see him in action was worth the loss of my wrist-cloth.

Tony shrugs. "It's my talent. We all have one. I'm agile."

I shake my head, my hands still raised as I edge around wondering if I can circle him. "You're amazing, you mean," I tell him. "But how I am supposed to win the game? You're so much faster than me."

He snorts. "And you're so much stronger than me," he counters, tossing the discarded cloth from my wrist onto the ground. "If you can grab me, it's all over."

I consider this while I watch for an opening. Maybe I can wrap my arms around him when he darts in again. "Don't suppose you'll *let* me grab you, huh? Just to be nice to the newbie?"

He makes a noise that isn't quite a chuckle and isn't quite a sneer, then he's coming in fast again, crouched low to the ground as though aiming for my knees—*or my stomach,* I realize. I bend to meet him, my hands already moving to clap around him once he's in grabbing range. No matter how fast he is, I just need to catch and hold him.

It's a good plan, and might have worked if he'd kept coming head-on. Instead he lunges to my left, his hands reaching for the knot of my sash. I stumble backwards, slapping a hand protectively over the knot. He lets his momentum carry him around my left side, slipping in behind me. I feel his hands on the back of my neck, reaching under my curls to find the cloth at my throat. "Being nice gets newbies dead," he hisses. "Being fast keeps them alive."

He's going to rip the cloth from my neck. *Then I'll be... what? Dead?* I'm pretty sure the game can't go on if I'm missing my head. Panic rises in my blood; even though I know I'm not in danger, I need to be better than this. Yet I can't think how to counter him when he's so fast. I'm strong, but that won't do me any good if I can't grab him. *Or does it?* In the arena, I'd used my body for more than just grabbing; I'd wielded myself like a weapon, throwing all my weight into the rock monster.

Sucking in a deep breath and praying I don't hurt Tony too much, I fling myself backwards and slam into him. We collide and I let myself go limp, bringing us both down in a crashing tangle of limbs. He yelps—the sound more angry than pained—and scrambles to get free of me but I have the advantage. Twisting around, I grapple with the struggling body under me, determined now to win.

I don't need to hold him down or stop him from moving; I just have to trap him long enough to get his flag. My hands scramble over his chest, sliding up to find his neck and the cloth tied there. His dark eyes meet mine, and for a heartbeat his struggles stop. Then he lunges upward against me, one knee slamming hard into my groin. As my world explodes with pain, his hands dart up to my neck and rip the sash away.

I roll off him, gasping for air. I'm laughing, even as tears stream down my cheeks from the pain. "Wow. *Wow.* I almost had you." I turn my head to see him lying on the sand next to me, sweat beaded on his forehead and his mouth set in a smug smile. "You didn't try to get away. Just went right for my throat."

He flashes a sharp grin at me, teeth flashing in the firelight. "That's why I'm alive, newbie."

I'm too impressed with him to be upset. "Man, you'd better get the best prize for killing me," I tease.

His dark eyes study my face. "How *did* you like your Prize, by the way? You didn't say earlier."

I shrug, leaning my head back into the soft sand. "Dunno. Didn't really do anything with her," I admit. Somehow it's easier to tell him if I don't have to look into his eyes.

"Don't you like girls?" he asks, sounding curious.

I chuckle at the question. "I like everyone." I turn to regard him with a wry grin, but he's not smiling back. He's watching me with an expression too solemn to bear, and I decide I have to make him laugh. I put on a very serious frown and try my best to look disappointed. "Anyway, I couldn't do anything with her."

He walks into the joke without realizing. "You couldn't? Why not?"

I give him my brightest smile. "Because I said I'd share with you, didn't I?"

Tony doesn't laugh at the joke, doesn't even smile. He just studies me with that serious expression, his mouth set in a line. "Huh," he says, the sound a soft puff of air between us. "Yeah. You did say that." He gives me a sidelong look, settling back into the sand. "You still thinking that's fair?"

106

I blink at him. Somewhere I must've lost my smile because now it returns, spreading slyly across my face. "Tell you what, the next time I get a Prize feel free to drop by. In fact, I *encourage* you to."

His lips part in readiness to speak—and I can tell from the warm flash of his eyes that it'll be good—when a surge of voices to our right cause him to jump. He clams up and his eyes take on a distant look; for a moment, I could throttle the other guys for choosing this moment to finish eating. But when I turn my head to see the approaching group, the grim look on Reese's face makes my stomach flip.

"What is it?" Matías stands straighter against the column that supports him, his face etched with worry.

Reese shakes his head, looking profoundly unhappy. "Handler gave a match notice when he picked up the bowls. Team-fight, but we don't know against what."

"Who's on the team?" Matías demands, his voice tight.

Christian—the handsome one with skin so much darker than my own and whose mouth is always set in a wry smile—isn't smiling now. "Me an' the newbie," he reports, giving me a pitying look.

"What?" Tony explodes, sitting bolt upright. "That's two bouts in a row for him! We haven't trained him yet! We haven't fitted him with armor! It's not remotely fair; he'll be going in tired."

"Tony, he didn't give any choice! No call for volunteers; just dropped off the names and left."

I listen with one ear to the rising argument, but the words wash over me in a meaningless roar. I'd known it would happen eventually, but I hadn't thought it would be this soon. *I'm going into the arena again.*

CHAPTER 11

Aniyah

Sunlight floods my senses as Sappho's cheery voice jolts me awake. "Wake up, Hana's back!" she sings out, throwing open the thick curtains around my bed. "She's back and she brought food and—oh!"

I groan and blink against the unwelcome light, trying to figure out where I am and whether all my bits are working correctly. I'm lying on my back with my neck twisted at a sharp angle to face Miyuki. Xie lies on xer side next to me, our faces only inches apart while xer arm is slung carelessly across my stomach. I feel soothed where xer arm is draped over me, a gentle goodness seeping in at xer touch.

"She what?" I mumble to Sappho. I close my eyes against the invading sun and try to stretch my back without disturbing Miyuki. My whole body is a mass of pain and stiffness, to the point where I'm unsure if I'll be able to move off this rock.

Sappho doesn't seem to hear me. "Are you two together?"

Her tone is faintly wounded, though I can't understand why. I turn my head to look at her and frown in puzzlement. She looks different from how I remember. When she moves, her body ripples as though she's a creature made from water; even when she stands motionless, flexibility is written in every supple curve of her body. Her stretching talent is so obvious now that I can't imagine why I needed a demonstration.

"Oh, Sappho. No one can say you didn't try." Heather's dry voice drifts from the table. "You've still got me, though. That has to count for something."

I twist to follow Heather's voice, rubbing my eyes when I see her. There's a new hardness etched into her shoulders, giving her a dull gloss around the edges. She looks as though she's been dipped in a substance that dried shiny and hard around her, a shell encasing her.

Nor are she and Sappho the only things I see differently now; the strange changes extend to the light around Heather and the table she leans upon. Looking around in fascination, I see changes in the whole cavern. Stone sparkles more brightly, sunlight glitters, and the golden doors at the far side of the cavern roil with a strange thrumming power under the surface of the metal. *What happened to my eyes?*

"Come and eat. We don't have a lot of time before the bout; you've already slept through first bell." A calm voice, almost stern, pierces the haze of my pain and confusion with its blessed familiarity: *Hana.*

"You're back," I breathe, not quite daring to believe it. I turn to pat Miyuki's cheek, feeling xer stir under my touch. "Miyuki, she's back." Xie, at least, seems the same as before; if xer skin glows faintly in the sun, I can pretend the subtle shimmer is a side-effect of the strange new light.

"Who's back?" Xie mumbles sleepily into xer arm, then sits bolt upright and looks around with startled eyes for something that isn't there.

"Your glasses are on your bed," I whisper up at xer. The grateful smile xie beams down on me in return makes my stomach flutter unexpectedly.

Miyuki has no trouble hopping down from the bed and retrieving xer glasses; once the frames are firmly perched on xer nose, xie runs fingers through the messy mop of xer hair and looks around the bright room with an expectant gaze. Getting up isn't nearly so easy for me. Unlike Miyuki,

I can't bend at the waist to sit, so I roll on my side to the edge of the bed. From there, I drop my legs to the floor and lever myself into a standing position. The movement isn't graceful, but it does the job.

The other girls are already at the table, and each is different from before. They have the same faces and bodies, but they seem more *real* under the bright sunlight. Chloe vibrates with strength and I sense lines of muscle running under her soft fat. Imani's face is as beautiful as ever, but now there's a glimmering shine to her skin—the hallmark of her ability to alter her appearance. Hana, lovely and alive, eats steaming brown mash from a bowl while a golden glow ripples through her body, searching for wounds to heal.

"Smells good," Miyuki observes, nodding at the bowl of mashed grains in the center of the table. I nod, still a little unsteady from rising, and pad over with tiny stiff steps. Miyuki wraps an arm around my waist to help steady me as we walk. "You're back," xie says warmly to Hana. "Are you okay? They said..." Xer eyes flick to Heather and the bandage wrapped around her arm.

"I'm fine," Hana says, spooning a handful of purple berries into her bowl and mashing them in a swirl with the brown grains. "I said I would be."

"How is the new boy?" Imani asks, her voice soft. "Is he okay?"

Hana shrugs. "He's decent so far," she says in a neutral tone. "New and confused. Not demanding yet. Might stay that way."

Chloe leans forward on her elbows, watching Hana with alert eyes. "Did you get any information out of him?"

"No, he'd already been wiped, like the others." She looks at Miyuki and me, her expression thoughtful. "He was brought in the same time you two were. I wonder if he was a friend or boyfriend of yours. I don't think he's related; when you were awake at first, Aniyah, you said you didn't have family nearby."

Miyuki looks up sharply from where xie has been stirring handfuls of pink seeds into xer bowl. "Could he be one of my relatives?"

110

"Maybe," Hana says with a shrug, returning to her bowl. "Without memories it's impossible to tell. But for what it's worth, he doesn't really look like either of you."

"What *does* he look like?" I ask, shifting on my cushion.

"Hmm. Taller than me, but not as tall as most of the boys. Skinny, sorta lanky, like he needs more food. Long bony arms I'd snap in a match, except apparently he's stronger than he looks. Still, I'd go for an elbow and see how he handled that. Smelled like sweat and sand, but they all do. Brown skin lighter than Imani's—lighter than Aniyah's, I think, but it's hard to tell in those dark rooms. Curls like Aniyah's, too, but longer down to his shoulders. His nose was a nose, but not like either of yours. And I couldn't tell the color of his eyes."

Miyuki digs intently into xer bowl, mixing the little puckered seeds with renewed purpose throughout this litany. "Well. We probably had lots of friends," xie observes when Hana finishes.

"You probably did," she agrees, "and it doesn't really matter now. Eat up; we have a bout to attend at third bell. I've got time for practice and a quick nap. You two should bathe and dress in clean clothes. The Master is particular about appearances."

I look up in alarm; in my current state, I'm struggling just to move. "Wait, what's being practiced?"

"*I'm* practicing kick-punching," Hana says patiently. She balls her hands into fists, and makes two slow jabs in the air: extending her arms to full length, twisting her wrists very slightly, and then drawing back to her chest. If she's aware of the glowing ripple that flickers over her arms, she doesn't show it. "You don't need to worry about that, unless you want to join in. We all pass time in different ways."

"Oh." I blink at the revelation that there is time to pass; somehow with all the talk of bouts and bells, I'd assumed my new life would be more structured. I let my gaze linger on her fists as she moves them again, gold rippling through her. My eyes catch something on the inside of her wrist, just under her diamond chains. She has a tattoo: an odd sequence of shapes that mean nothing to my mind. "What's that?"

"Hmm?" She looks up at me, then down at her wrist. Her fingers trace the little circle, the two dashes above, the two long lines beside, and the little swooping L that separates the lines.

"It's my name," she says quietly, her voice fond and faraway. "In a language only I remember. It means I'm number one. Better than everyone else." She flashes me a challenging grin and I can't argue with her confidence. She *is* better than everyone else, and it's impossible not to love her for it. "Now you two need to wash. Into the bath, and Chloe will show you how to dress for the arena. Hop to it, now."

I'm not sure why everyone is so certain we're dirty; we had a bath before sleeping, after all. But I'm in too much pain to argue. Imani helps me undress while Miyuki uses the restroom, then the three of us slip into the pool. Sappho joins us a little later, having shaken whatever mood was plaguing her. She laughs and jokes and gets into a splashing game with Miyuki, the two of them giggling when Sappho gets dunked.

I swim away from them, not wanting to get my hair wet, and let the stiffness in my muscles soak away. The water, like everything else in this place, looks different now. It sparkles strangely just under the surface and swirls in my hands when I cup the liquid to my face. The whorls in the water heal, though how I know this, I couldn't say. The healing is gradual, but now I understand why Heather douses her wounded arm in the shallow end and why Sappho wet the bandage when dressing her wound.

My changed eyes confuse me and I wonder if I ought to mention it to Miyuki or Hana. But so much else about this place is strange and puzzling that it seems silly to bring up one more thing. As for the healing water, I don't want to question the blessing lest it evaporate away. I don't feel completely free of pain in the bath and doubt I ever could, but at least I'll be able to walk to the arena on my own two feet.

The bath is over far too soon and Chloe takes me aside. I feel uncomfortable standing naked before her, but if she notices my scar she doesn't comment. "Dressing for the arena is different from dressing for in here," she explains, her voice brisk. "When we're in here, we just twist and knot and we're done. But out there the sun will blind and burn you. So we cover our arms and wear long skirts and a scarf to protect our hair."

She works as she talks, draping long swaths of gauze over me until I'm buried in a layered white dress with a hood to pull over my head and shade my eyes. "You see?" she says triumphantly as she turns me to gaze at my reflection in the pool. "Beautiful. Remember your gem-name out there, Alexandrite; but inside, you're always Aniyah. You'll do fine," she assures me before hurrying over to help Miyuki.

While the others fuss over us, Hana practices on the far side of the room: bouncing on her toes, rotating her wrists, and moving through a complicated routine of punching the air and lifting her knees high. I don't recognize any of it and just watching her makes my spine ache. She works until it's time for her to wash and dress in the same long swaths of gauze as the rest of us; seven identical sets of white robes with girls somewhere underneath.

When the golden doors finally scrape open, it's almost a relief for the waiting to be over. Miyuki stands with me near the table, squeezing my hand and tucking xer glasses carefully in xer robes. Heather, of all people, takes my other side. "You'll do fine," she murmurs to us, her voice a flat monotone. "Just don't scream. Bite your tongue instead, if you have to." This isn't reassuring at all, but before I can ask her what she means, *he* walks in and my breath is stolen away.

The creature is massive, taller even than Handler who trails behind him. He's shaped like us but everything about him is wrong. He's unnaturally white, as pale as our gowns, and his body is smooth without any hair at all. The place on his head where a face would be is featureless, having only a thin slit for a mouth and two flat holes for a nose. Around the perimeter of his empty face, jagged hooks of dark metal protrude from his skin.

113

He wears brown robes that cover him from shoulder to foot, but his arms are bare; it is there, where naked skin shows, that I see the pulsating glow. Blinding white light infests him, throbbing and squirming like a mountain of fat grubs. The same light runs through Handler, thrumming along the furrows cut into his face and hands like water racing through cracks.

"Is my spotter ready?" The creature's voice is devoid of any emotion. He turns his face to me, watching without eyes, and I bite my tongue as Heather suggested.

"She is only freshly awakened, Master," Hana says, bowing her head. "Her talent may not have surfaced."

His hand moves in a gesture that cuts away further protest. "I did not go to the trouble of procuring a spotter without intention to use her. What did we name her?"

"Alexandrite," Handler murmurs at his elbow. He focuses his attention on me, a frown creasing his mutilated face as he adds in a hissing order, "Girl, uncover your wrists so the Master can see your chains."

"For rarity," the creature muses, his flat voice bordering on the edge of boredom. "Alexandrite, do you see magic yet?"

Magic? Is that what's wrong with my eyes? My throat is dry and I can't imagine how to respond, but Miyuki nudges me with xer elbow. "I-I think so. Everything looks different since I woke up."

"Good. Very good. My mask," he adds, apparently no longer addressing me.

Handler draws a white disk from his robes. The towering creature takes the item in his pale hands and lifts it to his face, stretching the edges over the metal hooks protruding from his skin. When his hands pull away the disk remains, producing the semblance of a face. Holes are cut to give the impression of eyes, and a molded nose gives shape to the false image. The mouth is set in a curving smile that would be charming in any other context but here only increases the burning itch in my lungs to scream.

"We will be happy," murmurs the creature, turning to sweep out the golden doors. "Come, little spotter. Come, Prizes."

114

I shiver and Heather gives me a push to get me going. We're led through a curving hall dimly lit by guttering torches set in the walls. I feel my heartbeat in my spine with every step, spurred by the pain of walking and the stuffiness of the underground path. Faint magic flickers over the walls and ceiling; everything here seems made of the stuff, but nothing is as heavily imbued as the Master who leads us.

We round a corner and the hallway widens, providing a glimpse of huge black doors at the far end. The doors are covered in iron bindings carved in the same patterns as the ones on our golden doors. "Those are the boys' rooms," Imani whispers, stepping closer. "Handler may take you there later. Just stay calm and do whatever the boys want." Her tone tries to be reassuring but falls slightly flat.

The Master takes a sharp turn and leads us through a narrow hole in the cavern wall which turns out to contain a steep spiral staircase. We follow him up the steps, forced into a quick pace to match his strides. "We have a new challenger, girls. His master owed me a debt after the results of our previous bout, but with one new boy and two new girls to feed, I didn't want to add to the stables. Easier to schedule another match. Someone will die, and whoever survives will stay on as my property. Exciting for you girls, if we acquire a new boy for you to service."

He turns his head to look at me, the eyeless mask sending shivers down my spine. "I have been seeking a spotter for some time," he states, the white carved mouth of his mask at complete odds with his flat tone. "I did not want a girl. Girls are weak and stubborn and foolish. But we take spotters where we find them and you will earn your keep. Listen closely, girl. When we reach the top of the spire and emerge into sun, you will look down at the fighters in my arena and you will see their magic. Do you understand?"

My hands are clenched into fists at my side. I nod, not daring to trust my voice.

"Good. You will tell me what you see. I already know my boys, but challengers belong to the other faeries. I must know their talents accurately in order to set the betting, and their masters always lie. They downplay strengths to skew the odds, or they give me weaklings when I am owed proper fighters. One even tried to slip in an assassin. That was not amusing." For a moment his flat voice dips into anger, but then he shakes his head. "No, we are wearing the smiling mask. Ah, here we are."

At his final words, we reach the top of the spiral staircase and step out into bright sun and oppressive heat which makes me pant even harder. The stairs have not been easy for me, and Imani slips behind me to wrap an arm around my waist. I'm hurt that Miyuki has abandoned me, until I look around and see Hana helping xer up the last of the stairs. Miyuki squints anxiously into the light, and it hits me that xie can't see where we are without xer glasses. No wonder xie is frightened: we're bathed in blinding sunlight and surrounded by open air with only a long fall between us and the faraway ground.

We're standing in a spire that towers over a vast arena of dark sand and sharp stone. The area is bound by a ring of low cliffs, and the spire we've climbed is the highest peak in that ring. A wall rises at our back where the staircase vomited us forth. A low parapet sits before us with cushions for the girls to drape themselves on, and a colorful cloth canopy is erected over a golden throne which dominates the center of our platform; apart from these, we are in the open air. *It's a stadium,* I realize, the word leaping to my mind as I survey the area. *A stadium carved of stone.*

"Over here, spotter."

Handler speaks and I jump; in the imposing presence of the Master, I'd forgotten the existence of the creepy gray man. He takes me by the elbow and guides me to the low wall where I feel a panicked rush of vertigo. *He could throw me off with the slightest push.* He points with his bony finger, directing my gaze. "What do you see?" he demands.

The humming cliffs below me resolve into hundreds, maybe thousands, of people. Many are coated with the same blinding glow that infests our Master, while some boast equally strange and frightening bodies. Others

116

have softer hues and human faces, like myself and the girls behind me. Every member of the crowd peers out into the arena below, buzzing with anticipation for the expected show.

Below the audience, a huge iron gate is set into the far wall of the valley. Two boys stand near this gate, shading their eyes with upraised hands. I can see the shapes of their bodies and the set of their shoulders, but their faces are harder to make out at this distance. "Alexandrite?" prompts Handler, warning in his voice.

I narrow my eyes. I don't want to answer Handler or speak to him at all, but I must make myself useful if I want to keep myself and Miyuki safe. I focus on the boy who is closer, admiring his warm skin and light curls. He's *strong*; I see the way his wiry muscles glow in the sunlight, a warm golden brown strength that suffuses his arms and legs. "He's powerful. Much stronger than he looks."

Handler nods, watching me through his perpetually closed eyes. "Go on."

I suppress a shudder at his attention and focus on the second fighter. He's darker in color, his hair as black as the leather armor they've dressed him in. *He must be so hot out here,* I think, wondering how long these bouts last. I crane my head, squinting closer as I notice his outline seems fuzzy. A swirling black smoke tickles the edges of his body, dissipating whenever I look too closely.

"What is that?" Handler doesn't answer me, and I realize he's waiting to see if I can figure it out myself. There's an insubstantial feeling to the boy, as though he could be gone in the blink of an eye. "He's right there, but he might not be at any moment. He's like a wisp of smoke just before blowing away."

"He can relocate at will," Handler corrects, his voice lowered to a murmur. "Or you may say he breaches the distance between two points. You are not here for poetry, Alexandrite."

I look up at the urgency in his voice, shivering again as I feel the Master watching us. "And the challenger?" the pale creature cues, doing nothing to relax the knots of tension in my stomach.

Looking back at the valley, I see a second gate rising on the opposite side of the arena. A man stalks through; he's tall and broad-shouldered, with light brown hair and a short brown beard. It's hard to be certain from here, but he seems older than the two boys and moves with easy confidence.

"What do you see?" Handler hisses, gripping my elbow harder.

I shake my head, trying to dispel the cold fear his touch sends through me. I focus on the challenger and the soft glow that runs through him like a current. There's a greenish cast to it, but not like the leaves that cling to the fruits we eat; this green feels more like a threat, tugging at a lost memory. My mind calls up an image of something dangerous: a creature that slides through grass and bites bare feet.

"He's strong?" Handler prompts, nudging me from my trance. I can tell from his tone he already knows this, that strength is the extent of the challenger's advertised powers. This is what I'm here to confirm, so the fight can go ahead as planned.

"Yes, he's— he's strong," I whisper, shaking my head again. "But there's something else. Give me a moment!"

The crowd has already begun to roar. On the far side of the valley, the two boys cast about for their challenge. The man moves stealthily in their direction, staying close to the shadows of the stone spires scattered throughout the ring. The green light builds inside him as he moves, concentrating at his head.

"Oh. Oh, no! He spits venom!" I whirl to face the Master, my voice rising so he can hear me over the crowd. He can stop the fight, warn our fighters, or bring out more help so the odds are better for our two unsuspecting boys pitted against a killer fortified with deadly magic.

The white mask tilts, observing me with no trace of emotion. "Adjust the betting odds," he commands. Handler bows and scurries away while the pale creature settles himself in his throne to watch the show unfold.

CHAPTER 12

Keoki

After so much time spent underground, I'd forgotten how bright the sun could be. I shade my eyes as I scan the arena, looking for whatever we've been sent out to fight. Christian stands by my side performing the same search, his fingers running repeatedly over the little cross at his neck.

"Kid, I'm gonna apologize in advance," he says, his voice low under the rumble of the crowd. "I ain't as nice as Tony, so there's a better than average chance you're gonna die out here."

"That's fair," I tell him with a nod, because I figure there's no point in getting upset over things I can't change. "Uh, so, I didn't get much in the way of advice during practice. Is there some kind of plan you guys usually follow, or what?"

"Locate the bad guy. Find a weapon. Kill him. Don't die," he rattles off. "Order is kinda optional, though."

A pause drags out between us, the world silent save for the constant low roar of the audience. No footsteps stir the dark crumbly sand around us, and the only movement I see is the shimmer of hot air that hangs between the stone pillars dotting the valley. My lungs feel heavy, like I can't get enough air to breathe, and I don't know if the effect is from the heat or my own fear. *Or both*, I admit, struggling to own the pounding alarm in my ears without being controlled by it.

After more heartbeats than I can count, I twist my head to look at Christian. "I don't see anything."

He frowns, chewing on his lip just above the scruff that sprawls over his chin. "I don't either," he agrees, looking grim. "That means it's something we've gotta go out and find. Shit, I hate ambushes." He cracks his knuckles and stretches his arms until they pop, loosening up. "Okay, kid. I want you seven paces away from me, got it? Not behind me, but to my side. No good us both getting jumped at once. We'll circle around as we move in, slow and steady. They hide weapons up in those spires, so we're gonna have to run up a platform eventually and take what we can find. But until we see what we're up against, we move slow."

I take a deep breath, steadying myself. "Got it," I tell him. I walk several long strides to his left, stopping when I catch his approving nod. Then we move forward in silent unison, circling slowly around the edges of the arena as we approach the nearest outlying stone spire.

Nothing stirs around us, and the stillness unsettles me. *Is there really anything out here?* A sudden unwelcome thought occurs: I never asked if we're ever expected to fight each other. I shove the thought away, not wishing to dwell on it. There's *something* out here for us to fight; we just have to find it.

The nearest spire is a pillar of porous stone that stabs up through the ground and tapers to a jagged point high above us. At the base, you'd need four boys joining hands to surround the entire column, and even at its narrowest point I'd be hard-pressed to wrap my arms around the tip. A ramp spirals up around the stone, ending in a platform that sits at about my height from the very top, and which is level with the lowest benches carved into the cliffs where the audience sits to watch us.

We approach the spire with slow, silent steps. I cut a direct route while

Christian circles around to the right, trying to catch a glimpse of what might be hiding behind. He's four strides from the bottom of the ramp when a face pops around the side of the pillar. I catch a quick glimpse of brown hair framing tan skin and light gray eyes squinted against the sunlight. Then I hear a hacking hiss and the stranger spits a glob of transparent green mucus directly at Christian's face.

The attack takes place in the blink of an eye. I stumble forward with a vague idea of pushing Christian out of the projectile's path, but I'm much too far away to reach him in time. An inarticulate sound of annoyance rips from his throat, followed by a strange huffing sound like a sudden gust of wind. Christian disappears, with only a trace of black smoke to mark where he just stood. The mucus sails through the smoke, splatting harmlessly on the sand to sizzle in the sun.

"What the—" I stumble backwards, partly from surprise and partly to escape the range of the spitter now that I don't have a partner to push away. "Christian?" I call, uncertain whether to expect a response. I don't know what just happened, but I very much hope the other boy didn't suddenly cease to exist. Then those gray eyes focus on me and I don't have time to wonder. The spitter darts out from the shadows into the light, and I turn heel and run.

I'm relieved to find I'm as fast a runner as I'd hoped to be, my toes gripping the sand with easy familiarity. I chance a look over my shoulder to see the distance widening between me and the spitter; I'm faster than him, though not as much as I'd like. I can see him in greater detail now: he's bigger and taller, his legs and arms flexing with muscle as he runs. Looks might not mean everything out here, but knowing I'm stronger than I look isn't much comfort when the same might well apply to him.

What was that spit, and what happened to Christian? My lungs burn in the stifling heat, but I keep running. I'm rounding another pillar, hoping to run in its shade, when I hear a soft huff of air and strong hands reach out to grab my shoulders. "Here, newbie! Up the platform we go!"

The sudden sound of Christian's voice causes me to slip on the sand, pitching forward towards the ramp he's pulling me onto. He catches and steadies me briefly before pulling me along behind him. "Don't freak out on me, newbie. Keep an eye on that sh— Damn, he's ducked behind another pillar."

"What happened to you? Is that normal?" I whip my head about as we run, trying to pick out movement among the shadowy spires but finding nothing.

"The spit? Pretty sure it's corrosive, the way it was bubbling," he observes, his feet pounding hard against the wooden platform. "So, no. Not normal."

"I mean the smoke and the popping!" I'm trying not to panic, but I'm shaken by the sudden transition from being helpless to save him to seeing him poof back into existence right beside me.

"Oh, *that*. Yeah, that's normal." I can't see his face while he's running ahead of me, but I hear the smug grin in his voice. In any other circumstances I'd probably be annoyed, but right now his cockiness is unexpectedly soothing; if he's not panicking about his close call, I won't either.

"Okay. You can pop." I take a deep breath as we careen to a halt at the top of the platform, doubling over to rest my hands on my knees as I gasp for air. "Uh, any reason you didn't use it before? I mean, dude, you could've scouted the area a lot faster that way."

He snorts, not looking at me as his hands pat over the stone, exploring in methodical patterns. "I don't tell you how to muscle at things, do I, kid? My talent packs more punch if they don't know what I can do until I need to do it. Element of surprise. Watch for that shitface, will you? I don't want to get cornered up here."

I peer around the spire, searching the ground for our attacker. For a moment I think I see something move in the shadows two pillars over, but then everything is still again and I'm not sure it wasn't my imagination. "Over there! Maybe. I'm not sure. Are you finding anything?"

He pulls his arm out of a jagged crevice, careful not to cut himself on the edges. I remember during the last fight Tony had drawn a sword out of a similar crack, yet Christian's hand comes away empty. "Nothing," he reports, frowning as he chews on his lip. "Stay here, newbie. Keep an eye on the ramp. Don't let him sneak up on you."

"Where are you going?" We're at the very top of the platform, with no way down except to edge around me. The nearest platform is almost close enough to leap to, but I wouldn't want to take that chance.

Christian doesn't try to move around me, doesn't even pause long enough for me to finish my question. I'm looking right at him when he disappears; he's close enough to touch and then he's gone. Only the soft puff of air announces his departure, with just a wisp of black smoke marking the spot where he'd been. I jerk around, hearing the telltale puff from the next spire over. He pops out of the air and onto the platform, stepping effortlessly back into existence. Flattening himself against the stone, he squints at the ground while his hands begin the same search as before, with the same result: nothing.

He pops again, his parting wisp of smoke lingering in the air. Now that I know to follow the sound, it's easy to find where he emerges: another spire further down the row. He pats quickly over the rock, frowning as he does so; once again, he comes up empty. Another puff, another platform, another search; he repeats the pattern a dozen times around the arena, always watching the ground intently for a target I can no longer glimpse. It's difficult to judge his expression from here, but he looks increasingly grim. I can guess why: none of the stone spires has yielded any weapons.

The puff sounds near my ear and he's beside me again. His wry grin doesn't hide the fact that he's panting heavily; whatever he's doing to jump about like that, it isn't easy for him. "Well, kid, we've got some bad news."

"No weapons," I hazard.

"Not a single solitary blade," he agrees, shaking his head. "Nor a club, a sling, or even a nice heavy rock to drop on his head."

"Did you at least find him?" I ask, peering at the shadows. I feel exposed up here, knowing that he's probably watching us even as we fail to see him.

"Lost him," Christian says, glaring at the ground. "He's sticking to the shade. We need to keep moving; I don't want him sneaking up the ramp while we talk. C'mon."

He edges around me and we begin to jog down the spire. "Okay, you said we don't have any rocks, but would anything heavy do?" I cast around us, but there's nothing out here except sand and sun. "Uh. Maybe drop *me* on him? We find him and you pop us onto him before he has a chance to spit?" I don't really love this idea, but I *did* ride the stone giant without falling off and I'd rather be on top of the spitter than in front of him.

Christian gives a low whistle. "Damn, newbie, I don't know if that would actually work, but the crowd would love it. But, no, I can't carry people when I pop. Wish I could, but can't."

My shoulders sag, and I couldn't say whether I'm disappointed or relieved. "Okay. That's okay. That wasn't even my best plan. That was just, like, my first plan." We round another loop of the winding platform. "Uh, do you have a *usual* plan for this sort of thing? What do you guys normally do?"

"Told you," he says, his feet hitting the sand as we reach the bottom. "Get a weapon, then pop behind the guy and slit his throat. Worst case, we can strangl—"

His words are cut off as a hand snakes out from around the spire and grabs him by the neck of his leather armor. Christian is dragged into the shade by the bigger man, wriggling in an attempt to escape his grasp. "Run!" he orders, shooting me a dark glare.

I hesitate for the length of a breath; I don't want to leave him here and I can't imagine why he's asking me to. Then I turn on my heel, pounding back up the platform we just descended, fervently hoping this is the right thing to do. I hear the hacking sound again and my heart clenches in my chest, but there's no accompanying howl of pain or smell of burning skin. The crowd roars so loudly I can no longer hear my feet pounding the wooden ramp, and I pray they're roaring for Christian.

Did he pop away in time? Only then does it strike me: he couldn't pop free until I was safely away. If he'd disappeared while I was standing there, the guy would have got me instead. *Oh, shit! Christian, you'd better be okay.*

Rounding one loop of the ramp, I catch sight of them below. Christian is behind the challenger now, grappling with him as the man whips his head from side to side, trying to face him. A chunk of Christian's armor—the back plating—lies abandoned on the ground, twisted and smoking as the strange venom eats through the leather. As he grapples with the bigger man, his feet moving in a complicated dance to stay behind him, Christian tugs at the fabric covering his chest and pulls away a long length of cloth.

I can't imagine what he's doing—*undressing in the middle of a fight?*—until Christian tosses the loop of cloth around the man's head and pulls back hard with both hands. The cloth snaps under the man's chin, tightening around his neck; blood pools in his cheeks, turning his face red. He twists as Christian pulls him back, his leg sweeping Christian's out from under him and hauling him roughly down; but the challenger hits the ground hard, nothing between him and the sand. Christian pops back into existence behind him, taking up the cloth again as though the interruption had never happened.

He's good, I think, my eyes widening. With a talent like that and the creativity to use it, it's no wonder he's stayed alive. But this guy doesn't want to go down easy; he twists to face Christian, hacking another mouthful of venom which Christian narrowly poofs away from. The corrosive spit flies up to hit the rock beside me, and I jump as the stone dissolves with a hiss. The man clambers to his feet, glaring at me; then Christian is behind him again, his hands gripping the cloth tangled around the spitter's neck.

Considering that he's unarmed and fighting a stronger opponent, Christian is doing amazingly well; yet I don't think he can win as things stand. He can't strangle the guy to death when he has to keep popping away, and what happens when the spitter gets off a lucky shot, or if Christian doesn't manage to disappear in time? *I've got to help him, but how?* If I get close to them I'll be hit by the next glob of spit, and I don't want to see what it does to skin, not after the way it ate through the nearby rock. I peer warily at the edges of the sizzling hole, watching the venom dissolve the soft stone, and a new thought nibbles at me.

The spires aren't solid all the way through; they can't be, not with those holes all over, many large enough to conceal a weapon. How many holes did Christian stick his hand in while he was searching, always taking care not to scrape himself on the rough edges? *Crumbly edges like crumbly sand,* I think, flexing my feet and feeling the stuff cling between my toes. The sand is sharp and heavy, but breaks easily into smaller fragments. Would this stone break if enough strength were applied? I remember the rock monster under me and the way my arms felt, tearing away slabs of stone. I hear Tony: *You're one of the strong ones.*

I turn on my heel to run higher up the ramp, numb to the sounds of the crowd and the struggle below as I race to the top. *Hold on, Christian, just a little longer.* Blood pounds in my ears as I round the final curve and skid to a halt on the flat platform. I flatten myself against the rock and reach my hands around the spire, feeling for weak points in the stone: the empty hollow crevices. *Here and here,* I decide, bracing my hands against the column as I brace my feet against wood.

I push harder than I'd ever thought possible. My arms strain from it, the hidden muscles under my wiry frame rippling with power. I hear the crackling of rock under my assault and feel pieces crumble away beneath my hands. I let the little pebbles fall, pressing harder, moving with the stone. Beneath me, I hear the fight—the sounds of sizzling spit and puffs of air—but I grit my teeth and block out anything that isn't *this*. The world slows and narrows until there is only me and the stone I'm determined to defeat. I push again, harder, bracing my feet and shoving for all I'm worth.

The crackling builds from a soft intermittent noise to a constant groan, peaking in a sharp *crack*. The platform shifts under me and I hear my own shout of triumph as the pillar snaps in two. The top third of the spire shifts and begins to tip ponderously over, shuddering into a mass of large jagged boulders and crumbly pebbles. "Christian, get out of the way!" I yell, peering around broken stone to watch the two fighters below.

He looks up at my shout, his dark eyes widening as he sees the pillar bearing down on them both. The spitter looks up at the same moment, instantly moving to leap out of the way. I watch with horror as Christian tackles him, hauling him to the ground and holding him under the shadow of the falling stones. I don't even have time to scream before they both disappear under the mass of boulders, dark stone slamming into the sand and obliterating them both.

"Christian!" The cry rips out of me as the platform I'm standing on lurches sideways, almost throwing me off balance. I jerk my head down to stare at my feet as I hear the ominous sound of tearing wood. My stomach clenches sickeningly when I realize the falling pillar has taken most of the ramp with it. The section I'm standing on is still supported by four long poles but, with the rest of the ramp collapsing fast, the platform won't hold. I shout, but the sound is lost in the ecstatic screams of the crowd.

I have mere moments to make a decision. Planting my feet firmly, I kick off against the remains of the crumbling spire, throwing all my weight towards the nearest adjacent pillar and the undamaged ramp wrapped around it. The platform I'm standing on tears loose from the last of the dangling remains, the supporting poles wobbling in their foundations as the wood beneath my feet tilts in a long fall towards the ground. I flail in mid-air, hands wildly outstretched as I pray for luck to save me.

With a painful slam that reverberates through my arms, I hit my mark. My hands find the solid wood of the nearby ramp and I hang on for dear life. The platform I'd been riding carries on falling, slamming into the sand below and bursting into shattered fragments of wood and splinters. I take a deep breath, grateful for the privilege, as my hands scramble to hold their grip. The platform I'm grasping is blessedly stable, but my hands are slick with sweat and I struggle to pull myself up without losing my grip.

There's a soft stirring of air, almost like a breeze. Christian pops into existence on the ramp above me, his wry grin reaching new heights of smugness. His hands clasp my wrist and he begins the process of hauling me up onto the tiny platform; no small task, but one he manages with grace. "Damn, newbie, could you *be* any heavier?" he complains cheerily over the roar of the crowd. "I swear, you're half the size of Ruby but weigh twice as much. Explain that to me, I dare you."

CHAPTER 13

Aniyah

Not until the curly-haired boy is safely on the platform am I able to sink back onto the cushion where I've been kneeling. My legs tremble violently and my arms are useless and rubbery, unable to support me. Beside me, the other girls exhale in shared relief; we exchange quick looks, but no one feels safe speak in front of the Master.

Hana's face is outwardly as calm as ever, though anger smolders deep in her dark eyes. Heather looks bored, as does Sappho, but neither of them looks directly at the fighters, as if they can't bear to watch. Miyuki's expression is carefully neutral, and I know xie can't have seen much of what went on; Imani sits close to xer, her lips moving near xer ear as she whispers details. Chloe seems the most affected of us all, which surprises me given how calm she'd been earlier; her face is so pale that I think she might be ill.

The frightening creature who owns us sits motionless on his golden throne, his grinning white mask directed towards the center of the arena where the pillar crumbled and fell. "Master, shall I call the match?" Handler murmurs at his elbow, his face angled respectfully towards his feet.

"Yes," the Master replies, his voice flat and low. If he's derived any pleasure from watching a man dic, none shows in his tone or posture.

"Open the gate to bring them in. I'll need to repair the arena before the next match. Tiresome, but the crowd is pleased." His pale fingers tap the arm of his throne. "Obsidian continues to earn his keep," he observes, almost to himself. "The new one: what did we call him?"

"Granite, Master."

"Granite. He seems determined to draw a crowd. I am pleased. Send Prizes to them both." My spine stiffens at this reminder of why we are here, and the white mask turns to regard me. "Send the two newest. They need to be broken in." Hana closes her eyes, pain flashing over her face, but there is nothing she can say or do to countermand the order.

Handler bows. "Yes, Master. With your leave, I will take the girls down now." The creature waves his hand in dismissal, and Handler gestures for us to rise.

The others stand from their cushions, and I manage to do the same after a minor struggle—the trick turns out to be leaning forward on my hands and knees, working one leg up into a half-standing position, and then pushing off from the ground. Handler's mouth twists into a disapproving frown at my contortions, but the Master ignores us and his indifference is apparently enough to protect me from rebuke. *It's not like I asked for any of this,* I think, pushing the sour thought away before it can show on my face.

We're led back down the spiral staircase into the caverns, and my eyes struggle to adjust to the darkness after the dazzling light. I feel a cool body at my side and fingers snaking down to twine through mine; I squeeze Miyuki's hand, and hope my closeness will comfort xer. Then Hana is on the other side of us, pushing into the tight space between Miyuki and the wall as we wind down.

"You're going to be fine," she whispers, her voice low and urgent in the dark. "Your only job is to make them happy and stay safe. Talk to them, be yourselves, but keep polite. Don't act rude to them; don't get into any fights. You'll be fine," she repeats. I wonder whether she's trying to convince us or herself.

"Will we be together?" Miyuki asks, squeezing my hand tightly.

Hana shakes her head. "No, you'll—"

"We're here," Handler announces, cutting in. "The rest of you wait in the hall while I take these Prizes in."

He grabs me by the elbow, jarring me forward and causing me to stumble. I right myself before I can fall, and whip my head around to glare; an unwise but unthinking act. The sight of him causes fresh waves of fear to wash over me. The strange magic that runs through the furrows on his face and hands is brighter now without the searing light of the Master to overwhelm his glow.

"This way, Alexandrite," he orders, ignoring my stare. He doesn't acknowledge Miyuki, but yanks me hard enough to separate us, tearing xer hand away from mine.

We approach the huge black doors we saw earlier, Handler pulling me forward and Miyuki close behind. The iron bands wrapped around the doors glint with the same roiling magic which covers the golden doors of our cavern. The gleam moves like a current through the metal, and the cuts in Handler's face grow brighter as we approach. He reaches out to the doors and the cracks in his hands flare hotly. The currents flow faster—too fast for my eyes to follow—and the doors open to let us through.

It's some kind of connection, I realize, peering hard at him as he ushers us into a large open cave. I still don't know how to read the magic, but I can see that those eerie cuts in his hands and face and the matching scrolls on the doors all work together to let him through while keeping us trapped.

I don't relish the thought of being trapped anywhere, but especially not in the cavern Handler leads us through. Devoid of sun, the only light comes from torches set into stone columns clustered throughout the cave; heat and smoke fill the murky room and black soot clings to our long gowns. The dark emptiness stretching above us is a disorienting black void that bears no resemblance to a ceiling and leaves me feeling exposed and alone all at the same time.

When we round one of the columns I realize we're not the only people in this place. Seven boys stand in a cluster on the far side, talking excitedly. "—never seen anything like that! Never heard of anyone even *trying*. Fucking brilliant!"

A tall white-skinned boy with straight brown hair brushing the tips of his shoulders pounds the back of the fighter who nearly fell to his death. The shorter boy grins under the onslaught of rambunctious affection while my spine twitches in sympathy; he rubs his neck in a self-conscious gesture that clashes with the confidence in his smile. "Reese, it wasn't exactly smart. I almost splatted myself onto the sand, you know."

"Newbie, it was the flashiest damn kill in the last dozen fights." The other one from the arena, the one who can puff into smoke, stands nearby chuckling as he pulls off the remains of his armor. "It's a miracle the crowd didn't jump down to mob you."

"They always go wild for the strong ones," declares another boy. His hair is lighter, the same color as the sand filling a nearby pit, and his pale skin is strangely translucent when I peer at him, as though he's not quite solid. "We've got to figure out a way to teach talents. We don't *know* they can't be learned."

Several of the other boys laugh, excepting one with a young face and long black curls. "Maybe we could trade them," he says in a glum voice, scuffing at the floor with his foot. His shoulders hunch over as he folds his arms over his chest, and I catch the faintest glitter of rainbow color in his dark hair as we approach. "I'd love to get rid of— Oh! Girls!"

His eyes widen when he sees us, his head whipping up to toss back the mop of wild curls tumbling over his forehead. The other boys turn to face us; mouths snap shut, spines straighten, and chests are proudly thrown out. My stomach clenches at the way their gazes sweep openly over our bodies. They're not hostile, and some of them seem kind—a silent dark-haired boy meets my eyes with a gentle expression, and the tall one with the bright smile looks almost apologetic—but none of them look away. I feel naked;

a sensation not alleviated by the sandy-haired one staring at me as though trying to bore a hole through to the other side.

"Handler?" An older boy with tan skin and wavy brown hair steps forward, walking with a cane made from a thick glossy wood. "It's a little early for Prizes, isn't it?" His tone is mild and deferential, reminiscent of the way Hana speaks to our inhuman keeper, though without her falsetto affectation.

"Consider the extra time a gift from the Master, commensurate with how pleased he was by your show." Handler's voice is as cool as ever, but there's a hint of danger underneath cautioning the older boy against further questions. The boy drops his gaze in response to Handler's tone, nodding obediently.

Without warning, Handler yanks on my elbow and gives me a rough shove from behind. I stumble forward, my heart in my throat at the threat of the onrushing ground. Yet I'm saved from falling by the strong arms of the boy I've been propelled towards: the smoky fighter from the arena. "Alexandrite," Handler says by way of introduction. "Our newest and most valuable Prize. Don't use her too hard, Obsidian."

The young man's dark eyes flash at the injunction, but his smile remains bright and easy. "I'll take good care of her," he promises, and despite the lingering fear that always surrounds Handler, several of the other boys chuckle. I shiver in his arms and stare at my feet; more than anything, I don't want to be here.

"Quartz," Handler adds, herding Miyuki closer to the other fighter. He doesn't say any more, and his silence speaks loudly of the relative unimportance of *xer* well-being.

I risk a look at the boy, searching his face for a spark of recognition. *Did he really come in with us? Did we know each other?* His warm brown skin is a shade lighter than my own, but the tight tendrils of curls covering his head are almost exactly like mine; the only difference is that my curls are cut close to my head while his stick out wildly in all directions and tumble down to his shoulders. I like the look of him immediately, but he's as much a stranger to my wiped mind as Miyuki was.

He looks surprised to find Miyuki thrust into his arms, but doesn't argue with Handler. He doesn't speak at all, not even to reassure xer; he just nods his head in an easy-going manner. I try to catch his eye to communicate that xie is valuable to *me*, but he's watching the face of the silent boy, who is looking away in another direction entirely.

I don't want to leave Miyuki. I'm scared for xer, scared of what this boy might do to xer. But strong arms move to usher me away, and I know if I resist we'll be punished. Handler saw how we held on to each other and must have guessed we're friends. I can't expect mercy from him, not when the monster he serves was willing to let these boys die just to have fewer mouths to feed. So I close my eyes and let myself be led to a door that opens onto a tiny, humid cave. *Please be right, Hana. Please let us be okay.*

The boy to whom I've been given closes the door behind us. He leans me gently against the wall as if I'm a rigid piece of wood that might fall over if left to stand alone. "Stay here, okay?" he says, his voice low and warm in the darkness. "I'm still covered in grit after all that. Didn't expect girls so soon; usually Prizes aren't given out until after we've had a chance to wash and eat."

I should be worrying over what he might do to me; Heather's bloody demonstration with her arm dances behind my eyelids while Sappho's harrowing tale of sleep-strangling rings in my ears. But I'm too anxious about Miyuki to concentrate on myself, fearing what the other boy might be doing to xer right now. I open my eyes and focus on this one in the dim lighting, needing a distraction from the images in my mind.

Only once my eyes are open do I realize what sort of distraction is available. The fighter is stripping off his clothes, shaking sand out of his hair and rubbing grit off his skin with handfuls of cloth. His naked body flexes as he moves, muscle and sinew and scars appearing under the curling smoky magic that lingers on him. He's *beautiful*, and while he's the first naked man I remember seeing, the contours of his body are intimately familiar to me. I shouldn't stare, but I find myself unable to look away.

When the worst of the sand is scrubbed away, he reaches for a metal bowl full of water set into the wall. He tugs the bowl free and tips it over his head; water streams over every hard curve of him and he shakes his head to toss droplets from his hair. I press back into the door to avoid the splatter, and he grins at me before grabbing up a clean cloth and beginning to towel off.

He clicks the bowl back into the wall when he's finished and turns to face me, watching my face with undisguised mischief. I feel my cheeks heat in embarrassment at having been caught gawking. "Sorry," I mumble.

He laughs at my apology, a soft chuckle that ripples through his chest. "Don't be. It's a nicer reaction than I get from some of the other girls. What's your name, pretty girl? Sit on the bed with me?"

He crosses the room as he talks, sitting on a shelf set into the wall. He pats the bed in invitation and I repress a shudder imagining how it will feel against my back; the pad is barely a fingertip thicker than the ones in our sunlit cavern, and I don't relish the painful prospect of lying down. But Hana said not to act rudely, so I ease onto the shelf beside him and let my legs dangle over the side. "Um. Handler calls me Alexandrite."

"Alexandrite?" He rolls the word on his tongue, trying out the unfamiliar sound. "I'm Christian, Alexandrite. That 'Obsidian' stuff is for out there. In here it's just us." His dark eyes watch me, dancing suggestively around the word 'us', and my stomach flips again. "Sure there's nothing else you'd rather I call you?"

I shake my head, wary of this line of questioning. Hana said never to tell; Heather said we could be killed if the Master found out we know our names. I'm not sure if this boy has shown me trust by giving his name or if the rules are different for boys, but I won't take any chances.

Instead, I put on a smile. "You said, uh, the other girls don't like you?" I'm trying to banter with him as a distraction from his question and aiming to match his teasing tone, but in my nervous state my words come out sounding like an insult.

"Well, that depends on the girl." He grins and runs his hand up my arm, trailing goosebumps. "Ruby and I are *very* good friends." He gives me a sly wink, his hand moving to caress my back and massage my neck. His fingers find the tucks and folds of my robe as he works, pulling swaths of cloth away from my head and shoulders with confident grace; the long loose end of gauze tumbles down to trail over the lip of the bed and onto the floor. "Amethyst, eh. She helps me with my hair," he confides in a low chuckle. "Then we cuddle after."

Christian leans in then, his lips brushing over my shoulder. I shiver at the touch, but his hand on my back steadies me. "Mmm," he murmurs into my skin. "Emerald, not so much. Good girl, but she can't really feel anything, you know?" Warm lips trace over my collarbone, causing my breath to hitch. "I like a girl to feel things." Without warning, he nibbles at my neck. I jerk away in surprise and he draws back to watch me, his eyes full of amusement. "Don't you like nibbles, pretty girl?"

"I-I don't know." I'm struggling to keep my breathing even, to not squirm under his touch. The things he's doing are nice, even *good*; they're things I sense my body has done before. But my mind isn't in the same place as my body right now, and I don't know which one to listen to.

He grins at my answer. "Plenty of time to find out," he murmurs, leaning in to kiss my neck again. "Hmm. Who does that leave? Well, ha, Sapphire, but she's never looked at any boy the way you look at me, pretty girl. And Diamond, but the only time she looks at *anyone* that way, she's faking." He snorts, his tongue darting out to taste my skin as he moves up my jaw. "That girl wants bed-play about as much as I want a gut-wound. She hides it well, but I can tell."

I open my mouth to speak, but only a soft whimper escapes as his lips work their way up to my earlobe. He chuckles warmly and I feel the vibration of his laughter against my skin. I clear my throat and try again. "You can tell? You're good at knowing what people want?"

He draws back just far enough to lock eyes with me in the darkness, his grin bright and confident. "Yes," he murmurs, his breath sweet on my face. He places a hand on my hip, sliding fingers up my side and drawing a long shiver from me. "And I think, pretty girl, that you want *me*." He leans in and brushes his lips against mine.

I freeze at the suddenness of it, the sensation new to me and yet perfectly familiar. His lips are full and warm and soft, covering my own in a long kiss that quickly deepens from the initial light brush. My lips move with his in an instinctive memory, savoring the taste of him as my heart races. Then he's leaning me backwards onto the bed, moving me so gently that my back puts up only a token protest as his hands glide over my body in beautifully distracting ways.

I kiss him a little faster than before, feeling hot despite the coolness of the room. My hand reaches up to touch his face, but when I feel his skin under my fingertips everything seems wrong. The warmth in my blood fades, leaving a chill behind, and the heat pooling through my stomach curls into a painful knot.

What happened? I wrack my mind, trying to recapture the heat. I don't have a choice, after all; I have to go through with this, so I'd like to enjoy it if I can. By some miracle, this experience hasn't been what I'd feared; he hasn't hurt me or humiliated me in any way. He's been kind: polite and gentle and talkative with me. He's beautiful and clever and strong. He fought well in the arena, which is probably a good thing; it means he'll live longer and I won't have to watch him die. *Isn't all that enough?*

It's his face, I realize. *It's this bed.* The problem isn't what he is but rather what he's not: Miyuki.

I'd touched xer face when we woke in bed together. I'd held xer in my arms while we slept. I'd promised myself I'd shield xer from this place. Now xie has been torn from me and sent off with another boy who'd been more or less told by Handler that he can do whatever he likes with xer. How can I enjoy myself knowing xie is in danger? No matter how much my body responds to the touch of this boy, my mind is tied into miserable knots while I wait to see xer again.

I still have to do this. I won't let Miyuki be hurt because I put on a poor performance. But my lips falter in spite of my determination and the boy on top of me seems to notice. His kisses slow and gradually come to a halt, and he pulls back to study my face.

I'm relieved to see he doesn't look angry, just thoughtful and a little disappointed. "I'm sorry," I whisper, knowing I've screwed up but helpless to explain. "I *do* want you, Christian. I just—" I take a shaky breath and wonder if I can trust him with the truth. "I don't want *this*. Not right now."

He smiles down at me; not his laughing smile from before, but a softer expression. Gently, he shifts to lie beside me, relieving me from the painful pressure of his body. "It's okay," he tells me, kissing my forehead and smoothing a curl back from my face. "Like I said. It all depends on the girl."

I bite my lip, unsure how to take this. He doesn't look mad, but how can I be sure? I turn to face him, watching him in the dim light. "It isn't you," I promise, praying he'll believe me and won't be insulted. "It's me. It's this place. I'm still trying to wrap my head around it. It isn't anything wrong with you."

He chuckles again and gives me a quick squeezing hug, more friendly than fiery. "Never thought otherwise," he assures me, his grin as bright as ever. "Hey. Get some sleep. They'll bring food later if we're lucky, but you can never get enough sleep. You're safe with me. Ain't nothing gonna hurt you in here, pretty girl."

I don't think I can sleep. I'm not tired, I'm not comfortable, and I'm worried for Miyuki. But closing my eyes and listening to the water trickling down the cave walls is easier than trying to explain feelings I don't have words for. Nuzzling into his warm embrace, I breathe in the scent of his clean body and wondering if I'll ever feel safe enough to tell him my real name, and if he would live long enough afterwards to use it.

138

CHAPTER 14

Keoki

I'm still reeling from the shock of being alive. I've survived the arena a second time and my arms still tremble, though I think I managed to hide the worst of it from the other guys. I'm relieved to be shuffled into the privacy offered by my little cave, where I can shake all I want in the darkness. Here no one can read the emotions in my face as my brain replays on a loop the near-deaths Christian and I just experienced.

Well, almost no one. I have no idea what to do with the girl who's been shoved in here with me. I don't want to seem ungrateful, but I would almost rather she hadn't been awarded to me at all. I preferred the one who was presented to Christian, and when Handler gave me this one Tony wouldn't even meet my eye. I'd been serious before when I asked him to come and share, but he'd seemed no more interested in this girl than I am. So now I'm stuck here, without the Prize I wanted and no Tony coming to join me.

She's pretty, I guess. She has short black hair like Tony's, which falls into her eyes, but she keeps those eyes low and downcast, with none of the bright evaluation of her friend's piercing gaze. The other girl had studied us in the main cavern before Christian took her away, her eyes alighting from face to face around our circle. I'd shivered when she looked at me, feeling as though she could see into my heart. Handler had said she was valuable, but I could see that without being told.

In contrast, this one seems distant and faraway, like she's not quite here with me. She hasn't once looked up at my face; instead, she just stands silently in the center of the room, her hands fretting at the fabric of her dress. *Maybe she's nervous?* There's certainly no enthusiasm in her face or frame. I guess I can't blame her, since the lack of interest is mutual; I don't even remember her name, because I'd been watching the other girl when Handler introduced them. I feel guilty about that; it isn't her fault she's not her friend.

Taking a deep breath, I give her my best reassuring smile. "Hey, I don't know if they told you, but I'm kind of new to all this," I tell her. I stay close to the door, not wanting to frighten her further. "It sounds like we have plenty of time together, so we don't have to rush into anything." I hesitate on this last point; I'm not actually sure when Handler plans to collect her, but it sounded like it would be a long wait. "Do you want to sit down? Or do you need to use the bathroom?"

Her eyes remain downcast, yet her voice is louder than I'd expected: strong and thick, but with a tremor rippling through the words. "No. Thank you. Don't touch me. *Please.* I need you to keep your hands away, o-okay?" She falters on the last word as her voice cracks with rising panic.

I blink at her. "Uh, okay. You... You know I'm not going to hurt you, right?" I duck my head, trying to catch her eye, but she still doesn't look up. "Do you know Diamond? Because I told her—"

We're interrupted by a soft knock at the door. I turn to open it, frowning as I do. The last thing I want right now is another glimpse of Handler's creepy face, but maybe this intrusion could be a good thing. I could ask him to take the girl away, since she clearly doesn't want to be here. I could improvise a plausible reason that wouldn't get her into trouble: I'm hungry, maybe, or I'm cramping up after the bout.

Except it's not Handler on the other side. Tony slips through the cracked door, throwing his arms around my neck before I can react. He shoves the door closed with his foot as his lips press hotly against my mouth.

A moment before, I couldn't even recall the word 'kiss' but now the concept comes flooding back. My heart is pounding so loudly you could hear it from the arena because, *holy crap*, he does like me after all, he likes me back, he's kissing me and I didn't even need to get beaten up first, he's actually *kissing me*. My hands find his hips to pull him closer but he presses hard against me, pushing me backwards. I move with his guiding step, perfectly happy to let him take the lead here and everywhere else.

There's a soft gasp behind me, and I realize with belated guilt that the girl has been forced to scramble away from us as Tony pushes me towards her. I turn to see her backing into the far wall of the cave, her wide eyes containing a trace of panic. I can't think why she would be frightened of Tony, but Diamond had said some of the girls were new and easily scared. Probably she's afraid he jumps everyone like this, and she'd been keen not to be touched.

"Hey, it's okay," I tell her, raising my palms in a placating gesture. "This is my buddy, Tony. He's just, uh." I look back at him with a chuckle in my throat, blanking on the right words to explain how we went from wrestling in the sand earlier to kissing just now, his soft mouth moving over mine with painful urgency.

"Confused," he finishes for me, laughing softly. He throws her an easy grin, but his black eyes are unreadable in the dark. "Sorry. I thought she was answering the door for you, Keoki."

I blink at him as the world comes crashing down around my ears. "You thought... I was the girl? Here I figured you were just relieved to have me back alive." My words are light and teasing, but I'm cut by his reversal; if the kiss was a mistake, what does that mean? Did he not mean to do it or not *want* to do it? Will he not want to do it again?

He pauses long enough for me to wonder if he's heard what I said, then tosses his shaggy hair back and flashes the same smile he'd given her. "That, too. We all are. I've seen people break their legs falling from the platforms, and the Master almost never agrees to let us keep them alive. It'd be awful to lose you so soon, newbie. So, yeah, relief-kisses all around."

I'm not sure how to take this—nor how to tell him that I only want kisses from *him* right now—so I try to match his smile and easy stance. "Well, hopefully not *all* round," I point out, maintaining our joking tone. "It'd get kind of crowded in here if we added more people, don't you think? Everyone else can have fun doing whatever it is they're doing now."

He chuckles again and stretches his arms behind his head, balancing on the balls of his feet as if he's in practice or antsy to move. "Good point. Everyone else is relaxing. There are never two bouts in one cycle, so we're safe until first bell. Sleep, talk trash, practice; Teacher'll be in the sandpit, but it's up to us to show up and work. I said I wasn't feeling too good and was going to my room. Ended up here instead," he adds, giving me that lopsided arrogant grin of his.

"So no one knows you're here?" I wouldn't mind if the others knew, but I suppose there might be some rule against it. Tony may have agreed to share my Prizes, but no one ever actually said whether that's allowed.

He shakes his head, his eyes never leaving my face. "Nah. Our little secret. Handler said he'd bring food later, then check on you and Christian to make sure you're being treated right. We've got plenty of time to play together before I slip out." His eyes flick to the girl behind me. "The three of us, I mean."

I glance over my shoulder at the girl, still pressed against the far wall and watching Tony warily, then turn back to him, rubbing my neck. "Well, there's a problem with that. She doesn't want to be touched."

Tony's gaze doesn't meet mine, lingering on her instead. "Oh." His voice is quieter now, more serious. His smile fades into solemnity: sympathy tinged with disappointment. The disappointment hits me hardest; I'd invited him here for some fun and he'd slipped away to join me, only to have his hopes dashed.

He'll leave now. The realization makes my stomach clench. I'd thought I wanted to be alone, but that changed when he arrived. I don't want him to leave and I'm afraid if he does, he won't come back.

"Hey, there's always next time," I tell him, willing the statement to be true, hoping he'll agree with me. I need a sign that this isn't a one-time failed experiment that won't be tried again. "Right?"

He considers this in silence, his expression maddeningly blank. "Well, but *this* time was supposed to be fun," he points out. "You need something good to take your mind off that fight just now."

I blink at him. Of all the reasons for him to be disappointed, I hadn't ranked my own discomfort high on the list. "Uh, I mean." I cast a glance back at the wary girl. "She doesn't want to, so that's just how it is. I don't want anyone who isn't, uh, eager. You know?"

He nods at this, his face still solemn. "Yeah," he agrees quietly. He takes a deep breath, looking as though he's made a decision. "Maybe we can still make it fun for you," he murmurs, stepping closer. He slides his hand around the back of my neck and draws me forward, his lips finding mine again.

I freeze in place, not wanting to do anything to break this kiss. *Is this real? Is he really kissing me again?* There can't be any mistake this time, he *has* to want this, and after a single skipped heartbeat my mouth moves over his, matching his slow pace and opening at his gentle urging. His tongue flicks out in a quick teasing movement, caressing my lips where they part, and the sensation sends a sharp shiver down to my toes. He hesitates at my trembling, drawing back just enough to allow his dark eyes to scrutinize mine.

"You're making my knees weak," I confess, giving him a laughing smile to cover my own embarrassment. *I can push over a giant rock column in the arena, but I can't even stand up straight in here with him!*

He watches me for a long moment, and when he speaks his voice is husky. "Well, maybe we should get you into bed," he suggests. Then his solemn expression cracks into that lopsided smile, sending another shiver rippling through my legs. "Before you fall over, I mean."

My heart leaps into my throat at the suggestion; I'm not sure precisely what he wants to do with me in bed, just that I very much want to find out. My hands find his hips again, trying to pick up where we left off before. I step slowly backwards towards my bed, drawing him with me as I walk. His grin broadens and he slides his hands up my arms, guiding me with a firm grip so I don't back into the wall.

When he angles me down towards the niche that holds my bed, my eyes fall on the girl. Her eyes are still wide as she watches us. "Oh." I freeze and he nearly runs into me, taken by surprise at the sudden resistance. "Tony, what about *her*?"

He turns to look at her, frowning uncertainly. "Oh." He repeats my own doubtful noise, chewing over the logistics of one cave with three people in it. "Right," he says, making a decision. Releasing his hold on me, he moves quickly to the bed, gathering up the thin blanket and long pillow in his arms.

Approaching her slowly, he holds out the items like an offering. She blinks at him, not shying away but not jumping forward to take them either. "Here. You can make a little shelter on the floor," Tony urges, shaking the pillow at her. "And, uh, you can cover your ears. Sorry. We'll be real quiet."

She snorts, one hand flying up to cover her mouth and nose. "I'll manage," she tells him firmly, the hint of a smile flitting over her face. She takes the pillow and blanket, plops down on the floor with them, and wraps the blanket around her head and shoulders, disappearing inside.

Tony takes a step back, but his eyes linger on the blanket-lump and he hesitates. "Thanks," he says, rubbing the palm of his hand against his leg, looking a little nervous. "And you won't tell, will you?"

"Nothing for me to tell," she points out from her shelter. "I don't see anything."

He flashes a dazzling smile that would bowl me over had it been aimed at me. "You're a life-saver." He turns on his heel and hurries back to me, his hands already outstretched to press on my chest and lower me into bed. I sink back, feeling a strange sense of familiarity; Diamond had pushed me in much the same way, but he doesn't drop to his knees like she did.

Instead he stands over me, beautiful in the dim light. His scars stand out on his skin like paths I want to travel with my fingers. He grins with confidence and eagerness and giddy relief, throwing one last glance back at the pile of pillow and blanket and girl squatting against the far wall. "Sure you don't want to join us?" he teases, laughter bubbling up in his voice. "Last chance!"

The girl snorts again, sounding almost as amused as he is. "I'm fine over here, thanks," she says firmly, her voice muffled through the blanket.

I open my mouth to thank her and join in the teasing, but before I can draw a breath his lips are on mine again, his body leaning into me as he bends to kiss me. His hands pull at my clothes, dragging the wrappings away. I reach up to follow his example, pulling at his clothes with equal urgency.

Our kiss breaks for an unbearably long moment as we fumble through the worst of the knots. "Not there, here", he whispers, his low voice full of all the frustration I feel at being unable to render him naked faster. Then the cloth falls away and he's pressing me back on the bed, pushing me to lie down even as I pull him along with me because I'd rather have him fall on top of me than break the kiss again. He tumbles down heavily but I don't feel the slightest twinge of pain as he scrambles onto his side next to me.

I turn to face him, my lips seeking his again, my fingers exploring his body as quickly as I can: the soft skin of his back, laced with rough ridges of scars; the hard muscles in his arms, thicker than my own; the line of his hip pressed against mine. *Now this is a prize,* I think as he bites at my lower lip, causing a burst of hot need that pools in my stomach. *This is what I didn't have with Diamond: being wanted.*

"Thank you." It's a stupid thing to say; I feel foolish as I blurt out the words, gasping for breath between kisses. The words had fluttered through my mind and I'd opened my mouth without thinking. Yet he doesn't laugh at me, doesn't engage in any justified teasing. Instead, he draws back to study my face, his lips curved into that arrogant smile even as he pants for air.

"You're welcome." His hand snakes down my chest, gripping me where my skin is hottest, his fingers curling around me until I gasp—and not for air this time. "But I haven't done the thing you're supposed to thank me for," he adds, his smile widening. "Guess I should get on with that." His hand moves over me, drawing a long shudder through my legs and causing my eyes to clench shut at the unexpected intensity.

I groan and my hands fumble in their journey down his stomach, wanting to touch him in the same way he's touching me. If I can make him feel even half as good as I do right now, I'll consider that a victory. He hisses through clenched teeth when my fingers reach their destination, his dark eyes fluttering shut, and I'm pretty sure my own grin could give his arrogance a fair fight.

"Remind me sometime," I tease him, trying not to gasp as his hand continues to work on me, "to show you something I learned from Diamond."

I'm rewarded with a short bark of laughter, his fingers playing in a light teasing pattern before settling into a grip that takes my breath away. "Newbie," he gasps, "there is nothing Diamond can make you feel that I can't do better."

"*Keoki*," I correct him, giving him a mock frown as I play, one hand stroking the soft skin of his thigh just lightly enough to tickle.

"Keoki!" he gasps in agreement, squirming at my touch. "My point—ah!—stands."

I grin in the dark, enjoying the show, the way his solemn face flickers with little smiles and gasps as I touch him. "Does that mean you'll come back?" I whisper, giving him a shamelessly shy smile in the hope that he won't turn down my wide eyes. "To show me how much better you are?"

His soft growl is almost feral, like something I'd expect from a monster in the arena. "Keoki, the only reason I'm not showing off right now is because I need my lips up here to kiss you." His free hand snakes around behind the back of my head, tangling in my hair to drag me closer; his lips crush against mine hard enough to bruise, and I can't bring myself to care.

That's a promise, I think to myself, because I couldn't break away from our kiss even if I wanted to. *I'm holding you to that.* My fingers tighten around him, matching his movements and speed even if I can't copy his talent for precise touch. He groans into my mouth, his lips warm against mine, and then cries out very quietly, baring his teeth in a soft bite against my shoulder.

His hand doesn't stop moving, relentless in his determination to please me. It's almost a surprise—and yet perfectly familiar—when the surge of pleasure bubbles through me, and then I understand why he had to brace his teeth, because I feel I'm about to clench my jaw into dust from the intensity of it. "*Tony,*" I hiss, my hands on his back, pulling him into me, praying I'm not hurting him with my strength but *oh, yes!* it's so much better than anything I've ever felt before.

Then I'm letting him go, the blood rising to my cheeks in embarrassment. There's a flash of hurt in his dark eyes as I rush to scoot away from him. "I didn't hurt you, did I?" I gasp, my throat raw. "I know I'm strong— I didn't mean to— I'm sorry."

He stares at me for a long moment, then his face breaks into a smile so bright the cave is lighter for it. "Nah. You can't hurt me, newb— Keoki." He slides his arm under his head, using his elbow as a pillow while he gropes behind him for one of the long pieces of cloth to pull over us like a blanket. "Everything is good." Leaning in, he kisses me again: a slow, lingering kiss lasting longer than I can measure and still not long enough.

I bring my own arm up, mimicking his makeshift cushion. "And you'll come back?" I tease, though my heart is still racing with the fear that he won't. I don't want to put pressure on him, but I hate to think this might be a once-off thing.

Tony grins at me. "Count on it," he says with a chuckle, closing his eyes and pulling me closer. "Still got lots to show you."

CHAPTER 15

Aniyah

I don't remember falling asleep. At no point do my thoughts stop churning; I'm worried for Miyuki and what xie might be going through right now, and I long to be back together in the safety of our sunlit cavern in the company of Hana and the other girls. Yet I jerk awake from what feels like sleep at the sound of banging on the cave door.

"Christian!" A voice I don't recognize shouts cheerily from the other side. "Pull your dick out and come get food! We're not waiting on you!"

I open my eyes to find myself on a bed which is little more than a rocky shelf cut into the cave wall, the stone pressing mercilessly into my spine. The boy beside me is almost invisible in the darkness, but I feel his arm slung over my waist and hear his soft breath near my ear. I turn my head to find his dark eyes watching me through half-closed eyelids; he looks as drowsy as I feel, but his smile is warm.

"Hey, sleepy-head," he whispers, brushing a curl away from my eyes. "It's good you got some rest. This place saps it out of you, I swear. Makes the time seem funny. If it weren't for the bells, I think I'd lose myself. Speaking of, you slept right through them; you must have been tired!"

He says it like it's an accomplishment. I shake my head, grimacing at the stiff pain shooting through my neck and back at the movement. "No, I..." My voice trails away, lacking the words to describe how the constant ache in my muscles seems to drain all my energy. *Do the rest of them not feel this way?* I don't think they do, which in itself is troubling. *What's wrong with me? And why is the pain getting worse?*

"You hungry?" the boy asks, filling the silence with a smile. "For food, or the extremely handsome man in your bed?" He chuckles when my eyes widen. "No? You cut me to the bone, gorgeous. C'mon, we can at least get you some food." He pushes me with little gentle movements, and I manage to roll out of bed, my feet landing on the floor with more instinct than grace. He follows me out, stooping to grab up his clothes while I brush down my skirt and re-drape the folds of my hood back over my hair.

As my hands sweep over the white fabric I realize that every fold on my dress is still in place, every knot perfectly tied save for the few he loosened about my head and shoulders when we were kissing earlier. *He didn't try to undress me while I slept.* The realization brings gratitude, followed by a vague uneasiness. Somehow it seems strange to want to thank someone for not touching me in my sleep. *Or strangling me.* The memory of Sappho's grim story makes my stomach clench with fresh worry; more than anything, I need to know Miyuki is okay.

"Ready?" The boy straightens up, tucking in the last fold of his wrapped skirt. "Don't be scared. The other guys don't bite, and they don't want to hurt you. You're a goddess, gorgeous. All you gotta do is remember that. C'mon."

I'm dubious of this assessment but I follow him out the door into the cavern, blinking against torchlight which momentarily blinds me. When my vision clears, my first impulse is to turn on my heel; Handler stands near the center of the cave, his cart parked alongside the large sandpit. His hands and face are still alight with magic coursing through the cracks in his skin, and that familiar dread rolls off him, causing my heart to hammer my chest.

Boys squat on the floor around the cart, sitting as far back as they can from the reach of Handler's aura. Each holds a bowl filled with yellow grains and dark meat, which they scoop up greedily with their fingers. They seem comfortable sprawled on the floor and lounging against stalagmites that rise into the darkness, but my back aches at the sight and I find myself longing for the sparkling table and colorful cushions of our sunlit grotto. All eyes look up as we approach, and I have to force myself to keep walking; I can't tell whether they mean me harm, only that I don't like being the sudden focus of so many boys.

"Aw, Christian, you didn't have to tell her to put on clothes just to come eat! We're all friends here."

"Ha! Why should you losers get to see *my* Prize?"

"There's nothing wrong with sharing the wealth a little!"

I don't look at them, refusing to watch them stare at me. Instead, I focus on Handler, willing myself to gaze upon his carved face and the closed eyelids which never impede him. He seems different from earlier: calmer, more relaxed in his stance. *Is it because the Master isn't here?* The absence of the looming inhuman creature is certainly a weight off *my* shoulders. There's something I can't put my finger on, however, a change that nags at my mind as laughter washes over me, unheard and unheeded.

The sound of a door slamming shut causes me to jump, and I whirl to see the other boy from the arena standing near the far wall of the cavern, looking sheepish. Next to him stands Miyuki, clothed and calm, xer eyes downcast to hide the fact that xie can't see us clearly without xer glasses.

"Whoops!" he says, his voice carrying to the center of the cavern. "I don't know my own strength. I think the door's okay, though."

He wants to be the center of attention. Of course he does; he must be accustomed to it. Everything about him catches the eye, from the spray of frizzy curls that stick straight up in the air before spiraling down to his shoulders, to the lanky arms that dangle easily at his sides, to the warm golden strength that thrums confidently through his entire body. He didn't win in the arena by being sneaky or hiding away; he ran to the top of a spire and dropped the entire thing on another man's head. It stands to reason that he's now drawing attention back to himself, flaunting his presence and the prized beauty at his side.

He can show off all he wants; xie isn't his. I cross the cavern as quickly as I can, not quite running in my long dress. I see the boy's eyes widen as I run up to them—*Does he really think I'm coming for him?*—and then my arms are around Miyuki, whispering xer name in xer ear and holding xer as tightly as I can.

"Are you okay? He didn't hurt you? Are you all right?" Behind me I can hear the boys hooting and laughing, their voices rising in a cacophony of words.

"No fair! Newbie, you don't get *two* girls."

"He shouldn't get either. He and Christian need to share; they've had the girls for bells and bells."

"Speaking of bells, where's Tony? Is he still sick?"

"I'm right here, good grief. I *was* sleeping, until you shitfaces starting yelling. Is that food?"

"Tony! Don't sneak up behind me like that, my heart nearly stopped."

Miyuki turns xer lips to touch my ear. "I'm fine," xie whispers. "Are *you* okay?"

"Look, all I'm saying," one of the boys is louder now, his words hard to shut out, "is we should have a practice round to see who gets the girls until first bell. They can even choose the winners! Would you girls like that? Bunch of handsome guys fighting over you?"

"Prizes are awarded by the Master." Handler's cold voice cuts in, silencing the group in an instant. The full force of his dread spreads through the room, like icy fingernails slicing down my spine. I hold Miyuki closer and refuse to look at him; I don't think I could hide the hate in my eyes. "Granite, did you find this Prize satisfactory so far?"

My heart stops at Handler's question. I look up at the lanky boy, my back stiffening with fear. He looks befuddled, at a loss for speech in this moment when every word counts. His eyes find mine, and I etch every line of my face into a pleading expression I pray he can't mistake. *Please. Xie was wonderful, amazing, perfect, indescribable.* If I could beam my thoughts into his head, I would in a heartbeat.

"Aw, yeah," he begins slowly, rubbing his hand along the back of his neck and suddenly looking very shy. "That was something amazing. Never felt anything like it before. Uh, not that Diamond wasn't great, too," he adds in a rush, a broad grin stealing over his face, "but this was something special."

Handler's blank expression doesn't change. "Then she is performing correctly. Come and eat, then you may retire with her to continue your time."

"About that, Handler—"

Christian lounges against a rough stalagmite, lazily scooping grains to his lips. He looks relaxed, a languid bonelessness in his slouch. "I can't speak for the newbie, of course, but I used mine pretty rough. I mean," he flashes the tall man a dazzling smile, "not *too* rough; you did say you wanted her back in one piece. But she could use a long soak, and I could use a nap. The Master is generous, but I'm just one man."

"Girl deserves a guy who can fuck her more than once in a bell cycle," one of the boys mutters loudly enough for everyone to hear.

"It was twice, Lucas," Christian says calmly, taking another bite of his meal. "But your point is taken. We'll keep her away from your limp dick."

Handler ignores the bantering. "If you are finished with your Prize, she will be returned," he says coolly. His eyeless gaze drifts to the boy near us.

"Oh, uh, the same goes for me." The boy with the warm golden glow shakes his head. He gives Miyuki an apologetic look as he speaks, looking sheepish. "I mean, the bed's bigger with only one person, you know?"

"Then both Prizes will be returned," Handler announces. There is a chorus of groans, but not too loud; familiarity lessens the scent of fear around the man, but it's never fully gone.

I can barely breathe after that. We wait for the boys to finish unloading bowls of food which aren't offered to us. All the while I worry they'll change their minds, or convince Handler to change his; one of them in particular, a boy with dark hair and piercing eyes, stares at Miyuki until the others tease him for being jealous of the strong one for winning xer. I don't rest easily again until the cart is empty and Handler gestures curtly for us to follow, then I grip Miyuki's hand as we slip out into the long hall that separates the two caverns.

Returning to the sunlight of our cavern and the soft burble of the waterfall is like coming home. Curtains are already up for the girls to sleep, and heads poke out when the doors open: sleepy, anxious faces that brighten immediately when they see us. Handler makes a curt gesture and they slip back into their beds, obediently disappearing behind heavy fabric. Then he turns to us, his expression blank and cold. "Prizes must be clean and well-rested. Attend to your bodies." With that, he wheels the cart out of the room.

Miyuki's arms are around me the moment he's gone, and I melt gratefully into xer touch. "He didn't touch you, did he?" xie whispers, pulling back just enough to reach into xer robes and dig out xer glasses. Once the little squares sit firmly on xer face, xie studies me with worry in xer hazel eyes.

"No," I say softly, shaking my head. Then I feel the blood rising to my cheeks, blushing with the memory of sensations I don't know how to explain. "Well, yes. But it wasn't bad; it was okay. I'm okay. He was nice. What about yours? He didn't hurt you, honestly?"

Xie actually giggles, touching xer forehead giddily to mine. "He gave me his pillow and blanket after I asked him not to touch me. It was reckless and I didn't plan it, but I just *couldn't*. I couldn't stand the thought of his hands." Relief and reassurance mingle on xer lovely face. "He left me alone. I made a tent on the floor with the blanket."

I stare at xer, feeling my own laughter bubble up, trying to contain it so I don't disturb the others. "You're kidding!"

"Nope!" Miyuki grins, xer hand reaching up to touch my cheek. "Do you think we can go straight to bed?" xie whispers. "I just want to hold you."

My breath catches at the declaration, and I hesitate. "Well. Hah. Uh." I glance at the pool, the sparkling waters calling to me in the light. "I'd actually intended to soak some of the pain away, but." I take a deep breath, turning back to xer. "I think if I get in, I won't be able to get back out. So, bed it is."

Xer expression sobers and xie nods softly. "Aniyah, I have an idea. Come with me?"

I grin at this. "I'll follow you anywhere. Lead on," I say as xie pulls me gently by the hands to our bed. Xie lifts the curtain and we duck into the darkness, crowding around the little platform that is so much airier than the claustrophobic shelf I've just left.

"Take off your clothes and lie face down on the bed," xie whispers, patting the thin padded mattress.

I turn my head to stare at xer. "What?" Having successfully avoided being undressed earlier, the logistics of clothing now seem heavily fraught, imbued with greater meaning than before. I feel strangely shy, even knowing we've already bathed and slept together.

"You said you're hurting," xie says, xer voice soft in the darkness. "I might be able to help with that. But I won't do anything you don't want me to, I promise."

I take a deep breath and try to find the right perspective. *Xie's already seen me naked. Xie's been helping me get dressed since we got here. Xie isn't going to hurt me.* I smile a little at my own embarrassment. "Okay. I trust you," I tell xer, peeling the cloth wrapping away from my skin. My movements are slow, hampered by the stiffness in my limbs. The pain is worse now, and I think running to Miyuki earlier might have pulled something out of joint. *Worth it,* I decide, but every muscle in my body is screaming.

When I'm naked, I reach out to balance the palms of my hands on the bed. I pull myself up onto the platform, crawling into position until I can flop onto my stomach. My movements aren't graceful, and by the end of the procedure I'm glad Miyuki can't see my burning face in the darkness. I bury my head in my arms and try to block out the world. "Like this?"

"Exactly like that," xie murmurs. I feel warm hands gently touching my back, running down the length of my spine. It isn't a straight path, and xer hands move in a curving sweep to follow the twists and turns of my bent body. *Bent but not broken*, I remind myself, yet the throbbing pain makes that hard to believe. Surely nothing whole and healthy would hurt like this.

"Hold still, okay?" says Miyuki, moving around to stand near my head. Xer hands rest on my shoulders, not hurrying in whatever xie's planning to do. "Tell me if I hurt you or if you don't like it, and I'll stop." I nod my head into my arms, making a muffled sound of agreement and staying as motionless as I can.

Xie begins kneading my back slowly, moving in soft sweeping motions. The tightness in my muscles relaxes at xer touch faster than I'd have believed possible. By the time xie has made two full passes over my back I've melted into a relaxed puddle on the bed. Wherever xer fingers trail I feel a sweet numbness seep in, and when xer fingertips brush up my neck and over my scalp the rush of contentment is almost euphoric.

"How... are you doing that?" My voice trembles in the dark as I sigh with relief. The pain is still with me, lurking under the pleasure, but even a temporary reprieve threatens to bring tears to my eyes.

"I'm not sure." Xer hands sweep slowly down the length of my spine, tracing over the worst of the aches. "I don't think it's something I've done before; there's no memory guiding my hands. I just have very strong feelings about touch. About *being* touched, and how I want to touch you. When my hands are on your back, I can feel where the muscles are tight and bunched up and I know how to relax them."

"It's amazing," I whisper, turning my head to look at xer. Xie looks different in the darkness somehow, a dusting of dark gold glitter hanging about xer cheeks, as though the sparkling minerals in the cavern table had leaped up to lie alongside xer freckles. "Can I see your hands?" I ask, a hunch nibbling at my mind. Xie tilts xer head at me, but produces xer hands for inspection.

Xer hands have changed. They're completely covered in a thick coating of rich sandstone dust, rendering them almost invisible in the shelter of our curtains. The golden flakes cover xer hands and seep up into xer wrists, thinning as they spread farther from the tips of xer fingers. The sparkles thrum softly in a mass, beating with the pulse of xer heart, and shimmering flecks break away to sail through the air between us. When they land on my cheek or brush my shoulder, I feel a fresh surge of relief from the constant pain.

"What do you see?" xie breathes, watching my face.

"Magic." I crane my neck to look up at xer eyes. "Your hands. They're warm and good and covered in gold flecks. They're... soothing." This is undeniably true, but I hesitate over the word. It's entirely insufficient for what xie's already done, and there's more underneath; a magic I don't fully understand yet.

"I'm not sure what else," I admit, biting my lower lip. "I can *see* the magic, but knowing what it does is harder."

"Well, I'm in no rush to find out," xie teases, giving me a broad smile. Now that xie's not touching me, the glittering dust slows and ebbs, slinking back into xer fingertips. I understand now why I didn't see xer magic before. It's a subtle talent that stays hidden when not in use, and perhaps that's why the Master undervalued xer. "I know what I want to do, and that's all that matters to me. I want to touch you, heal you, soothe you."

I giggle at this, made giddy by the relief xie's granted me. "You already have," I point out with a grin, catching xer hand in my own. "Come to bed with me? You can't have gotten much sleep on that boy's floor, pillow or no pillow."

Miyuki's smile softens at the suggestion. Xer free hand flies to the neck of xer dress, the white cloth dusted with soot and sand and powdered stone. "You don't mind?" xie asks, looking almost shy as xie gazes down at me.

"Why would I mind?" I shake my head, grinning up at xer. "You didn't mind seeing me, did you?"

Xie colors a little, a warm flush rising to xer cheeks, and quickly unwraps the long swaths of cloth that cover xer from head to toe. Then xie slides into bed with me, catching up the blanket from the floor and slipping it over us to chase away the chill. "So, we survived another— what do they call it?" xie whispers as xie squeezes in close to me on the narrow platform. "Bell cycle?"

"Yeah." I let my arm slip over xer waist the way Christian had held me, determined to keep xer close enough so xie can't fall off the bed in xer sleep. "A bell cycle. We survived. We'll survive all of them, Miyuki. We're not going to die. We can make this work."

I touch my head to xer forehead, but there's something else I want to give xer, something I learned from that boy. I tilt my neck back to place a gentle kiss on xer forehead, wondering if my lips will feel as good on xer skin as his did on mine. Xie sucks in a tiny breath, holding still for a long moment that stretches out between us, then dips xer head to lay an identical kiss in the soft hollow of my collarbone.

Here in the darkness, I feel the stirring heat Christian awakened at first; a pooling in my lower stomach and legs. The throbbing ache demands attention but I don't want to move from this position, not now that I've finally found some comfort from the escalating pain. And though I slept earlier I find myself wanting to drift away again, lulled by the thought of sleeping while hurt is at bay. *How long do I have until it comes back?* There's no way of knowing, and the exquisite numbness weighs me down.

So I ignore the throbbing ache between my legs and just hold Miyuki close, covering xer forehead and hair with tiny kisses while xie places matching ones on my throat and neck. Eventually xer caresses slow and tail off as xer breathing deepens into an even snore. *Sleep,* I think at xer. *Dream of a better world than this one.* A world with beds big enough for both of us, soft as the air around us; one where we can kiss and touch and be together without a dozen drowsy ears listening to every sound we make.

CHAPTER 16

Keoki

"Three bouts in three cycles is highly unusual, Handler!"

I can hear anger in Matías' voice even as he tries to hide it. I close the door to my room quietly behind me, wishing I hadn't slept through first bell. I'd stupidly stayed up late after mealtime in the hopes that Tony might slip back into my room after everyone else went to bed. He hadn't shown, which meant all I'd gotten from my vigil was a lethargic stupor that dragged me obliviously through first bell, early feeding, and whatever has gotten Matías riled up.

Leaning against my door, I shake my head against an encroaching headache throbbing behind my temples and rub grit from my eyes. Everyone is gathered by the training pit where Handler has parked his food cart for the usual first bell serving. The guys are clumped in a tight group nearby, sitting on the ground or slouched against stalagmites. Nobody looks happy. Matías leans on his cane, standing as close to Handler as anyone ever willingly gets, his expression dark.

"Your concerns are noted, Teacher," Handler says, his sightless gaze settling on the smaller man, who is small only in comparison to the robed creature's stretched frame. "That is why we are not using the same fighters as before; Granite, Obsidian, and Basalt will be excused from the bout and allowed to rest." The perpetual coldness of Handler's voice seems slightly less chilly, and I wonder if the relative warmth is a result of Matías' anger or the reason he feels safe expressing it now.

I strain to listen, slinking closer to hear the argument while trying not to draw attention to myself. I'm only about half-successful in my attempt at stealth; Reese looks up from where he's leaning with his back against a stone pillar, and beckons me over. "Bad news?" I ask him, pitching my voice low. Reese shakes his head at me while making a sour face, which I interpret as 'yes'.

"Handler, it's not as simple as rotation," Matías argues, though his shoulders are already hunched forward in defeat. "The boys need rest, practice, entertainment. Can't the Master reschedule? The match would be better for the wait."

"You know he will not," Handler says flatly. "If rest is what is needed, we shall field Pumice. He has rested through the last eight matches."

I don't know who that is, but the silence from the other guys suddenly gets a lot louder as several of them hold their breath. *Which one is Pumice?* I wrack my brain; Tony and Christian and I have already been excused, which leaves Lucas, Justin, and Reese. I look up at Reese, whose face is twisted in a pained wince, but he doesn't return my gaze; he's too busy staring at Justin, who watches his feet moodily.

Matías speaks slowly, his voice hoarser than before. "Pumice doesn't play well to a crowd yet. We're still training him."

Handler waves his scarred hand. "Immaterial in this case. The match is a private one; the Master owes a favor to the Lady of the Silent Forest. She wishes to break in a new guardian she has obtained. I imagine she will like Pumice." His eyeless gaze slides to regard Justin, who still stares at his feet. "As pretty as he is, she might even make an offer to the Master for him. That would be a satisfying outcome for everyone."

Matías' shoulders sag further, his gaze trailing away from Handler's face to study the ground. "Make it a pair match," he insists, "like the last bout. He won't be worth offering for if he's hurt or killed. Send in another of my boys, and he can show off without getting wounded."

Handler considers this, the air around him cold with dread. "Do you have any volunteers?"

His question is met with deafening silence. Matías turns to look at us, but the eyes of the others drop away from his searching expression. "Scoria? Breccia?" he whispers, his gaze swiveling between Lucas and Reese.

Reese winces and looks away while Lucas shakes his head. "Not for a private match," he mutters, his eyes trained on the ground. "Not since the one that took Alpha. You saw how brutal that was."

Dude! I manage to stay silent, to not shout at them, but I can feel myself getting angry. Maybe it's not my place to call anyone out; I'm the newbie here, after all, and there's still so much I don't know. Yet I can't deal with the grim defeat on Matías' face, nor with the glum acceptance on Justin's. I'm pissed that the other guys don't want this kid to die but no one is willing to do anything to save him. I don't know what all this talk is about private matches, but I've already beaten two opponents. *What's one more?*

"If you need another fighter, I'm right here," I volunteer, straightening up against the pillar where I've been leaning.

Every head in the cavern twists to stare at me, which I admit I enjoy, especially since it's the first time Tony has looked my way since I walked in. His face pales and he shakes his head, hair falling into his eyes. "No, you're on rest, newbie," he says, his voice sloshing over me like cold water.

"Only if he wants to be," Matías says quickly, relief brightening his face. "He can fight if he feels up to it. How do you feel?"

"It doesn't matter how he feels!" Tony insists, his voice rising enough to echo. "He's only been here for two cycles! He doesn't have the experience to judge whether or not he's up for another fight."

"Dude, I'm right here," I tell him, heat rising in my cheeks. I already wasn't feeling wild about his failure to come back after eating, so listening to him insult me in front of the others isn't helping my mood. "You wanna tell me this stuff to my face?"

He whirls on me, his dark eyes flashing. "Keoki—"

Handler makes a cutting gesture with his hands, silencing the argument. "Enough. The volunteer is accepted. Head to the arena at once."

Beside me, Reese sighs and gives a gentle punch to my upper arm. "You got guts, newbie," he mutters, his usual bright smile faltering into more of a grimace. My gaze is fixed on Tony but he closes his eyes and turns away with a pained expression, unwilling to look at me. So I sigh and fall into step beside Reese, with Justin slouching along behind us as we head for the gates of the arena.

"So what's the big deal about private matches?" I ask as we walk, trying to sound nonchalant.

"You're going to do fine," Matías says, walking alongside. He's moving as quickly as we are, but the pain caused by his bad knee is etched in the furrow of his brow and he stabs the ground hard with his cane at each step. "Private matches are shown to a limited audience, usually just one or two guests and their retinues. They have a reputation for being dangerous because visibility is poor."

"Justin can help with that, can't you?" Reese says, nudging him with his elbow. "It'll be okay. Tony just worries."

He has a funny way of showing it, I think, but I shake off the hurt for now. "Okay, so. Low visibility? Is the sand all kicked up or— *whoa!*"

If I'd been paying attention, I might have noticed that the corridor from our cavern to the arena was longer than usual, the darkness of the tunnel stretching further than before. As it is, I nearly smack my face into the iron grille of the massive gate which separates our caves from the outside. I'm prevented from breaking my nose by Reese's strong arms, which pull me back before I can collide with the metal.

"Careful! They're just pulling it up now," he admonishes, steadying me as I blink in confusion at the gate which seemed to leap into existence in front of my eyes and is now rising into the air.

Where did that come from? The gate is halfway up, metal screeching against stone, before my brain catches on: there's no sunlight. There's no light outside at all, nothing to illuminate the bars and splash across the ground inside the gate. The sky is completely black. *Can it do that?* I'd have thought not, but now that it's here before me I'm not so sure. A sunless sky seems faintly familiar in a way I can't place.

"Be careful out there," warns Matías, looking grave as we step into the void and the gate clatters shut behind Justin and myself.

I take a deep breath and flex my feet, feeling the sand between my toes. *Okay, I can do this. This is no different from before. Except Christian and Tony aren't here to help.* The latter realization crowds into my brain too late to be helpful. In my rush to save Justin, I'd forgotten that my last two victories were more like me assisting the real victor. *But that's okay, I'm practically a veteran now.*

I turn to Justin, surprised to be able to see him; he's not sharply defined, but there's a glow on his skin that provides a hazy outline in the darkness. "Where's that light coming from?" I ask, blinking.

"Tower seats," he mutters, gesturing over my shoulder. I whirl on my heel to catch a silvery glow swelling to bright life in the sky, a light strangely familiar to my eyes. Shapes appear within the light: the distant outline of girls, the unearthly white giant who presides over our fights, and something which looks more like a rotten tree than a person, moving at a slow pace about the tower to peer into the arena below.

"What kind of lady is *that*?" The rash words are out of my mouth before my brain has a chance to catch up, and I hope they can't hear us from this distance. "Uh, never mind," I amend, turning back to Justin. "Okay, what is it you do? Reese said you could help with the darkness?" The silvery light is just enough to illuminate his face but little else; the pillars dotting the arena throw thick shadows, perfect for lurking. I think of the poison-spitter and try not to shudder at the thought of tracking someone like him in these conditions.

Justin makes a face at my question, his shoulders hunched in a defensive posture. "You're not gonna like it," he warns. He extends his hand into the empty air in front of him, palm up and open.

I wonder if I'm supposed to slap his hand or otherwise respond to this gesture. But he doesn't look at me; instead, he stares at his palm as concentration knits his brow. I follow his gaze and my eyes widen at the bizarre sight that greets me: the skin on his open hand is bulging and bubbling into little hills and valleys. Half a dozen thick pustules sprout, each of them filled almost to bursting with pus. The effect is super gross and kinda cool in an icky way, but *not* something I want to touch.

The strange pustules are also *glowing*. They throb with inner colors that shine through his skin: white and red and yellow and blue and green and a sort of pinkish-purple color I couldn't name if I tried. In the span of a few heartbeats, six separate bubbles have puffed up in his hand: each the size of an eyeball and rounded off at the bottom until the skin attaching them to his palm is so thin that it seems no thicker than a thread. "Dude," I breathe, my voice low in the dark, "what *are* those?"

"Lights," he mutters. With a flick of his wrist, the little yellow bubble snaps off his hand and flips to the ground. An explosion of color dazzles my eyes when the pustule hits the sand, leaving me rubbing away the afterimage. Sun yellows, sand yellows, bright yellows, soft yellows; every shade of yellow I can imagine bursts from the bubble. The part of my mind that isn't dwelling on our imminent deaths wonders how a tiny thing like that could contain such multitudes; I'd be impressed if I weren't so confused.

"Lights?" I stare at the golden sparkles that glitter in the sand around us. The force of their initial explosion is spent, but many of the specks still smolder with inner light. The smaller ones on the far edges of the explosion flicker and wink as they die out one by one, but the bigger clumps near the center of the blast radiate lingering light and warmth, tiny wisps of steam dancing in the air above them. "Are they hot?"

Justin shrugs. "They sting if you touch them."

That's it? Why would anyone put this kid in a fight? I don't give voice to my thoughts but the question shows in my eyes, highlighted by yellow embers coating the ground and the remaining baubles glowing brightly in his hand, even as his long fingers curl protectively over them.

"I was payment in a gambling debt," he volunteers, looking surly. "They tossed me into my first fight expecting me to die. I threw sparks into the guy's face and he stumbled. Fell off the platform we were running on and broke his neck. Didn't really count as a proper kill, but I survived; so here I am."

About to die again. He doesn't say it, but the grim certainty is etched in the hunch of his shoulders. I swallow, pressing down my own fears; not only am I out here without any help this time, but I have to keep this kid alive.

"Okay," I tell him, taking a deep breath. "We can do this. We can make this work. Look, how fast can you make more of those?"

"The lights? Pretty fast. Just need to pick off the last batch." He looks down at the glowing baubles attached to his hand by thin threads of skin; with his free hand he pinches them away to make room for more. "Want one? Anyone can throw them; air or ground, doesn't matter."

He holds out the red bubble and I take it gingerly between my fingers, unsettled at being offered a piece of his body. It doesn't feel like skin; the texture is a thin webbing surrounding tiny pebbles that jostle each other in their desire to escape. I wonder how hard I would have to squeeze to pop the casing, but I'm in no mood to burn myself.

"Cool. Here's the plan," I announce, trying to sound like I've got the situation under control. "We'll get to the platforms and find a weapon. A sword or whatever. You keep making lights and throwing them to light our way. If anything rushes us, throw lights in its face and we'll run."

He looks skeptical at my plan, but nods and moves a little closer to me. "You lead," he mutters, a fresh glow prickling in his hand as more bubbles ripple from his skin.

Pushing away my fear, I set out for the nearest spire. The pillar stabs high into the black sky, only faintly outlined by the silver glow above us. It's unsettling to creep through the arena like this; the silence weighs heavily and every shadow threatens to vomit forth monsters as we pass. The only sounds are the popping explosions of light Justin throws ahead and around us as we walk, lighting our path in the dark.

We're only a few steps from the bottom of the spire when I spot it: beady eyes glinting from the darkness and a thick shag of matted hair that sucks up every glint of light and returns emptiness. "There!" I hear my own shout from a distance, my hand whipping around in a tight arc. The red bubble hisses as it flies through the air and explodes in the face of the creature, crimson sparks flying in an explosion of light.

It howls, pain and anger mingling in an inhuman cry that echoes through the arena. An outline forms under the red sizzling sparks that coat its face and body: a monster on all fours, with long limbs and an elongated snout. Teeth glint in the light and wicked claws dig into the sand. The creature hurls itself at us and I brace for the impact, my arms outstretched to grab and throw; if I'm lucky, I can use its momentum against itself and buy time for us to run.

My fingers sink into coarse fur, but any hope I have of throwing the monster dies instantly: it's *heavy*. A mass of muscle and fury barrels into me with more power than I can shift. The creature swipes me aside with a single blow of its paw, claws digging into my belly. A gush of blood coats my stomach, shiny and black in the glow of the tower. I'm thrown stumbling away, my hands clutching at the wound, my head spinning. Then I hear Justin scream and the ugly wet sound of claws tearing through flesh.

No! I whirl around but a fresh wave of vertigo causes me to make one revolution too many. Blood spills over my fingers and my vision blurs. I hear thrashing in the darkness and screams, then I smell more blood than my own. *Justin!*

I take a stumbling step towards the violence—I don't know what I can do, but I've got to try—when I'm blinded by an explosion of noise and color. I fall back, blinking, as another howl of pain rips through the arena followed by the sound of feet stumbling on rocky sand. One last swipe at my eyes clears away the dancing spots and I see Justin running in the silvery light, badly wounded and stumbling with every step. The creature gallops behind him, waving its head and howling in fury.

It's blind, I realize, taking in the bright sparkles coating every inch of its face. Justin must have set off all his bubbles at once in its face as it mauled him. If he had his hands up to ward the thing away, it would have been the easiest way to wound it and escape.

Yet his talent wasn't enough to kill it, only slightly slow it down. The earlier plan flashes through my mind like a talisman: *Find a weapon, kill the creature, don't die.*

I turn on my heel, running as fast as I can towards the platform, hoping that Justin can stay ahead of the creature long enough for me to come to his aid. Even blinded, it runs after him unerringly and my mind worries at this as my hands scramble at the stone in search of a blade. Can it hear him? Surely not after that explosion, which left my own ears ringing. No, it's almost like it can—

Smell him. The answer burns into my mind as brightly as one of Justin's flashes. The creature can smell him—can smell the smoke and fire he makes. That's why it ran past me and leaped on him when I threw the first explosion in its face. It couldn't hunt by sight in the aftermath, but it could by scent.

I set that thing on him. The realization hits me as my hands close on a heavy club hidden in one of the holes of the spire, relief and guilt flooding me in equal measure. I yank it out and the dark wood glints in the silvery light. It's made from the same material as the cane Matías uses, but is much thicker and shaped with a round end for bludgeoning. I whirl on the platform, running as hard as I can, a fresh giddiness washing through me. I don't know how to use a sword like Tony, but I can use this.

Screams orient me to a nearby scuffle; Justin must have tried to double back to reach me. I see the dark shape of the creature mauling a body that thrashes in the sand, but I don't look too closely or listen or think of the smells. My senses sharpen into a focus that leaves nothing in my world except me, the monster, and the club in my hand. I leap, screaming and swinging, and feel the satisfying crunch of bone. I hear a howl and then another, interspersed with the thud of my club and the thrumming sensation in my arm.

I don't know how long the fight goes on, but it doesn't end quickly. Teeth flash in the silvery light and blood spills; first Justin's, then mine, and then the creature's own. I swing and swing again until eventually it falls. I barely manage to kick it off the other boy, even though my legs are bursting with more power than I'd have thought possible. Then I go on swinging. I remember the stone creature of my first fight an eternity ago, and how it lived after losing its head. I won't be fooled this time, and so I keep swinging.

Slowly, the fact penetrates my rage that I can see better than before. My arm slows as pain catches up with me, loss of blood making me sway where I stand. The sky lightens on the horizon and a soft orange-pink glow spreads out. The sun appears and begins to climb the sky in a smooth motion; a few long beats of my heart later, it hangs as high above us as it always has, spreading warmth and light onto the brown shale sand.

I look down at the mangled body lying on the sand. Black fur, long nose, beady eyes now empty and dead. It isn't a monster, it's just a bear. The word leaps to my mind as tears sting my eyes. It isn't even a particularly large bear; it's about as big as me, though fur might once have made it look bigger if it weren't matted down and clotted with blood. *My fault.* My stomach churns and I look away, seeking my companion and dreading what I might find.

Justin. I don't recognize him where he lies in the sand. He's coated with blood that still gurgles up from his wounds, his leg twisted under him at an angle that hurts just to look at it. Part of his cheek has been gouged away, leaving his face caked with blood and sand; thick claw marks rake across his arms and chest. My own wounds throb in sympathy and I double over, vomiting up what feels like every bite of food I've ever eaten.

CHAPTER 17

Aniyah

T he sun climbs high above our heads before coming to a halt directly over the arena. Light beats down upon us, illuminating the grisly scene below. I hear a gasp from someone behind me catching sight of the mangled bodies—not Miyuki, who can't see without xer glasses, but one of the others.

The match had been difficult to follow, between the silvery light spilling from the air above the Master's throne and the colorful explosions. The magical outlines of the boys guided my gaze in the dark, but the rest of the girls had to rely on senses other than sight. We heard the screams and smelled the blood. I could almost feel the tear of flesh with each wound, the brutality of the fight stealing my breath.

Now in sunlight we see the aftermath: a dead animal lying in a heap with two boys nearby. Only one of them is standing, and my eyes confirm what my magical sense already knew: it's the boy who was brought in with us, the handsome one who was kind to Miyuki. He staggers, retches, then collapses from his wounds. Blood seeps between the fingers clutched to his side.

"Well, *that* was disappointing." The creature that paces our tower sighs, her voice like a gust of dry wind emerging from the rotted wood of her throat. I had forgotten the word 'tree' until I saw her, and in that moment I knew what she ought to be and yet was not. Her wooden skin is pitted with holes and scars which weep thick amber sap, and the hair tumbling down her back is a curtain of rotten leaves, each little more than a tattered stem and their colors only a faint suggestion of once-vibrant crimson and orange.

"It was indeed." The Master's voice is still inhumanly flat, but he makes an attempt at solicitous sympathy to match the mask hiding his blank face. 'My gentleman's mask,' he'd called it when he and Handler came to collect us for the fight, though all his affected gentleness has so far been reserved for this strange fey visitor who feels fetid to the core. "Your last guardian was much better, yes? It is always vexing to lose good servants, and worse when finders provide inferior replacements."

"My last guardian was a treasure," she observes with another low sigh. "My last finder, too. I have had the most unlucky streak lately, losing them both. And now this one, too." Her lip peels back in an expression of disgust, flecks of her face breaking away as dry wood mimics the movement of skin without the necessary elasticity. "I suppose I could buy a new bear from you, but your technique is so rough! It is easier to start with a sapling and bend it to my specifications than to try changing one you've already altered."

He hesitates before he answers, and I tear my eyes away from the carnage to watch him work out a way to take this as a compliment. "Well, my arena is a rough place, as you know. Perhaps too rough for a lady." The disgust flaking from her lips doesn't subside. Inside, my mind screams at the banal horror playing out before me; those boys are dead or dying while our captor ineptly banters. He hurries to mollify her. "The next time I get a fresh batch, I could save them for you to consider."

She peers at him, not yet placated. "Next time? When do you expect that to be? Your stables seem rather full. Have you decided to build an extension, as I suggested?"

"My stables *were* full," he corrects. "I'll have to bring in new ones to replace these two." He sighs, his shoulders moving in a parody of emotion that doesn't reach the fixed smile on his mask. "The strong one was shaping up to be the crowd favorite, too. Such a shame."

The tree-woman brightens, relaxing the curl of her lip. "Well, a new batch to look over *would* be quite welcome. I will take you up on the offer." Her eyes drift over us then, her pupils dark weevil holes rotting at the edges. "Unless any of you girls would be interested in leaving with me?" Her voice softens into a cajoling croon. "You must get so bored being cooped up. How would you like the freedom of a forest?"

If we hadn't just witnessed an innocent bear being clubbed to death, the offer might have been more tantalizing; as it is, her words meet horrified silence. Even the creature who calls himself our master seems discomfited, though I imagine not for the same reason. "Ah, my girls are not for fighting. They are delicate luxuries. They would be useless to you, dear lady."

She laughs off his objection; a barking, mocking sound of wet wood crumbling with age. "Nonsense. I require only anger to work with, and I assure you these girls have more than enough of that." Her eyes narrow, scrutinizing each of us in turn. "All of them have potential," she murmurs, sounding torn. "And I wouldn't have to wait for your finder to bring in fresh ones. But there is still the matter of the roughness of your technique. You tear what you should shape; it's sloppy, verging on criminal."

A trickle of ire seeps into the Master's flat voice. "I *choose* not to shape them because humans are prettiest in their raw state. The girls remain attractive for their partners, and the fighters are pleasing to the audience. I see no reason to add fangs or fur to obscure their natural beauty." He pauses, making an effort to match his tone to the gentlemanly mask he wears. "But if you believe she would suit your needs, I might be persuaded to part with my newest. She was an extra brought in with my spotter."

My heart leaps into my throat; I don't have to wait for his gaze to settle on Miyuki to know who he means. Xer hand squeezes mine in a rush of panic. "You can't."

The words squeak out of my throat before I have a chance to think about what I'm doing, yet even when my mind catches up, I can't see a better plan. *What can they do that's worse than separating us?* I clear my throat, trying to ignore the effect of the two magical titans staring coldly at me. "You can't," I repeat. The words are barely more than a whisper, but what I lack in volume I make up by sounding reasonable; my voice shows no trace of the wild panic that throbs down my spine.

"I see." The white-masked creature towers over me. "Would you like to tell us why that is?" Light gathers in his hands, hot and dangerous; his voice is cold as death.

I swallow, picking my words with care. "Master, Quartz has healing hands," I tell him, doing my best to sound respectful. "If you let us go down there," I nod at the arena, "it might not be too late to save the crowd favorite. Maybe even both of them." Miyuki squeezes my hand hard enough to hurt, but I ignore xer; there'll be time to work a miracle once xie's not in danger of being sold off. "She can't do that if she leaves."

The smallest of frowns enters his voice. "You are wrong, spotter. True healers are a rare breed, nothing like this one."

"I've felt it!" I insist, striving for the perfect balance between respect and certainty, hoping he won't notice the sweat beading on my forehead. "I've *spotted* it!" I maintain eye contact with the empty holes in his mask. *I'm the expert here,* I think, willing the words into his mind. *You took me for a reason. Trust me. Believe in me.*

The tree-woman watches me with her rotten eyes, the stench of mildew growing stronger. "It is an abstract point," she declares, turning away from us and stepping closer to the edge of the parapet.

Our master raises a pale hand. "Lady—"

"Either she is common clay, in which case I will find richer soil among a fresh batch," she interrupts, her voice cool, "or she is a healer, in which case I have no use for her as a guardian. Send me a message when your finder brings you new material to work with; if there is aught good among the findings, I will pay well."

174

She steps lightly onto the lip of the parapet and over the side into empty air. I gasp, expecting to see her plummet to the ground below, but she does not. The cloak of leaves tumbling down her back in lieu of hair lengthens in an instant to cover her from head to toe, wrapping every inch of her until she is nothing more than a bundle of thick foliage. This mass hangs in the air for the length of a single breath, then explodes into a stream of individual leaves carried away on a gust of wind that wasn't there before.

With a low growl, the Master tears off his mask and throws it against the stone wall behind us where it shatters into a thousand fragments. "She is the worst of sisters." He turns back to me, the vast featureless stretch of his blank face more menacing than ever before. "And *you*. You just lost me a sale, spotter. I shall have to think on your punishment."

I hear Hana draw a breath behind me, and for a moment I'm shot through with panic that she'll defend me and bring down his wrath on her too. Yet it is Handler who speaks, unexpectedly coming to my aid. "Master, if I may? The Lady of the Silent Forest would have been angry with you anyway, when the product of the sale proved inferior. Perhaps our spotter's mistake is a blessing in disguise."

No one moves. My eyes flick to Handler in astonishment before I remember to lower them in a show of humility. *What is he doing?* The cycle before, he was shoving me along corridors and throwing me at boys; now he's protecting me. His hands are clasped in front of him and one finger worries at a mole on his wrist, stroking the dark bump in a nervous rhythm. I don't remember noticing any spots on his hands when I studied the magic thrumming through those carved patterns; the blemish makes him seem more human somehow, less imposing. Did I miss it at the time, or is he changing?

"You are right," the Master concedes after a fraught pause, folding himself back onto his huge throne. "And she was seeking *girls* as guardians. A cynical mind might conclude that she *wanted* an inferior product, so she would have a pretext to be angry with me. Very well. Your mistake is forgiven, spotter."

He turns his gaze away and I breathe again; Miyuki squeezes my hand and, out of the corner of my eye, I see Hana's shoulders relax in relief. "But you will not interfere the next time I offer that one for sale," he adds, his flat voice stern. "No wild tales of healing."

Next time. My heart leaps into my throat. The thought of being separated from Miyuki, of having xer torn away from me in a sale, is more than I know how to cope with.

Handler clears his throat. "Master," he murmurs, his low voice deferential, "in her inexperience the spotter has overestimated what Quartz can do, yet we *were* aware the girl possesses manipulation over muscular systems. Their finder reported she'd undergone training in a related field; she manifested some talent in pain reduction and injury management before alteration. He suggested she might have a soothing effect on the boys, yet it might be more profitable to put her to work healing them."

The Master drums his pale fingers against the arm of his throne. "We'll see how bad it is," he decides, rising in a stately motion. "If they're too far gone, I can always repurpose them as meat."

We leap to follow him, and I hear the grind of metal against stone in the arena below us: the gate is rising. I glance back over my shoulder to see the distant figures of boys spilling out of the caverns and running to their wounded comrades, then we're plunged into darkness as we begin to descend the tower stair.

Please be alive. Please be okay. The words echo in my head, as though I could make them live through willpower alone. I need those boys to be safe, and not just because one was kind to Miyuki; if xie can save them, then maybe the Master won't sell xer away.

Miyuki crowds close to me in the tight staircase, gripping my arm with xer nails. "Aniyah!" xie hisses in my ear. "I can't! You know I can't do this."

"You have to try!" I twist my head to look at xer in the darkness, hoping the panic I feel is written on my face for xer to read. "Miyuki, I don't have any other ideas!"

176

"Aniyah, my hands aren't going to help those boys!"

A warm body presses into us from behind and Imani's lovely face shines in the low torchlight as she inserts herself into our whispering conference. "I can set a bone," she hisses.

"What?" I blink at her, my foot almost missing the next step.

"I can set a bone! That boy's leg was broken, you could see; I can set it." Her eyes flick away from my gaze, suddenly shy. "I've done it before, for one of the girls. It was only a finger, but I knew how. I... I think I was studying it before I was brought here."

Miyuki stares at her, xer eyes wide. "You can heal him? Because I— They're acting like I've done this before, but I can't remember!"

Imani shakes her head. "No, I can't heal him, but I can help. I can set his leg. We can wrap up the cuts. Maybe Chloe could fetch some of the pool water? It heals wounds; the Master put it in to fix us up after the boys use us, but it works on everyone. If we combine the water with what I know and what you can do..." Her voice trails away.

"You have to direct us," I whisper to Miyuki, my heart beating faster. "It's your magic, which makes it your show. You'll tell us what to do; you'll be the expert. The healing will be your doing, and then he'll want to keep you."

Miyuki turns to look at me, alarm written on xer face. "What if he finds out we're faking?"

"We're not faking! The only thing that matters is his fighters are healed. You can do this, Miyuki, I *know* you can. I see your magic."

We spill out of the stairwell into the cavern corridor that separates our home from the boys' rooms. Ahead of us, the Master stalks in long strides to the huge black doors. One hand moves in a wide arc that sweeps the air in front of him and the carved doors fling open at his gesture, parting with more violent speed than Handler has ever achieved. We scurry in his wake into the smoky cavern, where the group of boys awaits.

On the ground before us lie two badly-wounded boys. One of them, the handsome one who was kind to Miyuki, clutches his stomach where blood seeps from jagged claw marks. He groans as a dark-eyed boy kneels beside him and holds his free hand, clenching hard enough to turn his own knuckles white.

Beside him lies his comrade from the arena. Caked with blood and sand, his face has been marred by the beast's teeth, and deep gashes have torn away much of his clothes and the flesh underneath. Three boys cluster around him while another leans against a nearby pillar with his eyes closed, unable to watch. At first blush I'm sure the injured boy is already gone but then he coughs, blood gurgling from the corner of his mouth. *He's alive,* I realize, my eyes widening with horror; I can't begin to imagine the pain he must be in.

The Master draws to a halt, tilting his head to consider the wounded fighters. "Heal the strong one," he orders, pointing a thin finger at the curly-haired boy. "Kill the weak one. He's too far gone to keep."

"Master!" The oldest boy straightens from where he leans on his cane. "Pumice survived his fight. It would be bad for morale to kill him now." His face is taut with worry, his words edging the border of disrespect.

"Morale is not worth the cost of keeping a fighter who cannot fight," the creature declares. "You know that best of all." The man winces and looks down at his cane, unable to protest further.

"Master," Handler says from my elbow, his voice low. "Should the girls be able to heal Pumice, he might still turn a profit. You have already sunk a certain cost into the boy; it would be a shame not to recoup it."

The faceless creature considers this. "Even so," he says, his flat voice more thoughtful, "I cannot continue to throw good resources away on a defective servant. Even if he recovers, the odds of him ever properly winning a fight are much too low."

Handler nods, ever subservient. "He might profit you in a non-fighting capacity, Master. If he were healed, you could sell him. Or he could be repurposed as a Prize girl; the boys are clearly very fond of him."

Eyes widen, and not just my own; several boys look offended or outright horrified at the notion, though one just blinks and tilts his head slightly. The Master drums his fingers against his robe as precious time slips by. "That would leave me with eight Prizes in my stable; more than I usually like to keep. But I suppose it's only a matter of time until one of the boys is too rough with a Prize and breaks her. Girls are so fragile."

He turns to Miyuki then, his eyeless gaze sending chills up my spine. "Heal them both," he orders in a tone that brooks no refusal before sweeping out of the room. The black doors slam shut behind him with an ear-shattering bang and he is gone, leaving us to perform miracles in his absence.

CHAPTER 18

Keoki

Was I asleep? I hadn't thought so, but I'd been in darkness and now I find myself in light, shaken by the slam of doors. A hand clasps mine and I turn my head to see dark eyes blinking back tears. "Tony," I whisper, feeling a goofy grin spread wide over my lips. "I thought you were mad at me."

"Stupid," he says softly, shaking his head. Hair falls over his eyes and he has to swipe it away. "I am. Now stay alive so I can beat you up in practice."

My grin widens as the firelight behind his head flickers into a warm halo, causing his skin to glow invitingly in the gloom. "Only if you promise to kiss it all better after," I tell him, hearing my words slur.

Worry creases his brow and he touches my cheek with the back of his hand. "You're burning up."

"Answer the question," I mumble, feeling sleep closing over me.

"Yes! Don't you fall asleep on me," he orders, slapping my cheek. The sting is barely noticeable above the dull pain dragging me down. "I will, but you have to stay awake."

"Okay, okay. 'S hard," I mutter. My eyelids feel as heavy as the iron gate to the arena, slipping shut despite my best attempt to please him. Above me I hear a buzz of words, the strange sound of girls' voices.

180

"Miyuki! Tell us how we can help you."

"I-I don't— That one is worse off. We need to set his leg and stop the bleeding. Amethyst, help me?"

"I'm here. We'll need wood to make a splint and cloth to wrap it. And we need to wash the wound."

"We'll get water from our pool. Handler, we can use your cart. Ruby and I can load it up with bowls."

"Diamond, I don't have the Master's approval—"

"And if his fighters die while you're asking him? C'mon, open the doors!"

"She's right, Handler. Scoria, Breccia, go help the girls fetch their water."

"Not to butt in, but has anyone noticed the strong one is fading fast? Someone should fix that; we'll be punished if *he* dies."

"Yes, I don't— Aniyah, help me, I need—" A panicked pause in the heavy air before the same voice barrels onward. "Alexandrite! Undress him so we can wash the wound when they come back with water. Sapphire, can you wrap his cuts like you did with Emerald's arm? Amethyst and I will take this one."

"This is going to hurt him. I need someone to hold him down so he doesn't thrash while I set the leg."

"I'm on it." I hear Christian's voice, warm and confident, followed by a grunting howl of pain that pierces my mental haze.

"Justin." His name slurs on my tongue, my mind fumbling with helpless urgency. "I've got to save him."

"He's gonna be okay." The most beautiful girl in the world—the one Christian got before, and it was so unfair—appears beside me. Tight corkscrew curls frame brown eyes that flash in the firelight. Her lips are soft and plump, and her skin is a dark burnished brown I could fall into and never return.

"Hi," I breathe, my heart pounding faster.

"Hold still," she says, not looking up at my face. Her hands work over me, pulling away bloody scraps of cloth that stick to my body and are embedded in my wounds. I wince at fresh waves of pain, and Tony squeezes my hand.

"There... There was a bear. Justin." My words slur again, pain muddying my mind. There was red fire and eyes that gleamed dangerously in the dark. But I was wrong; it was just an innocent animal. I have to tell her. I have to explain. She needs to know what I did, and how Justin got hurt because of me.

"I know." She doesn't meet my eyes as she works. "I saw. But you won. You saved your friend. You're both going to be okay." Only then does she look up at me, her brown eyes stern. "You're *not* allowed to die. Miyuki is going to heal you and you're going to be properly appreciative when the Master asks."

"He's not going to die," Tony agrees, his voice hoarse. "We'll heal him up and sing your praises. Promise."

She shoots him a grateful look, her eyes softening when she sees his hand holding mine. "Are you friends?" Before Tony can answer, there is a sudden sound of grinding doors and they look up. I hear the pounding of bare feet on stone and another girl runs into my blurred field of vision, a bundle of white in her arms.

"I got clean cloth," she reports, panting. "The others are coming with water. Handler is with them. Did you need help getting his clothes off? Oh, hello." She studies me with a detached expression, sparing a nod for Tony. "You're the new boy, huh?"

"Keoki," I croak out, studying her face. The beauty kneeling beside me continues to pick torn shreds out of my wounds, the accompanying jolts of agony helping to keep me awake. "What's your name?"

She ignores me, pressing her lips together as she considers my condition. "Wrapping him is gonna be a pain. How will we lift him?"

"I can't help there," the beauty says, her voice flat. "Maybe Ruby could—" Her words are cut off as another girl approaches. A familiar face this time, though when I last saw Diamond she looked very different than

182

she does now with two heavy bowls of water tucked under her arms and sweaty hair plastered to her brow.

"Handler's back so keep your voices down. He hasn't said anything about you two using your names, so I'm hoping he didn't notice, but we need to be careful he doesn't hear any more. Ruby's keeping him distracted, but I can move the boy; he's not *that* heavy. Sapphire, take these off me before I slosh." The inked girl hurries to fuss over the bowls, working out the best way to unburden her without losing all the water.

"He's heavy to *me*," my goddess mutters, shaking her head as she stands to help the others.

She rises slowly, and not in an elegant way; she moves as though every action were a deliberate choice. When she stands from where she kneels, her hands push off from the floor and I see pain flicker over her face, twisting her sweet lips from a smile to a grimace.

What's wrong with her? Can't they fix her? Everyone here seems so damaged. I remember the scars crisscrossing Tony's back, the sensation of the raised welts under my fingers. If I don't die from these wounds, I suppose I'll soon have scars of my own. I don't know how I feel about that, but I don't think I like the idea.

"Sapphire, I'll lift him, then you two get the cloth under him, okay?"

"I'll help," Tony announces, moving to slide his hands under my shoulders.

Even this slight jostling sends new waves of pain rippling from the gashes in my stomach. "Stop, no! Hurts," I gasp, panting in agony. I black out, but only for a moment; when I can see again, no one has moved from where they'd been. Their distorted voices wash over me.

"Fast as we can," Diamond says, ignoring my words and bracing her hands under my legs. "Sooner we get that cloth under him, the sooner we can wrap the wound and staunch the bleeding. One, two, three!"

I don't have the breath to scream, but gasp again as the world swims around me. I feel the bustle of the two girls —the beauty and her inked friend—passing something through the thin layer of air beneath me. Then I'm lowered back down and the world is only darkness and pain and a sense of time being lost.

"Hey! Don't fall asleep; come on, come back!" Tony's voice, pinched and worried, sounds very far away.

"I've got you. You're not leaving us. I know it hurts." A soft voice, low by my ear. Musical and warm, suffused with understanding. "Listen, don't resist the pain; it'll just overwhelm you and carry you away. Let your mind move with it."

Her words don't make sense at first. Images and sounds flutter disjointedly through my mind. A memory jars loose: a powerful image of rushing water carrying me away from shore. Fighting the water would only wear me out and so I swim with it, breaking away in small strokes.

I close my eyes, trying to follow the pain. *Where is it worst?* Here, along the deepest gash: a tear that crosses my chest and cuts down to my hip. I let my mind trace the outline; it sharpens under my attention, then begins to lessen. Like the current, once I've accepted the pain, I can take steps to lessen the worst of it. My breathing becomes shallow, restricting the movements of my chest; I force my shoulder to relax, loosening the muscles along my side. Working with the pain, instead of against it, *does* help.

"But I still hurt."

"I know," the girl says, her hands moving over me as she dresses my wounds. I hadn't meant to voice my thoughts, but when I open my eyes I see understanding in her gentle gaze. "I know it's awful, and so very unfair, but I need you to be strong now. So much depends on you getting better."

She's right; it *isn't* fair. A part of me wants to scream, to break things, to smash in the white featureless face of that creep who was here before—the one who ordered Justin's death as though it were nothing to him. But I can't even move, so I sigh and settle back. The inked girl begins the painful process of knotting my wrappings, and I focus on the beauty's face and voice to get me through these ministrations.

184

"You know my name?" It was music on her tongue, the three syllables flowing as smoothly as the soothing water she now pours over my wounds. I would have expected washing to be fresh agony, but the water tingles against my skin and soaks away the sharpest pain.

Her lips twitch at my question. "You introduced yourself to Sapphire," she reminds, nodding at the inked girl.

"Oh, right." I glance at the other girl, but she doesn't look up from her work. Diamond is gone; she must have left while the pain was still washing over me. Turning my head, I see her with the others working on Justin. "There are so many of you: Sapphire, Diamond, Amethyst, Emerald, Ruby." I frown up at her. "What's your name? You said 'Miyuki', and I thought I heard her say 'Aniyah'. Or should I just call you 'Beautiful'?"

The other girl, Sapphire, ties off the last of my wrappings with a surge of vigor that makes me wince under her attentions. "I gotta go help Diamond with the other one," she tells my girl, jerking her head in Justin's direction. "You got this one by yourself?"

"I'll be fine." The beauty smiles at the other girl, who promptly bounces up and darts away. My benefactress watches her go with a fond gaze before her eyes drift back to Tony and me. "My name?"

She hesitates for a long moment, her eyes flicking to the knot of girls behind her. "Yes. My name is Aniyah," she admits in a low murmur, her expression turning solemn. "But the Master calls me Alexandrite and I'm not supposed to know my real name. Please don't tell?" Her voice is a gentle song drifting over me. "I'd get in trouble if he found out. Killed, or worse."

"Really? We have the same thing. Was it written on your clothes?" Tony studies her, curiosity alight in his dark eyes. He glances at Handler on the other side of the cavern, pitching his voice so we can't be overheard. "I'm Basalt in the arena and this one here is Granite. But my real name is Anthony Suen. You can call me Tony, though. Everyone does."

Aniyah graces him with a warm smile. "It's nice to meet you, Tony." She looks down at the bowl of water in her lap, now half empty and swirled with my blood after repeated dippings with the cloth used to clean me. "Can I ask you to get me a fresh bowl from the cart? Standing is a bit of an effort for me."

He studies her for a long moment, his dark eyes peering from under his shaggy fringe, then he breaks into an easy grin, all lopsided arrogance. "I'd be happy to help. Stay here, I'll be right back." He pats me lightly on the shoulder and bounces up to stroll over to the silver cart.

She watches him go with a skeptical smile on her face, then turns back to me. Lowering her voice and not meeting my gaze, she murmurs, "Thank you. For Miyuki."

I nod, but the words don't make a lot of sense. "For what now?"

Her lovely face is written with a confusion that melts into hesitation. "My friend was, uh, assigned to you. Miyuki told me you didn't— You gave her your blanket and pillow. Thank you."

I blink, remembering the girl in my room and how Tony had given her those things. Did Aniyah misunderstand which boy gave out the blanket when Miyuki told her story, or did she take her promise of silence more seriously than I'd expected? I stammer, trying not take credit for something I didn't do. "Hey, it wasn't a problem. I don't touch girls who don't want to be touched."

I'm rewarded with a warm smile, the curl of her lips turning my legs to liquid where I lie. "I'm glad. I haven't met everyone here yet, but you seem nice. You and Tony and Christian."

I give her a winsome grin, trying to look dashing despite the pain. "Tony and I are really awesome," I tell her with a wink. "But Christian? I'm incredibly jealous of that guy." I wait a heartbeat for the delivery. "He got awarded the best girl. How is that fair?"

She blinks, staring at me for a moment. Then her smile widens and she bursts into laughter, struggling to conceal it so the others don't notice. "Does that work?" she demands, her brown eyes dancing. "Like, ever?"

My own grin is unrepentant. "Well, I don't know!" I chuckle, wincing at the accompanying wave of pain; no laughing until my chest heals up, I note with some sourness. "I only woke up three cycles ago."

She nods, her expression sobering. "I know," she whispers, dabbing at my chest with her wet cloth. "We came in at the same time, you and me and Miyuki." She gives me a sidelong glance, her eyes watchful. "The other girls thought we might all be friends, the three of us, but who knows?"

I stare at her, processing this. With all the near-death situations I've been dealing with, I haven't had a lot of time to think about the memories I don't seem to possess anymore, and whether one of those memories was of a pretty girl with perfect hair and a dazzling smile. "Aw, man," I breathe, "if I forgot something like that, that'd be the unluckiest thing ever; to have a girl like you and then lose her."

Her lips quirk again, and she shakes her head at me. "Stop it," she orders, her voice teasing. But her eyes don't dance this time, and I wonder if she's thinking the same thing. Even if we didn't lose each other, there's a good chance we've both lost *someone*.

Yet if we have, there's nothing that can be done about it now. I take her hand, trying not to grimace at the pain as I struggle through movements that were so thoughtlessly easy before. "Sorry. I won't melodrama at you. But, uh. Would you be open to exploring that idea sometime?" I give her another grin. "I seem to win a lot of fights. Should I ask for you next time?"

Aniyah stares. Her hand is soft in mine but slightly limp; not holding me, but not pulling away either. "Maybe," she says, five whole heartbeats later. Her eyes soften again, warm and gentle, and I see temptation there. "We'd be able to talk, at least," she hedges. Her fingers curl against my palm, stroking the skin and sending little shivers of pleasure up my arm in welcome contrast to the pain.

Another moan from Justin ruins the mood; we both start guiltily and she yanks her hand away. I turn my head to see the others finishing up with him, having apparently done all they can do. His leg has been laid out with two thin wooden poles on either side then wrapped heavily with cloth.

The wounds on his chest have been washed and bound in the same way as mine, and the jagged cuts on his face bandaged with gauze. He doesn't look well at all, but he's alive and no longer bleeding; that's got to count for something, right?

Until the Master sends him out again, I think, a gloomy mood descending.

Aniyah turns back to me, her brow knitted with distress. "I'd better get back to Miyuki," she murmurs. "I'll send Tony over to you, okay?" She says his name hesitantly, as if she doesn't feel the word is hers to use.

"Yeah." I give her a sympathetic wince as she rises in her careful way. "You do that. And we'll talk later?"

She hesitates for a moment before nodding. "I'd like that. But don't you die! I mean it."

"I won't," I promise, watching her walk away, then leaning my head back with a sigh.

CHAPTER 19

Aniyah

We stay with the boys until fourth bell, but everything is awkward and awful. Keoki is washed down twice more with healing water from the pool, but I don't return to his side or speak with him again. I'm too aware of Miyuki's bustling presence nearby, directing us as a group and working with xer healing hands.

Instead, I leave his care to Sappho, Hana, and Tony, who together replace his blood-soaked bandages at third bell and keep the fresh ones damp with the magical water we bring in on Handler's cart. Keoki seems uncomfortable on the floor and in too much pain to carry anywhere else, but otherwise stable. He even tries to joke with us, and grins in momentary triumph when he coaxes an eyeroll out of Chloe.

Aside from his jokes, which mostly fall flat, the mood in the cavern is somber. The other boy, Justin, flits in and out of consciousness, moaning weakly and thrashing the leg that isn't wrapped from ankle to thigh. Now that his bones are set and his other wounds bandaged, there isn't much more we can do. Boys hover around him and I manage to coax a sip of water down his throat, but only time will tell if he can be saved.

We do one thing right: we make Miyuki look good. After the bumpy start when Miyuki and I blurted out each other's names, xie swings into command. Xie tells us when to wash the boys, how to bandage them, and when to replace the first batch of stained cloths with fresh ones. For things xie needs help with—like splinting Justin's leg—or when xie absolutely needs xer glasses to see, we're careful to get Handler out of the room first, having him escort Hana and Chloe to the pool for more water.

The purpose of this play is to save Miyuki, but it isn't all an act. Xie focuses xer attention on the boys once they've been made stable, working xer magic to ease their pain. I watch as dark dust pours out from xer fingertips to coat xer hands. The glittering powder soaks into the patients as xie works and, though only I can see the magic, it is undeniably real. Keoki swears his pain drains away at xer touch, and Justin's moans quiet under xer attentions.

For a moment, I'm caught up in my own fiction: I almost believe Miyuki can work miracles, that xer magic can heal them. My eyes know better, though. The dust coating xer hands manipulates muscles and numbs nerves with growing power, but xie can't knit bones back together or close the ragged gashes carved into their skin. We've done all we can for them, and I fear it won't be enough. I ache for these boys to be saved. Keoki is goofy and adorable and, while I don't know Justin, he doesn't deserve to die like this.

My heart weighs heavily in my chest as Handler escorts us back to our grotto at fourth bell. We've already eaten with the boys, though no one was very hungry, so there isn't much left for us to do in this cycle except to put up the bed curtains. Handler makes sure we have enough material left over after what was used to bind Justin's leg to his splint, but his demeanor is once again frosty. The air around him bites with a fearful chill, and his thumb rubs in repetitive motions over the mole at his wrist.

"There will be punishments handed out later," he warns. "Alexandrite, you spoke over the Master in the arena. Decorum was forgotten." I hold my breath, wondering if the breach of protocol is confined to my rash words in front of the strange fey visitor or if this means Handler heard our real names being used. "If the *fighters* recover," he stresses the word, reminding us they're not simply boys and we're not here to be their friends, "the Master will be pleased; but the errors of this cycle must not be repeated."

Hana sets her mouth in a thin line but she maintains her persona of obedient acceptance. "Yes, Handler," she murmurs, her voice meek. I wonder the point of trying to fool him, when he must have heard her barking orders to unload the cart and seen the way she lifted Keoki with only Tony's help. No matter how much she might pretend otherwise, Hana is strong and defiant to her core. Still, Handler seems satisfied.

"You always know your place, Diamond," he observes, his carved hands grasping the bar of his cart as he wheels it to the doors. "Teach the other girls to do the same. As long as they are useful and obedient, they will be retained." His eyeless gaze turns back to regard Miyuki for a long moment, then the doors close behind him with a shuddering groan and he is gone.

Murder flares in Hana's eyes when she turns back to us, but she takes a deep breath to steady herself and the worst of the tension drains from her shoulders. "Everyone did good," she declares, her voice firm. "Aniyah, you took a gamble and it paid off. Now we just need to chase the win. When Handler brings food at first bell, we'll ask him to let Emma check on the boys. You and Imani can go with her. As long as we keep their wounds clean and watered, everything should be fine."

She doesn't sound entirely convinced, and I'm reminded of those same words, *You'll be fine*, when Miyuki and I were dragged away to be thrown to the fighters as Prizes. Hana doesn't mention our mistake with the names, but it's comforting to hear her say we did well. *If there was something better I could have done or said, Hana would tell me. We're all doing the best we can.* Now I just have to hope our best is enough to save Miyuki—and those boys, while I'm busy wishing.

"At first bell, then," Miyuki agrees with a nod. Xie turns to me. "Aniyah, you're hurting. Dip in the water, then my hands?"

I stare, taken aback by the steady assurance in xer no-nonsense tone. "How did you know?" I try to trace the pattern of xer talent, to tell whether it has expanded to visualize my pain the way I can see xer magic, but xer ability seems dormant and I see nothing unusual.

Miyuki gives me an exasperated look, cocking xer hip to one side. "Oh, let me think. Your walking is stilted, your shoulders are stiffer than our beds, and you grimace when you think no one is looking. And Aniyah, I love you—so don't take this personally—but you're reacting to everything a moment later than usual, like your brain and body have both slowed down. C'mon, let's get you in the pool and wash off all that blood."

Xie takes my hand, leading me to the water as I blink back my surprise. I thought I'd been subtle with each careful step, managing to hide the worst of the pain. I don't think the others noticed, which is by design and preference; I don't *want* to be fussed over. Yet somehow it's wonderful to let Miyuki take charge of me. There's a contradiction here I can't unravel and as xie helps me out of my blood-stained wrap and into the water, I wonder if perhaps I like xer pampering simply because it's coming from *xer*.

When we wade into the pool, I find I can move more easily. The water buoys me, granting a delicious sense of weightlessness. Tiny glittering sparkles bubble up from the depths to nibble away at my aches. As the pain ebbs, my mind clears, the thick porridge coating my brain rinsed away by the magic in the water.

"Over there?" I suggest, pitching my voice low so as not to be heard by the other girls. At the far side of the pool where the cavern wall glistens, there is a shadow cast by an overhanging ledge. The patch of shade isn't large, but it's dark enough to give us some privacy after this long cycle which has been so full of people. Right now, I want to be somewhere quiet where we can feel alone.

"Perfect," Miyuki agrees, xer smile softening as xie follows me out. Xie isn't as strong a swimmer as I am, and when we hit deep water xer head dips low as xie furiously treads in place. But when we reach the shade, we find a little underwater ledge extending a few feet from the wall and providing a rough seat to perch upon. Once we're seated, I lean back against the wall while Miyuki hugs xer legs to xer chest.

"So," xie says, drawing the syllable out in a long sigh. "Thank you."

I look up, surprised out of my silent retreat. "For what?" My thoughts catch up the moment the word leaves my mouth and my jaw drops open. "Oh, Miyuki. How could I not?"

Xie smiles at me, xer hazel eyes flashing behind xer glasses in the dim light. "Yeah, but I could've been nicer about it earlier. Sorry. I got caught up in the immediate *'oh shit'* problems. But I really appreciate what you did. Speaking up for me to the Master like that. You were brave and amazing."

My cheeks burn and I look down at my hands. "Miyuki, I... I can't lose you. I don't think I could handle this place without you here."

Xer soft giggle sends a fresh shiver up my spine. "My hands aren't *that* good," xie teases.

I look up and catch xer broad grin, so I know the words are a joke; yet I need xer to know for certain how I really feel. "No, really." I take a deep breath, averting my eyes again. "Miyuki, I care about you. I care about what happens to you. I want to keep you safe, to protect you. You're my friend and I want..."

My voice trails away, unable to put into words how I feel. *I want to kiss you and hold you and take you away from here. I want to have what we had before, when we knew each other and our memories were ours.* Whatever we had, it would have been happy and good, untainted by the dread which hangs over us now.

"What do you want, Aniyah?" xie prompts, xer voice soft.

"I want to protect you." The quiet repetition is all I can manage, my eyes glued firmly to the place where my elbows disappear into the sparkling water. "I want to be with you."

Miyuki slides xer hands down my arms until xie finds my hands in the water. Lacing xer fingers through mine, xie ducks xer head to catch my gaze. "Aniyah, why do you sound so ashamed? I'm glad you want to protect me. Don't you think *I* want to protect *you*?"

"Me?" I jerk my head up, thoroughly confused. "What is there to worry about with me? I'm the expensive one, the one they tell the boys not to hurt. I get to talk back when everyone else has to be silent." I almost spit the words, anger rising in my chest; anger at the Master, anger at Handler, but most of all anger with myself. "And I still went and nearly ruined everything by using the wrong name in front of Handler."

Xie snorts, shaking xer head. "Pretty sure I made the same mistake," xie points out with a grin, "along with telling my first boy not to so much as *touch* me because I was in such a panic at the thought. You're not the only one making mistakes, Ani."

"Yeah, but—" I begin, but xie leans forward to press xer forehead against mine and the words die in my throat at the tantalizing closeness of xer lips to my own.

"You're also the one who has to watch those ugly matches, instead of closing your eyes or turning away like the rest of us. You have to talk to that *thing* who seems perfectly willing to punish you or anyone else for saying things he doesn't like. And they don't do you any favors when they single you out to the boys as something special! Maybe they won't hurt you as much, but how much more will they expect from you as the expensive Prize? I could smack Handler for that," xie adds in a low growl.

I'm aware my grin has turned goofy but I don't care. "Really? You'd smack Handler for me?"

Xer hazel eyes roll derisively at me above a wry smile. "*Aniyah.* I'd do much worse than that for you. I told you earlier: I love you."

I feel my heart jump against my ribcage at xer words. Xie *did* say so earlier, and I'd been too deep in a haze of pain to react. *Miyuki loves me.* All the feelings I have for xer—all the affection, all the protective urges, and

194

perhaps the heat I felt before when we were in bed together—xie feels those things for me? My throat feels thick enough to cry and part of me wants to burst out laughing at my own absurdity. Of course Miyuki loves me. Hasn't xie been telling me so since we awoke? Coming to my bed to comfort me, healing me with xer hands, helping me every step of the way; if that's not love, I don't know what is.

Then the thought strikes me that we may have had this conversation before, in the time our memories forgot. The idea is so hilariously awful that I giggle in giddy abandon, imagining the two of us locked in a cycle of loving and forgetting and loving anew.

"I love you, too," I tell xer, gasping for air. "I'm sorry, I don't mean to laugh. It's just—" Another burst of giggles, worse now that I'm trying to stop. "I love you, and I'll tell you as many times as I have to. As often as you want me to. No matter how many times he makes us forget, I'll still love you."

Miyuki's smile widens to a beaming grin and xie playfully skims water up to splash my face. "As often as I want? Be careful making promises like that, Ani," xie teases. "I saw the way you were looking at that boy. How will you have time to play if all your time is promised to me and my thirst for love declarations?"

I sober instantly, xer words dousing me with colder water than this lukewarm pool. "I... I won't. Miyuki, I won't play with him." My gaze drops away again, unable to meet xer eyes. "Not if you don't want me to." The promise doesn't sit right in my stomach—I feel an instant surge of regret the moment I make it—but I can't bring myself to take it back. I don't want to hurt xer, whatever the cost.

"Aniyah." Miyuki reaches up to grasp my chin, gently guiding my eyes up to xers. With infinite slowness xie leans in, xer lips finding mine for a kiss.

Time stands still. There is only xer soft lips, xer warm breath, xer gentle fingers caressing my cheek. My hands slip around xer back, pulling xer closer with little nudges and encouragements, needing xer body as close as possible to mine. I move my lips over xers in slow exploration, tasting the salt on xer skin and the sweetness of xer tongue when it flicks unexpectedly against me. Far too soon xie pulls away from me, a warm smile on xer face that matches the dancing glitter in xer eyes.

"Was it something I said?" I murmur, feeling light-headed. I lick my lips, savoring the lingering taste and wanting more.

Miyuki caresses my cheek with a feathery stroke of xer fingers, amusement dancing on xer lips. "It was, actually. Aniyah, you're so sweet, but I don't need you to make promises like that. I don't *want* promises like that. I love you for who you are. You loving someone else doesn't change that. How could it?"

I think now my heart really is in my throat. I hadn't expected this, nor even known the possibility existed to be hoped for. "You don't mind?" I remember Sappho's disappointment on finding us together the morning of our second cycle and the way Heather had teased her for being glum. "You won't be upset?"

Miyuki laughs. "Over that skinny guy? No. Just don't expect me to understand what you see in him. Or *them*," xie adds, xer grin widening. "I noticed he has a friend. They might come as a package, you know."

I blink in surprise at xer. "How closely were you watching us?" True, I'd caught Tony clutching Keoki's hand, but he'd let go when Sappho ran up and I never saw him repeat the gesture. There'd been affection there, I was sure of it, but he'd hidden his feelings well.

"Hmm?" Xie smiles vaguely at the question. "Aniyah, I have good eyes—when I have my glasses on!" Nudging closer, xer lips find my ear and brush against the soft skin, sending fresh shivers down my spine. "Now, come here and let me show you what else I'm good at."

From xer tone of voice and the way xer lips linger against my skin, I have an inkling of what xie might mean. Heat rises in my stomach and pools in my legs, faster and more urgent than before. My breath catches;

196

though I don't know the exact specifics of what I want, I know I need xer. Still I hesitate. "Here? Now?" I don't know when or where else we could go, but I certainly don't want everyone watching.

Miyuki laughs softly into my neck, xer lips kissing in light patterns. "We're in the dark. Everyone's drifting off to bed. They can't see through the curtains." I look around the cavern to realize xie's right: Hana and Imani have disappeared into the shelter of their beds; Chloe is coming out of the toilet and moving in that direction; Sappho and Heather are drying off from the pool and redressing, not sparing a glance back for us.

"We'll have to be quiet," I tell xer nervously. We're already nearly on top of one another where we sit on the ledge but I scoot closer, needing to be as close to xer as possible.

"Maybe this will help," xie murmurs, leaning in to seal my lips with xers.

This kiss isn't like the one before; no soft silkiness to brush against, no slow learning movements. Xie covers my mouth with xer own, drinking down my surprised gasp like water. Xer hand rises to touch my nipple just above the surface of the water, eliciting a deeper groan for xer to swallow as a tremor ripples through me. "I want to touch you," xie whispers, xer voice a breath on my lips. "Please, can I?"

I nod, feeling feverish in the cooler water. "Yes. *Yes.* Touch me." Each word slips out in a quiet panting cadence. I want what xie wants, I want this and more, and I want it all as fast as xie will give it to me.

Miyuki giggles and shifts position, lifting and rearranging xerself until one leg curls around behind me. My own legs dangle over the ledge of our seat, pressing into xer as xie pulls me closer. "Let me in?" Xer whisper brushes my ear as fingers playfully urge my knees apart. Soft lips engulf my earlobe, and I have to cover my mouth with my hand to keep from gasping aloud.

"There, right there," I beg. It's not just what xie's doing with xer tongue, it's also what xer fingers are doing as they trace up my legs. They slide up my inner thighs, finding the center where heat pools and I can feel my own heartbeat. Xer thumb strokes gently over the spot and I think I'm about to melt; then xie wriggles a single long finger inside me and my hand tightens over my mouth.

In this moment, I don't even remember what pain is. There's only heat and pleasure and need as xer finger curls into me and strokes slowly from within. Xer thumb plays in long sweeping patterns while teeth and tongue caress my ear, nibbling at the soft lobe. I crane backwards, my back scraping against the cavern wall as I strain to press myself deeper onto xer finger; xie chuckles at my greediness and carefully works a second finger alongside the first.

"Miyuki!" The sound is a ragged gasp of near-panic. My hand is curled into a fist and half-stuffed in my mouth to stop any noise. I want to cry out, I want to thrash in the water, but I can't bear the thought of the others peering out to see me like this.

"I've got you," xie whispers. "Shh. Bite my shoulder, Aniyah. Let yourself go for me."

I barely manage not to scream when the coiling heat erupts. Warmth spreads through my legs and shoots up my back while my mind shatters with colors I thought existed only in the sparkling table. I cling to Miyuki, trembling violently as I suck on xer shoulder.

"I love you, Aniyah," xie repeats, rocking me as I shudder. Xie withdraws xer fingers—though my body seems loath to let them go—and pulls back just enough to kiss me. "Thank you."

I manage a shaky laugh, barely audible against the constant trickle of the nearby waterfall. "You shouldn't be thanking me yet," I whisper, feeling light-headed and giddy in the aftermath of the explosion.

"No?" Miyuki tilts xer head at me, looking curious. "When should I?"

I manage a deep breath, gulping in air as quietly as I can. "After I do all that to you. Starting now." I set my shoulders in determination and resolve to ignore the rubbery looseness of my limbs. "Maybe even *twice*."

Xie giggles and my stomach flips over in the best possible way. "Well, in that case I get one more go at you afterwards. Just to be fair. Then bed and massage and cuddles."

"Deal," I breathe. My fingers reach out, aching to feel the heat inside xer, and I know without a doubt I'm the biggest winner in the Arena.

CHAPTER 20

Keoki

I figured they'd carry us to our rooms but, before Handler leaves, Matías corners him into a tense conversation of which I overhear a few whispered phrases. 'Dangerous to move that leg' and 'easier to set one watch for two patients' drift back to me under the crackle of torches. I also catch urgent snatches involving blankets and a fire, food and water, though we've already eaten a brief joyless meal with the girls.

"The important thing is protecting the Master's investment," Matías insists, his knuckles pale where he grips the handle of his cane. "The sooner they're healed, the sooner they can go back to earning their keep." I don't hear Handler's answer but he returns after he's taken the girls away, his cart loaded with necessities.

Blankets are pulled off the cart, along with a large metal bowl full of tiny black stones and thick slices of wood. It takes four of the guys—Tony, Christian, Reese, and Lucas—all lifting together to get the bowl off the cart and positioned on the floor nearby. Once in place, Lucas pries a torch off the far wall and tosses it in; the slivers of wood flare up almost instantly, providing a cheery blaze that warms the cavern. Tony and Christian put down layers of blankets to make beds and Reese rolls up two more for pillows.

While the others make up our sleeping area, Matías unloads the lower tray of the cart where Handler has stacked bowls of water and steaming food. The carved creature watches him with his impatient eyeless gaze before turning to wheel away the emptied cart. *Good riddance*, I think, flopping my head back.

"Okay, one more lift," Matías announces when Handler has gone. "Tony and Reese, you two take Keoki's head and feet. Then the four of you can move Justin; I want all hands on him to keep that leg steady."

"Up you go, newbie." Tony's voice, cool and distant, comes from behind as his hands slip under my shoulders.

"This is gonna hurt," Reese warns, taking my feet and giving me a sympathetic smile. "But we'll get you on clean blankets and you'll be all set to sleep."

I take a shallow breath, flashing him a quick smile and then gritting my teeth. "Go for it."

"Ready, Tony? One, two, three." He counts, and on the third beat fire shoots through my chest. The pain is raw heat running under my skin, tearing my wounds open under their bindings. I bite the inside of my cheek until a trickle of blood runs over my tongue, but I manage not to scream.

"Down we go!" Reese's voice cuts through the haze as they lower me onto the blankets laid out near the fire. Tony squeezes my shoulder before letting go, silent sympathy flashing over his face as he rises to help the others move Justin. I give him a smile to let him know I'm okay, but feel the strain around my eyes.

Moving Justin from the puddle of drying blood to clean blankets is a four-person ordeal with Matías supervising. The wounded boy cries out in guttural whimpers as they move him, his agony as raw as ever but his voice hoarse after his earlier screaming. They lie him on the blankets near me where the fire can warm us both, but his head lolls away from the bright light.

The other guys plop down on the floor around us, sitting with their knees pulled up to their chests and looking grim. I turn my head to watch Matías, groaning when my shoulder muscles tighten. "So, uh, now that Handler's gone, how bad is he, really?" I nod towards Justin, dreading the answer.

Matías sighs and shakes his head, one hand absently massaging his knee as he stretches his leg. "He's pretty bad. I've seen worse wounds on fighters before, but Justin doesn't have a talent for healing."

"We kept him alive, though," Christian says. He's frowning as he tugs at one of his cornrows. I see a flash of bronze in his hand; the bead for the braid must have gotten jostled off during the lifting and carrying. "That's a start. Usually they kill anyone wounded this badly. Maybe time, and those girls, can fix him."

"Those girls aren't healers," Lucas snorts, scuffing the ground with the back of his heel. "A talent that removes pain isn't healing; it's just another way of giving pleasure. Might as well have that girl mouth-fuck Justin, for all the good it would do."

"The important thing," Reese cuts in, his voice tighter than usual, "is that everyone is alive and kept comfortable. Keoki isn't too badly hurt. I reckon you'll be up and moving around in a cycle or two," he predicts, nodding at me while mustering a smile. "We'll change Justin's bandages when they get dirty, and keep him doused in water. It'll all be *fine*."

"Until next bout," Tony adds, his voice so low I can barely hear him over the crackle of fire.

"Got news on that front," Matías says, looking up with an air of announcement. "Handler says there won't be any more bouts for a while. The Master wants everyone rested up for a big show he's planning."

Christian narrows his eyes. "Did he say what kind of big show?"

"Handler didn't know," Matías admits, shaking his head. "But he did say we'd have an Auction before then. A few cycles from now, when Keoki is feeling better. He wants to boost morale and clear accounts, to keep everyone competitive. So that's something to look forward to."

I don't understand the word 'Auction' in this context, but the mood in the cavern instantly lightens. Lucas perks up and Tony's shoulders relax, the tension rippling out of his arms. Christian leans back with a satisfied grin, hands laced behind his head.

"Man, we *need* an Auction," Christian observes, his rich voice thick with amusement. "Hardest thing is gonna be deciding."

"How *do* the accounts stand?" Lucas asks, leaning forward to focus on Matías. "Did Handler say anything about this bout? Was a kill awarded?"

Reese laughs and claps him heavily on the shoulder. "Worried the newbie has more kills on account than you?" Lucas shakes the hand away, watching Matías for an answer.

Matías seems uninterested in the subject; he shrugs and reaches for a nearby bowl of steaming grain, picking at the food with the tips of his fingers. "There was a kill. I doubt it was awarded to Justin, so I would think Keoki has three to his account now."

Lucas shoots an ugly glare at the ground while Christian chuckles warmly. "Three, huh? Isn't that how many *you* have on account, Lucas?"

Lucas opens his mouth to retort, but Matías cuts in. "I want everyone to rest up as much as possible. We don't know when this big show is and we've had fights dropped on us the cycle after an Auction before, so we need to be prepared. Practice, eat, and sleep. We'll take shifts to watch Justin and keep him drinking. Reese, fill one of these from a room fountain?" He hands an empty bowl to the other boy. "Everyone else should head to bed. Who's taking first watch out here? Reese?"

"I will," Tony says, reaching for one of the bowls of food. "I'm still hungry, anyway. No skin off my back if I stay up a bit longer."

"Just don't eat all the food yourself," Matías warns, a smile tugging at the edge of his lip. "Wake Reese when you get sleepy? Christian can take third watch, then Lucas. I'll take last watch before first bell." There is some token grumbling, quickly subsiding; the tangy scent of blood lingering in the air drains any will to argue.

Plan in place, Matías grips the center of his cane and wedges it into the cave floor, using the angle to lever himself up while holding his bowl with his free hand. The other boys grab food for themselves to take back to their rooms, though the bulk of the feast is left behind. Reese returns with water and manages to get several sips down Justin's throat before the wounded boy turns his head away, lost in a haze of agony.

Reese leaves the water bowl on the floor, pausing to squeeze my good shoulder. "You're gonna be fine, newbie," he promises. "Just focus on getting better, okay?" I grunt agreement and watch as he walks to his room with dragging footsteps. I wonder how hard he will take it if Justin dies before Reese wakes.

How often have they had to do this? The thought strikes me as Tony settles down near my makeshift bed, picking through the bowls in search of something he can't seem to find. I haven't even lost anyone yet, and already I feel like a part of me is about to snap. I can't imagine doing this again and again, watching friends die without any relief in sight.

"You hungry?" Tony asks, not looking at me. He's frowning as he picks through the bowls, his brow knit deeply with annoyance; he looks personally offended. "The food is always shit. They serve better stuff at auction, but it's still not *right*. Here, we'll have to make do."

Without waiting for an answer, he pulls a small bread roll from one of the bowls. I watch as he breaks it open from the bottom, his deft fingers tearing out the fluff at the center. He scoops up a hunk of meat from another bowl, shreds it, and stuffs the meat into the hollowed-out shell. "Here," he says, shoving his creation at me. "It's not quite right, but that's the best I can do."

I take the roll with what I hope is a properly grateful expression, trying not to grin at the adorable intensity written in his face and shoulders. "Thanks." I bite in, and my eyes flutter closed as the taste rolls over my tongue. The combination of crunchy crust with soft meat tugs at my memory, words and images and scents all roiling over each other. "It's a manapua?" I ask, the word warm and familiar on my lips.

Tony looks up in surprise, brushing hair from his eyes. "What? No, it's supposed to be a cha siu bao. Reese calls it a pork sandwich, but that's not the right word." He shrugs, glancing away. "Anyway, the taste isn't the way I want it. Never is."

I nod, too busy savoring another bite of the meat-filled roll to speak. He's right that it's not quite what it should be, but it's close enough to resurrect a memory. I find myself blinking back tears as I eat, frustrated by the gap between the way things are here and the way they *ought* to be.

When I look up, Tony is watching me with a grave expression, understanding in his dark eyes. "So," he says. His voice is soft, almost gentle, and he hands me another roll before biting into one of his own. "You gonna try to snag that girl at Auction? She was making all kinds of eyes at you."

I could kiss him for changing the subject, happy to talk about anything that will distract me from crying over my dinner like a fool. "The pretty goddess with the kinky hair? Oh, *yes*. Well, probably; first, someone needs to tell me what Auction actually is," I add, sticking my tongue out at him.

He chuckles, giving me a teasing grin. "I forget you're such a newbie, Newbie. Auction is a big party. We get to visit the girls' room. It's got a pool so you can take a real bath instead of just washing with the room fountains. They serve better food there. The girls dance and sing and flirt and stuff. Everyone picks a girl to take back to his room. More kills on your account means you get to pick first, but as long as there's enough girls to go around, no one goes without. It's a reminder to work hard."

My eyes are wide by the time he finishes; the whole thing sounds amazing. "Girls, food, *and* swimming? But we have to wait until I'm up and about? That's torture. So that's why Lucas was upset about my kills?"

Tony nods, poking through the bowls as he talks but failing to find anything else he wants to eat. "I dunno how Handler will decide which of you gets first choice if you two are tied. Lucas likes going first. He usually picks Emerald because he thinks she's pretty and she isn't too mouthy, but new girls are always popular for the variety. Plus, Handler said your crush was valuable. Did you catch her talent, by any chance? Might be a good one."

"She's the *best* one," I tell him, leaning back and smiling at the memory of her face. "Her talent is being perfect in every way. If I get her, you're gonna come share though, right? Pass the water."

He laughs at my question, passing over the water bowl and holding it so it doesn't splash on me when I lean up to drink. "Not during Auction! You're on your own then; I'm getting my own girl."

I hope my disappointment isn't written on my face; to fill the silence, I wipe my mouth with the back of my hand, moving slowly so as not to disturb the wounds on my chest and side. "Who are you gonna try to nab, if you're not planning to spend the time with me?"

"I'm in permanent competition with Reese over Diamond," he says lightly, leaning back on his elbows beside me. I can feel the closeness of his body heat near my skin, a feeling separate and distinct from the glow of the nearby fire. "She's almost as good a trainer as Matías. If Reese snaps her up first, maybe I'll pick the healer and give her my bed; she did us a solid, so I figure I kinda owe her."

Us. I nod, trying to stay cool and ignore the pounding of my heart in my chest when he says the word so casually. "She really did. She's cute, though; you think the competition will be fierce for her?"

Tony shrugs. "Hard to say. Christian's torn between Ruby and Amethyst; he'd pick Ruby every time without question, except Amethyst does his braids and it's about that time again. And neither of the new girls is Matías' type; he likes them older, since he's been here awhile and feels bad picking the younger ones. I think he'd opt out of Auction entirely except he really does want the sex. He just never gets emotional over the girls. Don't get me wrong; he's friendly with them, just never acts romantic like Christian and some of the other guys do. He doesn't fall for guys, either." His gaze slides away from mine. "Guess that makes him smarter than everybody else."

Silence stretches out for a long moment. I think about what it must mean to live in this place, making friends and lovers only to watch them die. My hand reaches out, seeking Tony's and finding it—warm and gentle, resting a few inches from mine. Strong, too, with calluses where he grips his sword in practice.

He doesn't pull away from my touch, and after a moment's hesitation his hand squeezes me. Liquid fire flows from his hand into mine, spreading through my body until I think I might melt into a puddle from the heat of him. "You will come and share, though?" I ask him, staring into the darkness above us. "Not at Auction, but some other time? She's so pretty and, well, I'd like that."

"Oh, sure," he answers, his voice matching mine in volume. He tucks his free hand behind his head, leaning back on it like a pillow. "If she'll let me. I liked her."

I turn my head to grin at him, relief flooding through me. "Dude, how can she *not* like you? Have you met you?" His wry smile sends another wave of heat through me; emboldened, I take a deep breath and plunge forward. "You could come visit other times, you know. Not just when I have a Prize." Anxious energy forms a knot in my stomach. "You, uh, didn't come back after Handler took the last one away."

He gives me a sheepish smile, almost wincing. "Yeah, I'm sorry about that. I got in bed after the girls left. Figured I'd lie there for a bit until the other guys were asleep, but I passed out instead." He squeezes my hand again, his dark eyes studying me. "I really *will* come visit, Keoki. It's just... we gotta be careful."

I watch him in the firelight, the flickering flames casting dancing shadows over his face. I hate that I can't lie on my side to see him more easily; I'm stuck flat on my back, my neck bending at an uncomfortable angle. "Okay," I say, nodding slowly. "Why, though? I noticed you act kinda different when the guys are around." *In a pretend-I-don't-exist kind of way,* I don't add aloud.

He takes a deep breath, reaching up with his free hand to rub his eyes. "If Handler finds out that we like each other, things could get real bad."

I frown. "Bad how?"

He shakes his head, his eyes fixed on the expanse above. "They use it against you. Schedule matches together, knowing you'll work extra hard to keep the other alive, and that it'll be more emotional if one of you dies. Might even schedule a one-on-one match us against each other, if they thought it would be dramatic enough." He shivers in spite of the heat.

I stare at him, bile rising in my throat. "Tony?" My voice sounds small to my ears. "Did they do that to you?"

He shakes his head but still doesn't look at me. "No. Matías said they did it once that he knows of. He was a newbie when it happened, and the whole stable nearly rioted over it. The Master purged a bunch of fighters and everyone calmed down, but it hasn't been done again." He takes a ragged breath and turns to face me, pain in his dark eyes. "But the thing about pairing people together for drama? Yeah."

Time slows as the implications of his words sink in and I begin to comprehend the pain etched onto his face. "Tony, I'm so sorry."

He squeezes my hand tighter. "It was a long time ago," he says. His voice is softer now, almost hoarse. "Matías and Reese are the only ones left who remember; everyone else has passed on and been replaced. It was a pretty good show for the audience. Not so much for me."

I swallow back the lump in my throat. I shouldn't make his grief all about me, but damned if I don't want to hug him to pieces right now. "I'm so sorry," I repeat, my thumb stroking his hand. "It's no wonder you're so, uh."

Amusement flickers in his dark eyes as he blinks back tears. "Guarded?" he prompts, smiling wryly at my having talked myself into a corner.

"I was gonna say 'quiet'," I insist, pulling out my most dignified voice for the full effect.

His grin widens but his expression is soft in the firelight. It's amazing how gentle he looks when we're alone and he allows his features to relax. I wish more than anything that I could take him away from this place. I'm not sure where we'd go or what it would look like, but he'd never have to wear that stony mask again.

"The guys are mostly okay, and they'd probably keep a secret," he adds, closing his eyes. "But some of the guys before were jerks about it, and I just don't want to deal with that again. Even Christian can say stupid shit sometimes. It's easier this way, with no one knowing."

I nod, determined to understand. I don't think stupid shit would bother *me*, but his comfort is more important than my ego. "Sorry I got cranky earlier, before my fight. I didn't realize."

He opens his eyes again, blinking back fresh tears. "I'm sorry, too. I knew Justin wouldn't be much help, and I was afraid you'd be killed out there. I'm glad you weren't, but." His gaze sweeps my bloodied bandages and the cuts that stretch from my shoulder to my waist. "It hurts that I can't protect you. That I can't protect *anyone*. If I'm not out there in the arena, there's nothing I can do but watch. I hate it."

"Hey." I tug on his hand, prompting him to move closer; he rolls until his face hovers over mine, his eyes studying my own. "I'm not gonna die. You won't lose me, Tony. I promise."

"You're reckless," he points out, giving me a wary look.

"I know." I laugh, shaking my head. "I admit it, you've got me there. But I don't want to hurt you. I won't be reckless like that again. Next time, I'll listen to you. I'll be really super careful. Honest."

"You promise?" The question hangs in the air between us, his lips less than a finger's breadth from my own.

"Promise," I breathe. With my good hand, I reach up to tangle my fingers in his hair. I mean to pull him down for a kiss, but he's there before me; his mouth covers mine in a long, slow, sweet kiss that drives away every thought of pain until there is only him and the fire and the warmth from them both.

"You promised," he whispers in a teasing tone, his dark eyes dancing at me. His lips brush against mine as he speaks, all feathery touch and soft anticipation before he leans in to claim another kiss, harder and more deliberate than the first.

I nod under the slow onslaught of his mouth, not wanting to break away but needing to reassure him, to make him *know* he won't be hurt the way he was before. "I did. I do. I swear." As I gasp out the words, I blink back tears of my own. My hand loosens its grip on his hair, and he turns his cheek into my palm as I slide my fingers down the length of his jaw. "I'm not gonna die, Tony."

"You'd better not," he agrees, his voice hoarse. "I'm getting kind of attached to you, Keoki. Now shut up and kiss me. We don't have nearly enough time until I have to wake Reese to take his watch."

I grin, my good hand moving to pull him closer. "We'd better make every kiss count, huh?" His leg is like fire pressed against mine and his hands trail liquid heat as they move over my arm and shoulder, avoiding my wounds yet determined to touch as much of me as possible. My mouth finds his in a series of desperate kisses that stretch and merge into one long embrace that, in a perfect world, would go on forever.

CHAPTER 21

Aniyah

When first bell chimes, I groan and pull our blanket over my head. I don't want to leave the bed; I feel sleepy and stupid and stiff all over. Miyuki and I stayed up long past the others and I can't bring myself to regret a moment of it, even if means I now have to face the cycle in a shambling stupor. Being tired is a small price to pay for the memory of Miyuki's soft little gasps as xie wriggled on my fingers.

I have fewer fond feelings towards the stiffness that thrums through my spine and reaches out with gaunt fingers to infect the rest of my body. The numb paralysis in my hips and legs frightens me. I don't know what is hidden under my scars, or the meaning of the tattoo scrawled on my hip—*bent not broken*—but each awakening in this place has been more painful than the last. It's harder to move, harder to twist and bend, harder to think; the constant dull ache crowds out all other thoughts.

I don't know why I'm getting worse, and this scares me. Does something about this place increase the pain that lives deep inside me, nestling in the core of my spine? Or did I have some means of decreasing it before, back in the home from which I was taken? I have to believe the dull agony threading through me isn't normal, because the alternative is more than I can bear.

We do leave the bed eventually, of course. Sappho's bright greeting and the sunlight she brings when she pulls down our bed curtains penetrate the blanket I've thrown up against the world. Miyuki coaxes me gently from our slab with kind words and soft kisses, xer hands never straying far from my back. Wherever xie touches me the ache eases, yet I notice the effect seems weaker now and its duration shorter. I'm grateful for xer touch and crave xer fingers in more ways than one, but the specter looms that my pain may soon be more than xie can banish.

It wasn't like this before. The thought repeats on a loop in my mind as I brood over the cold food Handler brings with the bell. The lethargic sameness of this place obliges me to repeat that fact, to hold onto it even as time seems to flatten. *It wasn't like this the first time I woke. Something is wrong.*

I look around the table at the faces of the other girls, wondering if they might know the answer. Hana knows so much about everything, and Imani knew how to set Justin's broken leg. But no one meets my eyes and the mood in our cavern is noticeably subdued since the last match. I look at the food before me, my resolve wavering. Even if everyone were in a talkative mood, I don't think they can help me with this. I'm not sure they'd even understand; none of them have scars that span the length of *their* bodies.

After we eat, Handler takes Miyuki to the boys' cavern. I'd planned to go with xer, to help with the healing and to see Keoki; but Handler is harsh again, cold and unfeeling when Hana questions him. "Prizes are valuables to be won," he declares, his unseeing gaze singling me out with an accusatory air. "They lose their luster when they become too familiar. Save your flirting for Auction." He grips Miyuki by the arm and ushers xer out, my heart in my throat at each careful step xie is forced to take without the aid of xer glasses.

I wait for their return, antsy through the slow progression of bells. When he finally brings xer back, xie is fine; tired and pale, but with a wry smile set firmly on xer face. I wait until Handler leaves before covering xer in hugs and anxious kisses, no longer caring if the other girls see. Xie wipes tears from the corners of xer eyes before putting xer glasses back on after the first rush of kisses, but there's not a trace of sorrow in xer beautiful face. "I missed you," xie whispers, leading me back to the pool and eventually to bed.

Another cycle passes, falling into the same numbing pattern as the one before. We rise to eat, Miyuki leaves to tend the fighters, and we wait for xer return. Hana exercises, Chloe cleans, Imani swims or tells stories she makes up, her animated face changing for the parts of the characters. She's always a young woman, and always lovely to my eyes, but otherwise her capacity for variety seems infinite. Sappho draws patterns in the dusty floor while Imani talks, and Heather sleeps—or pretends to.

When the stories are over and Imani returns to the pool to swim laps, I walk the length of the cavern, counting each step until the pain becomes too much and I slip into the healing waters. As I float in the deep end, I stare at the doors that keep us trapped here and wonder if anything could pry them open. Magic flickers over their surface, tendrils waiting for Handler to approach so they might reach out to caress his mutilated face and hands.

Time blurs, becoming difficult to mark, and I find myself counting events. I've woken six times in this place when Handler reports that 'Granite' has healed enough to move freely and an Auction will be held on the next cycle. The other girls seem to know what that means and nod in silent agreement. After he leaves, Hana sits down with us at the table and I can tell she's preparing for another of her explanations. From the determined set of her lips, I imagine this event is not one she anticipates with any pleasure.

"What *is* Auction?" Miyuki asks. "The boys were talking about it when I went to change Justin's bandages. Some of them teased me, asking whether they ought to pick me. I didn't know what they meant." I frown at the image of boys bothering xer. I'm just as ignorant as xie on what

'Auction' might mean, but the word is ugly in my mind, conjuring images of shouting and grabbing, captivity and misery.

"When the boys fight, they're awarded a point for each kill they make," Hana explains. "So one boy might have five points, and another only three. Every so often, an Auction is held to clear accounts. Back in Heather's time, that meant bringing girls out one at a time and letting boys bid on them as a competition." Her voice deepens, taking on a lower tenor as she acts out a demonstration. "Next up is Emerald. One point for Emerald! I bid two points! No, three points! Going once, going twice, sold for three points."

I blanch, my head jerking back as though I could avoid the event by moving away from the person explaining it. Hana nods, looking sympathetic. "Yeah," she agrees, "it wasn't fun. It was rowdy and sometimes violent; the boys would fight and Handler would have to break them up. It was supposed to be a relaxing event to motivate the fighters, but it just wound them up and made them angrier. So the Master changed the rules, about the time I was brought in. Every boy gets a girl, assuming there are enough to go around, and the boys take their pick in order of who has most points. The one with the highest score goes first and has the most options; the one with the fewest points has to take whoever is left over."

Miyuki's lips twist unhappily. "Do they line everyone up?"

Hana shakes her head, her wavy hair slipping over her shoulder. "No. They did for awhile, but it was awkward. Being chosen last isn't complimentary, and the boys got restless waiting their turn. At this point, Auction is more of a party. The fighters visit here; we talk and flirt while Handler serves better food than usual. The boys get to swim, which is good for everyone." She rolls her eyes, her nose wrinkling in distaste.

Chloe laughs as she strolls over to pick through the food strewn over the table. "They don't smell *that* bad, Hana," she teases, settling on a bowl of tiny purple grapes. "They do bathe in their rooms after the fights. Usually."

"Folks pair off," Imani murmurs. I turn to find her seated beside me, soaking in the conversation as she pats her short hair dry after her swim.

"The boys with the most points know in advance where they stand and have their pick in mind. Handler leaves the doors open during Auction, and people drift back to the boys' rooms without making a fuss." She shrugs, twisting a finger through her black ringlets one at a time. "Some of the boys used to get nervous before, when everything was a big show. This way is... more intimate. More comfortable."

I glance back at Miyuki, whose expression looks as *un*comfortable as I feel. "Do we get any kind of choice? At all?" I remember the pretty boy, Keoki, and how his eyes watched me wherever I moved in the cavern. I'd wanted to spend more time with him, and a party where we could chat together might be nice; but the thought of being stuck at that party with some other boy, unable to speak with the one I want, sounds utterly miserable to me.

"No," Heather says, her voice blunt as she lies unmoving on her bed. "You don't get a choice. You go with the one who picks you, and you do as he says, and you come back alive. That's your job. It doesn't matter that Chloe only wants the smoke-popper, or that Imani wants to be in love first, or that Sappho doesn't like being touched by boys, or that Hana doesn't want to be touched by anyone ever. You're not here to *choose*." She stares up at the ceiling, her green eyes desolate.

"There are ways," Hana corrects, not looking at Heather. "You're new here, so it will be harder for you, but there *are* ways to make them happy on your own terms. I teach fighting. Imani braids hair and tells stories. Sappho dances, and some of the boys like to watch her and touch themselves so she doesn't have to. You'll learn what you can do and most of them will adjust around you." She hesitates, choosing her words carefully. "Never forget we live and die around their happiness, but most of them don't *want* to hurt you."

"Until they don't get their way," Heather adds in an undertone that no one acknowledges.

We go to bed soon after, as no one wants to talk any more. Miyuki holds me close and moves xer hands over the throbbing spots in my lower back and upper shoulders. I watch xer face as xie works, concentration knitting xer freckled brow. The thought strikes me that I won't be able to protect xer during auction. Xie will be taken off alone just as xie was before. "Miyuki?" I whisper, my voice low in the shelter of the curtains.

"Mmm?"

"Who are you going to try to get?" I ask, studying xer with worried eyes. "At the Auction, I mean. You said the boys ask if they should pick you. Are you going to encourage one of them? Will you be okay?" I know I will be, if only because Handler told them to keep me in one piece, but my stomach clenches at the thought of one of those boys hurting xer. Xie had been so panicky at the prospect of being touched.

Miyuki shrugs, looking unconcerned. "I imagine they'll send me to Justin," xie says. Air rushes back into my lungs at the obvious solution; of course they'll pair him off with his healer. "If not, I'll ask for the friend of your new friend. He seemed polite."

I can't help but smile. "That's twice you've mentioned Tony, you know," I tease. "You *sure* you don't have a crush on him?"

Miyuki swats playfully at my shoulder. "I'm sure. Now hold still, Aniyah. I need to concentrate!"

When we wake at first bell, I could almost imagine this cycle is the same as any other were it not for the fresh rush of pain screaming through my spine. I don't know why, but every breath sends a sharp stab through my ribs. I choke down my pain, determined not to be a burden, and rise to eat before Miyuki leaves to tend the wounded. When the doors slam behind xer, I move slowly back to our bed, knowing there will be no walking for me this cycle. Yet I'm intercepted by the other girls, who herd me into the pool to wash for Auction.

The following session of washing bodies, scrubbing faces, and delicate hair care would be traumatic for me, but the liquid fire rippling from the base of my spine to the tip of my skull blocks out everything else. Once or twice I catch Hana looking at me with an alarmed expression, but she says nothing as I'm patted dry by Imani. Chloe then spends far too long dressing me, fussing over the hang of my clothes and the knotting at my waist until I sway on my feet and have to be helped to the table cushions.

I feel dizzy and the room spins around me. Imani sits nearby, rubbing gentle circles over my back until Miyuki returns. Xie looks around the room in unseeing confusion at my failure to approach xer on arrival, but Sappho surreptitiously leads xer to my side while Hana and Chloe unload dishes from Handler's cart. "The boys will be brought at fourth bell," he announces, giving Hana a stern look before sweeping out. Miyuki's glasses are on the moment the doors clang closed, xer arms wrapping protectively around me.

"Aniyah! Are you okay? What's wrong?" Deft fingers fly over my spine, searching for the pain.

I shake my head, dizziness making my tongue thick. "Missed you. 'S all." The slur in my voice startles me, and a rush of euphoria hits me as Miyuki's fingers grind hard into my skin.

"*Aniyah*. Baby, don't you pass out on me! Come on, sit up straight and I'll get what magic I can into you. Sappho, can you get a damp cloth? Thank you." Strong hands grip me, holding me up when all I want to do is slump over onto the table. I can feel my pain edging away under xer concentration but my mind struggles to clear.

"Miyuki, what am I going to do?" The slur is gone, but rising fear replaces the giddiness.

Xer hands don't pause for an instant, the glitter of xer magic pouring into me as fast as xie can work. "You're going to be fine," xie declares, and xer tone is so certain that I feel foolish imagining otherwise. "The boys will come soon, and we'll set you up with Keoki. He's doing so much better since you saw him last. You two can have a bite to eat and then go back to his room. He'll take care of you."

I twist to look at xer face, catching a worried glance between Miyuki and Hana. *We live and die around their happiness.* I hear her words echo in my head. But Keoki liked me, and he was nice to Miyuki and Hana. He won't care if I'm a little dizzy or if I can't do... whatever he might be expecting me to do. *Anyway, I'm too important to the Master to kill,* I remember, bitter bile in my throat.

"We're going to be fine," I manage to whisper, leaning into Miyuki's touch. "We all are."

Hana insists Miyuki clean up before the boys come, but xie bathes quickly and returns to wrap xer arms around me. "I love you," xie whispers again and again, xer voice fierce in my ear. A distant part of my mind wonders why xie is so worried; I'm the expensive one, after all. I ought to be worried about xer, not the other way around. I feel too dizzy to answer, so I just squeeze xer hand each time and nod against xer cheek. The room has stopped spinning, but every thought seems to come from a distance.

The golden doors grind against the floor as the fourth bell rings. Even before they've fully opened, I hear boys' voices, loud and giddy. They're different from before, no longer cowed and eager to obey our healer for the sake of their friends. Now they're a cacophony of joyful chaos, spilling into the room with eager grins and hooting as they peel off their clothes and leap into the pool. Christian, the beautiful one I was given to before, runs over and grabs Chloe by the hands. Laughing, he coaxes her into the pool and the pretty red-headed girl flashes a warm grin at the boys whenever they swim up to her.

I watch their antics with a detached smile, leaning back into Miyuki's embrace. The room is brighter than usual to my eyes, glittering harshly in every direction. My gaze finds the pretty curly-haired boy in the water, and a little jolt of electricity ripples through me when he looks at me. He grins, his smile wide and confident, and I'm glad to be sitting down because my knees turn to water. "You gonna be okay?" Miyuki murmurs in my ear as he rises naked from the pool and begins toweling off.

"I'll be okay," I promise, squeezing xer hand. "What will you do?"

Miyuki chuckles, rising to xer feet and adjusting xer clothes carefully. "I'm going to go talk to Handler. They didn't bring Justin because it's still not safe to move him. I'd like to change his bandages again."

Xie walks away with a purposeful stride, xer path taking xer directly alongside Keoki as he walks towards our table. I see xer mouth move, murmuring words to him, and I catch his cheerful nod. Then he's plopping down beside me, folding his leg underneath him and reaching for a nearby bowl of fruit like he's at home here.

"Heya," he says with an easy grin. He bites into a plump golden fruit and his eyes flutter closed for a moment. "*Wow*, this is good. Have you had one of these?" He pushes the bowl at me, his warm eyes watching me with interest.

I shake my head at him, feeling my smile spread slowly; I'm still disoriented and already missing Miyuki's healing touch. "I think the food is supposed to be for you," I point out. I reach up to push a curl away from my eyes, and his hand catches mine in midair. Heat flows through us where we touch, warm and liquid and good, then he palms a fresh fruit into my hand.

"Try one," he whispers, ducking his head like a conspirator. "I won't tell."

I bring the golden fruit to my lips and take a deep breath to savor the rich scent. The smell is heady and thick, a dark fullness that doesn't seem at home in this stony place where we live. My mind fills in shadows and shade, the darkness of the arena when the sun was blotted out for the Master's private match. I take a tiny bite and a moan escapes my throat as the rich juice bursts over my tongue.

"Isn't it, though?" He grins, watching my enjoyment with open pleasure before reaching out to touch my lips with the tip of his finger. "Drip," he explains. "So, uh, hey. Your friend says you feel a little out of—"

"Shove over, newbie." His remark is interrupted by a boy with sandy-brown hair who stalks up, the hint of a frown knitted on his brow. He shoots me a warmer smile, dipping into a bow as he waits for Keoki to move. "Scoria, at your service. They said your name was Alexandrite?"

I hesitate, not knowing how to answer, but Keoki breaks in before I speak. "Her name is 'mine'," he says, reaching for another fruit and not moving from his seat beside me. "At least for Auction, Lucas."

The older boy glares at him, anger flaring in his eyes at Keoki's casual tone. "You seem to have forgotten I have as many kills as you, newbie, and seniority to boot. She's not yours until I decide she's not mine." His hand, still damp from the dip in the pool, reaches out to caress my curls. I try not to flinch away at the unexpected contact but my stomach knots at the sensation of a stranger touching my hair.

"Wouldn't you rather have a veteran than a kid, pretty Prize?" Scoria— *or is it Lucas?*—smiles down at me and I try to smile back, but the politely bared teeth I offer up to him can't possibly reach my eyes. I feel a fresh wave of pain at being made to bend my neck like this and sway in my seat.

"Scoria!"

A bright voice breaks the gathering tension. Sappho trips up, her blue eyes glittering with laughter, and grabs his hand with both of hers. He glares at the interruption, but she doesn't seem to notice. "Scoria, you have to come help judge the game! We're gonna blindfold Emerald and kiss her. She has to guess who it is, but we need judges to make sure no one whispers the answers. C'mon, I get first kiss, but don't tell!"

The sandy-haired boy hesitates, but Sappho tugs at him again and he nods. "Sure. Yeah. Just for a few rounds, though. Is Diamond gonna kiss her, too?" Despite his frown, interest creeps into his voice as she leads him away.

"Oh, gosh, do you think we can get her to?" Sappho gushes, wrapping an arm around his waist. She glances back at me once, a triumphant grin on her face, and nods meaningfully at the wide open golden doors. I mouth a prayer of relief back at her. *Thank you. I'll make it up to you.*

I look back to Keoki, who watches the other boy being led away with a small smile on his face, seeming amused. "Hey." I reach out to cover his hand with mine, seeking his gaze. My heart is pounding in my throat; I know what I want, but it's harder to spit it out than I would have imagined. "Can we get out of here? Now? Get back to your room before anyone notices we're gone?"

His breath catches in his throat; I can see the moment when his chest breaks its normal rhythm. "Yeah," he agrees, nodding at me with suddenly solemn eyes. "Yeah, I think we can. You good to stand? Here, I've got you." Rising easily, he reaches down his hand to help me up. "Let's go, Aniyah."

CHAPTER 22

Keoki

My eyes need a moment to adjust when we plunge from the sunny grotto into the darkened hallway. I pull up beside the open golden doors, out of sight of the guys inside. Leaning against the wall, I watch the flickering torchlight as it casts dancing shadows over the corridor that stretches back to our cavern.

Aniyah halts when I do, drawing near until our arms touch. I turn my hand, seeking her dangling fingers and lacing mine through the spaces between them; for a moment we stand still in the quiet semi-darkness and enjoy the sensation of touching like this. Her hand is soft and delicate, lacking a fighter's calluses. She brushes her fingers against mine and I shiver at the silken pleasure that ripples through me.

"You said we could go back to your room?" she prompts, her smile curving up at the edges with a wry twist.

I could die from that smile. My voice is husky, pitched low to match her whisper. "I'd like that."

Yet I hesitate for the length of a heartbeat, wrestling with doubt. I remember being with Diamond after my first fight, and Miyuki after my second. I'm pretty sure Aniyah likes me the way Tony does—and the way

Diamond and Miyuki *didn't*—and she isn't just trying to please me, but I need to be certain.

"Only if you want to, though," I tell her, searching her eyes. "I could smuggle you into Christian's room, if you like him better. Or we could go back inside and I could keep Lucas off your back while you pick someone else, you·know?"

Her smile widens in a slow spread that threatens to stop my heart. "No, I want to go to *your* room," she says, meeting my eyes without hesitation. She giggles in the darkness. "I mean, I would have liked to swim in the pool with you and talked for a while, but your room was where I wanted to end up. Your friend just sped things along."

I take a deep breath and offer her a dazzling grin. "He does that," I tell her in a confiding tone, pushing off from the wall. "He's not bad, I shouldn't bust on him, but he tends to shit all over everyone's fun."

She giggles again, covering her mouth with her free hand. "We have one of those, too. I guess you'll meet Heather properly one of these cycles."

I can't remember which one is Heather but that doesn't stop me from chuckling, her good humor impossible to resist. I sweep my gaze over her in the dim light, partly for the pleasure of looking but also in search whatever illness Miyuki seemed to think had struck her friend. She'd whispered a warning to me when she passed, but Aniyah seems fine; she's happy and giggling, and doesn't seem ill. *Was it just nerves?*

She twists shyly away from my gaze, looking down the hall behind us in the opposite direction from our rooms. "What do you suppose is back there?" she murmurs, her voice dropping into a dreamy cadence.

I peer at the dark stretch of hallway that curves into darkness. "I don't know. You think there's another stable of fighters?"

It's a joke, but the thought hits me that this could be the case; there could be pockets of boys and girls all over this place, not just our own little group. Her eyes meet mine and I see the same thought written on her face, the dawning possibility that there might be more of us. "Do you wanna find out?" I whisper.

"Yes." The word is drawn out in a long hesitant whisper and when she takes a step in that direction, her movements are sluggish, as if she isn't quite sure of this decision now that she's made it. We haven't been expressly forbidden from wandering the halls, but that doesn't mean it isn't dangerous and I wonder if the same concern has occurred to her. If we're caught, there might be consequences.

"Oh, hey. Hold up." I reach out to touch her—not roughly, my fingers barely brush her arm above the elbow—but she sways and topples over, crumbling slowly to the ground.

I reach for her in a panic, trying to steady her; but her legs have gone limp and she continues to fall. I stoop as she crumples, sliding my hands over her body as I grapple for purchase; trusting to my strength, I manage to wrap my arms around her waist and hoist her up. I end up standing with a girl slung across my arms, wondering what exactly happened.

Aniyah gasps in a very delayed reaction. Her face is close enough to mine for me to feel her breath on my cheek, and as I peer at her in the dim light I realize her pupils are heavily dilated. She looks dizzy, her gaze focused on a point over my shoulder as though she can't find my face.

"Hey," I whisper, studying her with concern. "Are you okay? Miyuki said you were sick."

She sighs and leans into my chest. "I've been hurting bad all cycle. I got dizzy for a moment. It'll pass."

A loud burst of laughter can be heard from inside the sunlit grotto. Quickly, I turn in the direction of my room, carrying her in long strides to the best safety I can offer. "What do you mean you're hurting? Are you wounded? Should I get Miyuki to come heal you? She'd patch you right up."

She looks up at me with a soft smile. "You think so?"

"Yeah!" I give her an encouraging nod as we pass through the ugly iron doors to our cavern, now flung open. "She's done wonders with me and Justin. He still can't walk and doesn't wake up much, but you can tell he hurts a lot less than he otherwise would, you know? And she's so good to

224

me; touches the scars on my chest and the pain vanishes for a whole cycle. Amazing! She could help you— oh."

I cease singing her friend's praises as the obvious drives its way home. "But you already know she can do that," I add, giving her a lopsided grin and feeling awkward. "And she already knows you're in pain."

"I do and she does," Aniyah admits, her gentle smile never wavering. "I'm glad to hear she helps you so much, though. Please don't drop me," she adds as we reach the door to my room.

I chuckle, pushing the door open with my foot. "Drop you? Don't you know I'm the strongest dude here?"

Aniyah's lips quirk at the edges as she tries not to laugh. "Yes, I do have eyes in my head," she teases. "I just, uh, need you to know that if you drop me on this floor, it will probably kill me."

I wince and tighten my arms around her, carrying her to my bed. Once I've laid her down, I retreat to close the door; Tony said he wouldn't be coming, and I don't want Lucas dropping in to whine at us. Then I flop onto the floor beside the bed, looking up at her. She lies with her eyes open, studying the glowing ceiling.

"So, uh. Her magic doesn't work on you?" Looking up at those wide eyes, I feel a sudden pang of guilt. "Are Justin and me using it all up? The magic, I mean?"

She blinks, looking thoughtful. "Noooo," she says, the word rolling slowly off her tongue. "I don't think so, anyway. There's something wrong with me, but I'm not sure what."

I try not to grin. "That's ridiculous. There's nothing wrong with you. You're perfect."

I'd expected her to smile, but instead she sighs and shakes her head. "I'm not perfect, Keoki. I *hurt*, I couldn't begin to describe how much. I can't do things; I can't even do what I wanted to do with you. And I'm— Well, I suppose you'll see sooner or later. Help me."

I'm not sure what she's doing; her hips lift and she squirms in place while patting down her clothes. She pulls at knots in her wrapped fabric, and I realize she's trying to undress. *Oh. Okay, then.* I help her, unwinding gauze from under her as she lifts with her legs. My hands tremble from trying not to touch more than necessary; it's not that I don't *want* to touch her, but I feel like we've skipped a few steps.

She kicks her discarded clothes to the ground and lies on my thin mattress in naked glory. Her brown skin glistens with a soft sheen under the phosphorescent light and my eyes sweep over her in a slow caress of appreciation. I'm not sure what I've done to warrant this gift, but I'm not going to question it. When I reach her eyes, however, there's sadness in those infinite depths. "Aniyah? Are you okay?"

"Just... don't flinch." Before I can make sense of this, she turns her back to me and faces the wall of the niche.

I don't see it at first. My eyes are too full of the curve of her perfect ass, too busy tracing the line of her legs where they stretch down the length of my bed. Then she takes a deep breath and her sides tremble with anticipation—*or is it pain?*—and suddenly it's all I can see, expanding until it fills every inch of my vision: a long scar cut from shoulder to hip, curving around her side to disappear along her lower stomach.

I'd thought Tony's scars were painful to look at, and my own vanity had been wounded by the prospect of permanent marks on my chest. But this one overshadows any I've seen on the guys here; the dark line carved into Aniyah is thicker than my finger and longer than my arm.

"Baby," I breathe. I reach out to touch her, but end up hovering uncertainly in the air over her silken skin; I don't want to hurt her with my clumsy hands. "Who did this to you? Was it Handler? Can I kill him for you?"

She shakes her head, tiny curls brushing against her arm where she's stretched it out to use as a pillow. "I came here like this. I don't remember who did it, or why." My fingers close the gap of air between us and I stroke the dark line where it crosses her hip. The tissue is knotted and hard

226

under my touch, closed and healed rather than fresh and recent like my own wounds.

"And it hurts?"

Aniyah hesitates. "Not the scar itself. But something under the scar, yes. All the time, and it's getting worse. I feel dizzy and unbalanced; not constantly, but in waves. That's why I nearly fell in the hallway out there. Thank you for catching me," she adds, her voice low.

I let my fingers roam over her scar, wondering if I could know her by knowing this part of her. "And it won't let you do— What *did* you want to do with me?"

She shifts along the thin mattress, turning to look at me. Lying on her back allows me to see where the scar terminates; it ends in a thick knot of tissue a finger's length from her navel, resembling a second belly-button, but to the right of where it should be. "Sorry?" she asks, her eyes full of confusion.

"You said you couldn't do what you wanted to do with me," I remind her, watching her face with curious interest. "What did you want to do?"

Aniyah snorts and leans back against her arm. "Um. I don't know exactly, but not this! Not having to be carried around because I'll fall over otherwise. I wanted to have fun with you." An embarrassed smile flashes over her beautiful face. "I'm *supposed* to be pleasing you."

I lace my fingers through hers and lean against the bed. Sitting here on the floor, I could lie my head against her leg if I wanted or I could turn and kiss her thigh. Just being close to her—feeling the warmth of her skin, inhaling the sweet scent of her—is enough to take me from these caves. She doesn't belong in this place. We need a world where the sun is gentler and the sand is softer and the crowd is gone entirely.

"Well, you *do* please me, just by being here with me." My fingers stray to the leather on my wrist and the tiny engraved pick inside. I feel the tug of a hazy memory: strings under my fingers and words in my throat; words bolstered by the magic of the music in my hands.

The memory fades as I look up to find her watching me with a wry smile. "You're very kind. But I doubt this was what they had in mind when they brought us here to please you."

I grin, conceding the point. "Well, they don't need to know what we get up to in the dark. I'm serious; I *am* happy to be here. I like you." I lean closer, dropping my voice to a conspiratorial whisper. "And anyway, I've got someone keeping me pretty set in the pleasure department, you know? So you don't need to worry. I'm perfectly content right now, just hanging out with someone I like."

Her smile widens and her head tilts very slightly to the left, curiosity and delight flickering over her face. "Oh? Oh! It's that boy, isn't it? He was so miserable when you were wounded. Miyuki said you were friends."

Heat rushes to my cheeks. "I, uh. Yeah." I could kick myself; Tony asked me to keep a secret and I didn't last a single conversation without blurting it out. "Don't tell anyone? Tony thinks we could get into trouble."

Aniyah's gaze softens and she nods. "Promise," she whispers, making a gesture over her heart. "Does he— Does Tony know about me? Us?" She looks down at her naked body, suddenly shy.

"Does he know that I like you and you're the prettiest girl here? I think he probably noticed, yeah." I raise my fingers to her chin, encouraging her eyes to meet mine. "Uh, I kinda invited him to play with us next time. If there's a next time. And if you want that. The both of us, I mean."

She stares at me then bursts out laughing, clutching her stomach with her hands. "Next time?" she asks, sputtering to a halt, her eyes dancing with amusement. "We haven't done anything *this* time."

I lean in closer, one hand running along her leg in a long caress from knee to hip. "You want to fix that?"

Desire flares in her eyes but the expression on her face collapses into hopelessness. "Keoki, I *want* to, but I don't think I can move. I'm sorry."

"That's okay! I figure there's lots of things we can do that don't involve you moving."

228

"Name one." Her eyes glitter in the dark as her lips tug back into a smile at her challenge. I love that about her, I realize, my stomach flipping as I watch her face; no matter how awful everything is, no matter how much she hurts, she still finds humor in the situation. She's fragile on the outside but with a core stronger than the arena pillars. *She deserves better than this,* I think, gazing up at her. *We all do.*

"Lean back, baby," I whisper, placing my hands on her legs. "Turn just a little to the— there you go." She doesn't move much, letting me do most of the work of adjusting her. I part her legs and pull her forward off the bed until she's just hanging off the edge and her knees frame my face.

"Tell me what we're doing?" she whispers, a hint of panic in her voice.

"I've got you," I promise. I slide my hands under the soft round curve of her bottom, supporting her at the edge of the thin mattress. "Remember how strong I am? I won't let you fall."

I lean into her warmth and study her in the dim light. I'd been planning to do this ever since my first time with Diamond, figuring that if her mouth felt like liquid fire on my body then I would return the favor. But now that I'm here and in a front-row seat, I feel a sudden attack of nerves. *What if I do it wrong?* I dip my head closer and dart out my tongue, stroking in a long experimental trace.

The soft hiss that escapes her throat turns the knot in my stomach to liquid. Another long lick, my tongue flattening wide against her, and she whimpers. Her body rolls against my hands, straining to follow my tongue in its long meandering stroke. "Like this, Aniyah?" I whisper, leaning in to press my lips flat against her in a kiss that quickly morphs into a soft sucking nuzzle against her skin.

"Yes. *Yes.*" Her low whisper is barely audible over the burble of water in the fountain behind me. "Can you—?" She stirs, raising her head to look down at me with glazed eyes. "No, your hands are full," she mumbles. I'm about to ask what she needs—I'd have done so already except it would require moving my mouth away—but her hand snakes down to nestle near my lips, her fingers working with easy assurance.

I chuckle, the sound thrumming against her warm skin. "Yes, baby," I whisper, letting my lips rake over her skin. "Help me please you, okay?" I'm not sure if she can hear me over her breathing and I'm not waiting to find out; I duck my head and get back to work, alternating between the flat of my tongue and the very tip, trying to move in time with the little cries that rip from her throat.

When her knees tighten around my face, I find I can support her with just one hand. Since everything below her waist is already pretty busy and since everything above her waist is tantalizingly out of reach and since plunging my tongue into her while she cries for more has worked me up more than I could have dreamed, I let my free hand drop to my own business to play.

I hadn't intended to finish myself off; I don't have *any* goal in mind except to please her. But when she arches her neck, letting out a long guttural moan and her thighs clench tight enough around my head to make me see lights behind my eyes, I tumble over the edge of reason with her. In one moment, I'm kissing her body in long rough strokes because I need more than anything else to please her, then liquid fire pours through me and my kisses become raw gratitude expressed through mindless repetition.

Her fingers are in my hair and pulling me away when her voice penetrates my consciousness. "Stop, please, Keoki, oh my gosh, stop!" Her words are punctuated by hysterical giggles. I rise in a daze from the ground, letting her pull me onto the bed beside her. My jaw hurts and I feel belated sympathy for Diamond, but this was worth the lingering ache in my muscles.

I wrap my arms around Aniyah and study her face closely in the darkness. "Did I hurt you?"

"No!" She laughs again, limp in my arms. "No, it was very good. Thank you." Her eyes shine in the darkness. "I just had to stop after everything exploded. It was too much."

230

I grin at her explanation, turning my head to wipe my face on the mattress before leaning in to steal a kiss. "You're sure I didn't hurt you? Not just down there, but all over?"

Her sleepy smile is like sunshine in the darkness. "I feel weightless," she whispers, nuzzling into me. "You didn't hurt me at all. Promise."

I kiss her nose, relishing the rush of relief accompanying her words. "You'll be here at first bell, won't you?" Already the prospect of being separated stabs with almost physical pain. "You won't slip out? If we wake early enough, I might be able to do this again." I dangle the offer shamelessly, sore jaw be damned.

"Mmm." She hums in my arms, her eyes closed while a smile steals over her face. "Don't be counting on me to forget, Keoki." She yawns and drifts away, leaving me alone to count the moments as they slip away.

CHAPTER 23

Aniyah

I wake disoriented. Blinking up at the glowing ceiling, I try to steady my breathing. I'm stiff and sore, each of my limbs as solid as the stone bed underneath me. I wonder, not for the first time, whether I slept on stone in my earlier life or if, somewhere, there is a world with more comfortable bedding than this. I'm not sure what it would look like—*gauze strung in the air between pillars? towels fluffy enough to float in the pool?*—but I'd be willing to try anything at this point.

The boy beside me is snoring, his nose tucked into the elbow he's slung under his head. I smirk, wondering whether I ought to wake him. I haven't heard any bells, but there's a rustling of movement in the cavern outside and I wonder if Handler is setting out food. If he's here with his cart, then it must be close to first bell. I'd better get dressed, I decide; I don't want Handler banging on the door while I'm naked.

Problem is, I can't move my limbs or bend at the waist to sit up. I lie still, trying not to panic, and concentrate on flexing my fingers and toes. Over and over in slow repetition, I move my extremities and feel my muscles pull with the effort. *One. Two. Three. Ouch!* Prickles cover my legs, hot little stabbing pains. The panic I've been pushing back threatens to pounce; what if I'm stuck here, paralyzed forever?

C'mon. Shut up. Push! I shove against the stone with my fingers and manage to roll myself over the side of the bed. My legs swing around in time, for which I'm thankful, because the alternative is to fall flat on my face. I end up on my hands and knees on the floor; not graceful, but out of bed at least. Now that I'm warmed up I'm able to move my limbs, but every motion—every *breath*—is agony. Maybe this sharp increase in pain is my new reality, but I don't know how long I can survive like this. Something is going to give.

Shoving that thought aside, I scoop up my clothes and straighten with effort. I hear popping along my spine as I stand, but upright is still a victory. I can't move my arms around to manage the pretty twists and knots that Chloe draped me in before so I just wrap my clothes around me like a towel and tuck in the tail end of the sheet at the top, under my armpit. I'm decently covered and it's not like I'm supposed to be seducing anyone; Handler probably won't complain. *I hope.*

I hear first bell clang, followed by a low bellow from the cavern outside: "Prizes! Assemble for return to the vault." I turn to the door, but the boy on the bed stirs and catches my wrist.

"Mmph. Aniyah?" The words are mumbled into his arm, which glistens with a hint of drool. I try not to giggle, but he's adorable like this, especially in contrast to his previous bravado. I can't imagine he'll be good to pleasure anyone until after he's eaten and had a good stretch to wake up, the sleepy-head.

I reach out with my free hand and ruffle his long curls. "Handler's calling me, Keoki. I have to go. Do you want to come with? I imagine there's food."

He opens bleary eyes, blinking away the crust formed along his long eyelashes. "But you're so warm," he mutters. He seems to realize he's holding my wrist, thereby causing me to stoop over the wall niche holding the bed; he releases me with an apologetic grimace. "Sorry. Um. Shit. Do you *really* have to go?"

I blink at his plaintive tone. I hadn't been sad up to this point; I'd been focused on basic necessities like being able to move and dress and breathe without passing out from the pain. I'd been eager to get back to Miyuki, too; I need to hear xie had a safe time tending Justin or hanging out with Tony. What I'd *not* been focused on was this boy and whether I'll ever see him again. *He could die at any time. Or he could live, but I might never be sent to him. It's not like with Miyuki, where I see xer every cycle.*

"We'll do this again soon," I whisper, touching his curls with the tips of my fingers and hoping I'm not lying. "You'll win me in a match and we'll get to be together again. And you wanted Tony to meet me, right?"

He brightens, sitting up in bed and yawning until his jaw cracks. "Yeah, that's the plan. But, man, it seems like this went by way too fast, you know? I gotta ask Handler for longer next time. You said there's food?"

I grin at his easy acceptance and stand back so he can hop up. I can't help him dress—I can barely move to the door without groaning in pain—so I wait and smile at him whenever he looks at me with those warm eyes. He's sweet and I like him, and I hope he doesn't die. I remember Chloe's ashen face when the pillar fell on Christian and feel a stab of fear. This place is dangerous, and I already care about more people than I can protect. How do I keep myself alive, and Miyuki and Keoki and Tony? And what about the others? I don't want *anyone* to die, yet this place seems designed to destroy everything good.

"You ready? Sure?" Now that he's up and awake, he's all bounding energy again. He reaches for the door, but pauses before opening it. "One last thing," he announces with a sly grin before leaning in to steal a long kiss.

I giggle and push at him, trying not to laugh. "Hurry, we'll get in trouble!" He smirks shamelessly and pushes the door open, taking my hand as we stumble blinking into the torchlit cavern.

The scent of freshly-cooked food assaults my nose and causes my stomach to clench greedily. Meat dripping with hot grease, bowls of thick grain belching wisps of steam, and the yeasty aroma of fresh bread. Smaller bowls swim with syrupy fruit ready to be spread upon bread. It's a feast as good as anything I've seen here, all laid out on a silver cart that flashes firelight back at my sensitive eyes.

"Food for the boys," Handler says, his tone stern. His eyeless gaze picks out my face among the dancing shadows of the room, and I check my step as Keoki stumbles forward lured by the siren scent of the food.

"Aw, they can eat with us, can't they?" Keoki asks, plopping down and reaching for a basket of bread. "There's plenty here and they worked hard." I'm amazed he has the courage to talk back to Handler, though I notice Keoki doesn't meet his sightless gaze.

"The Prizes eat in their vault." Handler's voice is colder than deep water in shade. Even from this distance, I can feel a fresh wave of fear rolling from the tall man and I shiver.

A door opens and Miyuki emerges from a dark room, swipes of dried blood staining xer white clothes. Xie places xer hand along the wall and follows the curve of the cavern away from Justin's room. I stretch out my hand to catch xers; xie returns my squeeze with an easy smile while magical relief pours into my hand and works up my stiff arm and shoulders. "How is he?" I whisper, but xie just shakes xer head.

I'm about to press for details when another door opens across the cavern, the occupants summoned by Handler's command and the scent of food. Hana and an attractive white boy with an even whiter smile stumble out, looking utterly exhausted and coated in a thin sheen of sweat. The boy's grin broadens further at the sight of food and he punches her lightly in the upper arm before jogging off to join Keoki.

Chloe emerges with Christian from his room, the pair of them a tangle of entwined arms. Christian claims a long kiss, his hands tightening in her red hair, before reluctantly disengaging and working his way in the general direction of the food; from his unsteady walk, either he's love-struck to the point of dizziness or he got almost no sleep. I feel heat rise to my cheeks with unexpected embarrassment, feeling like I've failed by not keeping Keoki occupied longer. I hadn't thought he minded my falling asleep, but it's not like I asked.

The next two couples to emerge put my mind somewhat at ease. Imani steps out of a room as the boy behind her holds the door politely; when he walks out into the firelight, I recognize Tony. *Keoki's boy.* His expression is solemn but Imani whispers in his ear and his lips twitch. He nods and jogs off to join the other boys, his demeanor kind without being clingy. When the older boy with the cane emerges from his room with Heather slouching behind him, they both seem well-rested and ready enough to part ways: he leads her on his free arm to Handler, but she doesn't look his way or speak a word to anyone.

I'm sorry to leave the food and sorrier still to be parted from Keoki, but I have Miyuki's hand in mine and that more than makes up for anything I'm losing. I smile at xer and turn to guide xer out with Handler when I'm distracted by the sound of a door to our left. I'm turning my head towards the sound, trying to remember who is missing from our group, when Sappho emerges and the world crashes down around me.

She's been beaten. She hangs her head so that her hair falls to cover what it can, but ugly glimpses peer out with every step. The skin around her right eye is bruised a deep blood-red in a circle as wide as a fist. Her upper lip is split and coated in a thick film of dried blood. Her arms, legs, and knees sport purple and black bruises that stain her tattoos and cause her to shuffle in a pained, uneven gait. She stumbles over the threshold of the room and falls forward, the ground rushing up to meet her face.

I don't have the power to jump forward and wouldn't reach Sappho in time to catch her even if I did. Several of the boys leap to their feet and I hear Hana gasp, but it's Lucas who catches her; his hand snakes out from the dark to pull her back by the shoulder and steady her with a rough shake. He closes the door behind them. "You're fine," he tells her, his voice rough as stone. "Walk properly."

She shivers at his touch but stays upright. I swallow hard and realize Miyuki is squeezing my hand so hard it hurts; xie can't see most of this, but the tension in the room is palpable and xie would have noticed the shapes of the boys leaping up from their seats. Handler breaks the silence, his words freezing the blood in my veins.

"Your Prize is damaged, Scoria. Was she not to your liking?" His gaze lands on Sappho and she winces again. "That one has been with us a long time. Perhaps she has lost her luster. We could acquire a new Sapphire."

No one in the room breathes. Hana tightens her fists until pricks of blood appear under her short nails, the cuts healing instantly as golden magic thrums through her skin. I want her to save Sappho, to save *all* of us, but I realize with a sinking pain in my chest that she can't.

Motion catches my eye and I twist my head to see the boy with the cane step forward. It's just one step but the movement is enough to catch every gaze. He glares daggers at Lucas from the center of the cavern, and the sandy-haired boy has the good grace to look almost ashamed.

"Nah," Lucas says, clearing his throat and meeting Handler's face. "She was good. We had fun. You like to play rough, don't you, baby?"

He gives Sappho a little shake of the shoulders and she clenches her eyes tight. "Sure," she whispers, the word dropping like a stone from her lips.

Handler is silent for a moment that spins into an eternity. "Back to the vault," he barks, turning his empty cart and wheeling it towards the massive iron doors. The seven of us dart forward as quickly as we can, Hana and Imani taking Sappho between them, and leave the boys behind us without looking back.

Never has our room seemed more like home; the sunlit cavern with its babbling waters and sparkling table is a sanctuary, away from the smoky subterranean rooms where boys lurk. We tumble into our vault as soon as Handler opens the doors, Sappho and I limping, and Miyuki stumbling without the aid of xer glasses. The other girls help us to the table, but Hana straightens and frowns at Handler's back when he turns to go.

"You're coming back with food?" she asks, her tone carefully neutral.

"Eventually," he replies in a cold tone as the doors slam closed behind him.

My stomach cries in protest at the implication of his words, but there's little we can do. We're trapped in here, and he'll either bring us food or we will starve. I sink into the cushions by the table and slump over on my elbows, the muscles in my back screaming from the effort of our walk. Sappho sits nearby with her head hunched over her knees, silent and miserable.

"Hon, are you okay?" Imani whispers, settling down beside Sappho. She looks as though she'd like to hug her, but keeps her hands back for the moment; from the look of Sappho's bruises, there aren't many places available to touch without hurting her.

Hana sits cross-legged on the floor on the other side of the table. "What happened?"

Sappho takes a deep breath and shakes her head, staring at the floor between her feet. When she speaks, her voice is a slow mumble and we have to strain for each word. "During the Auction. I covered for Aniyah. Dragged him off so she could slip away. He figured out what I did. Got angry. Picked me. Did this."

Her words are a fist wrapped around my heart, squeezing with all its might. "Oh, *Sappho*. I didn't know. I didn't think. I'm so sorry, I— If I'd known, I never would have gone. I'm so *sorry*."

"I know," she whispers, closing her eyes. "You didn't make him lose his temper. He does that on his own."

Chloe vibrates with fury on the other side of me. She slams her fist into the ground and my eyes widen as a little crater forms in the solid rock. "That *ass*. He could have picked anyone else! He had the whole room to pick! So he didn't get one of the newbies, so what? He has to beat one of us up over it? And not Hana or me, not someone who could fight back. *Coward*." She all but spits the last word.

"He doesn't like it when he doesn't get his own way." Heather's voice floats over the table, dull and soft. "He wants to be in control. It frightens him when he's not."

Hana shakes her head. She's breathing through her nose trying to stay calm, but her eyes are as murderous as Chloe's. "He's always been a problem. Even when you cater to him, Heather, he still works out his aggression on you. Just because you can't feel it doesn't make it okay. Never has." She takes another long breath, her gaze studying Sappho's bruises. "But this crosses a line."

"What do we do?" Miyuki's voice at my elbow is steady steel, as sharp as an arena sword. "There's got to be something we can do, right?"

Heather perks at this, sitting up straight at the table and putting on her cheeriest smile. "Let's complain to Handler!" she suggests in a chirrupy tone. "I'm sure he cares! Oh, babe, no, don't start that," she adds in her normal tone as Sappho's expression crumples and tears come at last. "C'mon, let's get you in the pool. It's gonna be okay. You've seen worse on me, right? And I got better. You will too."

With a gentleness I wouldn't have thought she could display, Heather helps Sappho to her feet and leads her to the healing pool. Looking at her wounds, I can't imagine it will do a damn thing except to take the worst edge off, but I know as well as anyone here that's better than nothing. I turn back to the others, feeling utterly miserable.

"This is all my fault," I admit, unable to meet Hana's eyes. "Lucas was flirting with me. Or trying to. I wasn't feeling well and I just wanted to go with Keoki. Sappho rescued me and I ran off without even thinking. Of course he'd be mad."

Imani reaches out to touch my shoulder, her warm brown eyes brimming with sorrow. "Hon, how could you have known? We're told to please the boys. You *did* that. You went off with the one who asked. You made him happy. You couldn't know a different boy would hurt a different girl on account of you not being able to please two at once."

"But I—"

"Don't," Hana says, her curt voice cutting me off. "Look, even if you'd gone off with Lucas and even if he hadn't roughed *you* up, it's just as possible

Keoki would've hurt someone else because *he* didn't get you. That's always the risk we take: their disappointment and fear and anger and resentment get taken out on us. Don't try to take responsibility for it, because it doesn't work like that."

I look up, shaking my head slowly. "Keoki wouldn't do that," I tell her, but I hear the doubt in my voice. "He's not like that." At least, I don't think he would. I glance to Miyuki, searching xer eyes behind xer glasses, seeking confirmation that Keoki was kind to xer, that he never hurt xer. *How well do we really know him? Any of them?*

Miyuki frowns, lost in xer own thoughts. "There must be *something* we can do," xie insists. "He can't just get away with this like it's nothing."

Chloe laughs, but the sound is bitter and joyless. "There's plenty of things. None of them are fun."

"Tell me," Miyuki insists.

"You give them what they want," Imani murmurs, turning away from us to study the far wall.

I blink. "How is that revenge?"

"You fuck them," Hana says, her voice flat. "You find their weak points; they all have them. The arena is rough. They tear muscles or break bones, and rarely heal clean. Bad knees, bad elbows, soft spots around the ankles. You ride them hard and hit where it hurts. Chloe doesn't know her own strength. Imani uses her nails without thinking. Me, I have a bad habit of kneeing sensitive areas while in the throes of passion."

Imani sighs, magic rippling in her shifting face; I realize she's using her talent to keep her face steady. Somehow this seems sadder than if she'd just cried without reservation. "Hurting them is easy," she says, meeting my gaze. "Wounding them enough to make a difference in the arena is harder. But you learn. We all learned."

"How do you keep them from telling on you?" Miyuki demands, frowning at Hana. "Don't they complain to Handler?"

"You'd be surprised how few boys are willing to admit they can't handle a girl in bed," Chloe drawls, leaning back to stare up at the sunlight.

"It's still a risk," Miyuki argues, staring unhappily at xer hands. "There's got to be a better way to fight back."

I stand slowly, all my thoughts reserved for the nearby pool. I can't think about this now, and I'd be no good at fighting even if I could; I can barely move, let alone ride a boy to harm. *There's got to be a better way than this,* I think, almost echoing Miyuki's words. *There has to be somewhere better for all of us.*

CHAPTER 24

Keoki

The heavy iron doors clang shut behind Handler and the girls. For the space of a heartbeat the room is still as everyone stares at Lucas, then there is a burst of movement so fast my eyes can't track more than a blur. Matías zips through the space between the center of the cavern and the spot where Lucas hangs back by his door. I hear the crack of a hard slap, and Lucas reels away with his hand cradling his cheek.

"What were you *thinking*?" Fury explodes from Matías as he leans on his cane, panting with the exertion of his superhuman run.

Christian still stands where he leaped to his feet when the tattooed girl first stumbled forward and needed catching. He laces his fingers and stretches his hands out until the joints crack, giving Lucas a furious glare. "You hold him," Christian snaps at Matías. "I'll beat him up. Taste of what he gave that girl."

"Go fuck your hands, Christian," Lucas snaps, whipping around to scowl at him. "Everything's easy for you, isn't it? The rest of us don't have a favorite girl panting for it. You ever think about that, when Ruby's wrapped around you screaming for more? The rest of us are making do with girls who barely tolerate it!"

"Hey!" Matías barks for attention, and Lucas swivels reluctantly back to face him. "I asked you a question. *What were you thinking?*" Each word is a sentence of its own, spat out and left hanging in the air. Lucas doesn't answer him, glaring in defiance as the silence stretches out around us.

Matías takes a deep breath and leans harder on his cane; I'm not sure if he needs the extra support after the exertion of zipping over there or if he's trying to restrain himself from striking out again. "Lucas," he says, his voice straining to remain calm, "it's one thing to lose control when you're with Emerald. She can't feel anything, so she doesn't know to stop you—"

"Are we still pretending that's what happens? That those bruises he leaves on her are some kind of accident?" Christian crosses his arms over his chest and narrows his eyes at Lucas. "Because I don't know about the rest of you guys, but I'm sick of playing that game."

"It's another thing entirely," Matías presses on, ignoring Christian, "to play rough with the other girls. Sapphire feels pain, just like you or me! You can't tell me she didn't cry out, that you didn't know you were hurting her!" He flings an accusing finger at Lucas' door. "So what were you *doing* in there that she came out looking like that? You can answer me now or I can beat it out of you in the training pit."

Lucas sets his jaw at the threat, his eyes burning with fresh anger. "She needed to be taught a lesson."

The room stills again until the only thing I can hear is the roar of blood in my ears and the crackle of the torches. "You hit her on purpose," Matías says, his voice cold.

"I've been saying he does!" Christian explodes, turning away to pace the cavern. "There's a difference between rough sex and the shit he does!"

Reese looks up from where he's been sitting on the ground beside me, his face as pale as the sheet he's wearing. "I can't believe you hit Sapphire," he whispers, his voice hoarse. He meets Lucas' eyes for only a moment before his gaze drops to the ground again. "You hit her in the *face*."

Tony sits on my other side, gazing into the middle distance; he says nothing and his expression is as blank as the expanse of sand in the arena. I look to him for help, for *something*, but he doesn't even glance my way. I swallow hard, pushing down food that threatens to rise and feeling as sick as Reese sounds.

My voice is thick in my throat. "The fuck do you mean, you taught her a lesson? What kind of lesson does *that*?"

Lucas turns on me, fury on his face. "I'm surprised you're not smart enough to figure it out," he spits at me. "You thought you were pretty clever at auction, sneaking off with the new girl like that."

With that barb the pieces fall into place. Sapphire was the one who dragged Lucas away so Aniyah and I could leave. I hadn't thought it unusual at the time, figuring the girls looked out for each other. Aniyah was ill, so Miyuki warned me and Sapphire created a distraction. I hadn't expected Lucas to take it personally.

I take a deep gulp of air and try to stay calm. "Dude. She wanted me. I wanted her. It was as simple as that. Not a big conspiracy to fuck you over."

"*Dude.*" The word is a mocking hiss in his mouth. "What she wants doesn't matter. Our job is to go into the arena and risk our lives, whether *we* want to or not. Their job is to reward us for doing well, whether *they* want to or not. Any time they wanna switch, I am completely in favor of letting them go out and kill shit while I relax in the stands and stud for them after. You think any of them would take that offer?"

Reese pulls his legs to his chest and presses his face to his knees. His shoulders are trembling and I think he might actually vomit; when he speaks, his voice is choked. "Just because our lives are miserable doesn't mean we have to make theirs equally bad, no matter what Master and Handler say."

"They've given us a system," Lucas yells, his face reddening. "We have points! We go in order. The alternative is a violent free-for-all where we run in and carry the girls off to our rooms. You'd prefer that?"

"I had the same number of kills as you," I point out. The roar of blood in my ears is louder now. "And *I* was the one who left with your choice, not Sapphire. So because you have a fight with me, you beat up a defenseless girl?"

He narrows his eyes. "You and your girl didn't know the rules," he says, one shoulder rising in a shrug. "Sapphire did. She took away my choice, so I took her. She won't make that mistake again." He watches me for a long moment. "And I'd say you and your girl got the message as well, so that's three lessons for one beating. Out in the arena, that's a bargain."

Tony hops to his feet. I whip around to look at him, hope swelling in my chest as I harbor a wild fantasy that he'll make all this better. How, I'm not sure, but he'll do something and it'll be exactly the *right* thing. Deliver a stinging rebuke that shames Lucas into acknowledging the error of his ways, maybe, or beat into him a reminder of why he should never ever pull this shit again. I'd be good with either or both.

Instead he stares in the direction of the training pit, looking more bored than anything else. "I'm done eating," he announces. "Don't save any more for me." Then he stalks off, not looking back.

I gape after him and look back at Matías. The older boy rubs his eyes with his free hand and looks as weary as I've ever seen him. "He's right," he says, sounding unhappy about it. "Handler said there was a big show in the works. We still don't know when it is; could be later this cycle, or could be a dozen cycles from now. We won't know unless Handler decides to tell us in advance. All we can do is prepare; rest, eat, and train."

Reese reaches for another bowl but otherwise ignores the rest of us; I get the sense that he won't be speaking to anyone for a long time. Given that he was the most cheerful and talkative among us, his silence is more reproachful than any words he could say. *I* feel guilty, and I wasn't even the one hurting girls.

I look up to see Christian scowling at Lucas, who meets his gaze with answering acrimony. "You'd better start working on a good apology,"

Christian advises, his voice low and still very angry, "or hope you're lucky enough not to be sent Ruby before she decides to forgive you. You haven't seen her when she's mad, and believe me: you don't want to." That said, he flops back down to the ground and reaches for the food.

"So that's it?" I demand from Matías. "We're just going to go back to normal and pretend this never happened?"

Lucas narrows his eyes. "The fuck are you going to do about it, newbie?"

Matías turns away from the other boy and walks slowly back to where we sit. "It's done," he says. His voice is calm now, the worst of the anger dissipated. "There's nothing we can do to undo it. If he does it again, he's a dead man." The cold threat hangs in the air and Lucas looks away.

It's not enough. I'm so upset I could shout the words, but I bite them back. I hold my tongue more for Reese's sake than anything else, as he doesn't need me yelling at the top of my lungs when he's within arm's reach of me and still trembling. Yet the longer I hold it in, the louder the anger throbs in my blood; there are a million things I want to say and none of them will help anyone.

"I'm going to find Tony," I announce, shoving at the ground with all the force I'd like to use on Lucas and hopping to my feet. No one tries to stop me.

Tony isn't hard to find; he's in the center of the training pit, doing things with a sword that would take my breath away if I weren't so furious. He's graceful to a fault out in the pale sand, moving his legs and arms in slow motion as he practices stances I have no vocabulary for. *Whatever I was before this, I must not have been up on sword-fighting. Swordplay. Swordery.*

No, it's no good. It just isn't funny.

I stand there without speaking for more heartbeats than I can count, watching him practice. I wonder how much of this he knew before he was brought here and how much he was forced to learn in order to survive. The thought strikes me that I have it easier than he does; brute strength doesn't have a lot of finesse, but it's not hard to learn and I can't be easily disarmed.

Mostly I just have to hit things and not die. As far as talents go, I've been pretty lucky; luckier than Justin, at the very least.

"You get enough to eat?"

Tony doesn't look at me when he speaks, but there's no one else here. I nod and then shake my head, the gesture one of disbelief rather than denial. "What are you doing?" I ask, spreading my hands to encompass the training area. "Don't you care? You didn't say a word back there. Did you *see* what he did to her?"

He's quiet for another stretch of beats, working through a complicated set of lunges with the blade. His feet sweep the sand, leaving little trails that would tell the story of his movements if I were skilled enough to read them. He moves subtly away from the trails as he works, edging down the center of the pit, and I wonder if Matías will come by later to study his footprints and grade the perfection of his form.

"Did you know," he says, his voice low and even, "Sapphire's been here longer than I have? She's a good girl. Doesn't care for boys, never gets attached to one, but she's a good sport. She's bendy—that's her power—and she can *dance*. She does things with her hips that'll make your dick stand straight up. Doesn't mind you touching yourself while she does it, either. I've had her probably half a dozen times, and she was always sweet as fruit."

His feet sweep in a quick turn, punctuated by a deep thrust of his sword. "Yes. I fucking care."

I find myself blinking back tears because I'm so relieved to hear him say it. "I'm sorry," I tell him, feeling ashamed of my earlier berating. Of course he knows her better than I do; I'm the newbie and he's been here longer than most of the other guys. "Why didn't you say anything?"

I'm more curious than angry now, and I hope he can hear the change in my tone; at any rate, he doesn't seem to take offense. He works a shrug into his graceful movements. "Because Lucas is going to do what he does. If he won't listen to Matías and Christian and Reese and you, one more voice isn't going to make any difference."

I frown. His logic is sound, but it seems so cold. "So you're just giving up? Training out here because it's not worth the effort?" I don't like it, and don't know how to say so without sounding judgmental; just because something seems inevitable doesn't mean there's no point in voicing opposition.

He drops into a roll and comes up on one knee, sword thrusting at his invisible opponent. Sand streams from his shoulders and hair but he doesn't even blink, his eyes focused on the middle distance. "I train out here because eventually I'm going to be in the ring with Lucas," he says, his tone cool. "And I need to make damn sure I can survive on my own, after I let whatever we're facing kill him dead."

The blood drains from my face. "Oh," is all I can say. *That's one way to handle a problem.* After seeing Sapphire bruised and broken, and that fist-shaped ring around her eye, I'm not even sure it's the wrong way. "I... I'm gonna go check on Justin." I can't help Tony out here, anyway; I'd be useless with his sword practice at the best of times, and now is definitely not a good time in my head.

"Tell him I said 'Hi'," he says, as calm as the cavern air.

Justin's room is cool and dark. We moved him here when Matías and Miyuki decided it was safe to carry him to his bed. She'd been worried about leaving him to sleep on the hard floor, and Matías believed his wounds had been closed long enough that careful movement wouldn't tear them open. Four guys had worked together to carry him to bed; Matías had directed while I watched uselessly from the side. My wounds had closed faster than Justin's, but no one wanted to take any chances.

I knock on the door and let myself in, waiting on the inside step until my eyes adjust to the low light. In the glow of the phosphorescent moss he doesn't look good, but he looks better than before. The bandages encasing him are clean and white and damp, and I realize Miyuki must have changed them before she left. The dirty cloths are in a bundle in the far corner of his room, near the toilet; I ought to take them out for Handler to wheel away with the empty dishes.

For the moment, however, I just stand next to the bed and study his face. His cheek and most of the right side of his head is bandaged where the creature savaged him, and his nose has a long gash across the top. By some miracle his eyes weren't gouged out; from the wounds along his arms, it looks as if he threw them up to protect his face. I reach out to touch his forehead with the back of my hand: he's warm but not feverish. Matías said that was a good sign, and that the healing water was working. *Probably.*

He stirs at my touch. *Shit.* I shouldn't have bothered him. Miyuki keeps him in as deep a fog as she can manage and he must have just gotten a fresh dose before she left. Here I'm waking him up and shaving off precious sleep time until the next dose. I straighten up to leave, but he groans and mumbles something.

"What was that?" I stoop lower, craning my neck to see into the wall niche that houses his bed. "Sorry, I didn't hear you, buddy."

"Is food time?" The words are a soft slur, relaxed and pained at the same time. I wince and the fresh scars on my chest prickle with sympathy pains.

"Yeah, it is, actually. Ha, I probably should have remembered to bring the food with me, huh? Let me go fix you up a bowl and I'll be right back. It's actually pretty good this time."

His moan turns distinctly negative, the aural equivalent of a headshake. "No. Just... stay?"

I hesitate. I'm pretty sure he needs food, but I can't deny him this simple request. Either Matías will come by or Justin will eventually get hungry enough to let me pop out and fix up a meal for him. Either way, he'll be fed; the spread out there was big enough that the guys aren't going to eat it all. I hunker down on the floor next to the bed and reach up to touch his shoulder—one of the few places not covered in bandages.

"What's new?" Each word escapes slowly, slurred by the combination punch of his wounds and whatever Miyuki does with her hands to keep the pain in check. I shrug, trying to act cool while desperately wishing I knew.

"Uh. There's some kind of big thing coming up? Matías keeps talking about it. We're supposed to be resting and training and shit. But we have no idea when it's on and aren't going to know unless Handler stops being an ass. Same as usual, I gather?"

He doesn't respond, save for the soft wheeze of his breath in the dark. Time stretches out until I wonder if he's gone to sleep on me. I'm just about to try standing up when new words trickle out. "Am I part of it?"

I blink. The kid can't even get up out of bed, let alone go to the arena. If we tried to carry him there, he could die from his wounds opening before we got to the gate. Even if he were healed enough that the wounds wouldn't tear and bleed out, his leg is still splinted. He'd be about as much use in a fight as a corpse.

"Probably not? I mean, you're not really at your best right now."

My answer is weak, sure, but I'd expected him to feel a little relief. Instead he sighs, a soft puff of air that's as forlorn a sound as I've ever heard. "That's a good thing, isn't it?" I ask, looking at him.

Dark eyes watch me through barely-open lids. His lips move the least amount necessary to let him speak. "If I can't fight... they won't keep feeding me." Each word a slow effort, hardly more than a breath.

A lump forms in my throat, hard and painful. "Hey. It's gonna be okay, man," I tell him, the words rushing out automatically. "Really, I have a good feeling about this. Look, close your eyes and take a rest, okay? I'm gonna go get you some food. I'll be back in just a bit; you'll hardly notice I'm gone."

I slip out of the room before he can object and almost run to where the dishes are scattered across the floor. I'll fix up a bowl and count to one hundred. By the time I do that, the tears threatening to fall will have dried up and I'll be able to go back in there with a calm face.

CHAPTER 25

Aniyah

When Handler brings food at third bell, he doesn't take Miyuki away to tend Justin. Instead, he fixes his sightless gaze in my direction. "Alexandrite, come with me." His voice is quiet now, lacking the cold disdain threading through his words earlier. His arms drop to his sides, but one hand strays to rub at the mole on his other hand. The nervous tic is back, I note; I haven't seen him worry at his blemish since the bout when Justin and Keoki were injured and Miyuki was nearly sold away.

Now he wants me to go with him. That doesn't bode well. I frown and look at Hana, but she appears equally mystified. "Yes, sir," I mumble, as there's little else I can do. I manage to pull myself upright, but leaving food behind after such a long fast is almost as painful as the constant tension in my back. *Miyuki will save some for me,* I console myself, but the comfort is as cold as the food will be.

Of course, that's assuming I come back alive. I give Handler a wary glance as I follow him. He says nothing as he leads me out through the golden doors, his cart rattling on the floor with every step. In the outside hallway I turn to the right, expecting to be led to the boys' cavern or to climb the stairs leading up to the Master's pavilion. Instead, to my surprise, Handler turns down the left corridor, wheeling his cart towards the mysterious bend I'd wanted to explore with Keoki during Auction. "Keep up, Alexandrite."

I walk a little faster, each step sending a stab of pain through my shoulder blades. The left corridor follows a sloping curvature identical to the right, and torches set in the walls throw wild shadows around us as we walk. Without thinking, I draw a little closer to Handler. Waves of magical fear still roll from his shoulders like water streaming off a surfacing swimmer, but at least his fear is a familiar one, and preferable to the creeping dread of a summons to places unknown.

We round a bend and face a giant set of doors almost identical to the golden and black doors I've passed through so many times, but these are white and so ugly I wince to look at them. Their color and texture summons memories of bleached bone and the horns of dead things. Handler steps forward, and the magic flowing through the doors reaches out to embrace him. Tendrils of light fall into the cracks of his face and hands, flowing in a rapid current that picks up speed in the deep troughs lining his skin.

The magic pulses brighter as the flow accelerates until a crack ripples down the center of the massive doors. Handler presses the sides of the crack and the doors open, scraping against the floor and leaving a powdery residue that clings to my feet. *It's the same with all the doors. His body is the key.* How many magical doors are underground here with us, I wonder, and could we ever get through them to freedom?

The cavern that opens before us is large enough to hold both the boys' cave and our own vault with room to spare. Across from us is a set of identical white doors. To our left and right, facing one another across the expansive cavern, are heavy iron gates with bars which allow sunlight to stream through and spill over the floor. The gate to our left leads to the arena; I can see stadium seats from here. But the gate to our right lets out onto a new world: sun and sand and stone, as far as the eye can see.

"Alexandrite?" My attention is so enthralled by the right-hand gate that I don't immediately hear Handler beside me. "Alexandrite! I asked if you prefer to take the stairs or the ramp."

I blink and look around at him. The ceiling above us has four wide holes through which more sunlight streams into the cavern. Each of the holes is positioned over thick pillars stretching from ceiling to floor. As I peer at the dark stone, I realize that three of the pillars have been cut with stairs and the fourth one carved with a spiraling ramp that slopes to the top of the cavern. I look at Handler again, utterly confused. "The ramp?" I've no idea where we're going, but I don't want to climb steps to get there.

Abandoning his cart in the center of the room, he leads me up the ramp. Around the halfway mark, I realize this may not have been the brightest plan; there's no rail to hold onto and I'm desperately afraid I'll slip and fall. Panic rising, I reach out to grab his hand. He recoils and I feel a cold splash of fear, but I hold on fast and we keep trudging to the top. I'd rather die on my own terms than from falling down a ramp.

We emerge from the hole in the ceiling and I blink in the light. *We're in the Arena stands,* I realize, staring at the sand below. The entire edifice is empty and a lonely wind whistles through the abandoned seats. I glance back at Handler, whose hand I had dropped the moment we were on firm footing.

"Alexandrite." He watches me with his sightless gaze, one hand worrying at his mole. His tone is softer than usual, and I'm not sure whether that's a good sign or a very bad one. "You spoke back to the Master in front of a guest. You are therefore sentenced to clean-up duty in the stands."

I'd forgotten about my threatened punishment. I look around in confusion; the stands are already clean, with no debris that I can see. "With my bare hands?" I can't wash the seats without water, and even if there were anything to pick up, there is nowhere to put it.

"A guest of our Master—She of the Western Wastes—has reported losing a piece of jewelry, a silver necklace. She believes she lost it on her last visit here. It is a powerful magical item. You will use your talent to either find it or confirm that it is not here. When you are finished, you may return to the vault."

The stadium is enormous, with multiple levels of seats that wrap all the way around the giant arena. Just walking to the far end and back would exhaust me. I swallow, watching his blank face for any hint of compassion. "I have to find a necklace for this lady before I can eat or rest again?"

"No. You must find the necklace for our Master. I doubt he has any intention of returning it." Handler turns to leave, then looks back at me. "It is a mild punishment. I have known the Master to command much worse. I encourage you to work diligently. When you have finished, you may return to the entrance hall and wait there to be collected." He descends the ramp, leaving me alone in a world of stone and sand.

I sit on the nearest bench, trying to settle my thoughts. I'm hungry and tired, and already burning from the sun which beats down on me. I adjust my clothes, trying to create a hood for my face, but I have little material to work with; I didn't dress in layers, not knowing I would be brought up here. Silence weighs heavily on me and I miss Miyuki, I miss Hana, I miss anyone whose comfort would make this task seem less impossible.

Okay, try to look on the bright side. Maybe this is a good thing. Maybe I can use this opportunity to learn something about this place. I'm up here all by myself, unsupervised and with silence to think.

I peer out over the stadium, trying to overlay the world I see up here onto the life I know underground. The arena is a huge oval of dark sand dotted with pillars that stab up at random intervals, all of which are whole and unbroken with no trace of Keoki's handiwork during his fight with Christian. The sand spreading out below the pillars is framed by sheer cliffs which rise as high as the tops of the pillars before tapering up and out, creating staggered rows of seating which circle the Arena. That's where I am now: standing on these carved cliffs, looking down. Under my feet, beneath the seats, are the caverns where we live.

Here below the staircases is the entrance hall, as Handler called it. On the far side of the arena is the gate where the boys enter for the fights. The matching gate in the entrance hall below must be the challengers' gate; I remember the venom-spitting man who strutted in for my first fight. If challengers come in from the entrance hall, they must be entering *from* somewhere: presumably the open wasteland which I glimpsed.

Could we get out through the wasteland? Where is our vault? Midway in the cliffs between the entrance hall and the boys' gate, the Master's pavilion rises to tower over the surrounding seats. The steps we are forced to climb are carved into the sharp slope beneath the throne. In that same slope my eyes locate a large hole cut into the cliffs: the ceiling to our vault. That hole is where sunlight comes in.

If I'm right, our vault is halfway between the boys' cavern and the entrance hall. The wasteland outside hadn't looked promising, but the visitors to the stadium must live *somewhere*. Maybe they have underground homes beneath the sand, and we just have to find the right entrance. If we could get through the golden doors and out the entrance gate, there might be a chance for us. *But that's a lot of ifs. And none of this is worth anything if I can't get back to the others to tell them.*

I sigh and stand, shading my eyes as I look around. The stadium is coated with the same soft dusting of magic as our vault, and nothing jumps out at me from here. I decide to make a circuit around the stadium, walking the lower levels and looking up. If I'm lucky, I'll only need to make one circuit in order to find the necklace. If I'm not lucky, I don't want to think how many laps it will take to check each row.

Handler might have known worse punishments than this, but halfway around the right-hand side of the stands I'm forced to admit I can't imagine what they might be. Every step I take is agony, and each breath sends shooting pains through my back and sides. I could stop and rest, but if I sat down I'm not sure I could get back up again. Worse, the giddy dizziness I felt during Auction is back, and there's no rail separating the lowest edge of the cliffs from the arena below. One woozy tumble and I'll break my neck.

My greatest enemy out here is the sun. It beats down with a vengeance, making my skin prickle. It casts shadows along the seats, creating dark pools where the necklace might hide. It assaults my eyes, making them squint and water as I look up and down the rows, desperate to catch a glitter of metal or magic. And it hides the strange man until I've almost walked by him, his sudden appearance causing me to take a step back and nearly lose my footing on the rough stone.

He sits on the ground in an aisle between seating sections, looking entirely at ease in the shade. The man is dark, but unnaturally so; his skin is the ashen black of a torch completely burned up. He shimmers in the sun like the heat mirages that dance at the edge of my vision, the effect making him almost invisible. Above all, he ripples with pure magic, thicker than anything I've seen. His power doesn't register as liquid light, the way it does with the Master; this man's energy appears as a layer of mist that pulses over and under and through him. He is unmistakably strong, more so even than the monster who rules my existence.

"Who are you? What are you doing here?" Recognition of his power does nothing to hold my tongue. I'm exhausted, starving, hurting, and very dizzy, and I've almost fallen, thanks to him. At this point, I would almost welcome being killed out here for my rudeness; it would be quicker than a fall. He ignores me, however, his intent gaze locked on the arena below.

"Hey! I'm talking to you." I ease a step closer. "What are you doing up here? Did you forget to go home?" The idea seems ludicrous, but I can't imagine why else a guest would be up here in the stands.

He looks up at me with an odd frown on his face, the way you'd look at someone if you weren't sure they were talking to *you*. When he meets my gaze, his eyes widen and he leaps to his feet in one smooth movement. He's taller than I, and the height added by the stands causes him to tower over me.

"You can see me?" His voice is thick and guttural, the sound of torch-smoke if it could talk.

"Yes." I set my shoulders and try not to regret speaking. "What are you doing here?"

He studies me and I shiver despite the heat. The whites of his eyes swirl like mist and his irises are as clear as water. Nothing about his gaze is kind or human. "You should leave," he says, his voice cold. "You have seen nothing."

I have no idea what the Master will do if I go back empty-handed and I don't want to find out, so I take a deep breath and stand my ground. "I see *you*," I remind him. "Does the Master know you're here?"

Emotion flickers through his strange eyes, almost a grimace. Not fear, I decide, but annoyance, as though faced with a bothersome prospect. "He doesn't, does he?" I guess, watching his shadowy face. "You don't want him to."

A long moment passes while thick power throbs in the air around him. "I wonder if you realize how simple it would be to remove you from consideration altogether?" His tone is curious, almost verging on polite if he weren't threatening to kill me.

"If something happens to me, the Master will know someone was here," I point out, swallowing hard. "You know, there's a third option. Tell me who you are and what you're doing here and where you came from, and I'll keep your secret. I won't tell anyone about you." I'm not sure this is wise, but anything I can get out of him regarding the outside world is worth the risk.

Misty eyes watch me without blinking, until my own eyes start to water on his behalf. "I accept this deal," he murmurs. Before I can react, he reaches out to place two fingers on my lips. A shock flickers through me, white-hot but painless, and the moisture in my mouth turns to a gritty ash. When he pulls his hand away I erupt into painful coughing, each hack bringing up gray dust.

"What was that?" I demand, spitting grit into the stands.

"A deal." He watches, unruffled by my reaction. "You will tell no one about me, which makes things significantly more convenient."

I glare at him. I hadn't been intending to go back on my offer, but I also hadn't meant it literally; Miyuki wasn't included in my silence, nor Hana and Keoki. But I'd said what I had said, and his touch was magic; I'd have known that even if I hadn't coughed up ash. "You could have warned me," I point out, trying not to sound as angry as I feel.

"I chose not to. Now, to uphold my end of the deal. I am the faery who was born in the shadows and lives there still. I came from the west. I am here searching for a good vantage point."

Silence stretches out as I wait for elucidation. When nothing follows, I blink. "What kind of answers are those?"

"Valid ones." His stance is easier and his voice calmer. He looks more self-assured now that I no longer represent a threat, studying me with a distant curiosity rather than hostility.

"But you haven't told me anything! I don't even know your name! Only that you're a faery—", the word rolls awkwardly on my tongue, but it's the same one the Master uses for his own strange kind, "—and that you care about getting a good seat? That applies to everyone who comes here!"

His lips twitch very slightly. "I am not responsible for your inability to recognize the uniqueness of the identifier I gave you," he says with a shrug. "As for my motive for being here," his eyes sweep over the sands below us, "the Master of Masques has been ordered by one of our illustrious parents to present a feast when they arrive. I wish to observe the feeding from a discreet distance."

I frown, working my way through this. "You want to watch... your parent eat a meal?"

"Yes," he says, his unblinking gaze still locked on my face. He scrutinizes me until I feel naked; there's no lust in his swirling eyes, just merciless curiosity. "I have recently become interested in the dynamics of human cooperation in battlefield settings. I believe the Master of Masques intends to serve several servants at once for this meal; perhaps even his entire stable. If he is wise, he will retain *you*, but I have never known him to be wise."

The oppressive heat of the arena steals my breath away as the world crashes around my ears. "The food... for the feast... is us?" I can't breathe; the air is too hot in my lungs. The thought of Miyuki or Keoki being eaten as I watch is heart-rending. "No. *No.* He can't! I swore we wouldn't die here. We've got to get out!"

The creature makes a humming noise, neither agreement nor denial. "Interesting. Do you think you can?"

I stare at him. "We've got to! There are fourteen of us—thirteen, if you don't count Justin—and if we work together and use our powers, there's got to be a way!"

He snorts, amusement flickering over his face. "Your powers," he muses, reaching up a mist-shrouded hand to stroke at the line of his jaw. "You're a magic-spotter, aren't you?"

"Yes. I'm supposed to be rare." *Now, if only I can use that in some way,* I think, my mind racing.

"You are, but he altered you very roughly." His eyes narrow with interest. "The Master of Masques is infamous in these parts for his shoddy work with humans. No finesse at all, just drags your talents to the surface and calls the job done. You'd be far more powerful in the hands of a competent faery, but then we wouldn't have little anomalies like your ability to see someone straddling the shadow-realm."

He considers me for a long moment while I try and fail to calm the flood of thoughts and fears washing over me. "I've made up my mind," he announces, as though I'd been waiting patiently for him all this time rather than paralyzed with anxiety. "I will give you directions and aid in exchange for a favor to be named later. Do you accept this deal?"

I frown, tasting the lingering traces of ash in my mouth. "What kind of directions and aid? The answers you gave in our last deal were almost useless. I could promise you a favor and get nothing in return."

He raises an eyebrow. "If you are unsatisfied with my answers, perhaps you asked the wrong questions; yet here I thought you had learned much. As for my current offer, logic dictates that it would be in my best interests for you to survive, as otherwise my favor will die with you."

I shake my head. "I've already said we're going to escape. You could be hoping for a free favor when we've succeeded. Without any kind of conditions? No way. I won't hurt Miyuki for you. Or any of my friends. Or people in general. If I get away from this place, I don't want to see any more killing."

Pitiless eyes sweep over me. "You're not in any position to drive a hard bargain," he points out. "Since you are so concerned, however, I agree with your condition and will not require you to harm anyone. Make no mistake, human: without the help I am offering, you will never escape your master or his hungry parent. I am satisfied in either case; my interest is in observation, not your personal safety."

I can't trust him. I know this for a fact, as strongly as I know the word for the sun above us. He's the same kind of creature as the one who holds me captive, and there's never been a trace of sympathy in his eyes. Yet if he's telling the truth, I need all the help he's willing to give. I'd been desperate for a single fact about the outside world and now he's offering me detailed instructions. All I have to do is promise him my total obedience in an unknown task which, in the best possible scenario, I will live to regret.

Worst case, I kill myself after I get Miyuki to safety. I can live with that, so to speak.

I swallow back the lump in my throat. "Deal."

His lips part in a smile and I see teeth the color of gray ash. One hand reaches out to stroke my cheek and I'm frozen to the spot. "This is going to hurt," he says, as pain stabs me with the force of a steel spike.

Every color in the arena brightens slowly, building to a blinding climax. The sun becomes a searing ball of agony; the blue of the sky burns its imprint on my very soul. The man touching my cheek and rooting me to

260

the spot is a swirl of smoky gray, misty white, and a wild thread of black ember that ripples through him burning everything he touches. Out of the corner of my eye I see, in an inky corner of shadow, a flash of glittering silver that grows brighter alongside the pain. *The necklace.*

"That's better," the faery announces, his words reaching me from far away. "Now let's close that pesky little crack. I don't need you seeing me unless I want you to. Then we can discuss directions." The world grows brighter, my eyes screaming in pain as he fades from my sight. With all my effort I open my mouth wide enough for sound to escape, but the agonized howling in my mind emerges only as a soft wheeze.

No one is coming to help me.

CHAPTER 26

Keoki

When Matías said we should spend our time training in preparation for the upcoming match, I hadn't realized it would hurt so much. After returning to Justin with food and helping him choke down his meal, I come back out to the main cavern to find I've been matched with Tony. Matías has this idea that I need to learn to dodge blows better than I did during the match with the bear, when I pretty much *didn't*.

The session that follows is the opposite of fun on a couple of different levels: for one, I'm acutely aware Tony isn't learning from my uncreative flailing, which makes me feel like an inept waste of his time. For two, training to dodge involves being hit a lot. Not with a sword, but with a lightweight hollowed-out stick. After the fiftieth or sixtieth tap from that thing, the aches begin to add up, not helped by my repeated flinging of myself into the sand to avoid the stick.

Tony is a little too enthusiastic in his attempts to beat me senseless. I'm told they started him with sticks before he worked up to learning swords, and now he's feeling nostalgic. "Of course, that was before we figured out we could just practice on Reese," he says, shaking hair out of his eyes.

"Matías worries, but we haven't hurt him yet. Anyway, there's not enough time to take it slow. You get good fast or you get killed. Speaking of Reese, you really ought to take a turn at him."

"I ought to do what now?" I ask, and promptly take a stick to the face because I've stopped moving. That's how I end up with a sword in my hands facing down a grinning Reese.

"C'mon, newbie," he teases, wrapping cloth around his knuckles and balancing on the balls of his feet. "If you can cut me even once, I'll clean your room next time Handler brings round the mops and buckets." This is high stakes, I decide, and I want to show off after spending the whole cycle so far being pounded into the sand. I lunge at him with the blade, he dances backwards with a laugh, and we're off.

I still don't know Reese's talent. I'd seen him fight in practice, using his fists in conjunction with weapons I didn't have a word for: there were two of them, each looking like a short knife with a flat metal handle studded with spikes. Reese had gripped the flat handles in his fists in such a way that the spikes slid out of the gaps between his fingers, then Matías wrapped strips of cloth around each hand to keep everything in place. At the end of these preparations, he'd been equipped with two long blades that jutted out at a right angle to his fists and a punch that had the force of metal behind it and four wicked spikes in front.

Reese isn't using his weapons for our practice, presumably because I've aptly demonstrated I can't be trusted to get out of harm's way. We move around the pit at a steady pace; I swing and stab with a weapon I have no idea how to use while he jumps about grinning and avoiding my blows. Matías watches from the sidelines and explains how everything I'm doing is wrong. I take the criticism as best I can and keep chasing, determined to carve a proper cut into my friend since we've all agreed that's what friends do.

He isn't making it easy, though. Reese moves with practiced skill, even if he isn't inhumanly fast like Matías nor graceful in the same way as Tony.

He avoids my clumsy swings and thrusts with ease and even gets close enough to cuff me around the head a few times, the blows making my ears ring. I'm starting to think he's a bruiser like me—talented to the tune of smacking things really hard and having good-looking arms—when the sand shifts out from under his feet as he dances back and he falls hard on his ass.

I don't need Matías' encouraging yell to urge me forward. I pounce on Reese, raking the blade over the arm he's reflexively thrown up. "Ha! Gotcha!" I yell, then stop and blink, because Reese has rolled back in the sand while laughing and there isn't a scratch on him. Frowning, I scrape the edge of the blade over his exposed knee. Nothing happens. My frown escalates to a glare as I poke the tip of the sword directly into the top of his foot. It doesn't pierce his skin at all; it's like pushing into solid rock.

Only then do I understand what Tony meant and why newbies can practice with blades on Reese: he can't be cut.

"Reese, you cheater! Making a bet you can't lose is playing dirty," I point out, helping him up. He laughs his way through the rest of practice and is still chuckling when we yield the area to Lucas and Christian.

I don't stay to watch their match, not wanting to look at Lucas while I'm still angry, but when they come back to eat Lucas is bruised and battered and Christian looks pleased with himself. I'm still not happy, but I guess that's supposed to be that. *For everyone other than Tony, at least.*

We eat in silence and everything feels wrong. I can't shake a lingering dread as I drift off to bed, and even when Tony slips under the blanket to lie beside me it isn't as comforting as it should be. I pull him into a tight hug and bury my face in his neck, trying to imagine something other than Justin's puffy face or Sapphire's bruises.

I wake to the sound of first bell with a sharp pain in my stomach. I feel like I've just been punched by a stone-monster, which makes sense when I realize I've actually been kneed by Tony as he scrambles to climb over me.

"*Ow*, what the—" I gasp before he clamps a hand over my mouth and sinks further back into the darkness, pressing himself against the far side of the niche where my bed is carved into the cave wall.

"—you will be ready when I return."

"Yes, Handler."

Miyuki's voice floats through the opening door just before she's shoved into the room and the door slams shut behind her. She stumbles and I leap up intending to catch her, but I smack my head on the ceiling above the bed and end up crouched over, holding my head and moaning loudly.

"Ow, ow, ow, *ow*! Can we please start everything over?" I groan.

Miyuki takes me by the shoulders, guiding me back to bed. When I look up, I see the glitter of metal and glass on her face. "Are you always this jumpy when you wake up? It takes Aniyah— who's there?"

She gasps and draws back, her hands clenching into fists at her sides. "Oh! Hey, no, it's okay," I tell her. "It's only Tony. He didn't want Handler to see him, but you're fine."

Tony sticks his head out, letting the glow of light catch his face. "Hi," he says, looking sheepish. I can tell he's not thrilled to have been caught, but he runs a hand through his shaggy hair and makes the best of it. "You're here to check on Keoki?"

She doesn't relax, looking as if she might begin pacing the small room at any moment. "Well, that's how we convinced Handler to let me come. Imani gave me the right words to say: your scars are healed up but there's risk of infection and inflammation." She pronounces the words with care, and I wonder if they mean any more to her than the vague tugging sensation they have on my mind. "So he let me bring the healing water. It was the only way we could think to get a message to you guys."

"Oh, hey." I give her a warm grin, one I hope will be reassuring. "That was smart. We've been wondering how you're all doing. How's Sapphire?"

A queer look crosses her face, as though she didn't expect the question and it isn't quite welcome. "She'll be fine," she says, her voice tight. "I have to talk to you. Can I trust you? Both of you?"

I blink, not really understanding the question. "Um. Yes?"

Tony nods from his seat beside me, his chin resting on his knee and our blanket strategically positioned over his lap. "You keep our secret," he points out, his dark eyes solemn. "We'll keep yours."

Miyuki takes a deep breath. "We're escaping," she whispers, the words tumbling out. "Soon. We want you to come with us."

I don't understand for a moment; it's as if she's spoken a string of nonsense. Then the sound of Tony sucking air between his teeth brings home the gravity of her words. "How?" he demands, leaning forward. "When?"

"This cycle." Her voice is low and urgent. "We can't wait any longer than that. The others are resting now so we won't need to sleep later."

I shake my head, trying to put the pieces together. "What do you mean, you can't wait any longer? What's the rush?"

She runs a hand under her glasses, rubbing at her eyes. "Last cycle, Handler took Aniyah up to the arena to look for a necklace lost by a guest. While she was up there, she overheard voices; we think it was the Master talking to Handler. He said there's going to be a big event soon: a feast for one of his parents."

"Handler said something about that to Matías," Tony says, a deep crease etched into his brow. "He said there was a big match coming up; a bunch of us fighting to put on a show. Is the feast afterwards?"

Miyuki shakes her head, worry flashing in her eyes. "The way Aniyah overheard it, you guys *are* the feast. Maybe us, too; we don't want to wait around to find out for sure who's being eaten."

I sit up so straight I nearly hit the ceiling again. "They can't kill all of us at once, not without giving us a chance." But my stomach curls in on itself. Even one of us dying would be too much. *What if they take Tony?*

"Why couldn't they?" Tony's voice is low, his chin hooked on his knee as he stares into the middle distance. "Kill everyone and start over with a fresh batch. They might deem the cost acceptable if they know what we've been up to."

266

I frown at him. "We haven't been up to anything! We eat and sleep and train, just like they want."

"We don't always obey. We look for names before Handler takes away the clothes. We know how to have fun without Prizes, or without using them the way we're expected to. If those things are important to the Master and if Handler noticed..." He shakes his head, his expression grim. "Newbies wouldn't know to do any of that. A fresh batch would do whatever Handler said without question. They'd be too afraid not to."

"We're in danger for the same reasons," Miyuki agrees, her lips thin. "Hana gets the names from new girls before the Master erases their memories. It took them ages to come up with that idea, and we were careless the cycle we tended you and Justin. Handler was here, and we don't know if he noticed us using our real names. He hasn't said anything about it, but how can we be sure? If they decided to wipe everyone out, any new girls they collect wouldn't know how to save their names."

Tony leans forward, watching her intently. "So if we're gonna die in this feast anyway, maybe it *is* better to go out in an escape. You said this cycle. You have some kind of plan?"

Her voice drops lower, as though the walls themselves could hear us over the burble of the fountain. "The doors are magic. That's how they keep us trapped. But Aniyah sees magic, how it flows and works. That's why she's so important to the Master. She understands the doors and thinks she can get them to open without Handler's help." Miyuki hesitates, looking down at her hands. "She's not *sure*, though. So we've got two plans. If you guys are willing to help, we can try them both at the same time."

I look over at Tony to see if he's following all this stuff about magic doors; he's nodding along with her, so he's doing better than I am. *I wish Matías were here*, I think, frowning as I chew on my lower lip.

"What do we need to do?" Tony asks, ignoring me in his focus on the girl.

"If we can't get the doors open, then we're going to have to force

Handler to help. When he brings the third meal, you jump him. Make him open the doors. We'll work on our doors on our own. If both plans work, we'll meet in the hallway; if only one method works, it'll be up to that group to get the other one out."

"And if neither plan works, we're in deep shit," Tony notes, closing his eyes and leaning back with a sigh. "Especially us. It's not like we can hide an attack on Handler and pretend it never happened."

"You can always sell us out for a lesser punishment," Miyuki offers, her voice dry as sand.

"Hey! We wouldn't do that," I protest, shaking my head at her. I give Tony a light punch in the arm, wincing as my muscles scold me for last cycle's training. "One of those ought to work, right? Aniyah wouldn't say she could do something unless she believed it. And I'm pretty sure we can take Handler!"

Tony drums his fingers against the mattress. "Far as I know, no one's ever tried. He could be a total pushover or he could be stronger than all of us combined. Once we're through the doors, then what?"

"There's a gate to the outside," Miyuki whispers, leaning forward. "Aniyah saw it. And she can see an escape route from the way the magic flows through the land. A refuge from captivity." She's talking faster now, her voice urgent in the darkness. "Isn't that worth taking a risk? A place where we can be free? Where we can be who we want, *with* whoever we want, without being killed or sold or punished?"

Tony runs a hand through his hair, avoiding her gaze. "Shit." The word is a soft hiss between his teeth. "Yeah, it would be. But if we do this, it's for keeps; there's no turning back once we start."

"That's a good thing, right?" I find his hand under the thin blanket. "Hey, I know I was overconfident in the last match. I got wounded and made you worry about me and I'm sorry. But even if we're careful and do everything right—if we rest and train and eat and sleep and don't do anything stupid like volunteer for private matches—there's always the chance they'll send us out there to face something we can't handle. I've been dealing with that fear by not thinking about it, but I don't know how long that's gonna work, Tony."

He looks down, and I barrel forward because I'm afraid if I stop now I'll break down and cry. "You've seen Justin; I can't deal with the possibility that might happen to you. And it's not a question of skill; they didn't even leave weapons for Christian and me! What are we gonna do when pushing over a pillar doesn't work? Or I can't catch a platform on the way down and I break my legs off? Dude, are you gonna love me without my legs?" I duck my head, trying to meet his eyes. "Because I gotta say, I think my legs are one of my best features. I don't wanna take the chance of you seeing me without them on."

It works; he smiles. A grin spreads across his face and he raises his head to roll his eyes at me. "Keoki, as excellent as your legs are, I'm fairly certain their absence would not affect my feelings for you."

"Man, I don't know. I still think it's a risk not worth taking." Now it's my turn to look down, staring at the spot under the blanket where our fingers lace together. I drop the teasing tone and whisper. "You know, if she's right, we're dead anyway. I'd rather have a chance. What's the alternative, to get good enough at this that we land teaching jobs with Matías? Train newbies and watch them die? I wouldn't be happy like that, dude. I can't think *he* is."

He watches me for a long moment, his gaze holding mine until there's nothing in the room but him and the pain buried in his dark eyes. It seems a lifetime ago I thought him entirely unreadable and now I can see my own hurt mirrored in his eyes. The frustration of nothing here tasting the way it should. The uncertainty that comes with having extra words for things, words the other boys don't seem to have. The constant dread of never knowing when the next match will be and whether a friend will be taken away forever.

This is why they'd start over fresh, I think, leaning in on a sudden impulse to press my forehead against his. *The names are just a part of it. We're supposed to be strangers, and instead we care about each other. If we work together, like Miyuki says, what couldn't we do?*

Tony takes a deep breath and reluctantly pulls away from me. "You know, if we do this, we don't have a lot of time to prepare."

I grin at the decision in his voice. "So we *are* doing this?"

"Yes. We need to be smart about it, though. Miyuki, we'll take you out to talk to Matías—"

Miyuki interrupts, crossing her arms over her chest. "No."

I blink at her, confused. "No?"

She meets my questioning look with a firm gaze. "No. I'm not going to tell the other boys. That'll be your job, *after* Handler takes me back."

Tony frowns and for once he looks as lost as I feel. "Why does it matter who tells them the plan?"

"It's not a question of *who*, it's a question of *when*. After Handler leaves, you won't see him again until he brings the third meal."

I stare at her, my mouth slowly drooping open. "You think someone's gonna tell Handler what you're planning? But then why did you tell us?" I look over at Tony, his expression carefully blank.

"Aniyah and I trust you," she says, as though this were the most obvious thing in the world. "That doesn't mean we trust all of you. We're not going to risk Lucas telling Handler the plan. When you guys jump Handler, he can help or get out of the way. But he won't have a chance to sound a warning."

Heated words are forming on my lips, but Tony squeezes my hand hard before I can speak. "Okay. We get it. I don't think Lucas would do that," he adds, his calm voice free of judgment, "but it makes sense to be careful."

She gives him a sour look. "Don't tell me what Lucas would or wouldn't do. Don't expect any of us to trust him ever again." Her voice is low, with the air of having settled an argument. I glance at Tony for his reaction, but he simply nods.

Only with difficulty do I bite my tongue. Lucas hurt them, yes, and that was wrong, but it doesn't mean he'd ruin our chance to escape. Surely what he did isn't a good enough reason to waste crucial time. We're going to need to explain all this, to work out an attack strategy that will leave Handler incapacitated but not dead, and maybe catch some sleep since we won't be getting any after this goes down. That's a lot to fit between now and then, so it hurts to not be allowed to start until she leaves.

But one look at her face tells me I won't win her over. And while we could overrule her wishes and tell the guys now, it seems like a bad idea to kick off a cooperative escape plan by betraying the trust of half the group. So I sigh and lean back against the cave wall, wishing I didn't feel so tired. "What do we do in the meantime?"

Miyuki gives me an exasperated look. "After Handler takes me back, you guys need to collect enough weapons and armor for all of us to use. You'll also need to save the food bowls from second meal for carrying water, and you'll have to make slings or something to carry them. So cool your heels and help me and Tony make a list of everything we need and how we're going to get it out of here."

I offer my most plaintive pout in supplication. "Can we sleep a little longer first?"

She rolls her eyes but the effect is softened by her smile. "C'mon, now's your chance to show me you're worth half as much as Aniyah thinks you are."

CHAPTER 27

Aniyah

"W e'll need to wrap up the way we do for matches, completely covered with no skin showing; otherwise the sun will sear us and we'll be too weak to get very far." Imani gathers up armfuls of gauzy cloth as she talks, briskly dumping everything in a big pile on her bed.

"Damn, I didn't think to tell the boys that. I hope they're not going to run around topless, the way they usually do." Miyuki pushes xer glasses up xer nose, squinting as xie peers up at the sunlight pouring through the hole in our ceiling. "Did you sense any shade beyond the gate, Aniyah?"

"Only distantly, on the other side of the border. There might be a little at the cliffs, but I wouldn't count on that for shelter." The lies come effortlessly now, rolling from my tongue without hesitation.

I did *try* to tell the truth when I was brought back from the arena. I was woozy from what the shadowy man had done to me, my senses so heightened that the magic around me had become a constant assault of glittering light. Hana and Miyuki were there to catch me when I stumbled over the threshold of the golden doors and I opened my mouth to speak the truth, too weary to care about a vow I'd never intended to keep. Then

272

I tasted ash on my tongue and my throat dried until all I could do was sputter wordlessly.

Miyuki brought me water and stroked my shoulder as I gulped down the soothing liquid, but each fresh attempt to speak brought another round of shuddering coughs. Only when I gave up the effort and resolved to lie did the ash wash away. So I'd 'heard' the news of our doom, letting the others deduce that the speaker had been the Master. And I'd 'sensed' the path through the wasteland, rather than receive detailed instructions from an invisible voice as I lay faint beside a bench in the arena.

I don't know if these easy lies are part of the magic that seals the truth inside me or a facet of my own character; I only know that lying to Miyuki ought to be harder than this. Even knowing it's the best chance I have to save our lives, I'm uneasy with the deal I've struck. *I just need to get everyone out and safe,* I remind myself. *Once we're away from here, I can decide what to do about the shadow man.*

"We've got enough cloth to cover the boys," Hana says, breaking into my thoughts. "My real worry is water. Even if we cover up, the sun will suck the moisture out of us. We've seen boys faint from thirst in the arena; I don't want that happening to any of us."

"Handler only brought nine bowls with second meal," Sappho says, looking up from the table with a dejected expression. "I guess we're lucky he brought any at all."

It's hard not to wince at the pain in her voice. Her wounds are healing—the purple-red bruises have turned a mottled yellow-green at the edges—but her mood is still low. Not even the prospect of escape has lifted her distress and, though she's insisted that what happened was not my fault, I still feel guilty.

"If you count the ones we've been keeping by our beds, that makes fifteen." Chloe carries them in a stack to the table, separating the bowls into three neat little towers.

Heather looks up from her seat by Sappho, her chin resting on her hands. "That's two for everyone else to carry and three for me? Joy and rapture."

"The boys should bring enough water for themselves, as long as they don't flake out on us." Hana counts on her fingers with a frown. "Well. Not the wounded one, of course. And someone will have to carry him, so that's two boys not lugging water. But we'll make it work."

Imani surveys her pile of cloth and pulls out several long strips. "We can wrap up the food that Handler brought for second meal. The fruits will bruise, but if we're lucky the meat will dry in the heat. Anyway, we don't need it to last long, just until we get to the border." She looks up at me, and I see the lingering doubt in her eyes warring with hope. "After that we'll be safe, won't we?"

"I think so." I want to say more but my throat is pricking as I remember the strange words the faery man had whispered as a punctuation to his directions: *'When you reach the forest on the other side of the chasm then, if you humans wish deeply enough to cross over into freedom, you will do so.'*

Chloe doesn't look at us, preoccupied with more immediate concerns. She frowns at the bowls she's stacked. "We can make slings from the curtains to carry them, but sloshing will be a problem. Every step we take, water is gonna be slopping out over the tops."

"What if we leave them stacked?" Sappho's voice is soft, her hands reaching out to run over the bowls. "They've got that indented lip around the top rim that lets him stack everything on the cart. It's not a perfect seal and water would still get out, but it'd be a slower leak than an open bowl in each hand."

Hana makes a face and walks over to the table, picking up a bowl and measuring it with her hand. "Wrist to finger," she mutters. "And we've got fifteen? We could make a couple stacks of seven and eight, but they'll be heavy when they're full."

"Halter across the neck?" Miyuki suggests as xie adjusts xer glasses. Xer nose glistens with slippery sweat after spending half a cycle running around making preparations. "Who's going to carry it, though?"

274

"Maybe one of the boys?" I suggest, anxious to contribute. I'm watching from my bed where I've been ordered to rest, since I'll slow the group enough without wearing myself out packing. But I hate having to sit still while the others run around; I feel antsy and useless. "Keoki could—"

Chloe scoffs before I can finish, shaking her head with amusement. "Y'all, I can handle them myself. Get them filled and stacked and tied up and I'll carry them fine. Just make sure they're wrapped tight so they don't shift off each other when I move."

It isn't a perfect plan, but no one can think of a better way to carry the water. Miyuki and Hana fill the bowls at the pool and bring them back to my bed. Chloe rips curtains into strips of heavy fabric and I tie the strips around the stacked bowls, securing everything tightly. Then Imani wraps the two little towers until they're cushioned in a thick weave that allows only the slightest movement. The result isn't perfect, but as long as Chloe doesn't move too fast it'll probably be okay.

Under different circumstances, I'd find this work relaxing; as it is, my heart is pounding and my shoulders feel stiff as the stone beneath me. Time seems to pass much faster than I feel it should, which is vexing when every cycle up to this one has been spent longing for the bells to come sooner. Everything *must* be finished before the third meal, and the other girls whirl around the cavern as they wrap food in gauze bundles and drape cloth over every inch of their skin and mine.

At last, Hana judges the time close enough for us to take our places. Miyuki helps me off the bed, xer glasses catching the sunlight as we walk to the door. It occurs to me that if this works and we manage to escape, xie will never have to hide xer glasses again. It's a small thing next to all of us being free and alive, but longing tears spring to my eyes. *If we stay together and don't panic, we can do this.*

Miyuki guides me forward until we stand before the golden doors. Ever since my senses were sharpened by the shadowy faery—whom I've begun to call the 'Shadow Man' in my head—the doors have glowed like a beacon, shining brighter than the sun which spills through our ceiling. Tendrils of magic writhe over the surface, like shrunken arms flailing bonelessly for something to grasp. Their constant wriggling unnerves me and I hate standing this close.

"Okay, Aniyah, do what you have to do," Hana prompts, shouldering her sack of fruit.

I nod without turning away from the doors. I know how the magic works now. I can *see* it, as clearly as I see the freckles on Miyuki's face. I understand the way Handler reaches out to the magic and how it flows through him as a conduit. Now I just have to create that circuit myself. *What could go wrong?*

Holding my breath, I take a step forward. I stand alone in front of the doors and spread my arms, waiting for the writhing tendrils to notice me. A thick golden strand brushes against my face, too warm to be comfortable; I swallow hard and wait for the others to follow. They reach out now that they know I'm here, encircling my wrists and caressing my face.

I'm part of you, I think, willing the magic to understand. *You recognize me, don't you? We were made by the same Master. The twists and turns in your design are stamped on me as well. I see it now.* The magic pulses faster, perhaps in response to my thoughts or the stillness of my stance, and hot light flows over and through me. The door glows subtly brighter, and I wait for the crack to appear down the center.

Nothing happens. We wait, the tension in the room rising as breath is held and feet shuffle in place.

"Aniyah?" Hana's voice is low, verging on the edge of concerned.

"I don't know about you guys, but I'm super impressed," Heather drawls, setting her pack against her feet.

I shake my head and step back, grimacing with frustration. "It's trying to work! I can tell by the way it speeds up. It goes faster when it flows through someone, and flows fastest through *him*. The cuts in his face and hands, the patterns—" My voice trails off as I turn to face the others and my gaze catches the shimmer that dances unceasingly over Imani's face.

Imani's talent is to alter her face. They captured her so the boys would have variety in their beds, but she uses her talent to tell stories instead. She's entertained me over the long cycles when I waited for Miyuki to return, her face remaking itself for each speaker in her tales with almost limitless range. *And her body is stamped with the same magic as me and the doors.*

She watches me staring at her. "Aniyah? Can I help?"

I lick my lips as the idea solidifies in my head. "Imani, can you alter your face to be like Handler's? With the cuts? And maybe your hands as well?" The flickering magic dispersed over her body is concentrated in her face, but a glimmer stretches over her extremities. "Just enough to change the texture. That's all we need."

Imani takes a deep breath, looking unsure. "I'll try."

She closes her eyes, her breath deepening as though falling asleep. The magic in her face flares so brightly I have to avert my eyes; when I look back, cracks are forming. Hairline fractures spread over her face and thicken into furrows so deep I could press my finger into the rows. Smaller cuts ripple up her hands and over her wrists, the strain of producing them etched into her tense shoulders.

"Aniyah." Her voice is a whisper through clenched teeth. "I don't know how long I can hold this."

"You're doing fine! Let me just—" I jump forward, ignoring the accompanying twinge of pain in my lower back as something I'm just going to deal with later. I put my hands on her shoulders and guide her into position with her arms stretched out, letting the magic find her. "Hold still. It's going to be warm, but let it flow through you; don't fight it."

The tendrils find her faster than they did me. They reach out with greedy hunger, sinking into her face and hands. My heart pounds as the light coating the door brightens with fierce urgency. Imani gasps, the sound loud in the silence, and I tighten my grip on her shoulder. "Just a little longer. It's working!" The air throbs with heat as the magic glows red through the cracks in her skin, casting the same shimmer in the air as the torches lighting the hallways.

A dark crack bisects the golden doors and someone behind me sucks in a surprised mouthful of air. I'm turning to grin at Miyuki when the light pulses again, this time brightly enough to leave me blinded. Imani cries out in pain and collides with me as she's flung backwards. We go down in a tangle of limbs, my groan inaudible over the clamor of voices and the screech of doors being hauled open before they can close again.

"Exactly what is going on here?"

The unexpected sound of Handler's voice traces raw fear down my spine. I look up from where I've fallen with Imani unconscious on top of me, blinking my eyes against the golden afterimage burned into my sight. The hooded man stands in the hallway outside, his cart loaded with food. *He came to feed us first.* We'd assumed he would go to the boys first, serving us later; they were the most valuable, after all.

"Heather, take the door!"

Hana is the first to react, her shout rising over the sudden terrified silence. Handler sweeps past her and Chloe without a backward glance and she glares at his back in frustrated impotence, the two girls unable to move from where they'd leaped forward to grab the doors when Imani and I were flung away. If we don't keep them open, the doors will pull themselves closed and we'll be trapped again.

Heather doesn't seem to hear; she's frozen to the spot, staring at Handler with wide, unblinking eyes. Sappho jumps to her feet and rushes forward, but Handler backhands her with a wide sweep of his inhumanly long arms. She staggers before collapsing to the stone floor, clutching at the bruise over her eye. He doesn't even check his walk, continuing in his long stride until he reaches the spot where I scrabble against stone in an unsuccessful attempt to get out from under Imani.

"You," he growls, peering down at me with his sightless gaze. Fear rolls off him in waves, setting my teeth on chattering edge. "I knew you were going to be trouble. Come here." He stoops to grab my arm and cold terror shoots through me.

"Don't you touch her!" Miyuki yells in a voice hoarse with fury. Xie darts forward to grab his hands where he grips me. I see a flash of magic, the sparkles in xer hands flaring into the air and sinking into his skin. He reels away in shock, clutching his hands to his sides at an odd angle while his feet skitter too fast on the stone. Miyuki drops to xer knees, hands fumbling to help me up even as xer breathing is labored.

"What did you do?" I hiss, scrambling to my knees as Miyuki rolls Imani off me. Now that she's no longer on top of me, I see what tore her consciousness away: the magic flowing through her face and hands has burned her, leaving angry scars in place of the furrows. *Oh, no! Imani, this is all my fault. I am so sorry.*

"It's— I figured—" Miyuki's breath comes hard and fast, struggling to get the words out. "The things I do to your muscles to loosen them? I reversed it. Imani, hon, we need you to wake up now," xie adds, placing xer hands on either side of the dazed girl's face. "I can take the pain away, but you have to get up."

"Heather, snap out of it and take the door!" I look up at Hana's bellow to see alarm written on her face as Handler stumbles backwards into the hallway. "He'll get the Master if we don't stop him! *Heather!*"

"I got it," Chloe growls, her voice low under Hana's shout. In a blur of sudden movement, she kicks back hard against her door. I clap my hands over my ears in automatic response to the horrible grinding *crunch* that follows when metal meets stone with far more enthusiasm than either would desire. The door shudders and buckles at the point of the kick, sticking fast to the wall. Chloe strides after Handler, her expression furious.

He's taller than her by more than a head and still sweats magical fear from every pore, infecting anyone who draws close with paralyzing dread. But his hands hang stiffly at his side, completely useless to him now, and Chloe's anger seems to carry her over the cresting fear as though feeding on all lesser emotions. She grabs him by the robes, her fist crumpling the fabric in a tight knot and pulling him forward until he's forced to stoop down to her level.

"You ever wonder what the boys think just before they die?"

The tone of her question is calm, almost pleasant. Before he can answer she jerks his robes in a swift forward tug. A loud crunch resonates as his face slams hard into the floor, followed by a second when she places her foot on the back of his head and presses down in a quick stomp.

Liquid oozes from the mangled remains of his head, and she shakes her foot daintily as she steps out of the mess. "Heather, are you okay? You kinda froze up there."

The blond girl nods her head, closing her eyes as she swallows hard. "Yeah." She doesn't say more on the subject but Hana studies her with worried eyes.

"C'mon," Hana orders. "Help Imani and Sappho up, then we have to reach the boys. Shit, with Handler dead we don't have any other way to open the doors. We're just gonna have to do this again."

Imani stands with Miyuki's help; at Hana's words she runs a shaky hand over her tight curls. "I'm ready," she chokes out, but the scars on her face tell another story. I'm not even sure if she *can* form the furrows again, given the state of her burns.

"I'm okay too," Sappho manages, pulling herself to her feet with Heather's help. "It just hurt, that's all."

"Up, up, up, here we go," chants Hana, ushering us through the doors and around the corpse of our jailer before jogging down the hall to the boys' cavern. I try a tentative run and conclude that, while it hurts like hell, it won't kill me. My body will make me pay for this later, but I'll either be free or dead by then so it won't matter.

"Look, worst case maybe Chloe can kick the doors down," Sappho suggests as we run, wiping blood from her cheek where Handler struck her. "Maybe you guys can open them halfway and Chloe can—"

Her voice dies away as we round the bend in the long hallway and skid to a halt. In front of us are the enormous black doors to the boys' cavern, imposing in their solidity and frightening in the strange writhing pattern of their magic.

280

The doors are currently open, though closing fast with the ponderous screech of metal on stone. Through the rapidly disappearing crack in the center of the doors we catch a glimpse of Handler, robed and hooded, with a silver cart near at hand.

CHAPTER 28

Keoki

There isn't time to lead up to the whole escape plan; the moment the doors close behind Handler and Miyuki, I have to dive onto the food to keep the guys from tearing into it. "Hungry?" Christian asks, picking meat from a bowl he'd snatched up before I almost landed in his lap gathering dishes into my arms.

"No. Shut up and listen." I frown, panting to catch my breath, and look at Tony. "Maybe you should tell them."

He gives Matías a level look, ignoring the others. "The girls are going to escape. This cycle, at third meal. They want us to come with them. The healer told us." He takes a deep breath. "They think the big upcoming match isn't something we'll be allowed to survive: that our deaths are the whole *point* of it."

Matías looks unsteady as the blood drains from his face. "Do they have good reason to believe that?"

Tony shrugs and thins his lips. "One of them was on clean-up duty in the arena and overheard the Master talking; said he was setting up a big feast to *eat* all of us, if you can believe it. I guess he could've known she was there and set it up for her to hear, but it wouldn't make any sense for him to do that."

Reese stares at us. "So we're gonna go? Just like that? Has Diamond got a plan?"

"We have a list of stuff to bring," I tell him, laying out a sheet to spread food upon. "You think we can wrap everything in one bundle, Tony? Problem will be arranging things so we won't have to undo the whole pack if we want to take a bite off the top."

"Knot it up at multiple points, so a spill wouldn't lose everything," Tony advises. "And, yeah, just like that. The other new girl, the one they brought in with the healer, has a talent she thinks can get her through the doors. If so, they'll come and collect us; if not, they want us to make Handler open the doors."

Christian's eyebrows rise and he gives a low whistle. "Well, now. That's tempting."

"*Capture*," Matías says in a warning tone. "If we kill him, we're not getting through."

"Could kill him after," Lucas points out, looking thoughtful. "This is happening at third meal? Not a lot of time."

Reese hops to his feet. "Okay, what do we need to do?"

I hadn't realized how much I'd braced myself for an argument until my shoulders sag with relief. "Um. Weapons for everyone, doubled up because the girls want some for themselves. All the food and as much water as possible. And we'll need some poles to stretch cloth between so we can carry Justin."

"Wait, what?" Lucas looks up with a frown. "No, we're not taking him. That's ridiculous." Every eye in the cavern turns to stare at him and he bristles. "No! Are you all sun-struck? He's half-dead as it is, there's no way we can carry him to wherever we're going. Where *are* we going, anyway?"

Tony gives him a hard look. "The girl who opens doors is also a tracker. We're following her out. All of us."

Lucas' glare intensifies. "He's *dying*. Do you think it's better for him to die out there than in here, and slow us down while he's doing it? If we're going to run, we have one chance! This isn't practice, this is a real match, and if he was dumped into a match with any of us right now, we'd have to let him die." His head whips around to stare at Matías. "You know I'm right."

Matías takes a deep breath and his knuckles tighten on his cane. "We're taking him with us. I won't leave him behind to bear our punishment for leaving."

"We could kill hi—"

"*No.*" Matías turns away, an air of finality in the set of his shoulders. "Keoki, take Reese to my room. I keep a stash of poles for cutting into canes as the old ones wear out. There should be a couple long enough to make a stretcher. Christian, you and Tony are on weapon duty. Lucas, help me with the food."

I take off at a trot with Reese's footsteps close behind me. *Poles plus blanket equals stretcher,* I think as we burst into the room. *I'm strong. That's my talent, the thing I'm best at. I can take the brunt of the weight and Reese can take the other end.*

These reassurances do little to distract me from a whirl of worried images: Aniyah's perfect face creased with pain, Sapphire's bruises glaring in the firelight, Miyuki's irritated told-you-so expression. She hadn't been right about Lucas—he agreed right away to go, with no thought of selling us out to Handler—but I'd never expected an argument over leaving behind one of our own.

"Hey." Reese's voice breaks through my thoughts as we sort through the poles by Matías' bed, searching for the strongest. "This *is* gonna work, right? All that stuff the healer said to you? What's her name again?"

I look up to find him watching me in the dim light, his eyes wide with hope. "Her name's Miyuki. She's friends with Aniyah, the pretty one. I think it will work, yeah. If Aniyah says she can do something, I trust her. We've just gotta do our part. Like taking care of Justin," I add, studying his face for a reaction.

He snorts and turns away, stripping the bed of its blanket for the stretcher. "Are you asking my opinion? I'd leave Lucas behind before I'd be okay with leaving Justin," he says, his voice firm. "Do you think one blanket can bear the weight, or should I get the one from my room, too?"

The blankets are so thin that we end up using three, liberating the one from my room to layer over the rest. We wind fabric around the poles, then cut slits through the blankets and loop a sheet through the cuts, fastening knots as we go. We could make a better one if we had more time, but this will do. We carry Tony in a lap around the cavern to test it before lifting Justin out of bed and onto his new stretcher.

"Where are we going?" Justin asks, looking up at me with bleary eyes. He doesn't seem entirely here and his skin is clammy, beaded with sweat. I try not to recall Lucas' earlier words.

"We're going somewhere better, dude. There's three girls for every guy there, and not just during Auctions. The food is amazing, too. So you gotta hang on tight and not fall out, okay?"

Tony seems less certain of my brilliant plan. "We're gonna have to lash him to the stretcher," he decides, peering at Justin with a frown. "If we're running, we don't want him to bounce off."

"We need to hide him," Christian adds, looking around the cavern. "Behind that column? If we lay him out flat at an angle, Handler shouldn't see him from the door."

Reese's brow furrows. "How *are* we going to jump him? If we crowd up near the doors, he'll see us and might not come in. We usually stay pretty far back when he brings food; he's too creepy to get close."

Matías stares at the doors, looking thoughtful. "It'll be third meal when he comes. Everyone's always drifting around at that point; washing off from practice, or taking a shit, or changing into clean clothes for bed. He won't notice if a few of us aren't in the main cavern. Tony and Lucas will hide behind those pillars. Reese and Keoki and I will sit out here pretending everything is normal. Christian, you'll sit with us, but—"

"Be ready to pop. Got it."

I'm surprised at how quickly Matías formulates plans and how easily the guys leap to their posts. *They're used to working together in the arena,* I realize, *and Matías pounds it into them in practice. I'm the only one who's new at all this teamwork stuff.*

Their honed cooperation produces a blur of activity. Weapons, food, and water are hidden by the doors. Tony and Lucas slip behind nearby pillars, and I keep an eye on Justin where he dozes fitfully. Reese sits on the floor and begins teaching me a game of carved stones; I can't concentrate but we appear busy. Christian lounges close by, looking bored as he repeatedly tosses and catches his knife in one hand. When Matías is satisfied with our deployment, he sits and carves a new cane from a fresh pole while we wait.

Time drags to a halt until I wonder if the Master knows our plans and has called off the ringing of bells until he decides how to deal with us. When we hear the screech of doors against stone, it's the most beautiful sound in the world. Handler pushes his cart into the cavern while the doors close behind him and I stare so intently at the stones in front of me that my eyes threaten to pop out of my head. "Teacher, come unlo—"

The sentence ends in a gurgle as I hear the tiny puff of air that signals Christian's movement. I whip my head up to see Handler just inside the cavern, his hands outstretched in placation. Tony presses a sword into his right side, while Lucas pokes Handler from the opposite side with a spear as long as my arm, tipped with a sharp metal blade. Christian grips the taller man from behind, holding a knife to his throat.

"We're leaving," Matías says, stabbing his cane into the ground and pulling himself up. Reese and I rush to grab the stretcher, carrying Justin between us. "You're going to take us through the doors, Handler. Don't give us any trouble and we won't kill you."

"Understood." His voice is a low rasp and he holds perfectly still under Christian's blade save for a persistent tremble in his outstretched hands.

"Tony, pass out the packs," Matías orders, scooping up one of the

286

bundles to sling over his shoulder. "Keoki and Reese, you guys have a good grip on Justin? Good. Let's go. Handler, get the doors."

Handler hesitates while Tony drapes a sling around my neck: a bundle of tied spears identical to the one Lucas carries, selected in the belief that the girls would have an easier time with those than with swords. "The Master will not like this," Handler warns, turning to face the doors as Christian and Lucas move with him. His hands are still shaking. "There will be resistance."

"We figured it wasn't gonna be easy," Christian drawls, keeping the knife on his throat as he moves. "Doors. Now."

"Yes." His words are soft as he extends his hands closer to the door and his head cranes forward in spite of the knife. "I need to be close."

A tremor ripples through his body as his words slur into a pained sigh. The doors shudder and a crack splits down the center, followed by the familiar strain of metal grinding against stone. A sudden chorus of girls' voices bursts through the sliver of air that expands between the doors.

"I can't hear a thing on the other side. Do you think—"

"Wait, it's opening!"

"Get the doors! Hold them!"

"Keoki!"

My heart jumps at the sight of Aniyah through the doorway and I have to remind myself not to drop the stretcher and run to her. "I'm here! We're okay; we got Handler to open the doors."

"I've got the door, Hana, if you wanna deal with the new Handler." The girl with fiery red hair slumps against one half of the iron doors, pinning her side open. "Seems fair, since I got the last one."

"Looks like I don't need to just yet. Where are our weapons?" Diamond—no, I must get used to calling her Hana—strides through the doorway, scanning the cavern with purpose. When her eyes land on my pack, her frown evaporates and she hurries over to grab the spears from my back. "These'll do," she decides, pulling one from the bundle and tossing the rest to the tall tattooed girl. "Sappho, hand 'em out."

"We don't need Handler any more, do we?" Christian points out, his knife sliding just far enough into his captive to bead with blood along the edge.

"Wait, we do!" Aniyah stumbles forward, one arm outstretched to stop Christian and the other digging into the small of her back as she pants for breath. "There's another door and a gate beyond it; don't kill him!"

Matías strokes his fingers along his cane, grimacing as he does so. "We'll have to tie him up. I don't want him trying anything and we need all hands for our packs."

Handler moves his outstretched hands to meet in midair in front of him, ignoring the knife teasing open skin at his neck. He still trembles and, when he clasps his hands together, one thumb begins to worry at a large mole on his wrist. Aniyah halts in front of him, her shoulders heaving as she gulps in air. At the sight of his hands, her eyes open wide and she gasps. Reaching out, she takes his hand in hers and peers at the mole.

Alarm is etched on Miyuki's face. "Aniyah! What are you doing?"

She ignores her, looking at Handler. "You're the one," she says, frowning deeply. "Aren't you? The Handler who hasn't been totally horrible. You helped me, when he wanted to sell Miyuki and I argued with him; and you warned me when you took me up to the stands."

Handler holds still under her touch, hardly seeming to breathe. Behind me, Reese clears his throat. "Um, I'm confused?"

"There's more than one Handler." The words are strained as the girl with glossy black ringlets and slender arms limps into the light. A network of dark burns has been cut over her beautiful face and her liquid brown eyes brim with fresh pain. *Shit, how did that happen?*

"That doesn't mean we're making friends with any of them," Hana warns, hefting her spear.

Aniyah doesn't let go of his hand, turning to the other girl with a pleading expression. "Hana, please trust me? I *know*. This one isn't bad."

"I can get you through the gate, but we have to hurry."

288

Shivers run down my spine at the sound of his voice. I shouldn't fear him—we have him captive and bleeding and soon to be tied—yet helpless as he is, he's as creepy as ever. I can appreciate Christian's eagerness to be done with him after having had to stand so close to that.

"C'mon, then," says Aniyah in a brisk tone that brooks no argument, grasping his hand to pull him forward. "Christian, put away that knife."

Christian stares at her for a long moment, then shrugs and takes a step back. She nods at him and pulls Handler along with her, the tall man almost stumbling from the sudden yank on his arm. Hana and Matías both set their teeth in similar grimaces, but they follow without complaint.

"He's right about one thing," Hana mutters, hefting the bag she carries as she jogs to catch up with them. "We do have to hurry. Come on!"

I look at Tony, but he just shrugs and follows. He hasn't put up his sword, though, and I'm pretty sure he could take out Handler in the time it'd take to blink if the terrifying man decides to hurt Aniyah. I don't like it, but I guess we don't have much choice.

"You ready, dude?" I look at Reese, who meets my gaze with a wide grin.

"Guess this is it," he says, his muscles tensing as he lifts his end of the stretcher. Justin moans in his sleep but doesn't stir from where we've strapped him. "Do or die, right?"

"Let's go for the 'do' part." I lift with him, feeling the tension in the poles as I do. The stretcher doesn't fall apart, but the strain in the wood as the poles bend tells me the contraption won't last forever. *It just needs to last until we get out of here.* We take up the rear behind Lucas; it might be my imagination, but the girls seem to be giving him a wide berth.

"Move, move, move," Hana orders from the front, her words drifting back down the hallway to us. "Faster, don't drop anything! No, don't mind that, it's just the last Handler. He's dead; don't poke at it."

"Babe, did you do that?" The low whistle unmistakably belongs to Christian.

"He was in my way."

"*Move*, I said!"

We round the corner behind them and I see the source of the commotion: an overturned silver cart, identical to the one we left behind, one tiny broken wheel disappearing into a pool of blood. The source of the blood is a dead body lying near the doors to the girls' room, the head a mess of brain and shattered bone.

I look at Reese, relieved to find he looks as unsettled as I feel. "Keep up," Lucas hisses back at us before rounding the next corner and running smack into Tony, who has stopped moving and whips around to glare at him.

Reese and I edge the stretcher around the corridor until I see what has caused the others to stop: another set of enormous doors stands in our way. These doors are made of bleached bones that look as though they were scavenged from arena kills. The effect might have been cool, using the bones of our enemies to build with, except I'm pretty sure the Master wouldn't see any reason not to include our bones in the building process. Tony blanches at the sight of the doors, and I wonder if he's had the same thought.

"Go ahead," Aniyah says, her voice gentle as she urges Handler forward. He nods and reaches out with his hands, tilting his head to face the stark white doors. Tony tenses his sword-arm and beside him Lucas readies his spear. Matías takes a deep breath, his eyes avoiding the bones.

Despite Aniyah's trust, I'm expecting trickery. I look at Reese, wondering if we should set down the stretcher so we can join the fray in case of a fight, or if it would be better to keep hold of Justin and be ready to run. But the doors shudder and creep open in the same ponderous manner we're used to; no tricks, no alarms. Then Aniyah gasps and takes a step back, her eyes widening with alarm.

The newly-opened doors spill onto an expanse of sunlit cavern. On the right is a gate which appears to lead to a vast desert of *not-here*. Directly across the cavern from us lies a pair of matching bone-white doors. These doors are flung open and in the dark passageway beyond loom at least a dozen Handlers, clumped tightly together in the hallway.

290

Every single one of them stares at our group with closed eyes as they shamble towards us.

CHAPTER 29

Aniyah

There are more of them than there are of us.

After adjusting to the shock of more than one Handler, I'd slipped into an expectation of maybe four in total: one to serve us, one for the boys, and a couple in reserve to allow those two to rest. I hadn't imagined the Master would as many Handlers as the fighters and prizes they served, but we're faced by over a dozen robed giants crowding through the far hallway: a host of jailers roused to subdue us.

Their sheer number is startling enough but the sight of their magic sends me reeling backwards. Magical fear drips from their robes and pools onto the floor and their outstretched hands flicker with red-hot light. I open my mouth to yell a warning but as I back away, I slip on the bone dust beneath my feet. *This is going to hurt,* I think, feeling my stomach flip over and my muscles tense in anticipation of impact.

Yet I don't hit the floor. Strong arms catch me as a jolt of fresh fear stabs my heart, stoking the terror pounding in my blood. As my savior rights me, my eyes widen at the sight of Handler's mutilated face hovering close to mine. He steps away as soon as I've regained my footing and Miyuki rushes to steady me while glaring a warning at him. His expression doesn't change, but there's sense in the tilt of his head that he is watching us. Then he takes off at a run before any of us can react.

"Where's he going?" Sappho's voice is pinched with terror.

"Back to the others! Stop him!"

"We're safer without him; let him go."

Hana's warning and Matías' reassurance overlap each other by a heartbeat. For a moment we are paralyzed with indecision, unsure who to heed. Hana starts forward, abandoning the door she holds open, then stops two steps out and flings a hand behind her to catch the door again.

She's stopped because Handler *isn't* rejoining the others. Darting out into the wide cavern, he turns to the right and dashes towards the gate. I'm astonished at how fast he can run, his long stride carrying him over the distance before the other Handlers can spill from the far hallway. *What's he doing?* The answer arrives hard on the heels of the question: *He knows we have to get out of here. We can't fight them.*

"I'm going with him," I announce as I suck in a long breath and steel myself to run. I don't doubt my choice; I only hesitate from dread of pain: running has escalated from something I can grit my teeth and endure to an intense stab of dizzying agony with each step. *All I have to do is kick off and run full pelt,* I tell myself. *I can rest when we get to the gate.*

Miyuki catches me, holding me still as xie pumps what healing magic xie can through my clothes. "Wait, Aniyah! What are you doing?"

I turn to look at xer, frowning as I do. I could wriggle away, but the required movements will hurt. *Just like everything else.* "Miyuki, let go. I'm going after him. We have to get to the gate!"

Chloe shakes her head from where she props open the other door, sweat beading on her forehead even as she seems comfortable with the effort it takes to keep the heavy portal from closing. "Aniyah, sweetie, it could be some kind of trick. He only helped us with this door because we made him. We can't trust him."

I try not to squirm. "I *do* trust him! As much as—" I don't want to finish that thought, not here in front of the boys. *But what reason do we have to trust any of them, after what Lucas did to Sappho?* Keoki and Christian and Tony are safe, but the other boys are strangers to me and at least one of them has shown he doesn't think of us as equal partners in this prison. "I trust him, Chloe."

Miyuki's hands tighten on my waist and I see the question flicker through xer eyes. I shake my head at xer, begging that xie won't ask me to explain. I barely have the words to explain it to myself.

I'm not stupid; I know Handler is our jailer. I have little reason to assume he isn't complicit in the Master's treatment of us. Yet he was so nervous when he spoke up to protect Miyuki from being sold, and I'm certain he was risking the Master's wrath. I believe he's a captive here too, with a different job from the rest of us. Maybe the other Handlers are bad, but I cling to a thread of hope that this one is not.

Hana watches me with a stern expression, her eyes darting back to the Handlers spilling slowly from their hallway and spreading out in a frontal line of assault. "Aniyah, even if you're right about him, it's safer here. The hallway is more defensible. We can shove the weaker people to the back and let the fighters handle a smaller number here where they're forced to funnel in. Out in the open, it'll be harder to protect everyone."

I shake my head, feeling panic rise as our jailers plod closer. It isn't just the fear rolling from them that causes my blood to pound, it's something in their excruciatingly slow gait. I've never seen Handler move quickly until that run to the gate just now, but this exaggerated pace feels wrong. I peer at their feet looking for magic, only to see the flash of metal as a robe shifts around a plodding step.

They're shackled, I realize with horror. *Does he keep them like that when not in use, or does he know we're running away?* I ought to want to save them, to strip off their chains and take them with us, but those flickering red hands bring a lump to my throat and banish all charitable impulses in deference to survival. *If they want to come with us, they'll need to make the first step. But we have to go. Now.*

"Hana." My voice is low, pleading for her to trust me, to view this situation with all her experience of watching the arena fights. "I can *see* how strong they are. We can't hold off that many, and what if there are others on the way? What if the Master comes?" I see the waver in her eyes; I'll either convince her or I'll break away and run. She'd follow me, I'm sure of it; Hana wouldn't leave me behind.

I press on, urging harder. "If want to survive, we *must* run. We can't win this fight."

She looks again at our jailers, counting softly under her breath in a language I don't recognize as her expression hardens. "Okay. Everybody through the doors! Chloe, get going; I'll hold this one until everyone's gone through, then I'll bring up the rear."

Sounds of protest bubble up behind me: boys' voices that I don't bother to differentiate. They're accustomed to fighting, but Hana understands survival. She's taken the decision out of their hands by ordering Chloe on and announcing her intention to follow; the boys can either lose two of their fighters to hold the doors open or they can follow us in retreat. I don't stick around to find out, kicking away and running full pelt after Handler, the pounding of Miyuki's feet close behind me in pursuit.

Fresh agony stabs me with every step, but I'll suffer worse if the Handlers catch me. I skirt the side of the cavern, running as close to the wall and as far from our jailers as I can. Miyuki keeps pace beside me, placing xerself bodily between them and me. Tears blur my vision and my heart swells until I think it might burst. *When we get out of here, there'll be kisses,* I promise. *We just have to get out of here.*

We slam to a halt next to the enormous gate, breathing hard. "Please tell me you can open this," I beg Handler, digging my hand into the small of my back and blinking away new tears from the pain. I feel a flash of dizziness so intense that I have to lean against the wall to avoid falling over;

as the room spins, Miyuki presses xer hands into my back to steady me with more magic.

"I've opened the smaller locks," he says, his voice a soft pant laced with panic. "But I'll need help with the bigger ones. There! Can you see?" He gestures wildly at the wall against which I'm leaning.

I don't see anything resembling a lock, only the cavern wall which curves into a puckered tunnel to the outside world and the metal bars stabbing down from the ceiling to block our passage. The wall is made of crumbly stone peppered with craters that look like burst bubbles. I peer where Handler points and see light buried in a hole the size of my fist: magic as white as our robes and hot as the sun, flickering with hostility.

"How can we help?" I ask, but I'm cut off by an agonized yell behind us. The three of us whirl to look, the gate pressed against our backs as though we could slide through the bars if sufficiently motivated.

Chloe is closest to us and runs beside Keoki and the stretcher, ready to help if needed. Imani and Sappho lag close behind, escorted by Tony with his sword. Heather is after them, jogging with a flat expression as she steadfastly avoids looking at the encroaching Handlers. Lucas and Matías come after her, the older boy speed-walking with his cane in a way that makes me wince in sympathy.

Christian and Hana bring up the rear, or rather they did before one of the Handlers broke away from the larger group to attack them; he must have lunged forward, or maybe his chains were longer and left him less hobbled. When we whirl at the sound of the pained scream, we see Handler gripping Christian painfully by the shoulder just before the fighter crumples to the ground in spasms of agony. Red light flickers over him like a net, binding him in place and keeping him from popping away as it torments him.

Hana's hands come up as fists in front of her face, clutching the shaft of her spear as close to the blade as she can. I expect her to jab at the giant man but instead her leg flies up to hit him in a frontal half-kick, half-shove, moving him away from Christian. He stumbles back but doesn't falter,

296

his hands reaching for her. She ducks under his grasp and kicks again in two quick blows: one from the side that connects hard and fast, then a sweeping rounded kick that would take off his head if he were as short as the rest of us.

The kick sends him stumbling into a fall. Hana is there in a blink with her spear, striking with a weapon that has become an extension of her fists. He scrambles at the floor and I think he's dying—which doesn't bother me after what he's done to Christian—but then his hands find Christian's blade where it fell. I try to yell a warning, but all that comes out is a useless gasp as metal flashes through the air and Handler buries the knife deep in Hana's chest before collapsing in a pool of his own blood.

Sappho screams. Heather leaps forward to catch Hana as the smaller girl coughs and a gout of blood erupts to coat her chin. "Help... me... with him," Hana rasps out, her voice hoarse from the effort. Heather hesitates, but releases Hana so the two girls can stoop to pull Christian to his feet. The magical red net is already fading, leaving pain but not paralysis, and he is able to throw an arm over Heather's shoulders and walk. Hana limps beside them, all three moving to join us before the rest of the Handlers can cut them off.

"Hana, you've got to sit down. Your lungs—"

"I'm... fine." Hana cuts off Imani with a pained wave of her hand as they reach us. Tony jumps forward to help with Christian, leaning him against the wall by the gate. "Help me... pull this out."

Imani hesitates, her burned hands hovering over the hilt of the blade that protrudes from Hana's chest. "I don't think I should."

"Just. Do it." Behind them, the Handlers loom closer. Keoki and the other boy set Justin on the floor and take up position to fight, their expressions equally grim. Chloe looks between the encroaching threat and the reclining Christian before hefting her spear and moving to stand in front of him and Tony.

Imani takes a deep breath, looking profoundly unsure about what she's going to do. She grasps the hilt with both hands and pulls the knife out with a swift straight stroke. Blood gushes out of the wound and Hana drops to her knees. Miyuki and Sappho grab her on either side to prevent her from collapsing.

"Hana?" Imani asks, her voice very soft, as she clutches the knife.

A golden glow courses through Hana's body, so bright she resembles the sun itself. "I'm... fine. Still works. Ha." Imani's shoulders sag with relief and my lungs ache with the sudden influx of fresh life as I suck in gulps of clean air. "Give me a minute and I can fight with the others. Damn, I dropped my spear."

Sappho presses her weapon into Hana's hands with a shaky laugh as I feel a heavy clap on my shoulder. I turn to see our Handler watching me with urgency in his face. "I need your help," he repeats gravely, ignoring our elation. "It takes two to open the door, a fail-safe against escape. You must do whatever you did to open your door. That *was* you, was it not? The one you killed would not have done it for you."

I blink at him, fear muddling my head as the Handlers reach our tiny defensive knot and their magic threatens to overwhelm my thoughts. I hear the sounds of fighting behind me and it's the most nerve-wracking thing in the world *not* to look, not knowing when I'll feel a hand clutching my shoulder and a red net of pain dragging me to the floor.

"We opened the door, yes; but it wasn't me, it was Imani! I figured out how it worked, but she was the one who made the cracks in her skin to channel the magic. It burned her badly; she can't do it again."

His face crumbles, but Imani looks up from where she's examining a recovering Christian. He looks much better; he clutches his knife and eyes the fray with a look that shows he's aching to join in and help. "What's that, Aniyah? What did he say?"

I swallow hard and meet her eyes. "This gate needs two Handlers, not just one. But your hand. Imani, it burned." Ugly scars crisscross the silken

298

skin of her face and hands, the network of cracks marring the shifting silvery reflection of her magic.

She thins her lips, setting her teeth into a hard edge. "Why didn't you say so earlier?" she says, stretching out her hand. She concentrates, straining with the effort as pain flickers over her face. I look around for Miyuki in a growing panic; xie looks up from where xie stands protectively over Justin and takes in Imani's grimace at a glance. Darting over, xie places hands on Imani's outstretched arm, xer magic easing the worst of the agony as deep furrows are coaxed into the girl's hand with excruciating slowness.

"There," Handler rasps, pointing. "That hole. The one on this side is mine. On the count of three." He hesitates before turning to his designated hole. "It will hurt."

Imani nods curtly, not looking up from the hand on which she concentrates. The furrows are there and in the right patterns, but not as cleanly as before. Her burns extend into the cuts, and I see the wild flicker of magic as she struggles to hold the form she's taken. Her free hand clutches the changed one at the wrist, steadying herself as she moves towards the hole. "One," she counts, her voice tense. "Two. Thre— *ah!*"

Her last word rips away in a scream as she jams her fist into the lock. On the other side of me, Handler leans his head against the wall where his hand disappears while a low keening groan escapes his throat. I don't know which one to help and I'm not sure what help I could offer anyway—I'm barely strong enough to hold myself up—when the bars shudder and draw up into the ceiling with a heavy grinding rattle.

"Hurry!" Handler's shout is hoarse with pain. "We have to go now!"

"Hana! Keoki! We're leaving!" My shout reverberates through the cavern as Miyuki grabs my hand and pulls me forward through the open hallway. I don't want to leave everyone behind, but xie's right; I'm one of the slower ones, which means I have to go first or risk dragging the whole group behind with me. As we stumble out into the sun, a flurry of activity erupts behind us and blends into the sounds of battle.

"Tony, you got this? Reese and I will get Justin."

"I got it! Lucas, get Matías out."

"I'm fine. Help Christian."

"Don't need any help, guys. Shit, you'd think I took a knife to the chest or something. Baby, you getting your girl out?"

"We've got her. You better follow, or I'm not gonna be happy. Sappho, you got Imani?"

"She's hurting real bad, but we're holding up."

"Just a question, but does anyone know how to *close* the gates? You guys only killed five of them." A wet gurgle and the sound of a heavy thud causes Heather to amend this. "Six."

"I do." Handler's gasp is barely audible and I twist my head to look back at him as Miyuki pulls me inexorably forward. "Just get everyone through, quickly."

He sucks in a pained breath as Tony and Lucas back out of the cavern into the sun, the last of our group to stumble out. Their weapons are raised high against the Handlers who move in a crowd towards the gated tunnel, jostling each other as they push towards the traitor who presses his fist into the wall.

With a sharp cry of pain, our Handler yanks his fist from the lock and throws himself forward, rolling where he hits the ground and scrambling forward on his hands and knees. Bars rattle down with a menacing roar, driving towards the ground with lethal speed. The other Handlers draw back in alarm as Tony leaps forward with perfect grace, grabbing the taller man by the arms and dragging him away from the onrushing bars.

Metal slams into place with a grinding screech and the two men collapse wearily into the sand of the outside world.

CHAPTER 30

Keoki

We're trying to jostle Justin as little as possible, but nothing can keep me from Tony right now. A quick signal at Reese to lower the stretcher, then I'm striding to where Tony has fallen. I pull him to his feet, check to make sure he's still got all his limbs attached, and sweep him into a hard kiss. He stiffens in my arms for more heartbeats than my ego can bear to count before pressing into my kiss with equal force.

It doesn't matter who sees us now. We're free. I won't break the kiss to say it but from the way his lips move greedily over mine, I'm confident he's thinking the same thing.

A girl's voice pierces my happy haze, speaking long before I'm anywhere near done. "Well, that was thrilling, but how long will it take them to open the gate again? I ask merely out of curiosity." There's a spike of fear under her drawl and I reluctantly tear away from Tony. The speaker is the delicate blond girl with blank green eyes; she's ripping bits of skin from her fingers, her gaze tightly focused on her hands.

"They will not get through that gate."

Handler pulls himself to his feet, brushing at his robes with one hand.

No one rushes to help him, which isn't surprising because I can't imagine who would. *Except Aniyah.* I twist to look for her in alarm and find her leaning on Miyuki. She's panting, her face wan and her pupils dilated as if she's about to pass out. *Shit.* I can carry her, but I'm not sure who could take my end of Justin's stretcher.

"Why not?" Imani stands next to Hana, looking almost as bad as Aniyah. She clutches her hand, blood dripping between her fingers. "What's to stop them from opening the locks?" She laughs, the bitter sound carried on a gust of hot wind. "It'll be easier for them than it was for *me*."

Handler's expression is grim as he clutches his own hand in reflection of Imani's pain. "Yes. That is why I tore out as much of the lock as I could when I brought the gate down." He opens his wounded fist and allows a dozen tiny chunks of stone to tumble upon the sand. The tips of his fingers are charred and blackened.

"How long do we have?" Hana asks, her voice tight. She's standing on her own without aid, but her face is pale and she doesn't look entirely recovered from that stab she took to the chest.

"And how far do we have to travel?" Matías adds, his knuckles standing out against the grip on his cane. "Are we looking at a short sprint between here and survival, or a long route?"

Lucas snorts, doubled over to catch his breath after the fight and our subsequent retreat. "What's the difference?"

"Difference is how we pace ourselves, stupid, and how we ration the food and water," replies Christian. He flashes Lucas a mocking smile, but his eyes don't dance. I give him a worried look; although he swore he was fine, he's moving slower than usual.

"Matías can only manage short bursts before his knee gives out; you know that," Reese says, running fingers through his hair with a sigh. "And we'll have to conserve strength if we're carrying Justin a long way."

Handler shakes his head. "We do not have long before they reach us. They will pursue us through other exits and will be unshackled for the

302

chase. We must move." He doesn't budge from where he stands and an odd sheepishness creeps into his imposing demeanor. "I do not know the way or how far," he admits.

"I do." Aniyah sways on her feet, but her voice is clear over the hot wind. "I can lead us out of here. It's not close, I'm sorry," she adds, giving Matías a sympathetic look.

"Is it underground?" Reese asks, shielding his eyes against the sun as he scans the hilly desert horizon. Inhospitable rocks and blinding sunlight face us from every direction, with no obvious refuge in sight.

"Are there other people there? Is that where we came from?" Tony adds, eagerness creeping into his voice.

Aniyah hesitates and I can't tell if she's struggling to answer or just to stay upright. "The Master's land has borders. The arena—this ring of mountains here that forms the stadium—lies in the center of his territory. There's a mountain range in that direction marking a boundary to his land." With Miyuki's help, she turns and points into the distance. Through the shimmering heat a dark outline of jagged rock climbs into the sky.

"We have to hike over a mountain range?" Lucas asks, casting another dubious look at Justin's stretcher.

"No." She shakes her head and points to the left of the mountains. "There's a chasm with a river that marks a second border. Where those two boundaries collide, the river flows under the range and becomes an underground lake. There's no bridge over the chasm, but there is a crossing point where it meets the mountains: a shelf of rock we can use to cross over. On the other side of *that* is a forest, and freedom."

"It's a long way away," Matías observes in a quiet tone.

"I know," she agrees, meeting his gaze with understanding eyes. "But it's just one foot in front of the other." As if to demonstrate, she takes a tentative step ahead while leaning on Miyuki for support.

No one looks happy, but Tony nods and pulls away from my arms. "You get Justin, and I'll help Teacher?"

"Sounds like a plan." I watch him a moment longer, not wanting to move away. "Hey. Be careful, okay?"

His lips curl into a wry lopsided grin. "Should be telling *you* that, Newbie."

Miyuki's voice floats back to us from ahead, the girls moving as a close group while Handler tags a few steps behind. "You said the others would come after us. What about the Master? Is he likely to follow us?"

"I'd like to see him try," I mutter as I heft my side of the stretcher and nod for Reese to go first. "Bet the lot of us could kill him."

"The Master no longer leave the Arena," Handler answers, his voice faint on the air. "The bouts have made him rich, but his profits are in the form of promises and favors. He fears a rival might void their debt by sending assassins. We protect him, as well as maintaining the Arena and servicing his assets."

"Assets?" Sappho repeats, her voice hollow. "You mean us?"

"Yes. Fighters are the source of his income and Prizes are an investment. You are not cheap to acquire and maintain, but without rewards the fighters lose their flair. Audiences will not attend a boring show."

"And you help him," Miyuki adds, with less rancor in her voice than before. The words are almost a question, her voice rising at the end in a request for elaboration.

Handler is silent for so long I wonder if he heard her, but eventually his voice drifts back on the wind. "We are acquired in the same way you are. He carves our bodies into keys and twists our brains until we can hear his commands in our minds without the need for speech. He is rough and clumsy with us, and sometimes the change does not take as deeply as he intends." His voice trails away and he worries at his hands.

You still had it better than us, I think, staring at his back as we trudge over this infinity of sand and heat. All the same, I remember telling Tony how rough it would be to spend a lifetime sending kids to their doom in the arena. I'd been talking about Matías, but now I wonder how Handler felt during our battles.

"Ke... oki?" Justin's soft voice floats up from the stretcher and my attention snaps to him.

"Yeah, buddy? You doing okay? Ride isn't too rough, is it?" This can't be good for his leg; his bandages are stained with blood after the trauma of being set down and picked back up several times already.

"Where are we going?"

I keep my smile firmly affixed to my face. His eye is still swollen from where the bear clawed him, and the skin surrounding it is puffy and has a fresh shine. The wound looks unwholesome, like you could touch it and something awful would ooze out. He'd been attractive before, even pretty if it weren't for his perpetual pout; now he looks like death warmed over.

"Remember I told you, kid?" I try to sound as if this is no big deal. "My girl knows a way out, just past those mountains up ahead. You can't see them from the stretcher but they're not too far. Just you wait!"

He moans as his head sinks back and his eyes close. I keep walking, trying not to let my worries slow me. The sand beneath my feet is proper sand—soft and pale and tiny-grained—but there's no comfort in the familiarity. Maybe the fault lies in the wind; it's too arid, biting my skin and sucking greedily at every drop of moisture until my tongue swells. *I hope we brought enough water.*

The others aren't doing so well. Reese struggles with the weight of the stretcher causing him to sink into the sand with every step. Aniyah stumbles frequently, even with one arm draped around Miyuki for support. Hana and Imani both grit their teeth against lingering pain as they walk. Christian doesn't say a word about the paralysis he suffered, but he stays close to Chloe and she reaches out to steady him. Matías stabs his cane into the sand, his face composed but his pace gradually slowing as we approach the cliffs.

If any one person were slowing us down, we could carry them. I could hold Aniyah while Tony took the stretcher, or Chloe could sling Christian over her shoulder. But over half our group struggles with wounds or stumbles through the sand. I look over my shoulder with increasing frequency, searching the ugly lump of the arena for signs of pursuit, but I see nothing, which is deeply unsettling. *Surely he won't just let us go?*

We have a head start, though; maybe that's enough. Already the cliffs are closer and the oppressive heat seems to be lessening. Dark clouds spread overhead, filling the sky above us and blotting out the harsh sun. My brain instantly supplies the word, despite the fact that I've never seen a cloud in the sky here. Somehow they seemed so normal that I hadn't noticed them until now.

"It's getting darker," Imani observes softly. "Is that a good thing or a bad thing?"

"It's magic." Aniyah's tone would be awed if she wasn't panting so heavily; she leans her head back to look at the sky while Miyuki helps her forward with each step. "It's like a fight in the sky. The Master's magic is spreading out from the arena and meeting an opposing force from the other direction."

"Can you tell whose magic it is?" I call, walking a little faster. "Would they help us, do you think?"

She hesitates and shakes her head, curls dancing on the wind. "I can't tell whose it is, only that it's different from *his*. As different as water is from sand. But I don't think it's here for us. I think it's just... here."

"Wait! Do you hear that?" Tony pulls up short and cocks his head.

Reese doesn't stop which means I can't halt without upsetting the stretcher, but Matías leans on his cane and listens with one hand cupped to his ear. "Is that water?"

Heads nod with varying degrees of conviction. We pick up the pace and our road becomes easier as sand gives way to stone under our feet. The mountain range on our right towers above our heads until we're close enough to reach out and brush the sharp wall of stone; only then do we see what Tony heard.

The ground under our feet rises in a soft slope before giving way to a sudden drop. Below us spans a deep gorge that stretches to our left as far as the eye can see, the chasm marking a boundary between the Master's desert on our side and green forests on the other. Through the gorge flows a slow-moving sludge of a river: thick and ponderous with nothing appetizing in its oily appearance. It has a brackish smell and there's a stinging taste in the air of too much salt which burns my eyes.

On our right side, the jagged mountain range rises in an almost vertical cliff, impossible to climb. The gorge intersects the cliff directly, its tepid river disappearing into a tunnel beneath our feet. The top of the tunnel bulges out over the gorge like a hungry mouth—and this, I realize, is our path: a narrow strip of uneven stone spanning the two sides of the chasm, only just wide enough for us to walk across.

"Is that going to hold everybody?" Chloe eyes the ledge warily. She's the biggest of us and will have to hug the cliffs while walking the narrow path; one wrong step will end in plummeting to the water below. The fall looks lethal, but even if someone survived we have no way to haul them back up. They'd disappear with the slow-moving current into the mountain.

"Is there no way around?" A stupid question when the river stretches as far as I can see in one direction and the cliffs in the other, but I have to ask; I'm certain we can't get the stretcher across this ledge.

I'm not sure Aniyah hears me through her haze of pain. She points across the chasm at a line of dark trees rendered nearly invisible under a sky of black clouds. "Look! That's where we're heading. That's freedom."

"We cross here," Hana says, her voice firm. "But we do it smart. Maybe we can use the sheets and tie—"

An inhuman scream cuts her off and I nearly drop the stretcher as I whip around to scan the horizon behind us. It's as empty as the last time I checked, which seems impossible given how close the scream had been. Then the blond girl cries out and her finger stabs the air as she points to the cliffs above.

The Handlers are here, though they no longer resemble what they were before. They crawl out of the cliffs above us, burrowing up through jagged holes. Their robes are gone and their carved white skin gleams against the stone to which they cling in defiance of gravity. Mouths hang grotesquely open as they cry wordless guttural instructions to each other, and for the first time their eyes are open. Orbs of swirling black stare down at us, emotionless and flat. Not one of them blinks against the hot wind, nor do their eyes reflect any light. They look hungry and empty, and descend toward us with terrifying speed.

"New plan: we're running."

"Heather! No, wait—"

The blond girl doesn't listen to Hana, running onto the ledge before anyone can stop her. Her hands sink into the stone looking for purchase and red blood instantly stains her hands where the stone cuts her. She seems not to notice these wounds. Our own Handler hurries after her, hands reaching out to help, but the sight of him seems to send her into a deeper panic and she edges along the cliffs faster than before.

"Pair off!" Matías yells, blood draining from his face. "Keoki, can you ditch the stretcher and carry Justin?"

"I got him," I yell, setting down the contraption and using one of the spears to slit the bindings.

"Tony, you're with me," Matías hollers, already starting over the ledge. Tony is there in a heartbeat, clinging to the rocks with one hand and leaning the other behind Matías to steady him if he falters. "Christian, stay with—"

"Already there, Teacher," Christian yells, sticking close to his girl.

She doesn't begin to cross, instead scooping up the bundle of spears I dropped and hurling two at the nearest Handler. Her aim isn't particularly precise, but the force behind the throw covers a multitude of sins when the second spear pins his thigh to the stone. The creature thrashes and screams in pain, then stills as his blood stains the wall below and awareness flees his eyes.

"Careful!" Hana cautions, eyes down as she helps Imani onto the ledge after Tony and Matías. "We don't want to make the path slippery with blood!"

"Or falling bodies," Miyuki adds, her voice tight with determined calm. She holds Aniyah from the front while Reese moves to hold her from the side, and I could kiss him for jumping forward to help. I don't want to lose anyone out here, but Tony and Aniyah are on a special list of their own.

The tattooed girl, Sappho, slips onto the wall next to Reese; of all of us, she seems the most sure on her feet. When I rise with Justin on my back—lashed in place with ties salvaged from the stretcher—I could swear I see her fingers elongating and slipping into the cracks in the wall, gripping with inhuman dexterity.

I hear a puff of air and Christian appears, clinging to the rocks above us. He grips the nearest Handler and flings himself backwards off the wall, taking both himself and the Handler hurtling through empty air to the water below. I gasp, horrified to see Christian falling to his death; then I hear the puff again and see him reappear higher on the cliffs, already reaching out to grab another attacker by the shoulder.

"Holy *shit.*"

"I know." I hadn't meant to utter the words but Chloe nods with smug amusement, hefting another spear in her hands and watching the melee above; I realize she's saving the weapon as backup in case a Handler gets too close to the others. "Go on with your boy. We can hold them off and then follow."

"Gotcha." I clear my throat, my eyes wide as Christian once more flings himself and his target out from the ledge and into the water. There's a poetry to his killing that I would appreciate if I had the time. Taking a deep breath and trying to find a calm center inside me, I refocus on the cliff in front of my face and cling to stone as I step onto the ledge after Lucas.

Shiiiiiiiiiiit. I don't like this at all, I quickly decide. Justin wasn't heavy when I was safely standing on stone. But now that he's dangling in the air behind me with a river below plotting to eat us up, it feels like I'm wearing a mountain strapped to my back rather than a wounded kid who's barely eaten in the last cycle.

"Christian! Lower down! Keoki, watch it!"

Chloe screams a warning and the world slows. I can't look up to locate the danger, since tilting my head back would unbalance us and send me and Justin toppling over the edge. I turn my head slowly to the side, hoping to catch something in my peripheral vision as my other senses try to parse every sound and smell.

I catch a flash of white skin reaching down to grasp at Lucas. I expect Christian to leap in and save us, but hear a struggle higher up; it sounds as if Christian is stuck dealing with another threat. Lucas looks up, and the flash of helpless frustration on his face is a reflection of my own. *That thing is going to grab him or push him off, and then I'll be next. And there's not a damn thing we can do about it.*

"Keoki, duck!"

Sound explodes above us as a spear hits the Handler in his shoulder and he screams. He gropes for the blade and yanks it out with a triumphant howl, but loses his grip on the blood-soaked stone. I pull back and Lucas leans forward as the creature plummets between us; we have a brief moment to share a smirk before the falling Handler grabs at Lucas' ankle and the sandy-haired boy slips over the ledge with a gasp.

"Lucas!"

I grip stone until my fingers bleed, leaning back as far as I dare while my eyes dart wildly for sight of the other boy. There's a ripple in the water where the Handler fell, but nothing for Lucas. Then I see him gripping the wall below me, hanging a full body's length lower than my feet. He'll have to climb up, and from the way his muscles are straining to hold him in place, I don't think he can.

"What's happening back there?" Matías shouts, his voice tight with anxiety.

310

"Lucas fell, but he hasn't hit the water. We have to haul him up!" Even as I say it, I have no idea how to go about a rescue and have no answer when Tony hollers back the obvious question.

"How?"

Reese pauses in his trek across the ledge, one hand still outstretched behind Aniyah. "We could use the sheets?" he suggests, but his voice is doubtful. We've already cut most of the sheets into small strips for the stretcher and food we dropped on the other side of the gorge. We'd have to tie the strips together while Lucas holds on for his life, then trust the cloth not to tear under his weight.

"Christian could—"

"I can't pop anyone! I could pop down there beside him, but I can't bring him up with me. I could try to throw him to you, but..." His voice trails away. One of us would have to catch Lucas and there's not enough room on the ledge to brace. The attempt would most likely send Lucas and his rescuer over the edge.

The girl in front of me on the ledge has fallen silent, her breathing slow as she waits for Reese to begin moving again. Now that Lucas isn't blocking my view, I see her fingers have stretched into the rock and her toes have elongated to grip the stone. Tattoos stretch with her limber body. She's not merely agile; she's using her talent to cling to the stone face.

"You!" I stare at her and she turns her head slowly to face me. She doesn't adjust her position in the slightest when she turns; instead, her neck moves in ways that necks shouldn't until her blue eyes are level with mine. "You can save him," I tell her, hope rising in my chest.

She stares at me, her eyes dilated and unblinking. An ugly bruise flowers around one eye, and it hits me that the one who gave her that wound is now dangling below us. Her breathing is shallow and she speaks in a faraway whisper, as though she's somewhere else rather than here in this moment. "Save *him*?"

I swallow hard and chance a glance down; wild eyes stare up at me and I see his fingers begin to slip. "You stretch, right? You can climb down to save him. Or, how far can you stretch? You could reach down a hand to grab him and we could pull him up, or you could swing him over for Christian and Chloe to catch—"

My frantic suggestions slam to a halt as she shakes her head with such force I'm afraid she might lose her grip. Her movements are jerky and her whisper becomes a venomous hiss. "*You* save him. You do it, if he's so important to you."

From above comes a puff of air, a scramble against rock and an inhuman scream as Christian throws another Handler to his doom. I've lost count how many this makes, yet their numbers don't seem fewer. "I can't," I tell her, trying to keep my voice calm. I don't want to agitate her more than she already is; the last thing we need is to lose another person over the cliffs. "I can't save him, but you can. Sappho, right? You can save his life."

She narrows her eyes at me. "Maybe. But why would I *want* to?" Her words are harsh, deliberately so; beneath the cutting tone I hear her sharp panicked breathing. Her eyes have dilated into black orbs ringed with a slight hint of blue.

"He hurt you." I nod, trying to convey validation and understanding through my own rising panic. Little crumbling sounds rise from the cliff below and Lucas yelps as he scrambles for a firmer hold. He hasn't fallen yet, but we don't have long. "He hurt you, and when we all get out of this alive, I'm going to beat the shit out of him for what he did to you. But you can be better than him. You can save him, Sappho. He's one of us, a captive like the rest of us, and we all promised we'd escape together."

"He's not one of *us*." She cuts me off, every line in her body rigid with the strain of hugging the cliff wall. "He's one of *you*. I'm already better than he is, and I won't give him another chance to hurt me or anyone else ever again."

"Sappho—!"

As quick as a thought, her body ripples and begins to stretch. She reaches an extended arm around Reese and grips the stone on the other side of him. He freezes against the wall as a girl as wide and thin as a sheet slips around him, her body caressing him as if she had turned into clothing. Her foot is next, swinging around behind him to anchor into the stone on the other side, then the second hand follows and lastly her remaining foot. She continues on down the ledge after Aniyah and Miyuki, not looking back.

Reese's troubled eyes meet my own. "We have to do something—" I begin, but stop as I hear a gasp and the plop of a body falling into the thick water. We wait but nothing follows; no thrashing, no shouts, no sign of life whatsoever. Above us Christian is still fighting the Handlers but the sounds are distant now, almost inaudible over the crashing blood in my ears.

He's dead. Lucas is dead.

I hadn't liked him and he was no friend of mine. I'd listened to Tony plan his death in the arena and had voiced no objection. But that was when we were angry and he'd just beaten an innocent girl out of spite. I'd calmed down since then and assumed everyone else had as well. Maybe not enough to talk to Lucas again or seek out his company, but enough not to let him die just because he was an asshole.

I'd been wrong. I had misjudged the intensity of Sappho's anger and now Lucas was dead. I'd heard him hit the water and go under, and I'd been helpless to stop it. The desert heat is suddenly suffocating and mingles with the stench of the river to make my stomach churn. Justin feels like solid stone on my back and I grip the cliffs harder as a wave of nausea hits me. "I'm gonna throw up," I announce, the words slurred.

"Keoki, we have to go," Reese urges. "Justin *needs* you to keep going. We can't do anything for Lucas now." On my back, Justin stirs at the sound of his name. I know if he wakes and starts thrashing, we'll both die. I nod at Reese, take a deep breath, and find the next handhold down the line. We pick our way over the ledge, avoiding slick blood and ducking as Christian sends another Handler screeching into the river below.

CHAPTER 31

Aniyah

I hear the chaos of fighting behind us, but we keep moving forward. Miyuki urges me on from ahead and Sappho herds me from behind. We keep going, because there's nothing else we *can* do; our weapons are on the other side of the gorge and the three of us never knew how to use them in the first place. Hana and Tony meet us as we reach the end of the ledge, helping me over the last step before readying their weapons.

"Go," Hana orders. "We'll catch up. Run!"

It hurts my heart to leave them behind, but the best way we can help the fighters is to get ourselves out of danger so they don't have to protect us. Heather and Handler run ahead towards the tree line, her panicked feet flying as he tries to catch up. Imani and Matías lag behind, helping each other over uneven ground. Miyuki tightens xer protective grip on my arm, and we take off.

We jog because I've run all I can this cycle—maybe all I'll ever be able to run my entire life—and my spine feels like a column of flame inside me; pain licks out to reach every part of my body. We jog while the sounds of popping air and inhuman screams and splashing water fill our ears, then we hear shouts of retreat and the wails of Handlers closing fast behind us, and I discover I can run after all.

I risk a look back, turning my head and hoping I don't fall on my face. The rest of our group bears down on us at full speed, gulping air as they sprint and clutching their remaining weapons. Behind them seven Handlers give chase, their elongated limbs stretched to allow them to run on all fours. Chills ripple over my scalp and I try to run faster, but can feel myself nearing my limit.

We just have to reach that line of trees, I tell myself, beginning to stumble between strides. A hundred steps or a thousand, it doesn't matter if my body shuts down here. My foot catches in the sand and I sprawl forward, hands shooting forward to break my fall as I tumble into the black sand.

Black sand? I stare at the particles in my hands, too delicate to be any kind of sand at all. It's as magical as everything else out here, but it's the rival magic that lives in the forest ahead and spreads into the sky, warring with the Master's influence and creating clouds. *'When you reach the forest on the other side of the chasm then, if you humans wish deeply enough to cross over into freedom, you will do so.'*

The Shadow Man had said the chasm and mountains and trees were borders, marking the territory of a neighbor; some unknown faery with their own signature style of magic, uniquely different from the pattern stamped on us by the Master. This is the power I've seen as we traveled: the magic in the dark clouds clashing with the Master's blue sky, and here in the ground as black dirt mingling with yellow sand.

I feel hands on me as Miyuki and Sappho try to pull me to my feet and keep running, but my body is dead weight. "No, no," I gasp, waving them off. "Look! Look at the Handlers." The creatures have halted in their chase and pace the ground near the outermost tendrils of black soil. "They won't follow us here. We're safe."

I flop back, cramming air into my lungs. We need to get to the trees, but my body is in no condition to run another step. The others catch up with us and I hear the bark of orders and a babble of confused explanations, but the chaos washes over me. Nothing can penetrate my pain, not even the familiar fear as Handler draws towards us. Heather trots ahead of him, ignoring her bleeding scrapes.

Hana is doubled over, her hands on her knees as she pants for breath. "Why can't they run on the dirt?"

Handler answers, "This territory is in dispute. If the Master's agents cross over, it would be a declaration of war."

Chloe narrows her eyes at him. "How do you know? You said you'd never been out here."

"I understand their cries," he murmurs, sinking to his knees to rest. "I hear the orders they call to each other. They're instructed to wait and see what we do." As he speaks, the other Handlers settle into the yellow sand, lying flat on their pale stomachs and watching us with empty, unblinking eyes.

"Then we're safe?" Imani asks, a kernel of hope in her gentle voice. "We have time to rest and then just... stroll into the forest?"

Handler hesitates, reluctant to crush her optimism. "They may give chase if we continue moving in that direction. The Master requires fodder for his parent. A war might cost him the remaining handlers, or he might win and regain his stable of fighters and prizes. He must consider the odds of the gamble."

Matías leans against his cane and wipes sweat from his brow. "So we have a short time, but not a clear shot. Who is injured? Now's the chance to bandage up." Almost none of us is unbloodied, yet no one answers. He pauses for a moment and his expression turns somber. "Just the one fatality? Lucas... fell?"

Keoki's hands are working on the strips of cloth lashed around his shoulders and waist; they are tearing in places and pull painfully against his skin. Tony circles around behind him and together they lower Justin to the ground, checking that he's still breathing. Keoki straightens and looks directly at Sappho.

"Lucas fell," he repeats, echoing Matías' question. "But we could have saved him."

Hana narrows her eyes and moves between him and Sappho. "Do you have a point?"

Keoki seems stung by her protective stance, and maybe a little offended. He displays his palms outward in a peaceful gesture. "Look, I— I know he hurt her. Obviously." His eyes find the bruise that still blooms on her face, and the marks on her arms and legs that blend into her colorful tattoos. "But he was one of us. A captive, like the rest of us. We don't leave each other behind. Not if they're wounded, not even if they're a jerk. If we turn this into a free-for-all to settle old grudges, we'll be caught and then we all die."

Sappho spits at the ground. "He was one of you. Not one of *us*."

"We're all in this together!" His words ring out over the field, and a flock of birds rise from the trees ahead. Embarrassment flits over his face and he lowers his voice. "Why does it matter if he was a boy or a girl or whatever? We're all captives. We've all done stuff we're not proud of or happy about. I'm not saying he was right to hurt you, of course that was wrong; but he was still one of us."

Miyuki's hand tightens on my arm and xie opens xer mouth to speak but Hana is already stalking forward, shoving her face up into his. She doesn't shout, but each perfectly enunciated word is like a slap. "You think we all had the same captivity back there? You think because you fought in the arena that you know anything about what we went through? You only had to face monsters. We had to face *you*. All of you."

He doesn't stumble back from her, but I see the hurt in his eyes. "I... I asked," he whispers, his voice so low I have to strain to hear him. His eyes seek out Miyuki. "I never did anything without asking. And I tried to make it feel good when a girl said yes." He doesn't glance at me when he says this, avoiding my eyes as he looks anywhere but in my direction.

"We still didn't have the choices you had," Chloe says, her face as foreboding as the dark clouds roiling above us. "No, not even when you guys asked. You don't know what it's like, sleeping with someone who can have you killed with a word. You *can't* know what kind of pressure that puts on you."

"Or strung out for a beating," Sappho adds through clenched teeth.

"Or thrown into solitary without food or water," Heather chimes in, watching the stationary Handlers on the horizon as she picks at her bleeding fingers. "Really, the punishments were so creative. Remember when they drowned Peridot in our pool because a boy complained about her crying? Left her body in there for half a dozen cycles so we could watch it bloat up. Whatever happened to him? Chloe broke his leg, I think?"

"I did it," Hana says, her voice cold. She doesn't look away from Keoki. "Broke his knee. Right before a match, too. Never complained about another girl again."

Keoki flinches, turning his head away to gaze at the ground. "Lucas didn't do that, though," he says. His pleading voice is so low I have to strain to hear. "Lucas didn't get you punished or killed. He lost his temper and took it out on you instead of on me."

Imani sits on the other side of me, knees tucked under her chin. "No," she whispers. "Lucas beat girls when he was frustrated, which was pretty much all the time. So we had to decide—when we even had a *chance* to decide—whether to send him Hana or Heather. Hana would heal faster, but we were afraid she'd lose her temper and hit back. Which meant Heather got to go, and Sappho and I got to patch her up each time."

She looks up, her eyes wet with unshed tears. "I'm sure he was nice enough to you, Keoki, but he treated us differently. Believe me or don't, but it's true."

Miyuki's eyes are narrowed, glaring at Keoki while he stares at his feet. "He would have hurt Aniyah!" xie explodes. "If not at Auction, then later. Just to get to you. You can't tell me you don't care about that! If you don't believe us, ask your friend," xie adds, nodding xer chin in Tony's direction.

He meets xer gaze without hesitation. "Are *you* even remotely surprised by any of this?"

Tony shakes his head, dark hair brushing his eyes. "Not in the least." He looks at Keoki, his expression softening. "And maybe if everyone was safe and there weren't Handlers crawling all over the cliff and the footing was decent and Sappho was as strong as she is stretchy—*maybe* if all that was the case, I'd spare a lick of regret for how it went down. As it is... I don't." He shrugs and looks away, peering off into the distant forest.

I look around the faces of the five boys who are still alive and conscious. Tony isn't the only one who looks unconcerned; Christian gives a similar shrug when Keoki glances his way, and seems far more interested in his failing efforts to catch Chloe's eye. Reese, the boy who helped me across the ledge, doesn't meet Keoki's gaze. Only Matías looks as stung as Keoki, but he says nothing and seems lost in his own regrets.

"We're going to take a rest break," Hana declares, turning her back on the boys and stalking to where we sit in a clump on the ground. "Girls over here and boys over there. We're allowed a breather while we get our wounded in order. Eat and drink whatever didn't get left on the other side of the chasm." Keoki opens his mouth, a doubtful frown flickering over his face, but she shuts him down. "We're as free as you out here. You don't have to agree with our decisions, but you *will* respect us."

She throws herself on the ground next to us and begins stretching her legs, rubbing out the kinks before we start running again. Just the idea of getting up from this spot makes me want to roll over and die, but Miyuki runs xer hands over me and magic loosens my muscles from their angry clench. Sappho squats on the ground nearby, her head buried in her arms and her shoulders trembling; Heather sits alongside and drapes an arm over her in silent commiseration. Chloe unslings the water she's been hauling and passes around the half-empty vessels for us to drain.

I hear the tread of footsteps and open my eyes to see Reese approaching. He looks sheepish, one hand playing with a silver bracelet on his wrist. He meets my gaze with a little wincing smile, but doesn't slow his pace as expectant heads turn towards him.

Hana doesn't look up at the intrusion, continuing her stretches. "I said: only girls over here."

He clears his throat and nods, pushing a long strand of hair behind his ear. "Yeah, I—" He smiles, tension visible in his eyes. "That's why I came over. Uh. Surprise?"

Hana looks up at him with open exasperation. "I'm not in the mood for games, Reese," she says in a tight voice. "You're nice and you've got a decent left hook worth developing, but you're *not* a girl."

He stands his ground, staring at the bracelet on his wrist that he continues to fiddle with. "I mean. How can you be so sure, Hana?" he asks, striking a reasonable tone. "Did you ever ask me?"

Beside me, Miyuki sits up so swiftly you'd think cold water had been dumped on xer. Hana doesn't notice. "You were placed with the fighters. You're a boy. That's the rule."

Reese nods at this. "I'm a good fighter," he agrees. "But, I mean, so are you." He looks at Chloe who watches him with one hand on her hip, her expression skeptical. "And you. Doesn't mean you're not girls, right? And it doesn't mean the Master knew anything when he placed you."

Imani looks up, curiosity flickering over her burned features. "Why would you *want* to be a girl? Arena deaths are faster than what we have to look forward to. If the Master made a mistake with you, why would you want to join us?" She laughs, cradling her wounded hand. "Hana's wanted to fight in the arena since she was brought here. She'd trade places with you in a heartbeat. Most of us would."

He shakes his head, fumbling with his wrist; I lean on my elbows and catch the letters of his name in silver. "It's not about what I want to do. It's about who I *am*. Yeah, I'd rather fight than be given to a bunch of guys as a Prize! I can't think how awful it's been for you. But imagine the Master screwed up and placed *you* with the guys, only they didn't know. Imagine

320

they thought you were one of them and you couldn't tell them otherwise. Can you believe how relieved you'd be to get out of there? Living your life in hiding, knowing if they figured you out then guys like Lucas would..."

Reese's voice trails away under Hana's baffled gaze. Miyuki's hand has stilled on my back and xer breath is almost inaudible. "I believe you," xie murmurs, looking up from where xie sits. "And that *does* sound like the most miserable existence in the world." Xie turns xer head to look at Hana, who stares back in surprise.

"Emma?"

"I believe her," Miyuki repeats simply, shrugging xer shoulders. "I do."

Tears leap into Reese's eyes, his—no, *her*—expression crumpling at xer declaration. "Does that mean I can stay over here with you?"

Sappho doesn't raise her head, but unfolds one arm and reaches up. She grabs Reese by the wrist and hauls her down to sit on the ground with her and Heather, drawing her into the silent cuddle-pile they've formed there. "Nobody's going to hurt you," she whispers, her shoulders still trembling as she wraps a tattooed arm around the other girl. "We're not going back. Those boys won't touch us again, I promise."

Miyuki gives a little snort at this vow, but there's a smile on xer face as xie lies on the ground next to me. "Unless we want them to," xie whispers, watching me with amused eyes from behind xer glasses.

"Do *you* want them to?" I ask, raising an eyebrow at xer.

"Not in the slightest," xie replies instantly, xer smile widening. "I was speaking for you, Aniyah. How are you doing, by the way? Ready to stand up? I think our break may be almost over."

I groan, shaking my head and letting my hair drag over the ground. "Please don't make me get up ever again? We'll just stay here in neutral territory forever, and dig up food from the ground. That's where food comes from, doesn't it?"

"Hmm. I have a vague recollection—" Xie stops mid-sentence, a frown creeping over xer face. "Do you hear that?"

From the line of trees comes the sound of beating wings: birds are rising, as they did before when Keoki raised his voice. But we've been quiet out here, with no reason for the animals to spook from their rest. I drag myself to a sitting position while the others do the same, sitting or standing to look at the rising flock.

"Aniyah?" Keoki is at my side, helping me up with his gentle hands. "Can you see anything? Any magic?"

I lean against him, absurdly grateful for his strength; I really don't know if I'm going to be able to stay upright for much longer after all the running I've been doing. I peer forward, one hand against my forehead to shade my eyes from the remnants of sun that filter through the cloud cover.

There is movement among the trees; shapes the size of the stooped Handlers, but thicker. Their outlines resemble the bear from the arena, the one who mauled Justin and Keoki. The figures are black against the shadows, all but invisible save for the outline of magic rippling over them. *We didn't disturb the birds; they did.*

My head whips up to face Keoki. The blood drains from my face as new fear floods through me. "We have to run again."

CHAPTER 32

Keoki

A guttural howl erupts from the forest and more birds explode into the black sky, their indistinct forms blurring in the turbulent darkness. I look down at Aniyah, my heart racing with an animal instinct to flee from the predatory threat.

"Can you run?"

She could stand only with my help, so the desolate shake of her head doesn't surprise me. I close my eyes and waste a precious second wishing there were two of me instead of one. After all my lofty talk about not leaving anyone behind, am I going to be forced to choose between a dying kid and my girl?

"Stop standing around! I'll get your boy," Chloe snaps, pushing past me to reach Justin. "You guys owe me one after." I open my eyes to see her heft Justin in her arms like a stack of clothes and take off running; Christian is hot on her heels, his knife drawn and ready. *I need to stop forgetting she can do that.*

I blink and scoop Aniyah up in the same manner. She gasps and for a heartbeat I'm pleased to have impressed her—not the most appropriate thought in the face of danger, but I never claimed to have a talent for humility—then I see the pain on her face and I realize I've hurt her just by picking her up.

"Are you okay?" Even as I ask the question, I know there's nothing I can do for her if she's not.

Aniyah wraps her arms around my neck and holds on. "No, but it doesn't matter. Run, Keoki!"

She's right, and not just because of the howls which are increasing in frequency. I hear movement behind us and whip around to see Handlers crawling onto the forbidden soil, their tentative first steps quickly escalating to a loping run. *Okay, that's bad,* I think, whirling on my heel and taking off at a sprint.

We run. The four of us lag at the back of the group: me with Aniyah in my arms, Tony and Miyuki sprinting next to us. Tony reaches out to take Miyuki's hand, but she waves him away. "I need my hands!" she snaps, the words a breathless bark. "Keep yours on that sword." He shrugs and doesn't press the issue but falls back a step just in case, ready to catch her if she falls.

Chloe and Christian run ahead of us. If she's burdened by carrying Justin she doesn't show it, but she's forced to lag back to keep pace with Christian. He's visibly struggling, and every few steps he pops out of existence to reappear farther ahead; without his talent, I don't think he could keep up. He's not the only one having to dip heavily into his magic; Matías sprints with them, alternating between short bursts of blurring speed and a slower limping pace. His face is contorted with pain, but he's managing.

The other girls and Reese—who I guess is also a girl now, though I'm still kinda confused about that part—quickly out-distance the rest of us. Heather and Sappho are the fastest runners in our group, and it doesn't hurt to have Handler behind them with his magical fear urging them forward. I gulp in a breath to shout a warning not to get too close to the trees, then I hesitate. I'm worried about the girls facing the lurking beasts by themselves, yet dawdling until we catch up with them might not be a better course of action, given the Handlers hot on our heels. I have to trust Hana and Reese can take care of the others.

Then those indistinct shapes stream out of the forest and my heart leaps into my throat. Tony yells a warning, but it would be impossible for the girls to miss the emerging threat: strange creatures with glossy black fur, pointed ears laid flat against the skull, and thin hairless tails as long as my arm. Each of the creatures is bigger than any one of us, and they run on all fours with a gait fast enough to close the distance between the trees and the girls in a matter of heartbeats.

A yelp pierces the air and Imani sprawls onto the ground, her foot caught on a protruding root. Handler throws himself over the fallen girl, shielding her with his body, and Hana skids to a halt in front of them with her fists raised. Ahead, Heather and Sappho keep going, oblivious to the plight of their friend. Reese glances back, her eyes widening when she sees Hana has stopped. She hesitates, then chases after the two unarmed girls, gripping her weapons and calling for them to stop.

Tony quickens his pace, but I know we'll be too late. Blood is about to be shed in front of us and we're helpless to protect the people we care about. In a matter of heartbeats, the rampaging beasts will slam into Heather and Sappho and then race on to trample Imani. The only hope we have—and it's a slim one, given the size of the pack—is that Hana and Reese can hold the creatures long enough for us to catch up. All I can do is run faster, Aniyah wincing with every bounding step.

Just as the monsters charge into reach of the running girls, the pack parts like a stream around a stone. They race around Heather and Sappho and Reese, then part again to avoid Hana and Imani and Handler. They clearly *see* our group, and some even snap their teeth menacingly as they run by, but they don't attack the girls. Instead they charge forward without slowing, heading straight for us.

"Taking out the fighters first?" Tony guesses, his hand tightening on his sword. "Plan to pick off the weaker ones after?"

"Your sword," Miyuki pants in short gasps as she gulps for air. "Maybe they only attack what threatens them. Hana's lost her spear and Reese is wearing that fist-weapon. Maybe they didn't see them as a danger."

"Great. If we don't disarm, we're a threat; if we do disarm, we're easy pickings." I'm exaggerating, but only a little; I can fight unarmed and Tony and Christian wouldn't be helpless, but I don't like those odds.

Aniyah's gasp is shot through with pain. "No! Look, don't you see the leader? Follow its eyes. Behind us!"

I can't tell which one is the leader; they're all equally big and ugly. She points unsteadily at a creature running near the front of the pack, its gaze locked on something over my left shoulder. I turn my head to look and immediately snap back around; a Handler gallops close behind, gaining distance with every step we take.

"Faster," I pant, tightening my grip on Aniyah. "Don't attack, just run. Tony, take care of Miyuki!"

"I'm *fine*," she hisses through closed teeth. "Stop treating me like—"

Anything she says after that is lost in the howl that bubbles up from the leader's throat. The creatures stream around Chloe and the other guys before angling back into line to face us. I hunch my shoulders around Aniyah and duck my head with intent to barrel through, then I feel a powerful rush of wind above my head as the creatures leap over us. I turn just in time to see them pounce onto the pursuing Handlers.

My eyes are wide as serving bowls. "Is this a rescue?" I wonder, gulping air into my burning lungs.

"No. Keep running." Aniyah's fists are clenched so tightly I can smell blood seeping from fresh cuts. "Those Handlers are coated with the Master's energy. I think they're hunting the scent."

Miyuki thins her lips, looking grim. "Don't we have the same smell, just not as strong?"

Aniyah's miserable whimper is answer enough and I shake my head, tossing curls back from my eyes. "Tony was right, then; they're taking out the strong ones first. We gotta be out of here when they're done."

"The trees," Aniyah whispers, her eyes fluttering shut. "We have to get to the trees. We have to want to escape. If we want it badly enough, we will do it."

That shouldn't be a problem. Already Heather has reached the first of the trees, all but slamming into the wood as she wraps her arms around it, bracing against imaginary hands seeking to haul her away. "We're here!" Heather's yell reverberates through the forest, causing another eruption of birds. "We made it; we're here!" Her voice is ragged, cracking under strain. "We're *here!*"

Her last word is a scream. She pounds her fists into the tree, tearing away strips of bark with her bleeding hands. Sappho catches her a moment later, wrapping her arms around the frantic girl and pulling her away before she can harm herself further. "We're here, we're here," she soothes. "As soon as the others come, we can leave."

We're close enough now to hear her words on the breeze. I open my mouth wide as I run, inhaling the cool air of the forest. I don't understand how I recognize what I see and taste and hear and feel. In the Master's domain, I never felt water in the air like this or saw the warm brown bark of a tree or heard the rustle of leaves in a breeze. Yet I know these things, just as I know how to run on sand, the knowledge coming from a past I don't remember. Those memories were stolen away when I was taken.

"Did we come from this place?" Miyuki's murmur floats back to me as we slow to a halt with the rest of the group. Tony pants hard at my side, his head tilted back to look from the tree to the canopy above. Chloe leans against one of the thicker trees, breathing deeply, and Christian flops down onto the ground beside her. Hana circles a tree warily, while Imani pokes gingerly with her burned hands at the area Heather mutilated.

"No." Handler's voice is as raw as an open wound and he doubles over against his knees, gasping for breath. "I do not know where you are brought from, but it is not from this domain. You were harvested."

"Harvested from where?" Heather rounds on him, her eyes wide with frustration. "You must know something! Where do we come from? How do we get back there?"

"The place where humans come from," he says, his voice desolate. "I know no more. If we cannot find the way, my only hope is for the guardians of this forest to give me a clean death."

"Aniyah will know," Miyuki insists, peering with an anxious expression at the half-conscious girl in my arms. "Sweetie, can you hear me? We need to know what to do next."

I shift my arms until I hope she's in a more comfortable position, but her eyes remain closed to the world. "She's in a lot of pain, Miyuki. I don't think she's awake."

Worry flashes in her hazel eyes as she places hands on Aniyah's neck. "You have to wake up," she whispers. "I don't have much magic left. Please let this be enough! I promise more later."

Aniyah stirs as a low howl sends shivers down my back. The sounds of battle behind us have tailed off; minus a few scattered growls and one last gurgling scream from a Handler, things are now dangerously quiet. "Oh, that's not good," Tony observes, watching the field behind me.

Miyuki ignores him, grasping Aniyah's hands in her own and maintaining eye contact as she rouses. "Aniyah! We've reached the trees, just like you said. What's next? What does the magic tell you to do?"

Aniyah blinks bleary eyes. "We have to want to leave," she says, as though everything were perfectly simple.

A few of the others groan; Christian and Matías ready their weapons, eyes focused on the enemy behind. "Ani, we did that part," Miyuki says, her voice urgent. "What do we do after that? Where do we go?"

"That's all," Aniyah says, shaking her head. There's a faraway quality to her voice. "We just have to want it enough."

We're going to die here. The knowledge squeezes my heart. *We'll never get back to where we came from.* I don't even have a name for the place: it's just where-we-came-from, the place where words were learned. A lost home the dark area of my mind longs for, even while I have no memory of it.

No memory except the words. My head tilts to the right as a new thought nibbles at me. "Tony, give me your hand."

He blinks but reaches out to tangle his fingers in mine, careful not to disturb my grip on Aniyah. "Okay. Why?"

"Maybe..." The words come slower than I'd like, the thought rolling around my brain as it struggles to pick up speed. "Maybe it's not enough to want to leave. Maybe we have to want to *be* in a certain place: home."

Tony nods, but I can see he doesn't understand. "Keoki, I couldn't want to be home any harder than I already do."

"No, no, you're not getting it!" I shake my head at him, my adrenaline building. "Tell me a thing you miss about home. Hold my hand and tell me. I'll start." Words spill out of me. "Sand as soft as skin, not this coarse stuff. The roar of the crowd when you're winning, only it's not the crowd—it's water. Music you make with your hands, fingers against strings. You sing to it."

"Beds that don't hurt." Aniyah's mumble floats on the breeze, plaintive and soft. "Pillows as thick as your head, not just flat ones for sitting on the floor. You put them behind your back or under your knees. Pain that wasn't like this. Feeling *alive*, not just... waiting to die."

Miyuki reaches out to stroke Aniyah's cheek at the hesitation in this last recollection. "Kisses in the darkness," she whispers, her eyes shining with tears. "Laughter in the light. I was about to be free. So many things I wanted to tell you about us. I don't recall them all, but I remember the parts that matter."

There's a change in the air, a flickering spark and an acrid scent that tickles the nose. The howls behind us are fainter than before and seem farther away. Chloe looks up, her arms tight around Justin. "Soft fabric on my skin," she says, sounding dazed by the recollection. "Texture and color, not like these white curtains we're stuck wearing. Flashing lights and a smile each time. The smile was important, but I was good at it because I was happy."

Christian watches her with shining eyes, his own smile widening. "There were high places. Do you remember those? Not cramped down in those caves like we've been, but flying high in the sky, legs out behind you while your arms hold you up. Wings over your head and the whole world under you. Tell me someone else remembers how to fly?"

"I remember the food," Matías says, shaking his head and frowning at the ground. "The heat of fire like the torches in our cavern, but hotter and steadier. Food I made with my bare hands from little bits and pieces: grains smaller than our sand and a bit of water to hold them together. I'd punch everything down and it would rise back up into the softest bread you ever tasted. Like those clouds up there."

The acrid scent in the air is stronger now as words come faster, stories going down the line like a passed torch. "Training," Hana says, clenching her fists and letting a proud smile flicker over her face. "*Real* training with real teachers; honest sweat and a long bath after. I was going to be the best."

"Washing my hands," Imani muses. She looks down at her burned hands and laughs softly. "I know it sounds weird, but washing them over and over again, more times than you can count. There were rooms to check on, and people in them. They needed food or healing or just someone to talk to. I liked the older people the best. What about you, Reese?"

"The wind in my hair," Reese says immediately, the answer already on her tongue. "I was supposed to wear a—a helmet, I think. I hardly ever did."

Sappho's hand tightens on Reese's arm, her expression wistful. "Pictures," she whispers, "and words. I drew pretty things to put on my body. I miss that most of all."

"Pain." Heather's voice is hollow again and she doesn't look up. "Feeling. Any kind of sensation. I have the most intense dreams, but when I wake up they fade in the sun."

Handler nods at this, his expression matching hers. "Silence. Peace from the voices."

Tony is watching me, his eyes warm under the shock of dark bangs. "You're the last one," I tell him, my voice low in the charged air. "What does home mean to you?"

He closes his eyes and takes a deep breath. "Hot tar paving the ground, sticky on my shoes in summer. People everywhere, not just six or a dozen but crushing you on all sides. Food with an actual *taste* to it, hot enough to burn your tongue. Dancing a routine until you knew it by heart and could perform it in your sleep." He opens his eyes again and they glisten with tears in the dim light. "Being allowed to love."

I'd been holding everything together until his voice cracked on the last word. Tears spring to my eyes and I squeeze his fingers in mine. "Tony—" I start, but Hana hisses a warning shush and drops to a wary crouch.

"They're almost here," she whispers, eyes darting around. "Shit, I can't see them anymore!"

A wall of white mist has sprung up around us, courtesy of the thick moisture in the forest air. The fog muffles every sound; though I can still hear the heavy breathing of the approaching creatures, they seem drastically fewer in number, a mere two or three rather than the large pack at the outset. *Did the Handlers kill the rest?* I wonder if I should put Aniyah down to fight or keep her in my arms in case we need to run.

"Aniyah?" My voice drops to a whisper, though if they're hunting us by smell instead of sound my caution will do little good. "Sweetheart, can you see anything in this mist?" She stirs at the question and opens her eyes, a dreamy expression on her beautiful face; it's as if the pain has taken her so far away that it's not really pain anymore.

She gasps when she registers the mist, her eyes widening as her fingers reach out to the drifting tendrils. "*Magic*," she breathes. Her gaze drifts to the center of our group and lands on Heather, who has fallen to her knees and is murmuring something over and over into her clasped hands. "That's right, Heather," Aniyah mumbles with a smile. "Send your power around us."

"Ani, we need you to tell us where the creatu—"

"Keoki!"

At Matías' shout I whirl in time to see one of the creatures plunging through the wall of mist, charging straight at me. I stumble back a step, caught in a fatal hesitation: I can't fight with Aniyah in my arms but can't bring myself to drop her to the ground. It's a stupid hang-up—she'll die because I was unwilling to cause her pain—and I have just enough time left in my life to curse my poor decision-making.

"Hold still!"

A woman's voice I've never heard before is accompanied by a soft hiss whizzing by my ears, then I have the immense yet confusing pleasure of watching an arrow bury itself in the creature's chest while it runs. Momentum carries it forward while a red blossom of blood spreads over its skin, then the dying creature plants its face into the dirt and slides to a lifeless halt at our feet.

"Eight and eleven o'clock, Celia!" A second voice, as foreign as the first but masculine this time.

"Blocked. I'm circling arou—"

"Taking eight."

"Tyr!"

An explosion rings out behind me to the left; I drop into a crouch, clutching Aniyah to my chest. There's a howl of pain and another one of those creatures collapses to the ground in the thick mist; this one had not been charging at all, but attempting to sneak up on Sappho and Imani.

Two strangers now stand in the mist with us. One is a pale man with feathery-soft brown hair, a chin full of scruff and a sleek black-and-gray hunting rifle; the other is a woman with brown skin, hair that hangs down in a thick braid over her shoulder and what appears to be a bow with extra complicated bits tacked on.

"Drop to the ground and hold still!" The woman's order is a little late, but most of us have already taken her advice; only Matías still stands, his knee preventing him from crouching quickly or easily.

"Taking eleven." A jingling popping sound of metal against metal rings out. Silver leaps from the gun, followed by a flat click. The man swears and glares at the rifle in his hands, fussing at a lever that seems to be giving him trouble. Over my shoulder, between myself and Christian, I hear a low animal growl.

"Tyr."

"I hear it. The fucking thing's jammed."

"Goddammit."

She plants her feet and pulls her arm back to draw the bow, her breath slowing as the creature crouches to spring. It leaps as she releases, the arrow striking it in the shoulder and barely checking its step. I watch with my hands full, helpless to intervene, while the creature bounds in a direct line for Matías. Resignation is written on his face; after having drawn heavily on his talent in so short a time, I know he won't be able to dodge. The animal pounces, its teeth bared to tear out his throat.

Tony is there in a single swift movement, his sword flashing bright silver in the mist. The creature's head flies wide, hits the earth hard, and bounces twice before rolling to a halt. The headless body of the animal slumps to the ground and cuts a deep sliding furrow before coming to a stop at Matías' feet. He takes a deep breath and looks up at his savior with a shaky smile.

"Thank you, Anthony."

CHAPTER 33

Aniyah

"**I**s that all of them, Tyr?"

I open my eyes to find myself in a world unlike any I've seen before. The silver mist has faded away to reveal a changed landscape similar to the one we've just fled—the soil is dark and loamy and trees grow thick around us—yet their colors are a brand new palette to my eyes.

Everything is dull, but in the best possible way. The blinding brightness assaulting me from every direction since the Shadow Man altered my sight has softened to muted hues which no longer dazzle. The leafy canopy above us is a deep calming green, casting a dappled shade that shields us from the setting sun, itself a warm ochre that soothes my mind after the searing yellow constantly flooding our cavern.

The magic isn't gone. I remember how everything looked when I was first awakened by the Master, the flat emptiness surrounding me before my blossoming talent opened my eyes to what lay beneath. This new world isn't devoid of that vibrant flow, but the magic that courses through the land and trees is vastly different to what we've left behind. *If the other world belonged to faeries,* I decide, spreading my fingers and reaching out to touch the air, *this world must be where humans live.*

"Yeah, that's all of them."

I sit up straighter in Keoki's arms to get a better look at our rescuers, but feel a snap in my lower back and my vision blurs with new pain. My mind swirls into a strange blend of dizzy confusion and perfect lucidity; the world around me spins, yet my thoughts are of such sharp clarity they feel like daggers in my head.

The woman who saved us is dusted in a glimmer of faery magic. She's beautifully strong, as lean and muscular as any of our fighters, and she holds her weapon like an extension of her body. At the man's answer, she brings the bow around to a strap harness worn over her shoulder and secures the weapon with short practiced movements. "Only three guardians made it through. Not bad; we got lucky."

"Lucky would be if this expensive rubbish hadn't jammed on me." The man fusses with his gun without bothering to look up, then shoulders the rifle with a sound of disgust. "You were expecting more trouble?"

"Considering the size of the portal, yes." She turns to our group and makes eye contact with each of us, her gaze not lingering on any one person for long. Her voice is deep, almost stern; her tone not one you would argue with without a good reason. "My name is Celia. You're on the run from faeries? You're safe now. You've escaped the otherworld; you're earthside again and we're human, just like you."

"Or something very like," her companion mutters. His expression is bored as he looks us over, a low whistle escaping his lips. "Look how many there are. Got to be a baker's dozen, at least."

She ignores him. "We're here to take you to healers, then food and rest. Are any of you too wounded to walk or be carried a short distance?" Her eyes flick to me, though much of her attention seems settled on Tony and the sword he grips in his hands, the blade dripping with dark ichor.

Hesitation ripples through our group. Could safety really be so simple as this, or is it a trap? Keoki is the first to step forward, and I would be proud of him were it not for the fresh pain that tears me apart with his every jarring step. "Nice to meet you, ma'am. Can you help Aniyah? She's hurt bad."

"Hello, Aniyah. May I touch you?" Her hands reach out with exaggerated slowness, careful not to startle me; when I don't pull away, she gingerly feels around my neck. "Where does it hurt, hon? Think you can hang on until we get to our healers?"

There's no magic in her hands like Miyuki's; I try to nod and the world spins again. "I'm... I'm not fine, but I can hang on." My words slur in my ears, the 'm's and 'n's dragging out longer than they should. "Help Justin. He was mauled by a bear."

"We're going to help all of you; the question is where and in what order. Where's Justin?"

"Here." Chloe moves to stand beside us, clutching the unconscious boy in her arms. "He's not too well."

Celia sucks air between her teeth, her fingertips flying over his swollen face and bleeding leg. "Shit, he's in bad condition. Tyr, get down to the road and be ready to flag down Rose. They've gotta be close."

"It's a two-lane street without a single turnoff, Celia. And we'd barely pulled over before you jumped out and tore up here. They can't miss us, they're just running late." Leaves rustle nearby and I hear the snap of dry twigs under a heavy tread. "Speak of the devil. C'mon out, it's safe."

Sappho gasps and draws back as more strangers pour into our midst. Miyuki's hand grips my arm harder and Tony renews his hold on his sword, though none of the newcomers seems to pay him any mind. Two women and a man—at least, I *think* he's a man—emerge from the trees into the tiny clearing where we stand, each dusted in the same magic radiance as our two rescuers.

The women are a beautiful pair, contrasting and yet strangely similar. One has pale skin and the other is warm and dark, their tumbling locks a deep purple and dark red respectively. Their eyes are as vibrantly green as Heather's, and thick raised veins climb their arms and snake down their calves in a tangle of wild magic. Despite their smiles, there's danger inside them and yet I am not afraid. Drinking in the heady scent wafting across the clearing, I think they could kill me and I'd not begrudge them.

The man accompanying them is an even stranger specimen. He's covered from head to toe in silver, yet his arms and legs move with the fluidity of human skin and his face is detailed to the smallest eyelash. His smile is gentle as he looks over our group, and his eyes are sympathetic when they fall on Justin.

"Celia?" The woman with dark red hair leads the group, stepping forward through the trees. "Sorry, we weren't trying to barge up here. We were careful to watch for flying arrows, I swear."

The purple-headed girl's voice is light and teasing. "Clarent, you just can't step lightly, can you?"

"You wouldn't either, Lavs, if you were made of metal."

Celia waves them closer, worry creasing her brow. "Rose, we've got wounded. They said this boy was mauled, and he smells of infection. He'll need a shot; I don't want to risk the time it'll take to get him to Joel."

The woman's expression is grave as she rummages through a bag slung across her chest. "My name is Rose," she murmurs to the unconscious boy. "Everything is going to be fine."

Her voice is soothing in spite of the fact that Justin isn't awake to hear it. She produces a vial of glowing white liquid and holds it up in display, light catching the silver tip of a needle. "You're safe and we're going to get you healed. See this? This is something I made myself. It'll fix you up." She angles the needle into the flesh of his hip above the tattered bandages encasing his leg, and liquid magic drains into him.

Imani is the first to gasp, setting off a cascade of similar yelps as a dramatic transformation ripples over Justin. Light streams through his body, cleansing where it passes and drawing angry purple bruises from the surface of his skin. Cracking noises fill the clearing, like bones shifting against each other, yet his expression is serene. As we watch, the swelling around his eye deflates like a sigh, leaving his face smooth without a lingering blemish to mark the bear's attack.

His eyes flutter open as the others crowd around. "Huh? What happened?" he asks, mumbling sleepily in Chloe's arms. He watches with bemusement as Imani pulls away bandages and splinting to examine his leg, which appears to be whole and healthy. "I'm so hungry I could eat sand."

They healed him. They saved our lives and they healed him. They really are here to help us. The same thought seems to occur to everyone at once, setting off a babble of voices speaking over each other.

"Are we really out, then? Can he reach us here?"

"How safe are we? Like, forever-safe or just-for-now-safe?"

"Is this home? Why don't I remember it?"

"Where is this *exactly?*" Hana's voice cuts through the others, her eyes on Celia's face.

"Right now?" Celia nods in recognition of Hana's question over the cacophony. "We're at Eagle Mountain Lake just outside Azle, Texas. The lake area is northwest of the Dallas-Fort Worth metroplex, which is where we'll be taking you all to heal and rest." She shakes her head, sympathy stealing over the worn lines in her strong face. "Most of those words won't make sense to you, but that's normal."

"There are neither eagles nor mountains here, and it's not technically a lake," Tyr adds with a helpful smirk. "Gods, I can't get over how *human* they look, Celia. Except for that robed one and those chains on the girls, you'd hardly know where they've been. Clarent, are they really altered?"

"They are," the silver man says in response. "It's a rough sort of alteration, not quite finished." His eyes find me and then Justin, his smooth silver brow knitting in confusion. "They aren't all from the same domain, though."

"That happens," Celia says, looking unconcerned. "The important thing is we're all earthside. Earth is where you came from, where you were born human. Later you were taken and altered to live among faeries in the otherworld, but you never stopped being human. Honey, I don't think you should be doing that."

Heather is running her bleeding hands over a nearby tree, scraping her skin against the bark and leaving trails of blood where she touches. At Celia's admonishment she turns towards us, her expression animated with joy for the first time I've seen. "It's back," she breathes. "I can *feel* things! It's faint, but it's there."

Celia hesitates, choosing her next words with care. "Some of you may have lost some magic in the crossing over. If any of you has harmful or unwanted skills, Clarent here may be able to help. But first we need to get you to our healers. Can everyone walk? My truck is parked down the hill, and we've got Rose's vehicle."

"How we're going to transport them all is the question," Tyr points out, trudging away in the direction from which the newcomers had arrived. "Fourteen escapees? That's got to be a record haul."

The pretty purple-haired woman rolls her eyes. "The wounded girl can lie across the back seat with me." She flashes me a warm smile. "It's a smoother ride than Celia's truck, at least. I'm Lavender, by the way."

"We'll pile everyone else in the back of the pickup," Celia adds with a shrug. "Legal enough, with everyone over eighteen. You boys can ride in the back with them and keep 'em from falling out."

Miyuki frowns at the suggestion that we separate, but when xie speaks it's of a different concern. "Didn't you know how many of us there would be? You knew we were coming, didn't you? That's how you were here to save us and heal Justin."

Celia shakes her head, pushing branches out of the way so we can walk through without being scratched. "Nope, didn't know how many of you to expect," she says, her voice brusque. She shrugs her shoulders. "Got a sense that someone was heading in this direction with intent to escape, and I know roughly where the borders lie. Details like who's coming and how many and whether they'll make it..." Her voice trails away for a moment before she shrugs again and continues walking. "You did good."

Keoki ducks his head under the branch she lifts and ambles down the path towards a strange gray path that I belatedly identify as a road. I'm having trouble concentrating and try not to wince with every step; it's not his fault my body is on fire. "Ma'am?" he asks, glancing back at her as he walks. "The guy who took us: is he gonna want us back?"

Rose touches his shoulder and guides him so he doesn't block the path. "We'll talk about everything later," she promises, her gentle voice reassuring. Her fingers brush my skin and I feel a little tremor at her touch as new magic seeps into my skin and whispers comforting words my mind can't disentangle.

What an odd talent, I think, drifting on the waves of those whispered words. *It's as if her whole purpose is to be a comfort to others. Was she given to boys, like we were?*

"The answer is usually 'no'," she continues, giving Keoki a kind smile. "It depends on what you did over there and how important you were to them. Even if they do come for you, we have ways of protecting you. We help each other."

Heather snorts at her answer; the sound is recognizably Heather's scoff, yet infinitely happier than before. "We weren't important to him in the least," she declares, shaking stray leaves from her blond tresses as we tumble out onto the road. She stares for a moment at the red truck that squats by the side of the road—undeniably a truck and yet the only one we can recall seeing—but takes it in stride and turns back to Rose. "He hardly ever even saw us. Prizes were just for servicing the fighters, that's all."

Rose's face falls slightly; she tries to hide the pain in her eyes, but her smile isn't fast enough. "I see," she says, her smile encompassing a world of sympathy. "And the fighters?" Her gentle gaze moves over the armored members of our group.

Tony swipes a handful of leaves from the nearest tree to swab ineffectively at the blood on his sword. "We were there to put on shows. Fight for their entertainment. When we left, we'd all been scheduled to die in some sort of massacre. Can't think he'd go to all the trouble to get us back if he just plans to kill us right away."

The silver man winces, his metallic face etched with compassion. He offers his hand to Tony and helps him hop into the bed of the truck. "You're safe now," he promises. "You're back home and you don't need to fight again if you don't want to. No one here is going to try to kill you."

Lavender gives him a fond look and opens the door to a nearby vehicle; it is squat and hunched and bulky, and sports a battered spare tire on the back. "Clarent's right. I know it's disorienting the first day out, and you don't really remember anything—"

"Oh, but we have memories!"

All five of our rescuers stop mid-step to stare at Sappho. Rose wears an expression of naked hunger, while Lavender blinks. "You do?"

Sappho shifts on her feet, uncertain under the focus of so much attention. "Well, we saved some."

"We know our names," Imani explains, taking Clarent's hand gingerly with her burned fingers.

"And we know we came from the University; most of us, anyway." Chloe hops into the truck bed without difficulty, flinging a hand out behind her to help Christian up.

Celia stares at her. "How do you know that?"

"Hana woke us up before the Master wiped our memories," I explain. Keoki sets me on my feet as gently as he can, but the world whirls sickeningly and I have to cling to his arms. "She... saved everything she could."

Her eyebrows shoot up. "That is *impressive*." Three little words, but she packs a lot of meaning into them.

Hana looks down at her feet and shrugs. I suppose it's one thing to know you're impressive and another entirely to hear it from someone who understands more about this world than all of us combined. "We didn't save as much as we wanted, but we know Miyuki has family in the area and Aniyah doesn't."

Miyuki perks up at the subject. "Yes! I have a father willing to pay to get me and Aniyah back. We haven't been gone long. We should be able to find him, right?"

"And Keoki was brought in with us," I add in a weak voice. "He might have family of his own."

Tyr hops into the truck bed and offers a hand to Matías, his attention focused on Miyuki. "If they're recent nabs, they may not have faded yet," he muses.

"That's a myth," Lavender snaps, thinning her lips.

"Not to me, Thornbush." He settles into the truck bed with his back against the cab, not bothering to look her way.

Clarent speaks before Lavender can retort, his peaceful voice floating over the road as he helps Justin into the crowded pickup. "We can check the 'Missing Persons' site; it won't take long and can't hurt. We know their appearances weren't changed, if the girls saw new arrivals before they were altered. We can look through the pictures and see if there are any matches."

Rose nods, hunger still glinting in her eyes. "Elric could do it. It'd be faster than making new identities from scratch, right?"

"Even if we can find their families, their memories are still wiped," Celia says, a note of caution in her voice. "Reintegration would be difficult verging on impossible. Up you go, hon. The rest of you can fit on the bench in the cab with me," she adds, helping Reese into the truck.

Tyr snorts and stretches out his arm along the side of the truck bed. "Tell 'em they were brainwashed by a cult. They're dressed the part and humans will believe anything. You can send a siren along if you absolutely have to; no one ever tells them boo."

Lavender mimes for Keoki to help me into their vehicle. I do my best to follow their guidance, but my head is swimming with possibilities. *Miyuki and xer father. He must have been close to me. Would he know my parents?* I look at Celia as she helps Imani and Sappho slide into the cab of her truck.

"You *will* help us find our families?" My voice sounds far away to my own ears, spinning with the breeze of the forest behind us. "All our families?"

Celia hesitates until the girls are inside, then meets my eyes with her clear gaze. "We will try. The odds are not good and I am sorry for that. But we will make an effort to look and we will teach you how to keep looking if we are not successful. And no matter what you find, you have a family here with us."

Miyuki catches my eyes as Keoki helps me to lie on the back seat of the squat little vehicle, xer smile happier than I ever remember. *And each other,* xie mouths before blowing me a kiss. I can't reach into the air to catch it, but I know xie sees my answering grin.

Yes. We can make a family with each other.

CHAPTER 34

Keoki

Memories don't come flooding back, but everywhere I look there's something familiar. The sky darkens as we ride away, but not to the total blackness I experienced in the arena. Instead, it's a soft blend of blues and grays, dotted with yellow lights that dangle overhead as we drive: *streetlights*.

My eyes know these lights just as my skin knows the kiss of the warm night wind. The heady scent of summer grass, hot asphalt, and burning gasoline brings tears to my eyes. *We're home,* I think, one arm draped over the side of the truck and around Tony, while the other holds a blanket Celia brought out to cover our bloodstained clothes and armor. *Even if we don't remember it, we're still home.*

We drive through a quiet town that feels bigger than it looks and come out on the other side to a stretch of wide road that would be empty were it not for the truck under us, the sports utility vehicle in front, and two new vehicles that swing out behind us: a giant white camper, the kind you can live inside as long as you don't mind cramped spaces, and a blue mini-van that looks like it could easily hold all of us. Clarent, the silver guy sitting with Matías, lifts a hand to wave at them before giving the rest of us a warm smile.

"Friends of ours," he explains, his voice carried away by the night wind. "Celia calls people on her cellphone. I'm still learning mine," he adds, scrunching up his metal nose in annoyance.

We pull in beside a lake dotted with fire pits around the perimeter and an occasional small building jutting from the grass-speckled sand. We pile out as the van parks behind us and a pretty woman hops from the driver's seat. She's as lean as the nearby trees and her skin as roughly textured as their bark. A quick introduction is tossed in our direction—"Name's Pensri. Call me Pri."—then she begins hauling out canvas and poles from her van, tossing them onto the sand before staking them up.

The camper is close on her heels and pulls off the road in a wide turn. A man steps down and looks around for someone he doesn't see; he has skin so pale he almost glows in the moonlight. "Where is my patient?" he asks Celia, who's slamming the truck door behind her.

"Lynn, the girl is in Rose's car. After you've finished with her, I want individual checks on everyone, one at a time in the RV with you. Sorry to drag you out here. I didn't figure they'd want to be separated yet, and a camping site is the best place to hide a dozen kids in plain sight. Pri, you got our permits?" She stalks over to the woman, reaching to help with the tent poles.

"Reserved our spot on my phone," the visitor replies without looking up. Celia nods without another word, and the two women strike up a silent rhythm as they work.

The rest of the night is surreal, starting with the fact that there even *is* a night at all. We do what we can to help Celia and Pri set up the massive tent, while Handler moves slowly about the group, unchaining the girls one by one. Pri announces that she brought food, so we get to make a fire and roast hot dogs and burn them until the skin is crackly and crispy. Aniyah and Miyuki are with the healer for a long time, and I join the group conversation to cover the gnawing worry in my stomach that food can't fix. We share words and learn new ones, and tell our rescuers about the arena and what we can do.

When Aniyah finally comes out of the camper, she's walking on her own two feet. She's a little unsteady and holding Miyuki's hand, but her easy smile is back. I jump up to meet them and pull her into a gentle hug. "You look amazing. Are you all fixed up now, like Justin? I missed you."

Her grin widens but she shakes her head. "Um. No, not healed but better. I have a lot to think about, but it's going to be okay."

I want to ask her what she means by that, but the healer places a delicate hand on my shoulder. "You next. Come on. You can talk later." I shrug and follow him up the camper steps with a parting grin. It's not like she's going anywhere, not when this is home and we've finally found it.

The inside of the camper is only slightly less sweltering than the campsite outside, and I plop down onto a nearby bench. Lynn kneels on the floor in front of me without saying a word, his fingers reaching out to hover just above my feet. I'm about to ask what he's doing; then his hands begin to glow faintly and he guides them over my body with a frown of concentration. The thin layer of air between us remains intact as he stands and moves up my chest, ending his examination with both hands above my head.

"You're healthy as a horse," he announces, leaning back on his heels and brushing his no-longer-glowing hands on his pants. "Send the next one in when you leave. Thanks."

I blink at the sudden dismissal, but nod and step back out into the night. *Maybe things just aren't going to make sense for a while,* I conclude, catching Tony's eye and jerking my thumb back towards the camper door. "You're up, but ask him how healthy a horse is for me? Kinda important."

As the healer finishes with us, we drift to the tent in ones and twos. We spend the night lying on ground that is even harder than the rock beds we've left behind. The temperature isn't quite as hot as the arena, but the nearby lake adds a sticky layer of humidity to coat our skin. With so many of us crammed into such a small space, the ruckus of snores, snorts, and nightmare-tremors is loud enough to prevent almost any sleep at all.

346

I snuggle closer to Tony, listen to his heartbeat under my ear, and decide this is perfection.

This impression is reinforced when the sun comes up the next morning and we wake to the smoky scent of a fire, blended with sweet and savory aromas that make my stomach growl. We scramble out to find Tyr cooking skewered bacon while Pri uses tongs to turn over a loaf of foil containing a block of sliced bread, now turned into French toast through the magic of a liquid egg mix and frozen sliced strawberries. She helps us load food onto paper plates while Celia paces some distance away, her phone pressed to her ear.

"You're sure the pictures match?" A pause while the person at the other end talks and Celia tugs at her braid. "And it's just the one? I don't know if that makes things better or worse. No, we'll manage on our own; you get started on identities for the others. Yes, I'm aware it's a lot; Elric, I didn't bring in fourteen refugees to personally spite you. Take 'em a day at a time, and—" Another long pause. I look up from my bacon to see Celia rub her forehead while noise babbles into her ear. "No. *No.* Fine. Thank you, Elric."

She jams the phone into her pocket and strolls over to us. "What's going on?" Matías asks, looking up with alert interest where he sits with his cane. His knee seems the same as ever, so I guess the healer with the glowing hands wasn't as good as the girl who healed Justin.

"Everything is probably okay," Celia says, choosing her words with care. "I asked Elric to sweep the local 'Missing Persons' database; there's a public site he checks every so often. It is *very* rare for altereds to show up there, but you said you hadn't been gone long." This is directed at Miyuki, who is sitting straight as a spear.

"And?" she breathes, the food in her hands forgotten.

"We found an entry for one Emma, complete with a grainy photo which Elric insists matches the picture I texted him. She looks at Aniyah and myself. "You two are mentioned briefly by name in the notes. That's it; there's no separate report for either of you. You're both officially missing in the sense that you disappeared around the same time Emma did, but there's otherwise no trace of you in the system. If Elric hadn't been looking for her, he'd never have found you two."

I frown, trying to work this out. "What does that mean? Why does she have a report and we don't? What's wrong with me and Aniyah?"

Celia's furrowed brow indicates more concern than her easy stance lets on. "We don't know why altereds disappear without leaving the usual traces. In my experience *Emma* is the exception, not you and Aniyah. Maybe her family was somehow more resistant to the fade than most. I don't know."

"But we *can* go home?" Miyuki sets aside her plate and stands up, brushing her hands on her robes. "I can see my family?"

"It's up to you," Celia says, her voice gentle. "It will be difficult to reintegrate without memories, but Tyr's right that we can make up a story and bluff our way through. If we're going to do that, we ought to take you in now; the longer we wait, the worse it'll look if they retrace your steps. Disheveled and confused and found by the side of the road in white robes: all those details work for his kidnapped-by-a-cult story. I can't be the one to take you in, so I'll need to call one of our sirens to play the part."

The three of us look at each other. Miyuki reaches for Aniyah's hand and Tony slips his into mine for a quick squeeze. "Let's do it now," I vote, rewarded with a warm smile of approval from Miyuki.

We get up to hug the others and say goodbye for the next few hours, then Aniyah looks at Celia with a question in her bright eyes. "How long were we gone?"

"Twenty-seven days, according to the police report," she answers, her eyes on her phone where she's texting our proposed escort with directions to the lake.

Twenty-seven days. I've only just been reintroduced to the concept of days after the eternal sunlight of the arena, but the number seems staggeringly large. I spend the ride to the police station trying and failing to match the time we lost here to the time spent over there. *Did time pass differently while we were gone, or was I too disoriented to tell?*

348

I hadn't known what to expect when we reach the police station, yet they still manage to surprise me with their almost total indifference. The man at the front desk seems less concerned with us and more interested in getting the telephone number of our escort, a slender-limbed hypnotic-voiced girl with shimmering fish-scales spreading up the back of her neck and down her arms. She draws the attention of everyone within earshot, leaving little left over for our disheveled selves.

This pattern repeats as we're passed from officer to officer while they search for Miyuki's file, which seems to have gone missing. Long after my stomach begins reminding me about lunch, the officer we've ended up with decides we have been missing after all; this is convenient, because it matches our collective insistence that we've been kidnapped by persons unknown. Miyuki's file is found and turns out to be a slender printout with only the barest of details.

"Ah! Here we are," he says, stabbing a triumphant finger at the sparse notes. "Young woman reported missing by her mother. Normally we wait twenty-four hours to file a report, but when your father golfs with the mayor..." He chuckles and shakes his head. "We've been expecting a ransom demand."

"My girlfriend and I were kidnapped together," Miyuki says, feeling her way through our tenuous story with care. "Did anyone report her missing?" She stretches her hand out in an attempt to take the file, her fingers almost trembling with need; he ignores the gesture and takes a sip from his water bottle.

"Ann-i-yah?" He glances up at Aniyah before returning to his perusal. "Out-of-state student and roommate. We found your car at a bar downtown; first hint you two hadn't just driven out of town on a lark. Second was the 911 call we got from the same location. Ran the number on the cellphone; came back registered to..."

He hesitates, looking at my name on the page and then back at me. I nod for him to continue, confused by the pause. "...K-man here. We figured you three were bar-hopping together when you got nabbed. K-man shot off an emergency call before he was disconnected."

We exchange glances, unsure how much of this to believe. "We don't remember much of that night," Aniyah begins cautiously, to be interrupted by our escort.

"They were disoriented when I found them by the side of the road," says the siren, giving the officer a plaintive look. I still haven't caught her name, which is odd because I know she's given it several times. Her voice draws my attention every time she speaks, but it's like I'm too busy listening to the sound to hear her actual words. "Starved and beaten and dressed in funny-looking robes. Their scrapes and bruises made me think they might have been thrown from a car. I'm surprised they remember their own names."

He nods so vigorously I think his head might fall off. "Happens. College students are particularly susceptible to cults. You kids are lucky they got tired of waiting for a ransom and kicked you to the curb. We'll finish taking your statement and get you the name of a shrink you can talk to. Then we'll call your parents and get you a ride home. Wait here; I'll make sure the front desk has their numbers."

I don't know whether to feel relief or frustration at his lack of interest in the details of our ordeal. We give vague statements about beatings and meager food served out by strangers with veiled faces whilst being held in a cave we didn't recognize: easy half-truths Celia encouraged us to stick to. When I think I'm about to faint from hunger, they bring in three adults I don't recognize. Two of them rush to embrace Miyuki while the remaining one—a handsome man with dark skin and a kind smile softening his weathered face—wraps me in a tight bear-hug.

That's how I meet my father, George, for what feels to me like the first time.

My dad takes me to his home, which turns out to be *my* old home: a place I once lived in a bedroom filled with things that were mine. Everything

I touch feels familiar, yet I recognize none of it. I'm drawn to the guitar that stands at the foot of my bed, my hand reaching for the pick at my wrist; somehow my fingers know how to play even when my brain scrambles to catch up. Through muscle memory and a lot of bluffing, I'm able to fake my way through eighty percent of each day.

When I can't fake something, Dad frowns but says he understands. The words *cult* and *head-injury* and *traumatic disorder* get thrown around when he thinks I can't hear. He spends a lot of time on the phone with police, doctors, school officials, and my mother, Kailani. My mind whispers *makuahine* the first time I hear her warm voice on the line, and I learn she lives in Hawai'i. I don't remember Hawai'i, but as soon as I see pictures on the internet the sounds and scents of home come flooding back.

This is how I learn how to trigger memories in little ways: foods Dad makes for me, each bite an explosion of savory familiarity; the clothes tucked farthest back in my closet, scented with old shampoo; the texture of white sand I keep in a jar under my bed. Over the weeks, I piece old half-memories together like a jigsaw, trying to match them up with the things I've experienced. Sometimes I'm frustrated with how slowly I'm integrating back into my old life, but at least I *have* good recollections to comfort me. Images from the arena stalk me at night, turning my dreams to nightmares until I wake in a cold sweat. I tremble until I remember where I am, or until Tony, my new boyfriend, reaches over to pull me into a tight hug.

I'm surprised to learn I'd been a student before I was taken, and then surprised by my own reaction. Somehow I'd internalized the notion that my mind and body were for fighting, and it's strange now to be faced with a world of choices about my future. I've missed the start date for the autumn semester and am too 'traumatized' for late enrollment—a word that neatly sums up the fact that I have to be reminded of what I've been majoring in for the past three years—but there's nothing stopping me from enrolling again in the spring. I have a legal identity, a home, and people who care about me.

Nor, as it turns out, do I have to stay here in Texas.

A couple months after I come out, Dad tells me he's planning to move back to Hawai'i. He says he misses Makuahine and that my absence made him rethink his priorities. He offers to take me with him and I'm tempted. I want to see the home I don't remember and become acquainted with it all over again. I want to see Makuahine, not just for a visit or over a call; I'd like to actually live with her, see her every day, and hug her whenever I can. I talk to Celia after one of the altered meetings, and she reckons I'd be as safe there as anywhere else, if not safer. When she shakes my hand and walks off, I realize I'm disappointed by her answer.

I have friends here. I have a boyfriend whom I bring home to meet Dad, then take out on the town for dinner and a movie. We drag ourselves to his brand-new apartment at sleep-o'clock and collapse on his bed: a very big bed, I'm delighted to see. When the sun rises, we vote for sexy shower times. I like that part *very* much. We have a girl friend who might or might not be a girlfriend, who is happy to drop by on weekends to watch television and roll around on the big bed with us. If I moved away, I would be leaving behind people who have accompanied me through something no one else understands.

It takes me two weeks to tell Dad what I realize I've known much longer: I'm staying in Texas. My school is here, and so is my boyfriend. He can't hide his disappointment at my decision and asks me about a million times if I'm sure, but when push comes to shove he says he understands. He hugs me and shakes Tony's hand, and tells me he'll see me again soon when I come to visit. He says to follow my dreams, be happy, and become the man I want to be. I laugh and tell him I'm happy right now and I like who I am, so I'm ahead of the game there.

The funny thing is, I'm telling the truth: I *am* happy. I'm not glad I was taken to the Arena, and I'll never forgive my memories being torn from me, but I've made lemonade out of my lemons. I like the person I am and learn to manage my fears. I still dream of the arena, but the nightmares are

352

gone. No longer do I run from nameless terrors stalking me; instead I chase the creature who took us, gripping a jagged blade in my hand. When I wake, I pull Tony closer or kiss Aniyah's forehead if she's staying overnight.

Sometimes after I wake, the adrenaline doesn't let me go back to sleep. I'll stumble to the kitchen for water, and more often than not I'll run into someone on the fold-out couch. Some nights it's Miyuki, other times Justin or Christian or Reese. All the ex-fighters and prizes have a key to our apartment. The girls tend to stay in their own places and invite us over rather than dropping by to hang out at ours, but they're not complete strangers; Christian brings Chloe with him, and when Reese drops in Heather and Sappho tag along.

On nights when someone visits, I slide onto the couch beside them. We flip on the television and watch something that isn't a sea of bloody sand and bad memories. If one of us needs to cry, we hold each other until the flood has abated. Hot drinks and warm blankets are brought out when the weather turns colder. As a coping mechanism, it works for now. If we can stick together, I like to believe it'll keep working forever.

CHAPTER 35

Aniyah

When we're taken from the police station to John's house, we learn to our surprise that it is *only* John's house. Miyuki and xer mother, Yumiko, do not live there even though rooms are furnished for both of them. Yumiko rents a small studio apartment on the opposite side of town, and Miyuki lived with me in a shared two-bedroom unit near the university campus before we were kidnapped.

We're informed over dinner that John has taken over the rent on our apartment. He'd refused to allow anyone to touch our belongings beyond the cursory investigation conducted by the police at his insistence. As a result, though he doesn't know it, our old living space is now a museum showcasing lives we don't remember: hundreds of preserved exhibits ready for us to paw through in an attempt to find ourselves.

I'm grateful to John; he didn't have to pay our rent, keep our things or hound the police into filing a report. If he hadn't, Celia wouldn't have found us in the system and we wouldn't be here right now eating dinner and imagining what our old apartment might hold. Keoki's father knew *he* was gone but knew nothing of us, and my own parents hadn't realized I was missing until the police called them.

I'd talked with them over the phone from the station and they'd sounded relieved though not particularly worried. There was a fuzziness at the edge of their recollection, and at points in the conversation they seemed to have forgotten I'd been gone at all. My feelings might have been hurt had I not myself so thoroughly forgotten *them*, and their placidity has the feel of magic about it.

I believe we made the right decision in coming forward to resume our old lives, but we hit a hiccup at bedtime. John is first alarmed and then solidly disapproving when Miyuki expects me to stay in xer room overnight rather than in a guest room. Only Yumiko's intervention prevents an argument and I am given an air mattress in Miyuki's study, which is attached to xer bedroom via a connecting bathroom. Everyone pretends I'm not sneaking into xer bed the moment the lights go out, but John develops an unsettling habit of watching me over breakfast and speaking to me only when directly spoken to.

I don't mind being a shadow in their household but Miyuki is livid at my treatment and urges our immediate relocation. I'm frightened by the prospect of living on our own with no memories to guide us, but I'm more afraid my presence will cause Miyuki's relationship with xer father to deteriorate. So two weeks after we escape, John agrees to help us to move back into our apartment on the understanding that he will continue paying the rent until we're ready to go back to work. The offer seems charitable to me, but Miyuki chews xer lip and I can see xer wondering what strings might be attached.

Despite these hurdles on our course to reintegration, I know how lucky we are; Keoki, Miyuki, and I are the only ones from the arena whose families Celia has found. Until new identities can be crafted, the others are obliged to stay as guests of people like us: humans who were kidnapped and altered into half-faery creatures. Some of the altered look wild and weird and some appear as normal as we do, but all have the telltale glow of magic to my eyes. They have stories similar to ours: stripped of their memories, they were held captive until they managed to escape to the earthside world they remembered only in shards of belief and dreams.

The promised new identities are agonizingly slow to arrive, but by the two month anniversary of our escape we all have paying work and living arrangements not dependent on charity. Miyuki and I return to our old jobs while the others find work around the metroplex. They rent places of their own which I find myself visiting on a semi-regular basis. We've been through a shared experience which has knit us together regardless of personality or preference, though I notice it takes longer for some of the girls to warm to the boys than it does for Miyuki and myself. This is another manner in which we're lucky, I know; we weren't harmed in the same ways the other girls were. I try not to take our fortune for granted.

Tony is the first to find his own place. We visit the apartment when he first rents it, bringing a potted basil plant to place in the kitchen window. Looking around the empty rooms, Miyuki notes with a wry grin that he's rented an awfully big place for a single guy. Tony ignores xer and offers me another slice of the pizza he's ordered from the place down the street, some little hole-in-the-wall joint that he swears makes the only proper pizza in the city. Keoki moves in with him two weeks later when his dad goes back to Hawaii, and Miyuki pretends innocent surprise at this development before shooing me out the door to visit.

"Wouldn't you like to come with?" We haven't talked about our relationship since the escape, not wanting to poke at a good thing that seemed to be working. My palms are sweating and already I feel pangs of guilt. I *do* want to go, but not if it would mean losing Miyuki.

Xie just laughs and flops onto the couch. "I'd rather watch television, take a hot bath, and go to bed early," xie says, rolling xer eyes over a teasing smirk. "See you tomorrow, Aniyah."

I push away the worst of the guilt while playing with Keoki and Tony, and the kisses I receive in the morning from Miyuki dissolve the last traces of worry. "Just don't plan to stay overnight when Justin and Matías get a place together," xie teases, stripping me down for a second shower. "I don't think your boys could handle the competition." I laugh and don't stop until xie covers my mouth with kisses.

Xie turns out to be wrong; Justin moves in with Imani. She says she needed a roommate while finding a medical school to attend and that Justin promised to behave. She hands me a cup of blueberry tea from the microwave and I watch her joyful face as she tells me about schooling options in the area. She's more animated than ever before, and I'm so relieved the healers were able to soothe the burns she suffered during our escape. Her lovely brown skin bears no blemish and she glitters with magic as she talks.

"You know you can always crash with us, don't you?" I tell her when I can get a word in edgewise. "Any time, no matter what." I want to ask if she's sure about this move; after all, Justin is one of the fighters, and much taller than she. Looking into her bright eyes, however, I already know the answer.

"I know," she says, giving me a warm grin and reaching across the table to squeeze my hand. "Thank you. I'll be fine, really. I know how to take care of myself."

Justin seems sanguine about their living situation, though I don't know him well enough to ask. I can see him from the tiny kitchen where Imani and I sit, sprawled out on their couch with his leg propped up as he watches his phone. His wounds have healed, but every so often his hand drifts to his cheek where the bear mauled him or rubs absently at his knee. His eyes are calm, but I wonder if some part of him needs reassurance that all his limbs are present and functioning.

He speaks at a lull in the conversation, without looking up from his phone. "If you're going to Chloe's place any time soon, tell Christian he has to pay his half of the Netflix subscription before I'll give him the password. No movies for them until then, and no, I don't feel bad even a little."

I roll my eyes even though he isn't watching. "I only go there every other week, but I'll tell him if I see him."

Chloe did the same as Tony and rented an apartment bigger than she needed; the only thing stopping Christian from moving in on the first day was Chloe herself. She kept him waiting three weeks after she signed the lease while he lived in Celia's house and occasionally fretted over her impending decision. When she did make the offer for him to move in, it was without fanfare: she showed up at Celia's and asked whether he wanted her to carry his bags. The way he tells it, he gave her a winning grin and said he'd be much obliged.

She's the one who takes us shopping for clothes, and I'm grateful for all the assistance I can get. Finding outfits that don't hurt my back is a challenge, but Chloe is determined we'll find what I need or die trying. "It's not that I don't love him," she tells me from the other side of the dressing-room door, as I struggle to pull a new dress over my head without snagging my hair. "You know I do; but over there I had no choice at all. I needed to be sure this was *my* decision and not just what I was used to."

"I understand," I tell her, my voice muffled in the closeness of the stall, but I'm not entirely sure I do. I think of Christian and how kind he'd been to me, how he made me feel warm all over yet wouldn't press further without my agreement. I can't imagine him making me feel like I didn't have a choice—but maybe it's not about him at all. We woke in that place without any sense of ourselves, and were told to obey orders or suffer the consequences. Choice was taken away from us by the Master, and maybe there was only so much the boys could do to give it back.

"Besides," she adds, and I can practically hear her rolling her eyes, "if I'd let him move in right away, he'd have slipped immediately into boyfriend mode. I don't *want* a boyfriend just yet! I've got loads of options for lovers if I want, and I'm still deciding when and where to take them on my terms. I love everything about him and me and us together but I'm not like Hana, you know? Come out so I can see how it looks."

358

"No, the zipper is stuck and everything is hot and sticky. I swear the air conditioning is broken. Anyway, no one is like Hana. Did you hear she got a job in banking? Just walked into an interview and lied her face off."

The story quickly becomes legend in our group for its sheer audacity. After landing an entry job in banking through a combination of guts and blatant bald-faced lying about her experience, Hana rents a cozy little apartment all to herself and takes up kickboxing on nights and weekends. After her first session the teacher moves her up from basic self-defense to advanced classes whilst scolding her for not mentioning having previous experience under her belt.

I visit the gym hoping to catch up with her after a bout and am amazed to find her grinning from ear to ear, happier than I've ever seen her. "Wow, Hana, you look great! Positively glowing, even."

"That's the sweat," she observes with a laugh, rubbing down her hair with a towel. "Did you *see* me, though? Pretty sure I've been taking classes since I was a kid. I've got a weird eclectic range with some gaps, which suggests I jumped around between teachers. Would make sense if my family moved around a lot, like an army brat or traveling sales or something. Not sure yet, but I'm getting a handle on it. Training for the Olympics right now, though that's gonna take some time."

I stare at her, wondering if I've misheard. "You're training for the Olympics? Like, to compete? Uh, Hana, how is that supposed to work? You're not exactly legally you."

She shrugs and looks unconcerned. "I'll figure something out when I get there. Who knows? By that time I may have found my family. You and Miyuki were the first, but there's no reason you should be the last. Have you talked to Sappho? She's trying to run hers down through a tattoo artist grapevine. Thinks she might have found a friend of a friend who recognizes her ink, but she isn't sure." She dabs moisture from her brow and shakes her head in exasperation. "Not sure her head's really in the search right now, given how distracted she is with Reese."

I hadn't heard this new angle to the drama of Sappho, but it doesn't surprise me in the least. On coming out earthside, she'd been briefly distraught to learn that the name tattooed on her skin was not her own but that of a famous poet whose words she'd borrowed. She'd locked herself sobbing in her room before deciding she *preferred* using a name she'd chosen rather than one given at birth. She was determined to share this trait with Reese, who seemed bemused by the attention but agreed that, yes, her silver-beaded name was probably her own choice, at least as far as she knew. Sappho had been delighted and—after pointing out that Heather's name wasn't hers by birth either—had insisted the three of them rent an apartment together and make a fresh start.

Sappho apprentices at a local tattoo parlor where she turns out to have a steady hand with a needle. She stumbles onto a quote which she wants to ink above my scar where it bends around my side and up my shoulder: *'scars have the strange power to remind us that our past is real'*. I laugh and tell her I'll think about it. I'm glad to see Sappho finding joy and throwing herself into life. She'd seemed so broken after Lucas hurt her, and I hadn't been sure whether his death would help or harm. I didn't blame her for what she'd done, and anyone who might have had lingering doubts on the subject came round real fast once Hana made it clear that a problem with one of us was a problem with all of us. Before long, Christian and Keoki and Tony were frequent visitors in the three girls' spacious apartment, stealing food and hogging the television and generally being a puppyish underfoot nuisance while watching sports and reminiscing with Reese.

I'd had little interaction with Reese in captivity, but she seems happy to be out. Instead of getting a car like the rest of us, she buys a used motorcycle and never looks happier than when she's in her leathers, helmet under her arm and ready to ride. She finds work with a local team of women roofers, figuring her impenetrable skin might be an asset in an industry noted for sharp nails and staple guns—and it's not like she isn't already accustomed to working in the midday heat. Heather also takes a job with the roofers but stays inside answering phones and being a pretty face for the customers; if asked, she always says in her wry drawl that she's sweated enough for one lifetime.

Like her roommates, Heather seems healthier now, even if she shows her contentedness in smaller, less obvious ways. She takes an interest in her wardrobe once she has money to spend, focusing on a variety of fabric textures now that her skin can once more feel sensation. She glows less strongly than the rest of us since our escape. At one of our group meetings, Celia confirms what I noticed after our escape: she believes Heather lost some of her magic while powering the portal that brought us over. Heather is close to ecstatic at this announcement. "Good riddance to bad rubbish," she declares, heading to the potluck table to shamelessly beg the remaining half of an apple pie to take home with her roommates.

The one person who never visits the girls' apartment is Handler. Maybe he feels he wouldn't be welcome, though I notice he doesn't socialize much at all. He attends the meetings because Celia says we ought to in that tone of hers that deters argument, but he doesn't talk during open-microphone time and he never lingers around the potluck tables after the meeting is adjourned. Many of the other altereds avoid him, disliking the fear that still rolls from his body like an ever-present cloak, though I notice a couple of the less savory of our peers go out of their way to give him a kind word. He's polite and nods at their attempts at conversation, but even in their company he never looks comfortable.

Through the grapevine, I hear Handler finds a house of his own to rent. I don't ask where the money comes from, but I can't imagine what he could do for a living when even humans avoid him. I write down his address, shove the paper into my purse, and fret for days over whether to visit him. I've gone to see every other member of our group when they found a place, so why should he be any different? He was a captive like the rest of us, even if we didn't know that until the end, and he helped us escape. There's no reason for me to avoid him, not really. Eventually I pick up some cheap cupcakes at the grocery store and drive over there, gripping the steering wheel tightly, determined not to think too hard about what I'm doing.

His face is as inscrutable as ever, but I think he's surprised to find me on his step. The etched lines in his skin failed to respond to Lynn's healing, so the fearful whorls and strange patterns still remain for altered eyes to see. Humans see only the weathered lines of hard living and a tight squint of eyes against the light. At least he is able to open his eyes, as the throbbing darkness behind his lids drained away in the portal, but his pupils are too big and dark and his squinting gaze unsettlingly direct.

"Can I... help you?" There is hesitation in his voice, the sound of someone who knows they have nothing to offer. I almost wince in sympathy, but I don't want him to see pain on my face when I'm certain he'd misinterpret the emotion. So instead I smile and pretend nothing is wrong.

"I brought you some cupcakes," I tell him, shoving the pastries forward to create a barrier between us. "As a house-warming present." The silence stretches out as he stares at me in confusion. "I bought them," I add helplessly, as if the plastic container festooned with stickers wasn't a dead giveaway. "I still don't know how to— The oven in the apartment is a little touchy."

I'm drowning in awkwardness, and perhaps my distress is what rouses him to save me. Carved hands reach to take the gift from my grip and he nods solemnly. "Thank you." Another long stretch of silence follows, punctuated by the pounding of my heart as I breathe in the familiar fear, stale and old, like ancient cologne seeped into his clothes. "Would you like to come in? I have milk."

The offer is given reluctantly, as though he's afraid I'll feel pressured to say yes, and I find myself hesitating as I wonder if he'd prefer me to say no. I nod slowly. "I like milk."

He shows me to the living room and I find a seat on a recliner, the armrests on either side of me forming a comforting bubble of personal space. Milk is set on the coffee table alongside my cupcakes, then he sits on

362

a threadbare old couch and turns his head away to look out the window. There's a bird feeder there, but mostly I think he's giving me privacy from those direct eyes of his.

We eat in silence—two cupcakes apiece—and then sit in continued silence. Somewhere in the house a clock ticks. I fidget with my hands and wonder if I should just go, but then I look up to find his gaze on me: curious, but not unkind. "I brought a book," I tell him, touching the bag across my shoulder, and he nods as if this explains everything.

I drop by his house once a week after that, though we never really converse beyond the bare minimum of niceties. He's not unhappy, I come to realize; he's simply not a social person. We sit in his living room and he smokes and watches the birds while I read my book. It's a strange ritual, but it makes me happy; I feel comfortable in his presence, despite the familiar fear. And it's nice to see him happy in his own way, shrouded in the scented smoke of his cigarillos, content to be relieved of the burden of herding a bunch of college kids to their deaths.

Miyuki doesn't understand my visits, but at least one other person from the Arena comes to see Handler. I run into Matías one day, just as he's leaving. I've got my book bag with me—the one that straps across my body and doesn't pull too hard on my spine as long as I don't get greedy with books—and I see him navigating the steps carefully with his cane. He nods at me and gives me a sad sort of smile, the kind of greeting you'd give to someone going through the same hard times as yourself.

"Matías! Hey! Um, how are you doing?" I'm used to hugging the other girls and sometimes Christian and Justin, but this doesn't feel like a hugging situation. I'm suddenly very aware of my hands and unsure where to put them; I end up clutching the strap of my bag with both hands.

He nods in an easygoing way and stops walking to lean on his cane. "I'm good, really! I got an apartment with another altered, a guy I met at one of the meetings. He needed someone to go halves on a place he'd picked out, and I needed a roommate, so it worked out pretty good. You?"

I shrug. "Pretty good? Miyuki and I are living at our old place and still trying to sort everything out. Planning to go back to school in the spring. You should come over to Sappho's place; I never see you on pizza night."

He nods at the invitation, avoiding my gaze. "Yeah, Tony's been on at me about that," he admits, reaching up to rub the back of his neck. "I know I should but, uh. I didn't want to make it awkward." His gaze slides back to the house behind him and he bites his lip. "Neither of us does. You know how it is."

I blink at him. "No? I mean, I understand why Handler doesn't visit, but you were one of the fighters, right?" I'm confused now, because I had thought Matías was a retired fighter kept on to teach the other boys after an injury left him unable to compete.

He smiles, but the expression doesn't reach his eyes. "Well, yeah, I was. But I guess I'm not so clear anymore on the difference between a captive who *feeds* the fighters before they're sent to be killed versus a captive who *trains* the fighters before they're sent to be killed." He runs a hand through his hair, looking sheepish. "Everything seemed clearer over there. Now there's time to think, and maybe I think too much. Sorry. I'll, uh, try to drop by."

I'm at a loss; now I really do want to hug him but I'm afraid the act would physically hurt one or both of us. "I can tell you the other boys miss you, for what it's worth. I know they'd like to see you. They talk like your training saved their lives, you know." He doesn't reply but his smile is warmer as he turns to go. My eyes are drawn to the movement of his cane and I open my mouth again without thinking. "Matías, did Celia not offer to heal you?"

I see a brief flash of weariness in his eyes and I feel an answering stab of guilt, understanding all too well the desire to *not* keep explaining the same intimate details to strangers. "She did, yeah," he says, his tone light in contrast to the stiffness around his shoulders. "I said I was good. I get around just fine on my cane and the pain isn't too bad with the medication I'm on. And, well, it's kinda hard to explain."

"I'm sorry," I blurt out, wishing I hadn't said anything. "I didn't mean to be rude, I just wondered."

"It's okay." He looks down at his leg, a melancholy smile dancing over his lips. "Getting my knee busted saved my life. Took me out of the fights and into teaching. And I don't think the Master would want me back in this condition; he already thought I was dead weight. So, for a lot of reasons, I decided not to mess with things yet. Maybe later. Hey, I gotta go; I'm teaching a cooking class up at the grocery market. Come by some time and I'll get you a discount seat!"

I watch him walk to his car, blinking against the setting sun. There are a million questions I want to ask him but never will. They would be too invasive, like the questions my co-workers ask me. But I can't imagine leaving my body the way it is, not even if it would keep me safe from being taken again. Perhaps it makes a difference not being in pain, but that's a state I can't seem to achieve. I'm much better now than I was in the otherworld, especially near the end when—according to Lynn—I was going through withdrawal after being without my medication for so long.

I found my prescription in a nightstand drawer in the apartment, and Lynn confirmed it was one of the strongest a doctor could prescribe. Those pills made it worth coming forward to assume our past identities, but even they can't erase the pain. My doctor says we're 'managing' the pain, and tells me that hurting for the rest of my life is a reality I have to accept. Miyuki works xer hands over me at night and I thank every star in the sky that xie is willing to help me in the way xie does. But sometimes I stand in the shower and cry, letting the hot water hide the tears I can't hold in. I'm not staying this way. I can't.

I've talked to Lynn and he's put me in contact with other healers in our group. Some heal with magic, others in more mundane ways. They all agree I can be helped—magic is, after all, *magic*—but there's some disagreement over how to accomplish this. The scar that stretches from shoulder to hip was created when three metal rods were bolted into my curved spine; these need to come out before flooding my system with regenerative magic. Getting the rods out isn't hard, but I need to survive the procedure. We're still in discussion but I'm not going to wait forever. I'm going to be healed, one way or another.

My spine isn't the only body part that vexes me since our escape. At night I lie awake thinking about my changed eyes and the bargain I struck in exchange for their refinement. I swore never to tell anyone about the Shadow Man, and to do him a favor which he could name later. Our agreement still magically seals my lips, and this is upsetting; I hate keeping secrets from Miyuki, and I'd like to tell Celia what happened. I hope it might never arise; after all, the Shadow Man lives in the otherworld, far away from us. Favor or not, I can't imagine I'll ever hear from him again, not when I have nothing of value to take.

Those sleepless nights become fewer and farther between. As the summer ebbs and autumn breathes life into the metroplex, I wake happy more often than not. Miyuki loves me and I love xer, and I have more fun than I'd thought possible with Keoki and Tony. I have friends who've been through hell with me. I have a job, I'm enrolled in classes, and I'm putting together the pieces of my life more successfully every day. Some parts don't make much sense, but we're managing. Miyuki finds a laptop case in xer closet but no laptop, and I have a shelf of notebooks near my bed which seems to be missing a few near the middle. But we'll find the schoolmate we lent these things to or the repair shop where xer computer resides. *We've got this.*

I repeat the motto to myself as I pull into the parking lot and step out of my car. Evening comes earlier now in the autumn and I squint against an orange sky. I'd been meaning to visit this place for some time, but kept putting off the trip in favor of more important things. Maybe I was afraid of what I would find. I dust down my jeans, straighten to the sound of my spine crackling all the way down and walk to the door, pushing it open as if it were second nature to me.

366

I'm early enough that the bar is empty save for one man behind the counter. He's not just any man, though. To my altered eyes, he's one of the most beautiful people I've ever seen. He's tall and lithe, with blond hair so rich it glimmers in the light like real gold. He isn't pretty like Miyuki or cute like Keoki or handsome like Tony; he's beautiful in the way a painting or a statue is beautiful. I wouldn't kiss him any more than I'd kiss the *Mona Lisa*, but I could stare at him for hours.

He looks up when I walk in, the automatic smile on his face faltering midway through forming. "Can I... help you?"

He's one of us. I can't breathe for excitement and look around the room to make sure we're alone. "Yes! You're an altered, too? I had no idea one of us worked here! I'm Aniyah. I was taken a while back and they found my car outside your bar, so I was just wondering if you or anyone else here knew me." I give him a sheepish smile, letting him see my embarrassment. "You know how it is; memory gone, trying to piece things together."

He blinks once, very slowly, then sympathy blossoms on his face. "*Aniyah!* I knew you looked familiar. Yes, you visited here over the summer! Mostly on music nights, to see the boy bands." He gives me a mischievous wink that is trying too hard, but in a good way; as if, by acting corny and undignified, he could subsume all my embarrassment into himself as a kindness to me. "Celia mentioned we had new escapees and might have hunters on the prowl in the area, but I never realized *you'd* been taken, dear."

Wiping his hands on the cloth he'd been using to polish glasses, he reaches out glittering fingers in offer to shake my own. His smile is like warm summer rain after weeks of drought, welcoming and kind; even though we've just met, I can imagine being friends with this person. I take his hand and we shake like normal people do while an automatic smile spreads over my face in response to his own.

"I'm Timothy, by the way. It's so good to meet you again."

Note to the Reader

Thank you for reading this book! I hope you have enjoyed it and you are very welcome to leave a review or recommend this novel to a friend; reviews and recommendations are the lifeblood of indie authors and I cannot thank my reviewers enough for their kind words. If I may, I would like to insert a brief note on genders in this novel and how best to label the characters in reviews.

Emma Miyuki is a transgender person, which is a person whose gender does not match the gender assigned to them at birth. Miyuki was incorrectly assigned female at birth (AFAB) but is actually a nonbinary gender, i.e. neither a man nor a woman. Miyuki's specific nonbinary gender identification (for there are several!) is a demigirl. Miyuki answers to xie/xer pronouns and she/her pronouns, but prefers the former to the latter. A sample sentence introducing Miyuki to another reader might be: "Miyuki is a transgender demigirl who uses xie/xer pronouns," or simply, "Miyuki is nonbinary."

Reese is also a transgender person, specifically a trans woman who was erroneously assigned male at birth (AMAB). Reese was not 'born a boy' nor did she 'change' her gender at any point in her life; she has always been a girl, even if rest of the world has not always recognized that fact. Please only refer to Reese with she/her pronouns! If you consider Reese's gender identity a 'spoiler', then it would be better not to reference her at all in reviews rather than concealing her gender with incorrect he/him pronouns. Thank you for being considerate; sensitive reviews for books with trans characters are easier for trans readers to navigate.

Bless you again for reading my work! More resources on transgender characters and how to write about them are available at GLAAD.org and Nonbinary.org for those who are interested. I owe a debt of gratitude to Vee (@FindMeReading) of GayYA.Org for sharing their poignant thoughts regarding how trans characters are handled in book reviews and how we can better serve our community.

Acknowledgements

This book would not have been possible without the loving kindness of more people than I can count in a lifetime. I am grateful to my chosen family and friends on Twitter, who believed in me and nurtured me during my coming out as genderqueer. I am indebted to the community of readers on my blog, who buoy my spirits on even the worst days. My very survival would not be possible without the members of my family who help me through the ups and downs of my disability without complaint and laugh at my jokes even when they aren't particularly funny. I am blessed.

Particular thanks must go to the friends and colleagues who read and shaped this work prior to publication. Kristy Griffin Green and Thomas, my wonderful writing partners, touched every page of this book and are the dearest of friends. Nikki Murray, Smilodon Meow, Lutecia Sciavone, Rachel, Jules Bristow, and of course S. Qiouyi Lu worked tirelessly as beta and sensitivity readers for the material. Much of what is good in this book is due to these people; anything bad which remains is on my head.

Thank you for reading and supporting me in my work. Blessed be.

About the Author

ANA MARDOLL is a writer and activist who lives in the dusty Texas wilderness with two spoiled cats. Her favorite employment is weaving new tellings of old fairy tales, fashioning beautiful creations to bring comfort on cold nights. She is the author of the Earthside series, the Rewoven Tales novels, and several short stories.

Aside from reading and writing, Ana enjoys games of almost every flavor and frequently posts videos of gaming sessions on YouTube. After coming out as genderqueer in 2015, Ana answers to both xie/xer and she/her pronouns.

Website: www.AnaMardoll.com
Twitter: @AnaMardoll
YouTube: www.YouTube.com/c/AnaMardoll

Arena Captives

Prizes
- Aniyah, the Alexandrite Prize
- Chloe, the Ruby Prize
- Emma Miyuki, the Quartz Prize
- Hana, the Diamond Prize
- Heather, the Emerald Prize
- Imani, the Amethyst Prize
- Sappho, the Sapphire Prize

Fighters
- Anthony 'Tony' Suen, the Basalt Fighter
- Christian, the Obsidian Fighter
- Justin, the Pumice Fighter
- Keoki, the Granite Fighter
- Lucas, the Scoria Fighter
- Matías, the Teacher
- Reese, the Breccia Fighter

Content Notes

Content notes (sometimes referred to as 'trigger warnings') are intended to help trauma survivors avoid being surprised by story elements which may trigger them. These content notes may allude to story spoilers, which is why they have been placed at the back of the book. The content note system used in this book is the one created by the Fireside Fiction Company, and used here with permission from the owner. This book and the author are not affiliated with the Fireside Fiction Company in any way.

The content notes for this book include:

Animal Abuse •• one moderate intensity scene
Domestic Violence •• moderate intensity references
Self-Harm •• one moderate intensity scene
Sexual Assault •• moderate intensity references
Torture •• low intensity references
Violence •• multiple moderate intensity scenes